# DEATH ANGEL

# DEATH ANGEL

### A NOVEL

# MARTHA POWERS

{ 1 }

**⊙ceanview Publishing**

IPSWICH, MASSACHUSETTS

This book is a work of fiction. Names, characters, places, and incidents either
are the products of the author's imagination or are used fictitiously.
Any resemblance to actual events or locales or persons,
living or dead, is entirely coincidental.

ISBN-10: 1-933515-03-1
ISBN-13: 978-1-933515-03-8

Published in the United States by Oceanview Publishing,
Ipswich, Massachusetts
www.oceanviewpub.com

Distributed by Midpoint Trade Books
www.midpointtradebooks.com

2 4 6 8 10 9 7 5 3 1

PRINTED IN THE UNITED STATES OF AMERICA

To Bill
Thirty-five years. A helluva journey!

and

To Lorraine Pickard
A great friend who believed in this project.

# ACKNOWLEDGMENTS

Many thanks to Pat and Bob Gussin and to Sue Greger of Ocean-view Publishing for your generous invitation to be involved in such an exciting adventure. To Dave Wolfram, brother, friend, and critic, who has made me laugh over the years from the Circus Court to the Christmas wreath. To Joanne Strecker for having a delight-fully devious mind, and for helping me get the medical details right. To the Shop and Write ladies for all the laughs and advice and for nagging me to get off the golf course and back to the computer. To everyone at the Vero Beach Book Center for their support and encouragement and for creating a warm and knowledgeable atmos-phere for both readers and authors. And especially to the Chicago mother whose tragic loss and hunger for justice was the inspiration for this book.

# THE DARK ANGEL

Dark Angel with thine aching lust
To rid the world of penitence:
Malicious Angel, who still dost
My soul such subtile violence!

Because of thee, no thought, no thing
Abides for me undesecrate:
Dark Angel, ever on the wing,
Who never reachest me too late!

When music sounds, then changest thou
Its silvery to a sultry fire:
Nor will thine envious heart allow
Delight untortured by desire.

Through thee, the gracious Muses turn
To Furies, O mine Enemy!
And all the things of beauty burn
With flames of evil ecstasy.

Because of thee, the land of dreams
Becomes a gathering-place of fears:
Until tormented slumber seems
One vehemence of useless tears.

— Lionel Johnson

# DEATH ANGEL

# PROLOGUE

HE NOSED THE CAR INTO THE EMPTY PARKING LOT and stopped when the tires touched the concrete curb. His head was motionless, but his eyes flicked along the bank of evergreens edging the forest preserve. Clenching both hands at the top of the steering wheel, he straightened his arms and pressed his back against the seat. The impulse was so strong.

He expelled the air from his lungs in a slow, steady stream, then opened his door and walked around the front to the passenger side of the car. Once more he eyed the empty paths leading into the woods. Aware of danger, his mouth was dry. His hand moved to the door latch. The sharp click of the car door shattered the afternoon quiet.

The little girl slid out of the car. Her white sneakers scuffed the gravel and sent up a small cloud of dust. She tilted her head and squinted up against the glare of the sun.

He held out his hand and smiled. With one hand she tugged at the strand of black hair alongside her cheek and then, placed her other hand in his. Turning, they walked into the woods.

# ONE

Kate Warner opened the door, flapping the towel to clear the clouds of steam from the bathroom. She'd raced home after work, looking forward to a long shower. The air conditioning at the library hadn't been turned on yet, so it had been hot and sticky working in the small conference room. She cocked her head, straining to hear any sound from downstairs. All was quiet. It must not be as late as she thought.

She dried herself, and turned on the hair dryer, using her free hand to pull on her canvas shoes. The steady stream of air blew her ash-brown hair in a cloud around her head and she leaned closer to the mirror, frowning at the dry skin between her eyebrows. She'd have to start using a moisturizer. Thirty-one wasn't too old. She turned sideways, checking for signs of sagging breasts or buttocks, satisfied that she hadn't deteriorated since the last time she'd looked.

Shutting off the dryer, she brushed her hair away from her face, letting it fall straight, the curled ends grazing her shoulders. After putting on fresh clothes, she turned off the light and crossed the bedroom toward the upstairs hall on the way scooping up her watch and earrings. She slipped the gold hoops into her ears as she started down the stairs. A quick glance at her watch. Three ten. Five minutes before the school bus came.

Richard hadn't wanted her to take the job, but for once she had stood her ground. With Jenny in school, the demands of the household were cut in half and, since he had never approved of her going out to lunch or doing volunteer work, she was at loose ends. Besides, she felt as if her brain were atrophying. She hadn't worked since she was married and found the part-time job at the library a perfect way to ease back into the workforce. Helping the senior citizens in the computer training classes was something she really enjoyed. As she explained to Richard, she would only work when Jenny was in school.

Opening the front door, she stepped outside. She shaded her eyes with her hand, squinting down the empty street, watching for the school bus.

Last year Kate had walked to the corner to meet the bus, but since her eighth birthday, Jenny had insisted that only babies had their mothers meet the bus. Richard had agreed that Jenny needed to learn independence, and what better place than in a small town like Pickard?

Kate sniffed the air. It was already the middle of May, but this was the first really beautiful day. Illinois had had a wet and chilly spring. She loved the balmy days before the summer heat and hoped this weather would continue.

Down the block, the school bus came into sight, slowing for the stop at the corner. The doors opened and she could see Jenny in her yellow jacket standing inside on the top step.

The phone rang. Kate waved to Jenny and, leaving the door open, she walked back through the hall to the kitchen. She listened to the recorded message announcing that her prescription was ready at the pharmacy. Hanging up, she returned to the front porch.

The street was empty.

The bus was gone and Jenny was nowhere in sight.

Several times Jenny had stopped to play with one of her friends and Kate had to remind her that she needed to come home first, just to check in. Being the last house before the cul de sac offered too much temptation for distraction. Especially when the weather was fine.

"You're in big trouble, Jennifer Louise," Kate muttered.

She left the front door unlocked and hurried down the stairs. Walking briskly, she checked the yards as she passed each house but didn't see anyone outside playing. She reached the corner and looked both ways. There were several children walking along the sidewalk on the next block, but she didn't see Jenny in her yellow jacket. Her chest tightened as she fought the uneasiness that filled her.

Taking a deep breath, she looked around. At the corner on the side street, a blue nylon backpack lay on the ground, pushed under the edge of the hedge that lined the sidewalk. She scooped it up, ripping open the Velcro flap to check inside. "Jennifer Warner" was written in block letters on the nametag. Where was Jenny?

"Jenny!" She shouted the name, turning her head from side to side as she scanned the area. She hurried along the side street, calling as she went. "Jenny!"

Halfway down the block, Kate saw the watercolor.

The paper was caught in the hedge. The wind pinned it against the leafless branches. Across the top, "Spring Is Here" was printed in bold letters. The contrast between the black letters and the red watercolor house with the crooked green roof was stark. Beside the house stood a brown animal, more llama than dog. Jenny always painted her dogs that way. Even when Kate had shown her how a dog should look, she continued to paint the llama-like creatures, because they looked funnier.

Snatching up the painting, she stared at it for a moment, then opened her mouth as she gasped for air. Her heart pounded enough to break her ribs.

*Dear God, where was Jenny?*

Kate began to run, holding the backpack and the picture against her chest as she raced home. Stumbling up the stairs, she wrenched the door open and shoved it closed before running along the hall to the kitchen. She placed the picture on the countertop, lined it up against the edge, and stroked her fingertips across Jenny's signature.

She bit her lip in indecision. Shouldn't she call the neighbors or search outside. A sense of dread invaded her. Jenny never would have left her picture and backpack. She raised her hand and dialed 911.

"Pickard Police Department."

She opened her mouth, but the muscles in her throat refused to work.

"Pickard Police Department," the voice repeated.

"It's my daughter, J . . . Jenny."

"Has there been an accident, ma'am?"

"No. Something's happened to her. I saw her get off the bus, but she just disappeared."

"What do you mean, she disappeared?"

"I found her backpack. And her watercolor. But I can't find Jenny." It was an effort to speak. Her mouth trembled after each syllable, so she tried to keep her answers short in order to maintain control.

"All right, ma'am. Let me get some information." The male voice was firm and reasonable. "Nice and slow now."

"Oh God, I'm so frightened!" Tears trickled down her cheeks, but the sheer act of speaking her fears aloud had a calming effect. She drew a shuddering breath. "Sorry. I'm okay."

"I understand you're upset, but you'll need to stay calm. Now then, your name and address?"

*Please hurry*, Kate begged as she rattled off the information.

"How old is Jenny?"

"Eight. She'll be nine in September."

"Would you describe her, please?"

"She has shoulder-length black hair. It's straight but it curls at the ends. Her eyes are blue. Her skin is sort of an ivory color."

"Height?"

Kate put her hand just below her bosom in order to measure. Her mouth pulled tight in a grimace as she remembered Jenny hugging her before she left for school. For a moment she was unable to speak for the vividness of the little body pressed to her own. Voice hoarse, she spoke into the receiver. "She's about three and a half feet. Just little, very little."

"Okay I've got that. What was she wearing?"

Kate closed her eyes, picturing Jenny at breakfast. "She had on a blue and gray plaid jumper. White short-sleeved blouse with an appliquéd pink rose on the collar. White sneakers with blue shoelaces and white knee socks." She wiped away the tears on her chin with the back of her hand. "And a yellow nylon jacket. Bright yellow."

"Was she wearing any jewelry?"

"Yes. A bracelet. Gold links with one guardian angel charm. The initials JLW are on the back of the charm."

6

"All right, Mrs. Warner. Are you at home now?"

"Yes. I'm here."

"I've already dispatched a car, and in the meantime we'll send this information out on the radio. I want you to go through each room of the house to see if your daughter might have come in while you were out looking for her. Be sure to check the closets and under the beds. Attic and basement too, if you have them."

"And I'll look outside, too."

"Just inside, Mrs. Warner," directed the steady voice. "I know you want to run around the neighborhood and look, but we need you near the phone. In case your daughter calls. Do you understand?"

"Yes, but please hurry."

"Don't worry, Mrs. Warner. We'll find Jenny."

At the last, she heard some warmth in the voice on the other end of the phone. Kate replaced the receiver and ran her fingers over the cold plastic surface as though to let go would break the tenuous bond she had to another person.

She had finished searching the house when the police arrived.

Kate explained to the two police officers how she had found Jenny's watercolor and backpack. Feeling a kinship with the female officer, she spoke directly to her.

"I know something's happened to her." Kate's mouth trembled.

Officer Gates nodded in sympathy. "I know you're worried sick but believe me, Mrs. Warner, this time of year we always get a lot of calls. It's the change in weather. The kids get to playing outside and lose track of the time."

Kate turned to the other police officer for confirmation. His gray hair, potbelly, and ruddy face should have reassured her, but his expression was closed, giving nothing away. He reached in his shirt pocket for a pencil, cradled a clipboard in his left arm, and without meeting her eyes began to ask questions, printing each answer awkwardly, as if he had just learned to write. At the end he sighed, returned the pencil to his pocket and asked for a picture of Jenny.

"We have one of those child ID kits," Kate said. She opened the desk drawer and reached inside for the folder. Her hand shook as she handed it to the older officer. "We put a new picture in a couple months ago when we went to the zoo. It was cold that day so her cheeks are too red but otherwise she looks the same."

"This'll be a big help, Mrs. Warner," Officer Gates said.

"She brought the kit home from school. We didn't think we'd ever need it, but we kept it up to date anyway." Kate's voice trailed away, and in silence she walked the police officers to the door.

*Move! Get out of here!*

The words were silent, reverberating inside his head, but, numb to everything except the horror of his actions, his body refused to respond. A tremor started in his hands, advancing up his arms in a wave so strong he stared down to see if there was something traveling across his skin.

His body shook and a cry started in his chest, bitten off when he ground his teeth together. The truncated sound broke through his inertia and he blinked, then turned his head from side to side to survey the area around the car. The picnic area adjacent to the parking lot of the forest preserve was empty.

*No witnesses. Thank God!*

Fear of discovery spurred him to action and with great effort he raised his hand to turn the key. He gripped the steering wheel with one hand and in slow motion eased the lever into reverse. The car lurched backward with a squeal of tires. He slammed on the brakes, choked back a curse and once more changed gears, this time accelerating slightly. Sweat broke out on his forehead as he struggled to control his speed. He wanted to mash his foot to the floor and tear away but knew such action would increase the risk of being seen and remembered.

*Slow. There's a car ahead. Turn your head as you pass.*

His brain issued commands and his body obeyed.

*Don't speed. Turn right. Slow for the light.*

When he left the forest preserve and entered the suburban streets, the tension began to ease. The grid-patterned streets brought him a sense of balance and, with each turn, he could feel the muscles of his neck and shoulders relax. His breathing deepened, no longer shallow or gasping. He drove with no destination in mind, aware of a gnawing sense of urgency to distance himself from the forest preserve.

*No one must know. No one must know, no one must know, no one!*

The words crescendoed in a jumble of unintelligible sounds until the noise made him sick to his stomach. He opened his mouth, inhaling to dissipate the nausea.

*Gas station. Slow.*

He pulled the car against the side wall of the building, away from the front windows, which had a floor-to-ceiling view of the gas pumps. He shut off the engine and hurried toward the restroom. His movements were wooden, his knee joints frozen in an effort to keep his body upright. As he eased inside the bathroom, he risked a quick look around but there was no one in sight. He shoved the bolt across to secure the door.

Bile rose, burning a pathway up his throat. He made it to the toilet just in time, bending over as the vomit spewed from his mouth and his nose. His stomach convulsed and he gagged, fighting to catch his breath before he threw up again. He wrapped his arms around his torso, hugging his body against the force of the spasms that ripped through his abdomen.

Afterwards he struggled across to the washbasin. He turned on the tap and scooped up water to wash his face and rinse away the bitter taste. When his mouth began to feel cleaner, he cupped his hands and lapped at the water with his tongue, gulping and slurping to quench his raging thirst.

He never should have stopped, but the urges were strong. Just one touch had ripped away his control and by giving in to impulse, the ending was inevitable. He couldn't change what he'd done. What mattered now was that he get away.

Hunched over the sink, he rested on his arms, letting the water run over his fingers. His eyes were closed and he rocked back and forth, willing his body to pick up the strong cadence of his heart.

He heard a metallic clink and froze. He raised his head, but the sound was not repeated. As he leaned forward, he heard it again and looked down. A short length of gold chain was caught on his jacket and struck against the porcelain with the light tinkle of a string of bells. In his mind, small hands pushed against his chest and he sucked in his breath at the instant reminder of the body squirming against his own.

Disentangling the child's bracelet, he cradled it in his hand where it glistened against the wet skin. The clasp was broken, the opening bent at an angle, but the gold charm, a winged angel, was still attached.

Holding the bracelet between thumb and index finger, he placed it in a paper towel and rubbed it free of fingerprints, then wadded it inside the paper and pushed the bundle down among the other trash in the wastebasket.

The moment his fingers lost contact with the bracelet, he was struck by such a strong sense of loss that he rooted through the rubbish until he found it again.

He knew the danger of keeping such an object. The bracelet was physical evidence that could destroy him, but perhaps it would be worth the risk if he used it as a reminder that he must never again give in to impulse. The gold links would become a sacred ring. His talisman.

Sliding the bracelet into his pant's pocket, his fingers rustled among the empty candy wrappers until he found a full one. His thumbnail forced its way beneath the cellophane to push the candy free. He pulled it out and pushed it between his lips, coaxing it into the center of his nested tongue. He sucked it, the pervasive butterscotch flavor banishing the acrid taste in his mouth.

He straightened his back, dropped his shoulders, and blew out two steadying gusts of air, like an athlete preparing for an event. His hands were steady as he unbolted the door.

When Kate heard the key in the front door, she remained in her chair. From the living room, she watched as the door opened and Richard stepped into the hall. For an instant she clung to her belief in miracles hoping that Jenny would appear behind his tall, slim figure.

"Kate?"

Richard's deep voice broke the spell that immobilized her, and she sagged against the back of the chair with a sigh. The sound caught Richard's attention, and he flipped the light switch beside the door.

"What are you doing sitting in the dark?"

Although it was still light outside, the house was shadowed with the approach of evening. He dropped his briefcase beside the hall table and entered the living room, turning on lights as he came toward her. When she didn't speak, his expression changed to one of alarm.

"What is it, Kate? What's wrong?"

"Jenny's missing."

"What do you mean missing?"

In short, blunt sentences Kate told him about searching for Jenny, finding her watercolor, and calling the police.

"Dear God, Kate, why didn't you call me?"

Kate flinched at the tone in his voice then realized part of his anger was fear. "I tried calling you. Your cell phone was off."

Richard reached into the pocket of his jacket and jerked out the phone, eyebrows bunched together as he stared down at the display. "I don't remember turning it off. I'm so sorry."

He crossed to her, pulled her out of the chair, and wrapped his arms around her. She rested her forehead against his chest squeezing her eyes shut as if she could block out the world. She felt a tremor in his body and pushed away before she lost any hope of composure.

"Tell me what's happened. Start from the beginning."

His voice was hoarse as he eased her back into the chair and he pulled up the ottoman so he could face her. When she finished, he rubbed her hands between his as if he sensed the chill that invaded her body.

"She must be playing somewhere," he said. "This has happened before. You need to impress on her again that she needs to follow the rules. Independence brings responsibility."

Kate pressed back a spurt of anger at his comment and spoke firmly. "This is different, Richard. Jenny wouldn't leave her backpack on the ground and she never would have left her watercolor."

"You're right," he conceded. "This whole thing scares the hell out of me. What are the police doing? When did you talk to them last?"

"About an hour ago. I think it was five thirty or five forty-five. They said they'd call as soon as they knew anything."

"Have you called her friends from school?"

"Yes. I even called the school and checked with the bus driver. He said she got off the bus, but doesn't know what happened after that."

"Did you call Bethanne Peters' house? They always walk home together."

"Yes. Bethanne was sick today and didn't go to school. I called all the houses on both our street and on Corydon. No one saw Jenny."

Kate's voice broke. She pressed her fist against her mouth to keep from screaming.

"Nothing could have happened to Jenny in broad daylight. She's got to be somewhere playing," Richard said.

She stared up at him, stunned at his refusal to believe anything else. One look at the lines across his forehead and his tight mouth told her that despite his brisk assurances, he was as terrified as she was. The light outside had taken on a red-orange tint, and she could feel the chill of evening reach into the room.

"Look, Kate, I'm going to change my clothes," Richard said. "Then if Jenny's not back, I'll call the police again. We'll find Jenny."

She followed him to the hall and waited beside the newel post as he went upstairs. She stared down at her watch. It was almost seven. Jenny had been missing since three-fifteen.

Walter Hepburn tried to pace his breathing to the steady thump of his running shoes on the cinder path of the forest preserve. Sweat trickled under the band at his forehead and slid down his temple, leaving the skin tight and itchy. His glasses began to fog as each damp puff of air rasped from his throat. He hated to stop when his rhythm was just beginning to gel. He raised his arm in front of his face and squinted at his wristwatch. Seven o'clock. A few more minutes and then he'd stop.

The toe of his sneaker stubbed on a tree root. He stumbled and lost his balance. Throwing out his hands, he dropped to his knees and fell forward. His glasses flipped off into the shrubbery as he sprawled face down on the trail.

The breath was knocked out of him and he rolled over on his back, gasping for air. Slowly he sat up and, still breathing heavily, felt along his legs, relieved to discover nothing but bruises. If he hadn't been wearing running gloves, the gravel would have scraped the palms of his hands.

He stood up, gingerly shook out his legs, then bent at the waist.

He wiggled his arms and turned his head slowly from side to side. Bunched muscles eased as he rolled his shoulders and scanned the edge of the trail for his glasses. Damn. Without them, he wouldn't be able to drive.

"And for Christ's sake don't step on them," he muttered as he cautiously parted the bushes beside the path.

He searched the ground in sections and cursed at the thick undergrowth. The sun was low in the sky and the shadows had deepened. He was afraid to move too quickly in case he overlooked the glasses in his hurry.

Should've had orange frames. Should've carried an extra pair. Should've exercised more and then he wouldn't have gained weight and been forced to jog to get the lard off.

He was about two feet off the trail when he spotted a glint ahead. Amazed that the glasses had gone so far, he parted the bushes, reached down, and grasped the plastic earpieces. He spit on the lenses and rubbed them clean on the bottom of his sweatshirt. Putting them on, he smiled as his blurred vision cleared.

The brilliant yellow color was stark against the greens and blacks of the early spring woods. Curiosity drew Walter deeper into the underbrush. His eyes focused on the bright material and grew wide as he pulled aside the last branches.

She lay on her back, arms flung wide as if she would embrace the sky. The plaid jumper was bunched up around her hips, the image of innocent sleep marred by the smear of red on her inner thighs. The side of her head was misshapen and blood mingled with the black hair that covered her cheek. Her blue eyes were open, but the horror of her final agony was not visible in the glazed expression.

Light ricocheted off the wall of trees as the police cameras recorded the grim scene. The repeated flashes were like strobe lights creating the illusion of movement where none existed. Muted voices rose above the sound of snapping twigs as the photographers worked around the body.

"It's all yours, Jamison. I'll do the rest when the paramedics arrive," the medical examiner said.

Patrolman Jamison watched as the doctor moved away from the

ring of lights. He nodded to the evidence technicians who approached the body. Seven-thirty. Where the hell was Chief Leidecker anyway? The M.E. and the crime scene guys had gotten here, so what the hell was the hold up with the chief?

His eyes shifted to the back of his squad car where the jogger was sitting, head resting against the back of the seat.

"Did it have to be me he flagged down?" Jamison grumbled.

When he'd called into the station, they told him not to let the guy out of his sight. Until Leidecker arrived, he was in charge, so he'd better do everything according to the book.

"Leidecker'll chew my ass if I screw this up," Jamison muttered.

Two months on the force hadn't prepared him for violent crime. Speeders and addicts, that's all he'd handled. But once he saw the yellow windbreaker, he'd known it was the missing kid. His eyes followed the movements of the two men working over the body. God, only eight-years-old. He shifted his feet and coughed to disguise his shudder of distaste as plastic bags were slipped over the little girl's hands.

Richard paced, moving back and forth between the living room and the kitchen then back again to the front door. Kate remained in the living room, clinging to the arms of the upholstered chair. If she let go, she knew she would lose any control she had over her emotions.

Nothing in her life had prepared her to deal with this. It could not be happening. The police would find Jenny. It was a mistake. She had tried to be a good person. She and Richard and Jenny were a family and she had worked hard to make their world warm and loving and safe. They were protected from bad things. If she remembered that, everything would turn out fine.

She prayed. Meaningless words. She wanted to bargain with God but was afraid to even think about what she could offer for the safe return of her daughter. She recited the prayers she had learned as a child, taking comfort from the familiarity of ritual.

The call from the hospital came at eight-thirty.

Jenny had been found.

# Two

Police Chief Carl Leidecker made his way back to the squad car, slammed the door, and automatically reached for the pack of cigarettes on the console. His fingers closed over a package of gum and he swore. He'd quit when he turned forty. Two years and the compulsion was still there. He tore off the wrapper and wadded the silver foil into a ball, flicking it out the open window of the car and cramming the stick of gum into his mouth.

His teeth jarred together as he stared at the trees lining the parking lot of the forest preserve. The city had spent a lot of money planting flowers and shrubs, putting fresh wood chips on the trails, and picking up the trash. Before the divorce, he and Mary Clare used to picnic in the Chicago parks. None as nice as this one. Death was never acceptable, but rape and murder in such a place was sacrilegious.

Located thirty miles from Chicago, Pickard had always had the atmosphere of a small country village. He'd taken the job of chief of police in order to get away from the brutality of crime in Chicago. He should have remembered that evil was universal.

He turned the key in the ignition and backed up slowly, muttering under his breath at the small group of onlookers who stood just beyond the yellow tape that blocked off the outer reaches of the crime scene. Voyeurs and thrill seekers. Earlier there had been a carnival atmosphere, but when the covered stretcher containing the body of the child had been put into the ambulance, the spectators quieted and huddled together as if for warmth in the gathering chill of night.

The ambulance pulled away. Caught in the red glow of the whirling lights, the crowd appeared motionless, reminding Leidecker of a stop action scene from a horror film.

After viewing the crime scene, he'd talked to the jogger who'd found the body. Unfortunately he was so into his run that he hadn't seen anyone or heard anything until he'd lost his glasses. He was pretty shaken up, so after a few more questions, Carl had let him go home.

The chewing gum turned hard and Carl spit the wad into the night then threw the car into gear.

It was time to go to the hospital. Since becoming the chief of police six years earlier, Carl had made it a practice to go to the hospital whenever there was a fatality and the police were involved. Traffic-related deaths were the only ones he'd had to deal with. This was different.

It was never easy talking to the parents after the death of a child, but in this case it would be particularly difficult, since he knew both Kate and Richard Warner from church. He and Richard had worked on the fund-raising committee, and he'd been to the Warner's house several times for meetings.

The hospital doors slid open automatically with an asthmatic wheeze. Rubber matting muffled the sound of his heels as he approached the nurses' station. He was not surprised to see Marge Carrier, the head nurse, waiting for him. In a small town, news travels fast.

"This way, Carl."

She preceded him along the hallway. There was a stiffness to her white uniformed back that reminded Carl that Marge's granddaughter was the same age as Jennifer Warner. She stopped at a door with a nameplate that read: DR. MICHAEL KENNEDY.

"Dr. Kennedy said to bring you to his office." She tapped lightly and without waiting for a response turned the handle and swung the door open.

Mike came around from behind the desk and met Carl halfway across the carpet. They shook hands.

"Thanks for coming, Carl. Have a seat," he said, waving to one of the chairs pulled up in front of the desk.

Carl sank into the leather chair and stared across at the doctor.

He knew Mike mainly from the golf course. They'd played together in several charity events. There was an air of reassurance about him that immediately put people at ease. Perhaps it was his size. He was easily six foot, heavily built, the buttons of his white coat straining slightly across his midsection. Beneath the overhead fluorescent lights his brown hair held red tints. It was thick and worn on the shaggy side, standing away from his head as if he had a habit of running his hands through it. The pallor of his skin accentuated the freckles that covered his face.

"Since I know the Warners, the hospital asked if I'd act as liaison. Here's my card." He waited while Carl jotted the numbers onto his clipboard notes, then sat down behind the desk. "If you have questions or need anything from the staff, I'm the one who's supposed to expedite things. We haven't had a lot of experience with this . . . ."

Mike's words trickled away and he made no attempt to complete the sentence. He rubbed his face with one hand, then reached around to massage the back of his neck.

"I briefed the men who accompanied the body," Carl said. "They know exactly what guidelines to follow. Everything will be done by the book. We want to do everything possible to make sure the perpetrator is brought to justice."

The formal phrases lowered the emotional level in the room and set the focus on procedure.

"Sorry," Mike said. "This is still hard to take in. Richard called me when he found out that Jenny had been brought here. All he'd been told was that there had been an accident."

"There's no good way to get this kind of news," Carl said. "Are Kate and Richard here?"

Mike nodded.

"You know I'll have to talk to Kate. She's the one who reported Jenny missing."

"Can't it wait?"

"No. It's got to be done now while all the details are fresh."

"They're pretty cut up so go as easy as you can. Besides being a doctor, I'm their friend. Richard and I go back a long way. We were roommates in college. I'm Jenny's godfather."

Poor bastard! Mike's words explained the wealth of emotion Carl had sensed just below the surface. "Were you Jenny's pediatrician?"

"No. Geriatrics. I deal well with my older patients. Jenny says it's the freckles."

At mention of the murdered child's name, a bleak expression crossed his face. Before he could say anything else, the phone on the desk rang. Mike snatched up the receiver, spoke briefly, and then rose from his chair.

"The hospital chaplain has just left Kate and Richard. I'll take you down there. I won't come in, but if you need me just pick up the phone and page me."

He crossed the room in long, restless strides, leading Carl along the hall to the staff lounge. They stood at the door, watching as Richard leaned over Kate, his words a quiet murmur in the room. Carl entered, waiting until Richard became aware of his presence and rose to his feet.

Richard's athletic body and five-foot-eleven frame appeared bowed by the tragedy of his daughter's death. Beneath curly black hair, his tanned hawkish face looked skeletal, blue eyes lackluster. In his jeans and sweater, he looked youthful, but he moved stiffly as if he had aged overnight. The man was in the zombie stage, too stunned to take in the long-term effects of the tragedy. Perhaps the body reacted that way as a form of protection. Carl couldn't begin to imagine how one coped with the pain.

He crossed the room and reached out to shake hands. "God, I'm sorry."

"I know." Richard nodded as if he understood all that was left unsaid.

Kate had not changed positions since his entry. She sat primly on the edge of the couch, feet together, and hands folded in her lap. Her head was bent, any expression hidden behind the curtain of brown hair that fell on either side of her face.

Carl leaned down toward her. "Kate?"

She didn't move, and he wondered if he had spoken too softly. The fingers of her hands tightened around each other. She raised her head slowly as if the weight were too much for her slender neck to bear.

Her eyes searched his face and he could see that it was an effort for her to concentrate.

"She's a little groggy," Richard said at his shoulder. "Mike gave her something after we heard about Jenny." His voice broke and it was a moment before he could continue. "Kate, it's Carl Leidecker. He's going to help us."

Her brown eyes were enormous. She blinked rapidly, as if to help her focus. She started to rise and Carl held out his hand for her to grasp.

"Oh, Carl. How could anyone hurt Jenny?" she asked.

"I don't know, Kate. We're trying to find out, but we're going to need your help." Although she did not pull away, Carl could feel her withdrawal. "That's the only way we're going to find the killer. Do you understand?"

Her response was a whisper. "Yes."

She released his hand as if to distance herself from him and sat down. Richard looked uncertain for a moment and then perched on the overstuffed arm of the couch, near enough to offer comfort, yet free to move at will. Carl pulled up a chair.

Questioning Kate about the events leading up to her 911 call was difficult. Several times he had to repeat the questions. Occasionally in the midst of a reply, her words would become halting, fading into silence until she looked up in bewilderment unable to grasp the thread of her answer.

Carl turned to Richard with relief. In contrast to Kate's responses, his words were bursts of energy, punctuated by restless gestures. He gave a crisp summary of his actions during the day.

Through each of their recitals, Carl took notes. Despite his resolve to remain impersonal, he could not keep from thinking about the last time he had seen Jennifer Warner.

It was in February after Sunday Mass. The Girl Scouts were sponsoring a Valentine's Day bake sale in the choir room. The smell of coffee and fresh baked goods drew him in, and he recognized Jenny behind the Brownie Scout table. He asked her what she had baked. Self-consciously she pointed to the peanut butter cookies. When he bought three plates full, Jenny's eyes opened wide in astonishment and her mouth stretched in a grin of delight.

When Carl had seen her body at the crime scene, Jenny's mouth had been bruised, lips split by her attacker.

"I think that's it for now," he said. His words came out more harshly than he intended and Kate's head jerked up, her eyes fluttering in confusion. In a softer tone, "I have everything I need for the moment."

Both Kate and Richard rose to their feet. Now that the questioning was over they were reluctant to let him leave. Their business with him was unfinished; he was their hope of a solution. Carl shook Richard's hand and took Kate's hands in both of his. Her cold fingers clutched at him as if to steady herself.

"I realize it's little comfort, but the entire police force will be working on this."

Richard put his arm around Kate's shoulders, and she released her grip on Carl's hands. He walked to the door and exited without looking back.

When Carl had moved to Pickard, he'd felt a sense of community that he'd never had in Chicago. This was his town. As police chief he was responsible for public safety. No matter what it took, he'd find the bastard who killed Jennifer Warner.


The following morning Carl turned into Kate and Richard's street, a quiet residential area in the older section of Pickard. A clutter of vehicles lined the street half way up the block to the cul de sac.

*Dammit!*

Two mobile TV vans from Chicago were parked beneath the trees, while other reporters and photographers huddled in groups on the lawn and sidewalks. He drew his car up to the curb and they converged on him like a pack of snapping pit bulls.

"Chief Leidecker! Chief Leidecker!"

Voices shouted at him as he opened the car door; a microphone and several tape recorders were shoved in his face. Wanting to set the ground rules immediately, he remained perfectly still, waiting until the frenzied group had quieted before he spoke.

"All right, folks, listen up. I'm going to give all of you ten minutes to clear out of here. After that I'm going to haul your butts in for obstructing traffic." He ignored the groaning objections and glared at the cameraman who was closest to him until the man backed up a little. "This is not Chicago. In Pickard we expect a certain show of decency. These people have suffered a terrible loss. I know you're looking for a story, but for the moment this place is off limits. After I talk to the Warners, I'll be more than happy to meet with all of you back at the station and answer your questions. Now get moving."

"Have you got any suspects?"

"Is the coroner's report in?"

"Is it true this is just one of a series of child murders in Pickard?"

Carl did not even acknowledge the questions, reaching inside the car for the radio to order backup to the area. He leaned casually against the car door, watching the activity as the crowd dispersed and the exodus began. By the time two patrol cars arrived, there were only a few neighbors standing around and these stragglers broke apart and hurried indoors. After giving the men instructions to block off the street to the media, he picked up his leather notebook and started up the walk.

Neatly trimmed bushes hugged the two-story Tudor and the green of tulips and daffodils was already showing in the stone-edged gardens on either side of the front stairs. The house had been painted recently and the cream-colored flower boxes beneath the front windows were still empty. Carl wondered if the boxes would ever hold flowers again.

Moving briskly, he brushed a piece of lint from his uniform sleeve, straightened his shoulders, and pushed the doorbell. After a moment, a short, matronly woman pulled the door inward. Her body barred his entrance and warily she peeked around him at the empty street.

"Thank goodness, they're gone. It's been a zoo all morning."

"Sorry, ma'am. My men will keep the street clear," he said, adding, "Chief Leidecker to see the Warners."

He stepped forward, forcing the woman to pull the door wider to permit him entry. The phone was ringing and in the back of the house he could hear the low murmur of voices.

"Please come in. I'm the Warner's next door neighbor. This is all so god-awful." Her voice shook and her face took on a pinched look.

"I'll get Richard. They just got back from the funeral home, and we're trying to get Kate to eat something. She hasn't been able to keep anything down since it happened and she's going to need strength to get through the next couple of days."

As if she realized that she was beginning to babble, she snapped her mouth shut, turned on her heel, and hurried toward the back of the house. Left alone, Carl surveyed the living room, soothed by the warmth evident in the arrangement of the furnishings. The upholstery fabrics and draperies were varied tones of yellow and cream. The only bright splash of color in the room was the red in the painting that hung above the fireplace.

Carl remembered seeing the picture. He had commented on it, and Kate had told him with pardonable pride that Richard had painted it. Moving closer to the mantel, he stared up at the rain scene, a moment in time caught forever in swirling brushstrokes on the canvas.

Beneath red umbrellas, two figures in yellow slickers and black boots splashed in a puddle. The woman's face was in shadow, but the child's laughing features were so meticulously painted that Carl imagined he could hear her girlish shrieks in the corners of the room. With a sickening feeling in the pit of his stomach, he realized that the child would never laugh again.

Jenny Warner, the model for the picture, was dead.

Carl turned his back and faced the archway as footsteps sounded in the hall and the telephone shrilled. Richard Warner came into view just as the doorbell rang, a quieter echo to the strident tone of the phone.

"Good God, now what!" Richard said, rubbing a hand across his forehead. He reached toward the doorknob, hesitated for a moment, then snatched the door open. The conversation was unintelligible, but Richard's rigid back reflected the controlled pain just beneath the surface.

"Thank you for coming, Joe," He accepted the plastic-wrapped plate thrust into his hand, and began to ease the front door closed. "I know Kate will appreciate the cake."

Once the door was closed he stood uncertainly with the plate in his hand, then set it on the mahogany table in the hall, and turned once more toward the living room, extending his hand as he crossed the carpeting. "Carl. Sorry to keep you waiting, but this place is bedlam."

"Please, don't give it a thought."

"Marian told me that you got rid of those ghouls out front."

"We'll try to keep the media at a distance, but it won't last."

"Bastards almost mobbed us when we went to the funeral home."

Richard's voice was savage and as Carl opened his mouth to reply, the phone rang again.

"It's been like this ever since we came home last night. Joe Bushnell, the guy who just brought the cake, lives at the end of the block with his wife. I know people are trying to show their concern, but it's about to drive me out of my mind. Come into my studio. There's no phone in there."

Richard moved to a door at the back of the living room. Carl followed, entering what appeared to be a converted porch. Draperies covered the windows on two sides, but were open over the windows that faced out onto a fenced backyard. Aside from shelves along the wall that were crowded with books and papers, the room was surprisingly neat. An easel with a covered canvas stood in one corner, and facing the backyard, was a drafting table and stool. Two easy chairs were tucked in a corner and Richard indicated to Carl that he should take one.

"Kate will be along in a moment. She's having some soup and I told her she had to finish it before she could join us."

Carl took in the strained air and the nervous energy carefully held in check. Before he could respond, Richard hurried into speech.

"Thank you for expediting everything with the funeral home." His voice shook slightly, but after a shuddered breath, he managed to continue. "As it stands now there'll be a wake tomorrow and the funeral will be Friday. Everyone has been so understanding."

"I'm glad." Inadequate words.

"Richard?"

Carl had not been aware of Kate's arrival until she spoke. One hand held to the framework of the door and the other pressed against her throat. Her face was devoid of color except for a bright slash of lipstick. With her brown hair tied with a rubber band behind her head, she looked like a teenager rather than a woman in her thirties.

"Come and sit down, Kate." Richard drew her into the room, easing her toward one of the chairs and standing over her until she settled into the cushions. "Did you finish your soup?" he asked as if she were a child.

"Most of it," she said, her voice a bare whisper.

The few times that Carl had seen Kate and Richard together, he had been surprised at their interaction. They were a loving couple, but it was clear that Richard was the more dominant in the marriage. She was always gracious, but in Richard's company she concentrated on anticipating his needs. Her plain clothing and lack of makeup did little to enhance the beauty that Carl saw in her. He wondered if her preference to remain in the shadows was her idea or Richard's.

Carl sorted through his notes, giving them a chance to prepare themselves for his questions. Asking them to repeat everything that happened the day Jenny disappeared would be painful, but he knew from experience that each repetition would be less hurtful.

Throughout their recital of events, Carl heard the constant ring of the phone, a muted reminder of the world outside the closed door of the studio. Richard appeared unaffected by the chaos beyond the room. He seemed able to focus on the events of the moment to the exclusion of all else. Kate flinched at each sound. Occasionally she closed her eyes, taking a deep, steadying breath until the lines and furrows smoothed away leaving her face expressionless. Only then did she re-open her eyes. Emotions once more controlled.

Carl finished scratching notes on the yellow, lined sheets in his notebook. He reached into the folder at the back and pulled out a sealed envelope.

"This is a copy of the preliminary autopsy report." He tried to ignore the horror on their faces, letting the honesty in his words reach out to the couple. "I know you're not ready to read this now, but later you may want to see it. It's better to know exactly what happened than to imagine even worse things. No one can hurt Jenny anymore. I know you're in agony, but it's necessary to find the man who killed her. Let your anger help you fight the grief."

He handed the envelope to Richard, who folded it with meticulous care and put it in the pocket of his shirt. Kate turned away as if the sight of such a document was too distasteful for her to bear.

Carl didn't give them time to dwell on what might be in the report. "I'm sure you're appalled by the cameras and reporters. We'll try to keep things under control but you need to know that some of it's necessary and actually serves a purpose. We'll be taking our own film of people at the funeral home, the church, and the cemetery. Later we'll go back and, with your help, identify everyone who was present."

"You think the murderer would show up?" Richard asked.

"More than likely. Or so the psychiatrists would have us believe." Keeping his voice neutral, Carl continued, "I know you've got a lot to do but I'll need a list of names from you sometime today."

After a sideways glance at his wife, Richard asked, "Is this something that could wait?"

"No, I'm afraid not. It shouldn't take you long. We need the names of everyone either of you spoke to the day of Jenny's disappearance. Added to that I'd like a list of the people you know or have frequent contact with. Doctors. Dentists. For the present, just people in Pickard."

"You mean — our friends?" Kate asked.

"Yes." He kept his response to the single syllable. Everyone wanted crime to be committed by strangers.

"Surely you don't think someone we know would have h-hurt Jenny?" she asked.

"It's something we can't rule out. Although it's possible that the attacker was a transient, we have to go on the assumption that it was someone Jenny knew. So far we've had neither report nor sign of a forcible abduction. At this point the evidence suggests that she went willingly with her killer."

He watched both parents as the impact of his words sank in. The nightmare situation had just gotten worse. The thought that someone they knew might have committed such a crime was another cruelty added to the death of their child.

"Do either of you recall any time that you were uncomfortable with anyone's relationship with Jenny?"

"No, of course not." Kate shook her head, shrinking against the cushioned back of the chair.

"Did Jenny seem unusually shy with any of your friends or acquaintances?"

"No." Richard's response was brusque.

"I know this is distasteful, but it must be faced. In light of what's happened, you need to think back. Perhaps something happened that at the time you dismissed as nothing of importance. Don't drive yourselves crazy but give it some thought and let me know if anything comes to mind," Carl said. "Do you have any questions?"

Richard spoke up immediately. "You say you've had no reports of an abduction. But what if someone saw something but doesn't know it's important?"

"Don't worry. Officers have gone door to door all around the bus stop, especially on the side street where the watercolor was found. We questioned all of the occupants in the households. That brings up something I need to ask you." He reached into the folder again and withdrew another sheet of paper. "In the pocket of Jenny's windbreaker there was a piece of hard candy. She had been sucking it and put it back into the original wrapper. It's an imported brand of butterscotch candy called ButterSkots. Are you familiar with it?"

"ButterSkots? No, I never heard of it," Richard said.

"Jenny hated butterscotch," Kate said, sitting forward in her chair, her face alive with eagerness for the first time in the interview. "She always spit it out. If you're suggesting that someone might have offered Jenny candy in order to grab her, you're way off base, Carl. She'd had all the 'Stranger Danger' lectures. She knew enough not to be enticed by the offer of a piece of candy."

"It may have no bearing at all on what happened. I'll check with her teacher to see if she got it at school. One more thing. When you reported Jenny missing, you described what she was wearing but in going over the list there's an item not accounted for. You said she was wearing a bracelet."

Carl flattened out the piece of paper and ran his finger under the section as he read the description. "One bracelet. Gold links with one charm of a guardian angel. The initials JLW on the back of the charm."

Kate's eyes filled with tears. She nodded her head but was unable to speak.

Richard, voice tight, answered for her. "I gave her the bracelet last Christmas."

"The bracelet didn't show up on the list of her belongings. Are you positive she had it on when she left for school?"

"Yes," Kate said. "I remember distinctly because it caught on the sleeve of her windbreaker when she was getting ready to leave."

"Do you have a picture of the bracelet or could you make a drawing of the charm?"

If anything, Kate's face went paler. She reached into the neckline of her blouse and pulled out a gold necklace. Her fingers shook as she undid the clasp and extended it to Carl.

"The charm is just like Jenny's. Richard gave each of us one."

Carl took the necklace, holding the charm in the palm of his hand. Still warm from the heat of Kate's body, the winged angel felt alive.

"Would you mind if I borrowed this?" When she shook her head, he placed the necklace in the breast pocket of his uniform and buttoned the flap. "You'll get this back and in the meantime I'll take very good care of it." Carl wrote a note at the bottom of the page, then closed the notebook and stood up. "That's it for now."

Before Kate could rise, Richard was at her side, helping her up, holding her in the protective circle of his arm. They walked with Carl back through the living room. They remained in a silent triangle, having no social amenities to get them past the awkward phrases of grief. Carl opened the front door, then turned in the doorway to face Kate and Richard.

"I'll keep you posted," he said.

With a brisk nod of his head, he walked to his squad car. The street was empty but a flutter of the curtains across the street gave evidence of the avid curiosity that always surrounded a tragedy. He'd have to send several officers to the funeral home and to the church the day of the funeral for crowd control. He couldn't protect the Warners from reporters for long, but he'd try.

Reminded that he'd promised to make a press statement back at

27

the station, he sat for a moment trying to decide how much information he could hold back without the reporters crying foul. He had a nagging feeling that something he'd heard since the discovery of the murder didn't ring true. Picking up his folder he skimmed his notes, flipping pages and stopping at random, hoping that something would trigger his memory. So many interviews. Every investigation was a morass of paperwork.

Paperwork. Work. His head jerked up, eyes unfocused, thoughts coalescing into a question. He returned to his notes, searching each page, stopping once, moving forward to stop again.

It was a triviality. Probably just a throwaway comment. But if it wasn't, it opened up a frightening possibility. It would only take one call to verify. Like a child who suspected a monster under his bed, he was reluctant to check. He tossed the leather folder on the seat and started the car.

Knowing he'd have to do it eventually, Carl reached for his cell phone.

# THREE

Kate shed no tears at the wake.

By detaching herself from the process, she was able to calmly greet those who came to pay their respects, with only an occasional break in her composure. She stood beside the closed casket, periodically stroking the satiny surface as if in some way she could touch the child lying within the cushioned interior. In the quiet moments she stared at Jenny's picture nestled in the spray of coral roses and babies breath, praying silently that it was only a nightmare.

Her prayers went unanswered.

For most of the evening, Richard stood beside her, supporting her with a touch or a glance but occasionally, when restlessness overcame him, he left her to roam the fringes of the large room, acknowledging the comments of friends and acquaintances but avoiding any real conversations. Worried about him, she followed him with her eyes.

He's shrunk, she noted with concern. It wasn't just that he was weighted down by the tragedy, but in some real sense he had shriveled. The spark of vitality that originally had drawn her to him was dimmed.

She could still remember the first time that she'd seen him. Fresh out of college, she had been hired as a copywriter for Mayerling Ltd., a Chicago advertising agency. On her first day of work, she had arrived early and wandered the silent halls looking for someone to tell her where to go. In the conference room, a man paced in front of a storyboard, practicing his presentation of an ad campaign. Standing unnoticed in the doorway, she watched in fascination as he waved his arms to punctuate the words he mumbled under his breath.

At twenty-six, Richard Warner had been striking rather than handsome, tall with broad shoulders, no hips, and a loose-limbed walk. Bony wrists stuck out of his shirtsleeves and his hands were large, the fingers long and gracefully shaped. He had thin, almost ascetic features. El Greco would have loved to paint him, she thought.

There was an aura of excitement around him and in that instant she fell in love. She wanted to be a part of his world. She was drawn to his strength as well. He took control of her life, which had been unfocused since the death of her father the year before. Six months later they married.

During eleven years of marriage, Richard had been in charge. He was never domineering, but always gave her the feeling she was protected and treasured. Her father had controlled her life after her mother died when Kate was twelve. He had been a loving but demanding parent, selecting her class subjects, her clothes, and her friends. Her father had been the major influence in her life, and without his guidance she had felt lost. Kate stepped into the wifely role with ease, grateful that Richard was willing to make the decisions in their lives.

Even though she did not believe it, Kate loved the fact that Richard thought she was beautiful. She suspected with his artist's eye, he had different standards than the rest of the world. He taught her how to dress and chose clothes that gave her confidence in her appearance and style. If she had beauty, Richard had given it to her.

She had been so lost in her thoughts, she was startled when Mike Kennedy appeared at her side.

"How's my girl?" he asked.

He opened his mouth to speak again but this time there were no words. He held out his arms. Letting down her guard for a moment, Kate drew strength from his embrace. She closed her eyes, rested her head against his chest, and wished he could block out the world forever. A tear slid out of the corner of her eye. She took a shuddering breath and stepped back.

"Where's Chessy?"

"Right here, Kate." The normally throaty voice of Mike's girl-friend was tight with tears. "Oh, God, I'm sorry."

Two years earlier when Mike had brought her to the house for dinner, Kate had liked the long-haired brunette with the plain face, the breathtaking dimensions and the incongruous name of Chesa-peake Chesney. Chessy was the nutritionist at the hospital who teased Mike that his main interest was not in her but in her cooking skills.

Kate pressed the other woman's hands in a quick gesture of friend-ship. "Thank you for coming."

Chessy reached into her purse and pulled out a linen handker-chief, scrubbing her eyes and blowing her nose. "Is there anything we can do?"

"Nothing really. Tomorrow is the funeral at St. Madelaine's." Kate stopped talking, swallowing and blinking her eyes several times before she could continue.

"How are you managing with all this furor going on outside? Re-porters. Curiosity seekers. It's incredible."

"The funeral home sent a limo for us this morning and smuggled us in a side door. On the one hand I hate the publicity, but on the other I keep thinking it might prompt people to come forward with any in-formation that might help the case."

Chessy turned to answer a question from Mike and, for a moment, Kate was alone, her back to the majority of the people in the room. A wave of uneasiness crept up her spine. She fixed her eyes on the cruci-fix above the casket and fought back a sense of panic.

"Kate?" Carl Leidecker's voice at her shoulder made her jump.

The muscles in Kate's throat constricted as she turned to face him. She nodded as he took her hand and spoke quietly to her. She didn't take in the content of the words, only the comfort in his voice.

The strength in his fingers surprised Kate. Outwardly he didn't look particularly strong. He was an inch or two shorter than Richard, slight of build, with studied, almost plodding, movements.

Kate wondered if he had adopted the slow, methodical actions to cover a mind both quick and subtle. The other times she had met him, he kept in the background, offering information only when prodded.

He was a private person, perhaps made so because of his job. His firm grip communicated a strength of purpose and commitment to Kate. If it were at all possible, Carl Leidecker would find Jenny's killer.

Again a shiver of apprehension chilled her. She released his hand, breaking the tenuous connection.

Leidecker moved to the back of the room, speaking only to the people who approached him, shaking his head often in answer to their questions. Throughout the evening, Kate remained aware of him. His eyes were hooded beneath lowered brows, his very stillness an indication that he was unobtrusively observing the faces of the gathered mourners.

To Kate, it seemed that everyone in Pickard had come to the funeral home. Mayor Frank Etzel and his assistant Joseph Garvey came with their wives. She had never met either of the men but appreciated their attendance. Neighbors, friends, acquaintances from church and the library. Even strangers held her hand and whispered words of condolence. The death of a child was a shared pain.

She was touched by the number of people from Richard's office who had made the effort to attend the wake. Christian Mayerling, Richard's boss, arrived early in the evening. His carriage was stiff, muscles rippling in his jawline as he patted Richard awkwardly on the shoulder.

At fifty-five, Chris was tall and whipcord thin, with an elegance that was part upbringing and part affectation. He came from a wealthy family, well-connected in Chicago. Just recently he had moved to an exclusive hi-rise on Round Lake, so they saw more of him than they had when he lived in the city. He had a full head of black hair with wings of white at the temples that accentuated his striking good looks.

"God Almighty, Kate, what can I say?" He grasped both her hands, pressing them convulsively. "Is there anything I can do?"

"There's nothing, Chris, but thanks for offering. Your flowers are lovely," she said, nodding at the enormous basket of spring flowers on the pedestal beside the casket. "Jenny loved daffodils."

"I was hoping so. One of the pictures in Richard's office shows her with an armful."

Kate remembered the picture and her eyes filled with tears. Chris turned to Richard, while Kate tried to gather the remnants of her composure. She checked her watch. Eight. One more hour.

Watching Richard she was struck by how alone she was. Most of the people in the room were friends of his. She had no immediate family and he had not encouraged her to socialize with either the school parents or anyone at the library. She had always felt her life was full. She had been busy with Jenny and Richard, never realizing that except for Mike and Chessy and Marian Grainger she had few real friends. How would she fill her life now that Jenny was gone?

*Be careful. The COP has arrived.*

He could feel his body tensing the moment Leidecker entered the room. No emotion visible on the COP face except when the shadowing lids lifted and a flash of expression quivered across the surface.

The COP stood at the back of the room: a guard on patrol. Probing eyes. Sweeping around the room like the searchlights in a prison camp. Progressing slowly, evaluating, and weighing.

He was grateful he had not brought the talisman.

Just before he came to the funeral home he had taken it out of the secret place. The metal looked dull. He rubbed the bracelet against his pant leg to polish it.

He raised it to his eyes. The gold links appeared brighter. Once again he rubbed it against his leg. He stroked more vigorously and beneath the material of his pants he could feel the heat against his leg. His erection was immediate.

Time had been short. He couldn't continue to explore his rising excitement and the prickly sensations quivering beneath his skin. He'd debated taking the bracelet with him but knew it was safer where it was. Later.

He returned to the moment and his own wrenching sorrow as he stared at the tiny casket. Realization of his precarious position sent a spurt of anger through his body that temporarily blocked the pain.

What had she done with the candy wrapper? Had she dropped it in the woods? It wasn't in the ashtray or wedged behind the car seat.

He'd searched the entire car and couldn't find it. If the police had found the wrapper maybe they wouldn't think anything about it. Kids always carried candy in their pockets.

He couldn't afford to make another mistake. He had to go on the assumption that the police found the wrapper and get rid of the rest of them. Or at least keep them hidden. Too many secrets. His brain felt overloaded with everything he had to remember.

It was done. Nothing could change what had happened. All that mattered at the moment was to protect himself. And the COP was his greatest danger.

COP *eyes see too much.*

Kate had heard of out-of-body experiences and wondered if that was what was happening. She was present at the funeral service but it was as if she were not a part of the proceedings. The pew beneath her was unyielding, yet she had no sense of the solid oak against her thighs. The organ music came from a distance, the sounds muted and wavery as though she were underwater.

> Jenny loved me in the springtime
> When the buds were on the trees
> Once the chill winds bared the branches
> Jenny left me in the fall.

Kate closed her eyes and tried to remember if those were actually the words of the song. Was it a song? Maybe it was a poem. She couldn't recall where she had heard it. Over and over, she rolled each syllable inside her head. It was very important to recall the exact sequence of the words. She fixed her eyes on a spot above Father Blaney's head and ran through the lyrics again. She wished she could say them out loud.

She opened her mouth to speak but some slight motion must have penetrated Richard's consciousness because he turned to her and reached over to pat her knee. She closed her mouth. Directing her eyes to the large crucifix suspended over the altar, she concentrated on the details of the hanging Christ, noting the contrast between the black

34

iron spikes and the white skin of the porcelain hands. She closed her mind to the words of the funeral service.

She glanced down at Richard's hand resting on her knee, her own fingers clenched around his wrist. She was cold, and it frightened her that Richard's proximity brought her no warmth. In the days since Jenny's death, he had touched her and held her but he could not reach below the surface to give her comfort. It was almost as if Jenny's absence had opened a void between them that could never again be filled.

Her eyes flickered to the tiny coffin standing isolated in front of the altar. She averted her gaze, listening to the words filling her mind.

> Jenny wandered free and happy
> Dashing through the summer sunshine
> Even though she's gone forever
> I can still hear Jenny's call.

It didn't sound right. Kate started over but as she repeated the second verse, she stumbled over the word "forever." She tried moving her mouth to form the sounds but her lips were unyielding.

*Oh please God please God please God.*

The organ chords trembled at the beginning of another hymn. Richard stood and his hand dropped away from her. Kate pressed back against the wooden seat. She wanted to remain where she was, sitting perfectly still until she became invisible. She didn't want to participate.

Even as rebellion built within her, she knew such behavior would draw the eyes of the congregation and that she could not permit. She could bear the furtive glances, but not the full weight of all that attention.

She stood. One. Two. Three. Six tile roses edged the doorway into the chancery.

> Jenny smiled at all the young men
> Flocking round her day and night
> In her eyes I saw the message
> Jenny loved me best of all.

Movement on the edge of her vision broke through her concentration. Carl Leidecker slipped in the side door and walked toward the back of the church. For the funeral, he was dressed in a dark suit, but despite the plain clothes she knew he was attending in an official capacity, watching their friends and neighbors, eyes once more full of questions.

Questions. Endless questions and still no answers.

Kate gripped the wooden handrail of the pew, absorbing the vibrations of sound through her palms. Father Blaney left the altar and approached the coffin. A whimper slipped through her control and she reached out in panic for Richard, plucking at the sleeve of his suit. His head was bowed and his whole body shook. She enclosed his fingers in her own, clinging to him, as they followed the casket up the aisle.

The doors of the church opened and Kate flinched. Police, reporters, and a group of onlookers waited on the sidewalk. Cameramen jostled for position on the stairs, one lens no more than two feet away. Kate instinctively brought her hand up to shield her face. Richard pulled her against his side, shouldering his way through the crowd to where the coffin was being placed inside the hearse.

One. Two. Kate focused on the cars drawn up at the curb. Nineteen. Twenty. And others in the parking lot, marked with the purple funeral stickers to indicate they would be going to the cemetery. Kate remembered how for months after her cousin Connie's funeral, a residue of glue had stuck to the windshield, catching at the rubber edge of the wipers whenever it rained.

The back door of the hearse closed with a leaden sound, and Richard led her to the funeral home limousine. The crowd of reporters surged forward, pressing against the sides of the car, and she shrank against Richard, closing her eyes to block out the avid curiosity on the faces outside the windows.

She shed no tears during the ceremony at the graveside, received no comfort from the traditional words. None of it had any relationship to Jenny of the twinkly eyes. Jenny, of the dirt-streaked face and straggly black pigtails. Jenny, of the restless feet and lithe body.

After the service, Kate and Richard were led to a police car for the drive home. Once more the street was blocked off and Kate was grateful for the protection. The clamor of the press and the gawkers had been terrifying.

Leidecker's patrol car was parked in front of the house. By the time they pulled into the driveway Carl was already opening the door beside Kate. He held out his hand, but she didn't move.

"Is there any news?" she asked.

Leidecker squatted on his heels so that his face was level with hers. His expression was full of compassion and she sensed his apology for this intrusion. "Nothing conclusive, Kate. It's going to take time."

She looked at him, waiting for him to continue.

In answer to her unspoken question, Carl said, "There are a few things I need to clear up."

Richard leaned across Kate. "It's been a very long day. Couldn't this wait until tomorrow?"

"No." Carl's glance moved from Kate to Richard. His expression hardened. "Although it's not strictly necessary, in my opinion, Richard, you should consider having a lawyer present."

# FOUR

It took a moment for the import of Carl's words to register with Kate. "What . . . what's going on?" Her head swiveled between the two men in her confusion. "Richard?"

After a moment of absolute stillness, he blinked, eyes now shuttered as he turned his head away from her, one hand gripping the door handle of the car with whitened fingers. The silence was claustrophobic. In rising panic, she clutched Richard's arm. His rigid body relaxed at her touch.

"Let's go into the house, Kate," he said, opening his door.

He got out, leaving her alone and disoriented. At her side, Carl once more extended his hand. Frightened by the police chief's attitude, she waved him away and struggled out of the car.

Her legs threatened to buckle under her. She locked her knees until Richard was beside her and then took his arm, leaning against him for support. Her emotions were so close to the surface that she barely controlled the urge to run away.

Richard unlocked the front door and she entered, all too conscious of Leidecker's footsteps behind her. She led the way to the family room at the back of the house.

She opened the curtains across the patio doors and stared outside at the late afternoon sunshine that highlighted the newly budding trees in the backyard. At the cemetery, she had dreaded returning to the emptiness of the house. The fear and confusion at Leidecker's intrusion superseded her despair. At least for the moment. Fighting for control, she turned to face the others.

"Now, Carl," she said, moving to stand beside Richard. "What exactly is going on here?"

"Sorry, Kate," Leidecker said. "Several questions have come up that need to be answered."

"Again?" Kate asked. "Haven't you asked the same questions over and over enough times?"

She didn't know why she was reacting so strongly to Leidecker's presence, but she had a real sense of danger.

"Go away," she said. "Come back tomorrow and we'll talk." Richard moved restlessly at her side and she turned to him, tears of frustration filling her eyes. "Make them go away, Richard."

"It's all right, Kate," he said. "Let's just get it over with."

Before she could speak, Richard led her over to the couch. His expression was forbidding. She suspected that he dreaded talking about Jenny's death as much as she did but maybe he was right. Putting it off until later wouldn't make it any easier. She glared at Leidecker, hating him for causing such pain. Lips pressed together to keep them from trembling, she sat down without further comment. Richard stood beside the arm of the couch.

Without waiting for an invitation, Carl sat down in an overstuffed chair facing the couch. He appeared relaxed, his hands folded loosely on top of a leather notebook on his lap.

"Before we begin," he said, "is there anyone you would like to have present?"

"You mean a lawyer," Richard snapped. Kate moved at his side, and he pressed her shoulder to silence her. "I appreciate the courtesy, but I can't think of any reason we would need one. As you may recall it is our daughter who has been killed. I assume that we are not suspects."

"At this stage, everyone is a suspect."

The words were quietly spoken but nonetheless dramatic. In the charged silence, the phone rang and Kate jumped as if she had been scalded. No one moved. The second ring broke the spell, and Richard hurried into the kitchen cutting off the shrill sound in the middle of the third ring.

The tension that had been building dissipated. Kate sank into the corner of the couch, drawing her feet up in preparation for the coming ordeal.

"The answering machine will pick up, so we won't be disturbed," Richard said returning to the room. He eyed Kate, relief showing on his face at her composure. He sat on the couch beside her and turned his attention to Carl. "Now, how can we help you?"

"I'd like each of you to repeat the events of Tuesday, May 16th." At Kate's grimace, he nodded in silent agreement. "I know you've told the story before but you've had some time to think about it and perhaps you've remembered something that you didn't think to mention before. I realize how difficult this is but it must be done."

Objecting was fruitless. It would only prolong the agony. At first she spoke slowly, but eventually she became caught up in the narrative and the effort to control the painful remembrance of that day. Her words were stilted and when she faltered, she felt Richard's hand on her shoulder and took comfort from his presence.

She was aware of Carl but did not talk directly to him. It was easier to speak to the walls of the room. For the most part she concentrated on the sound of her own voice and the rhythm of her breathing. At the completion of her narrative, she looked across at Carl.

"You're doing fine, Kate. Just a few more questions." His voice was brisk, acknowledging her effort. "Do you recall seeing anyone you knew as you walked toward the corner or on the side street?"

"No. No one."

"Any cars along the street. Either parked and/or driving past?"

Kate closed her eyes, trying to picture the scene. "I suppose I saw cars, but nothing that struck me as either familiar or unusual."

"We've gone over the list of people you called or who called you that evening, and the approximate times you spoke to them. If you could both look it over and see if it's correct or if other names might have been forgotten."

Carl opened the leather folder and extracted a white sheet of paper. He leaned forward and handed Kate the list.

The letters blurred and she forced herself to stare at the first name on the list until it became clear. Barbara Morrisey. Jenny's teacher. She concentrated as she looked at each entry then wordlessly handed the paper to Richard. Closing her eyes she tried to think of anyone's name she had not included. Finally she opened her eyes and stared across at Carl.

"I can't think of anyone else."

"Richard?"

"It seems as if everyone is here. I'm not positive they're in the right order, but by and large I think it's complete."

Richard handed the list back to Carl, who folded it and slid it into the front pocket of the leather folder. Kate watched as the police chief checked through the yellow, lined pages of the note pad. His finger paused beside one of the handwritten notes. He reached into the inside of his uniform jacket to remove a pen, tested the point on a corner of the page.

She let her mind wander to the sounds outside. The dull putt-putt of a neighbor's lawn mower and the sharp yip of a dog were comfortably familiar. It was hard to believe that life went on when her whole world had been ripped apart.

"Now let's go through your day again, please," Carl said.

Kate brought her attention back to Richard. When he spoke, his voice was impassive, almost a monotone. Her eyes moved to Carl. His loose-limbed posture appeared unchanged until she noticed the contrast between his relaxed appearance and the rigidity of his fingers holding the shank of the pen.

"What time was it when you and Kate arrived at the hospital?" he asked.

"I think it was eight-fifteen or eight-thirty. Is that about right, Kate?"

Richard's eyes sought hers and she automatically nodded.

"I think so. Mike would know what time we got there." She turned to Carl. "Richard called him when we learned that Jenny had been taken to the Pickard Hospital."

"You called him before you left the house?"

"We didn't know then what had happened. We didn't want Jenny to be alone," Kate said.

She pressed her lips together, blinking rapidly to dissipate the sudden flood of tears that blurred her vision. She inhaled deeply. As her lungs filled, she lifted her chin, once more in control. Richard extended his hand and she grasped it like a lifeline.

"As it turned out, Mike was already at the hospital, but he didn't know Jenny was there. I told him. Then we left."

"You drove to the hospital together?"

"Yes," Richard said. "In my car."

"You work in Chicago?"

"Yes. At Mayerling, an advertising agency. Chris Mayerling is the owner and president of the agency. I'm the creative director and one of three vice presidents."

"Where did you work prior to Mayerling's?"

"It was my first job out of school. I went to Case Western Reserve in Cleveland, Ohio. My major was art and I took my junior year in Rome. I ran into Chris in a bar near the Spanish Steps. I was into political cartooning at the time and he liked my work. When I went to Chicago during spring break my senior year, I called him for an interview. He hired me, subject to graduation, and I've been there for fifteen years."

Kate shook her head at the reminder of the passage of time. She had never had enough time, until now. How would she fill the minutes and hours and years ahead? She shifted, forcing her attention back to the questioning.

"Do you drive into Chicago?"

"I take the Metra train. It's about an hour and fifteen minutes from Round Lake Beach. I hate driving into Chicago and only do it if I know I'll be working late. During an ad campaign, the hours can get pretty long."

"Are you in the midst of a campaign now?" Carl asked, his head cocked to the side, eyebrows raised in curiosity.

"No." Richard sighed. "We just completed our fall campaign for Aqua Power. They've got a line of fishing boats and boat motors."

Carl referred to his notes. "Do you take a specific train when you commute?"

"Yes. Usually the 7:12 in the morning, and try to get out of the office in time to catch the 5:00. It's an express and gets me home around 6:45."

"You leave your car at the train station?"

"Yes. I park it along the tracks on Main."

Kate was becoming more uncomfortable with the tone of the questions, but Richard seemed unfazed. Perhaps she was just being overly sensitive.

Carl flipped a page, running his finger down the yellow, lined paper, stopping close to the bottom. "Were you in the office all morning?"

"Yes."

The single syllable was drawn out. Richard's voice was strained and Kate stared at him, surprised at the flush of color high on his cheekbones.

Something was wrong.

Her eyes flashed to Carl. She didn't know when he'd changed position but he was no longer lounging back in the easy chair but sitting upright, feet flat on the floor, the hand holding the pencil poised above the yellow pad of paper.

"What time did you leave for lunch?"

"Around noon."

"Could you be more specific?"

"No," Richard responded shortly. "You could ask my assistant, Candy Marshall."

"She said you left while she was at lunch."

Richard's head jerked up and for a long moment he stared intently into the police chief's expressionless face. Kate glanced from her husband to Carl, hoping to discover some clue as to why Richard had reacted so strongly. Both men ignored her, their eyes locked in a non-verbal challenge that ended when Richard dropped his gaze to the coffee table.

"Were you in your office on Tuesday afternoon?"

"No."

His response shocked her. "Richard?"

He turned, reaching out to squeeze her hand. The gesture did little to reassure her.

"Perhaps you could give me some idea of how you spent your afternoon," Carl said.

With a final squeeze of her fingers, Richard released Kate's hand

and pushed himself to his feet, walked to the patio doors, and stared out at the backyard. When he turned back to the room, his body was outlined against the light, the shadowed features of his face almost skeletal.

"This is probably going to sound stupid," Richard said, "but I don't know where I was most of the afternoon."

He flopped down on the cushions. He rubbed his hands back and forth along his pant legs, then propped the ankle of his left leg on his right knee, pleating and straightening the material along the cuff. Satisfied with the arrangement, he put his foot back on the floor.

He leaned forward, arms braced on his knees. He faced Carl directly; eyes steady. His forehead was puckered as he stared across at the police chief who waited in silence.

"It's hard to explain the kind of pressure that builds up during the last days of a major campaign. Everything goes wrong. Film gets lost; scripts need rewriting; artwork stinks. The deadline is constantly hanging over your head. Every phase has to be approved by me. I'm the one responsible if the client hates it."

Richard paused, his eyes focused on the police chief's inscrutable face. "Once the presentation is over, there's a tremendous letdown. Usually I've been penned up in the agency for long hours, and when it's over I feel claustrophobic. It's almost like I'm suffocating."

Kate had been aware of Richard's restlessness, but she had never heard him describe it. He was such a driven person that at times she wondered how much he was in touch with his own motivations.

"On Monday there were a lot of details to wind up, but I was really anxious to get away from the office. I probably would have left in the afternoon, but it started to rain. Tuesday, however, was magnificent. Spring was really in the air. Just looking out the window was almost painful, so at lunch I packed it in. I took the 1:25 train to Round Lake Beach, picked up the car, and just spent the afternoon driving around."

"Could you give me a list of the places you went and the times you were there?" Carl's voice was nonjudgmental, neither accepting nor rejecting Richard's explanations.

"No, I can't." He shook his head. "I just started driving. I went northwest but beyond that I haven't the slightest idea where I was."

"Did you have lunch?"

"Yes. At a McDonald's. Until I saw the sign I didn't even realize I was hungry. And no, I haven't any idea where it was or what time it was."

"I see. During this part of the day is there anyone who would be able to vouch for your presence?"

The question jolted Kate.

"Excuse me," she interrupted before Richard could respond. "What is that supposed to mean?"

"Now, Kate —" Richard began.

He reached out to her, but she batted his hand away almost as if he were attempting to gag her. Her concentration on Carl was complete.

"What are you suggesting?" she asked.

Carl sighed. "I am not suggesting anything, Kate. This is no different from any other crime. We need to have an accurate picture of where everyone was during the time of Jenny's disappearance. All I am asking is if there was anyone who could corroborate Richard's story."

Despite the neutrality of Carl's words, she sensed a subtle shift in the tone of his voice. She glanced at Richard to see if he had detected the change. His expression was noncommittal and for a moment she wondered if she had been mistaken. No. She had a gut feeling that something was wrong.

"To answer your question, I can't think of anyone who could verify my whereabouts."

Silence built up after Richard's statement. Carl glanced back through his notes.

"At the hospital you said that you had just gotten home from work when you discovered that Jenny was missing." More pages flipped. "On Wednesday you repeated the same thing. When asked how you had spent the day, you said 'at the office.' Why didn't you mention that you left the office for lunch and did not return?"

"It didn't seem important." The words were spoken in a burst of exasperation. Watching Richard's face, Kate couldn't tell if he was more annoyed than concerned by the police chief's questions. "The only thing that mattered was that Jenny was missing. When we talked to you at the hospital, I never thought about it. Later it seemed like more trouble than it was worth to explain."

The very blandness of Carl's face suggested he did not find Richard's explanation particularly credible. For Kate it was totally consistent with his character. Richard brought all his energy and talents to the project at hand, which was why he was so good at his job. He could focus on one thing, relegating everything else to the background.

Kate could just imagine that since it had no bearing on Jenny's disappearance, Richard's whereabouts during the day would have little meaning for him. Jenny was the only thing that mattered. Suddenly Kate realized the source of her own uneasiness.

Carl was treating Richard as if he were guilty of some crime.

My God! Surely he didn't think that Richard had anything to do with Jenny's death. The man who murdered Jenny was a monster. What kind of warped mind did Carl have that he could contemplate a father doing such horrible things to his own child? The mere thought was an obscenity.

"That's enough."

Richard and Carl froze at her unexpected words.

"Kate?"

She ignored Richard, speaking directly to Carl. "We will not answer any more questions. How dare you treat us as if we have done something wrong? I don't know if we're within our rights to refuse to continue this interview, but I want you out of this house."

"Kate, please don't get upset," Richard said. "I know this is awful, but he's doing his job."

She was infuriated at his inability to see the connection between Carl's questions and his own danger. "Richard, listen to what I'm saying. The interview is over."

It was obvious Richard was stunned by her implacability, but one look at Leidecker convinced Kate that he had expected the termination. He gave an abrupt nod and rose to his feet.

"You have the right to postpone this meeting. I'll call tomorrow to reschedule it. In the meantime I suggest you seek legal counsel."

With those ominous words, he left the room, leaving Kate to stare at Richard in bewilderment and rising fear.

46

At the sound of the front door closing, Richard leaped to his feet. "Christ Almighty, Kate! What's the matter with you?"

"Don't you yell at me! Don't you understand what was happening?" Her voice was shrill and she pressed her lips together to keep from screaming. "Carl was almost accusing you of lying. Why on earth didn't you say you'd taken the afternoon off? There's no crime in that. How could you believe that they wouldn't find out you weren't at the office?"

"It just never occurred to me to explain." He paced in front of the couch. "How could I be expected to think about anything at the hospital when Jenny was —" He waved his hand helplessly, his voice thick with tears.

Kate cupped a hand over her mouth to keep herself from crying out. She was so close to hysteria she knew if she lost control now, she might not be able to stop screaming. Breathing in short, jerking gasps, she waited for him to continue.

"The next day all that mattered was to find out who had killed Jenny. It didn't seem important where I was. And now Carl thinks I'm involved, doesn't he?"

"Forget what Carl thinks," she snapped.

He stopped pacing, facing her across the glass-topped coffee table. "Honest to God, Kate, losing Jenny is tearing me apart."

"Richard, I know you're hurting. Everyone is. But for now we have to forget everything and focus on finding Jenny's killer. Talk to Carl tomorrow."

"You just threw the man out of the house."

"I know I'm not acting consistently, but I really felt you were in danger."

"Carl doesn't understand that I wasn't trying to hide where I was the day of Jenny's disappearance," he repeated stubbornly.

"Then you'll have to explain it again. You've got to make sure he understands. So what if he thinks you're crazy for driving around all day. It could have been worse. Just imagine if you'd gone to the forest preserve."

Richard's eyes went blank. His very stillness alarmed her and she rephrased her words. "You weren't in the forest preserve, were you?"

"No. Of course not. I spent the afternoon driving around. I never got out of the car." Kate opened her mouth but before she could speak, Richard held up his hand for silence. "Enough, Kate. Let it rest for a while. We're both tired and the last thing we need is to question each other. That's Leidecker's job. I think we need something to eat and a good stiff drink. You stay where you are. I'll get it."

Without another word, he turned on his heel and left the room. In the kitchen she could hear the rattle of dishes and the opening of the refrigerator. She remained where she was, her mouth partially open, her eyes fixed on the empty doorway. Awareness seeped into her consciousness with the corrosive power of acid.

Richard was lying.

# FIVE

RICHARD WAS LYING. Kate knew it the moment he spoke.

She was so used to analyzing his moods that, over the years, she had become accustomed to listening to the nuances in his voice. Stress was evident in his inflection, and she knew that he wasn't telling the whole story. He was holding something back.

Pulling her knees up against her stomach, she curled into the corner of the couch, resting her cheek against her arm. Her eyes burned and she closed them.

At times it was difficult to return to the world. The safety of the darkness was seductive. She would not stay long. She only needed some time to gather her strength.

*Oh God, please help me. The nightmare is all around me and I cannot find my way.*

She remembered praying in much the same way when her father died. He had been big and bluff; a giant of a man to a motherless girl. She remembered how he came to all her swim meets, cheering her on to the finish line. He'd wrap her in a towel and congratulate her and then explain how she could improve the next time. Until she met Richard, her father had provided her with advice and a sense of direction.

*Oh, Daddy, where are you? I need your guidance.*

Footsteps approached as Richard returned from the kitchen. She could not face him yet. She was too close to panic. She fought to keep her breathing in a steady rhythm.

She heard the clink of china as Richard set some dishes on the coffee table. He didn't speak, but she could feel his presence beside the couch and knew he was staring down at her. It took tremendous effort to feign sleep. He moved across the room, and when he returned his hands were gentle as he tucked the Afghan around her. When he left the room, a tear slid out of the corner of her eye, rolling down her cheek until it was absorbed in the material of her sleeve.

*Not Richard. Please God, not Richard.*

As repugnant as it was, she knew she had to consider whether Richard had killed Jenny.

She knew it was possible that a man might rape a child. But his own daughter? God knew there were enough stories on television about incest and sexual abuse that she couldn't pretend such a thing didn't exist. She had never had the slightest feeling of discomfort with Richard's relationship with Jenny. He hugged her and kissed her and comforted her. None of this had ever seemed inappropriate.

She would have known if anything was wrong, wouldn't she?

Unable to answer in the affirmative, she had to accept the fact that perhaps, under some sort of psychological breakdown, Richard might have attacked Jenny. But he could never have killed her!

In some ways Jenny was a clone of Richard. In his eyes, she was a work of art, and he was far too narcissistic to destroy such an incredible creation.

Kate had always wanted children and Jenny's birth was a much anticipated event. When they decided to have another child, however, Kate had difficulty conceiving. According to the doctor, Jenny's conception had been a delightful miracle, but Kate might not be so lucky again. She had discussed with Richard whether they should consider going the route of fertility doctors, but they decided to leave it in God's hands. An only child herself, Kate had always hoped for a house full of children.

Not so Richard. Jenny was enough. He could concentrate all his energies on his daughter, filling her with ideas and carefully nurturing her talents. Jenny was Richard's ticket to immortality. With additional children, his gift to the world would be fragmented, watered down.

No matter what he was keeping back, Kate believed he had nothing to do with Jenny's death.

God, she was tired.

Resentment flashed through her. In her grief, she had counted on Richard's support. Something had shifted in their relationship. It was as if their roles had reversed. She had always been contented letting Richard take the lead, now it was as though he had lost his way. She had never been the one to take action. She didn't know if she could.

*Backbone, Kate. You have a job to do.*

She could almost hear her father's voice chiding her for shirking her responsibilities. She was Richard's wife. Whatever help he needed she would give. Having reconfirmed her support, she relaxed, letting herself drift naturally into sleep.

Kate threw back the Afghan as she clawed her way up out of the nightmare. She lay on her back, blinking her eyes in the darkness, trying to find some point of familiarity to anchor herself in safety. Her panted breath was loud in the night silence.

She didn't try to hold on to the dream. It was about Jenny, and she did not want to remember what had taken place in the irrational world of her mind. Better to block it all out.

Instinctively she sought comfort from Richard's presence. She reached out but her hand encountered only space. Fear of being alone brought her fully awake.

She was lying on the couch in the family room.

It was night and the room was in darkness. Richard sat in the lounge chair beside the couch, his back to the patio doors, his face in shadow. His feet and legs were bare and he was wearing a bathrobe over his shorts.

"Couldn't sleep?" she asked, propping herself up on her arm.

"No. Too wound up." Richard's voice was disembodied in the darkened room. "I called Mike and talked to him about Leidecker's interview. Apparently he had already taken a statement of sorts from Mike."

"From Mike? What for?"

"It appears that everyone we know is under suspicion of one kind or another. Mike played it down, but I could tell it was bothering him. I gather Leidecker was trying to confirm the time we called him and when we got to the hospital. What seemed to trouble Mike was that Carl grilled him pretty intensely on my college life and single days. He also asked if Mike had ever seen any evidence that Jenny had been abused."

"Dear God!"

"Apparently Mike read him the riot act and Leidecker believed him. Doctors have credibility with the police." His softly spoken words were bitter.

She edged her legs over the side of the couch and sat up, flexing her shoulders to release the stiffness from her cramped position. She held up her arm, and in the glow of moonlight filtering through the patio doors, she could just make out the numbers on her watch. One-thirty.

"Mike thinks I should talk to a lawyer."

"He does?" Kate's heart jolted at their friend's confirmation of the gravity of the situation.

"Yes." Richard's voice was noncommittal. "Suggested I see Stacie Wolfram. He dated her a couple of years ago. Says she's a first-class criminal lawyer."

"I vaguely remember her. Cute and very funny. Didn't she play beach volleyball?"

Richard snorted. "That's how Mike met her. At any rate, he called her and she'll see me tomorrow at four." He glanced at the darkened windows and grimaced. "I guess that's today."

"Do you want me to go with you?"

"No." The single word was edged with anger. He took a steadying breath and stared at her, his expression bleak in the semi-darkness of the room. "I'd like to spare you any more hurt, Kate. I wish I could make all of this go away, but I can't. No matter what Leidecker thinks, I had nothing to do with Jenny's death. Do you believe me?"

Despite the pain in his voice, Kate did not answer immediately. She turned toward the window so that the moonlight would illuminate her face. Richard could read her expressions as easily as she could gauge the shadings in his voice, and it was imperative that there be no suspicion between them. When she spoke, her words were specific as she tried to give him the assurances that he needed.

"I believe that you had nothing to do with Jenny's death."

"Thank you, Kate."

"Let's go to bed," she said, rising and holding out her hand.

She undressed quickly and slipped beneath the covers, opening her arms as Richard pressed against her. There was nothing sexual in the embrace. Kate could not have borne that. Long after his breathing had softened in sleep, she held him.

Dry-eyed she stared into the darkness, her arms aching for the child she would never hold again.


"Judas Priest, Bea!" Carl Leidecker glowered down at the mug in his hand. "Can't anyone around here make decent coffee?"

"That's probably left over from last night. Amy'll be in shortly and she'll make a fresh pot." Bea Johnson smoothed a hand over her crisp gray curls, avoiding his eyes.

"Couldn't you make a pot? I'd do it, but I don't know how to run the machine."

Besides being the assistant chief of police, Bea made the best coffee in the department.

"Typical male copout." She snorted at the pleading look on Carl's face. With ill grace she got to her feet, snatched the extended mug, and stalked to the door of his office. "You owe me, Leidecker."

"Anything. I swear it." He grinned after her departing figure.

Bea was forty-nine, divorced, and had three college-aged children. She'd gone to the police academy in Milwaukee and worked as a cop for a year before she was married and moved to Pickard and stayed home with her kids. When she turned thirty, her husband left her for a twenty-one-year-old secretary in his office. She'd cried for a month then talked Chief Corcoran into hiring her. She'd been with the department for nineteen years.

Eight years earlier, Carl had been hired as assistant chief of police with the understanding that he'd take over when Chief Corcoran retired. He had two years to evaluate the department before he became chief.

When he became chief, he asked Bea to be his assistant. She took the job with two conditions. She wanted her salary doubled and an understanding that she could quit at fifty.

At the time, it was easy to agree, but now Bea was forty-nine and Carl wondered if he or the department could do without her.

He leaned back in his desk chair and stared through the glass partition at the activity in the outer offices of the police station. It was barely seven. People were beginning to drift in for the seven-thirty briefing. Noise and conversation mingled in a low, unintelligible murmur.

One of the first things Carl had done as police chief was to establish procedures to handle violent crime. Pickard had 36,000 residents and a fifty-person police force. In normal circumstances, the town was adequately manned. With so many people involved in the Warner case, their resources would be strained. He and Bea had been working since six o'clock, reviewing the progress and adding to the assignments of the five-member crisis team.

Deputy Lieutenant Bob Jackson, a soft-spoken, humorless African-American, was the most senior of the team. When Carl had been brought to Pickard over Bob's head, the man had held no resentment. He'd acknowledged that the town wasn't ready for a black police chief, and he was too old to fight the system. Bob had proven to be an indefatigable worker.

Detective Diego Garcia was on the team because he had an eye for out-of-place details which sometimes made the difference in solving a crime.

After some consideration, Detective Anthony Torrentino had been added. Tony dressed and acted like a Chicago mobster, but he had the tenacity of a rat terrier when he was involved in a case.

The fourth member of the team was Sergeant Jas Walker. Working as a Chicago police photographer, he'd earned the nickname "Squint" and had been lured to Pickard when Carl became chief.

After looking over the facilities, Squint had set up a first-rate photo lab, and had trained a group of officers in photography procedures.

Owing to the nature of this crime, Ellen Fredricks, the youth officer, had been added to the team. Although she was younger than the others, she was tough enough and intelligent enough not to be intimidated.

When Bea returned, Carl eagerly accepted the mug of coffee, took a careful sip of the steaming contents and sighed in appreciation.

"Where were we?" she asked as she pulled her chair up to the desk and looked back over her notes.

"I want Diego to coordinate all the door-to-door interviews. Tell him to go over them to see if he can pick up anything that might be useful."

"He'll bellyache. He prefers to be out on the street."

"Don't we all. Sweet talk him. Once this phase is over, I'll get him on something else."

She grimaced but nodded in agreement. She handed him several typed sheets. "This is Ellen's interview with the victim's teacher."

"Good. Tell her I talked to Father Blaney at St. Madelaine's. He and the principal, Miss —" Carl leafed through the stack of papers on his left until he found the note he wanted. "Aha. Miss McGough will talk to the children at a special assembly this morning. Both the school psychologist and the social worker suggested that normal routine be followed for the remainder of the day. They'll treat individual problems as they come up."

"Okay. Ellen's going back to the school today to interview some of the children in the victim's class."

"Make sure we get a list of all the pupils and all the staff. Anyone who would have a reason to be at the school. Nurse, janitors, coaches, bus drivers, deliveries. You know the drill."

"Got it," she said. "Bob Jackson's in charge of the interviews at Mr. Warner's office and at the hospital."

"How about Tony for priors?"

"Just seeing his ugly mug should make any previous offender confess to jay walking. Do you think it's a repeater?"

"I don't know. I talked to the crime lab boys in Chicago last night. They're going to run it to see if the MO fits. Same with the suburbs on the north side of Chicago." His expression hardened. "I've a gut feeling that it was a one-shot deal. If it had been planned, there would have been more of an attempt to hide the body. My guess is it was someone the kid knew. Once he'd raped her, he panicked, and killed her."

He took a sip of the coffee then continued. "While Ellen's at the school, have her check to see if the Warner kid ever showed any signs of abuse." Bea looked up, her face a question. "We don't want to overlook the possibility that it's an escalation of an ongoing situation."

"All right." Bea wrote a note in the margin of the paper, underlining it twice. "I notice you're running a pretty heavy check on Richard Warner. It's early days yet to zero in on anyone. Once that happens, everyone gets a blind spot and we could miss something major."

Carl's voice was cold. "If you're suggesting that my own personal agenda is clouding my judgment, forget it. I'm open at this point. However just because Warner is the victim's father doesn't automatically keep him off the list of suspects. He lied about where he was on the day of the murder and I want to know why."

Bea held up both hands in surrender. "I'm not criticizing."

"Like hell." There was a moment of tense silence as their eyes met. Carl jerked his head in an abrupt nod. "I'll keep your concerns in mind."

"Good." She ran a finger down the list on the top of her papers, pausing at the last item. "I talked to Squint last night. He'll have individual photos in the computer today after two."

"He'll have pictures from the funeral home, church, and the cemetery?"

"Yes. And he's trying to get footage from the other media. Those he won't have right away."

"That's all right. The shrinks say there's always a chance, even if he's a stranger, that he'll show up at the funeral or cemetery." Carl pushed his chair away from the desk. "Once we identify the majority of the people we'll have a preliminary list to work from."

"For the unknowns, we'll have everyone in the department take a

56

look. If one of us can't ID them, they're probably not local." She gathered her papers together into a neat pile then sat back in her chair. "Anything else?"

"The crisis team will meet after lunch. Say one-thirty. Until further notice, we'll use the conference room as our command post. We can add personnel as we need it."

"We've had to double the personnel on phones due to the number of tips, sightings, and assorted bizarre calls."

"The whole town's jumpy. I talked to Mayor Etzel last night and we're going to schedule a press conference for later today." He ran a finger down the scribbled notes on his daily agenda then shook his head. "I don't have a time listed. Late afternoon I'd guess. He wants to catch the commuter news at six."

"Good. The reporters have been bugging us for another statement."

"Any questions from the outside, refer to Hayden in PR. At briefing this morning remind the troops if there's a leak I'll have their balls. In the case of the ladies, you think of something creative. No talking at home about the details."

"Got it." Bea stood up, stretched, turning as the door of the office opened and Dana Adams, the watch commander, stepped inside and closed the door.

"Sorry to interrupt, Chief, but I think you better hear this. We just got a call from a woman who says she saw the guy that killed the Warner kid."

# Six

"Someone saw the killer?"

"Maybe." Dana's breathing was ragged as if she'd run from the communications room. "Lady called in. Said she just read the story in the paper, and she might've seen the kidnapping."

"A kook?" Carl asked.

"I've logged in at least eight of those," Dana said. "This one might be the goods. She was pretty hesitant. Kept apologizing for not calling sooner. At any rate, I told her that I'd send someone right over to talk to her. Thought you might like to go yourself."

"Damn straight," Carl said, pushing himself to his feet. "Got the name and address?"

Dana held out a small piece of paper. "A Mrs. Nell Doutt. Sounds like a little old lady."

Bea took the paper. "It's on Corydon. The street where Mrs. Warner found the watercolor."

Carl took the paper, eyeballed it, and then stood up. "Make sure not a word of this gets out until after I've talked to her."

"No problem." Dana touched her temple in a two fingered salute as she left.

Carl grabbed his uniform jacket, picked up his leather notebook, and started out the door. He straight-armed the door to the parking lot, car keys already in his hand.

He cursed as the light in the center of town turned red. He

resisted the urge to flip on the siren, settling back against the seat and trying to relax the muscles in his jaw.

It only took five minutes to get to the address, an old, but well-kept, two-and-a-half-story clapboard house. Stately elms lined the sidewalks, and there were four or five cars parked along the street. He pulled against the curb, walked up the front walk, and rang the bell. Nothing happened. Carl was just reaching for the bell to ring again when the door slowly opened. Standing inside, leaning heavily on a metal walker, was a tall, white-haired woman.

"Mrs. Doutt? I'm Chief Leidecker."

"Yes. Come in please."

She led him toward the living room. Although the room was tastefully furnished, it appeared crowded because of the profusion of photographs and small ceramic animals scattered on every surface. She stopped in front of a wing chair and Carl waited as she jockeyed her walker into position so that she could sit down. Once seated, she smiled warmly.

"Men in uniform always seem to have impeccable manners," she said, waving Carl to a chair.

"I gather you might have seen something that could be helpful in our investigation of the Warner child's death," Carl said.

"I am so sorry that I didn't call sooner. It was my grandson's birthday on Tuesday. My son-in-law picked me up after work, and I stayed at my daughter's in Rockford until last night. It wasn't until I saw the paper this morning that I thought I might have seen the child who was killed."

Restraining his impatience, Carl spoke quietly. "What were you doing when you first saw her?"

"I was washing the windows." She chuckled at Carl's raised eyebrow. "Since I broke my hip I've been confined to the house and bored to boot. I have a girl who comes in and cleans but she's just good for the surface of things. The windows were thick with winter grit and Tuesday was the most glorious day. I thought if I just washed these." She pointed to the windows in the alcove. "I had just finished the first one when I saw the child."

"Could you describe her for me?"

"She had black hair, shoulder length. A sweet face, although I couldn't see it very clearly. She was wearing a school uniform. St. Madelaine's. White knee socks and white tennis shoes."

"Anything else?"

"A bright yellow jacket. That's what made her so noticeable."

She paused, leaning her head against the back of the chair. Her eyes were open but focused out the window as if she were seeing it again.

"She was chasing a piece of paper down the street. The wind had caught it, and each time she reached for it a gust would carry it further. She was laughing. She made such a joyful picture that I couldn't help but smile as I watched her. She grabbed for it several times and on the last attempt she tripped and fell on her knee."

"Can you remember which knee?"

Her eyes narrowed in concentration, but the answer was definite when she spoke. "Her right."

When Carl had examined the child's body with the coroner, he had noted the scrape on the girl's right knee and assumed it had happened during the attack. Physical details like this had been withheld from the media. This information plus the yellow windbreaker made it almost a certainty that Mrs. Doutt had seen Jennifer Warner.

"It was right in front of the window and I could see that she'd skinned her knee and was crying. I put down my things and went to the door. Because of my walker, it took a minute or two before I could get to the front door. By that time the child was standing beside a car parked at the curb. The door on the passenger side was open and she got in. A man's hand reached across her and closed the car door. Through the rear window I could see them talking. Then the car pulled away."

Silence filled the room when the woman finished. Carl shifted in his chair, letting Mrs. Doutt relax now that the initial portion of the interview was completed.

"Where exactly was the car?"

She looked out the window. "Right where that red car is now."

"Do you remember what kind it was or the color?"

"Dark colored. I don't think it was black, but it could have been. It looked new. I don't know much about car models these days. I was really watching the child not the car." She pressed her lips together in agitation.

"It's perfectly understandable, Mrs. Doutt. Can you remember if it was a two-door or a four-door?"

"I want to say two, but it could have been four. I just don't remember."

"Would you say that the size or shape of the car was similar to any of the cars parked outside now."

Once more Mrs. Doutt stared out the window, eyes focusing on the street. She shook her head.

"I'd say it was about the size of the blue one." She pointed. "But I can't swear to it."

"That's fine. We're just hoping for impressions now. I don't suppose you saw the license plate?"

"Oh, I'm sorry. I forgot to mention that." She held up her hand as Carl stared at her. "It's not much help. All I saw was PF. No numbers."

"Don't apologize, Mrs. Doutt. That's a real break. It proves that the car was local."

The Pickard Federal Bank had put on a big campaign to celebrate the fiftieth anniversary of the incorporation of Pickard. Special license plates with the seal of the town and the letters PF and four numbers could be picked up at the bank. Carl figured half the cars in town carried the local plates. A dark car with PF plates. Not great, but a far cry from a blank.

"Just a few more questions if you don't mind. You say when you got to the front door the child was standing beside the open passenger door of the car. Were they talking?"

"Yes. But I couldn't hear their voices."

"Then after she got into the car, he reached across her and closed the door. Did you see his hand? A sleeve?"

Mrs. Doutt looked startled as if her memory had just come clear. "Why, yes, I did. He was wearing a suit or at least a sports coat. I don't know what color. Not tan. Not light-toned. I could see in the back window and I saw a white collar above the collar of the jacket."

"Very good. They were still talking?"

"Yes. At least he was. I could see his head move as if he was speaking to her."

"Was he wearing a hat?"

"No."

"Hair color?"

"Dark. Maybe brown." Her porcelain skin had a crepe-like quality as she squinted in concentration. "I could only see the back of his head, but from what I remember, it was short. Cut close to the head."

Carl knew better than to rely too heavily on the old woman's description, but he could feel the excitement building at the amount of information she'd provided. Slowly the picture of a man in a suit or sports jacket with well-groomed, dark hair, driving a fairly new car was forming. Not the drooling, disreputable pervert that most people pictured when such a crime was committed.

"I'm curious, Mrs. Doutt," Carl said. "Did you have any feeling of unease or discomfort as you watched the man talking to the child?"

"No. In actual fact I felt relieved that she was with someone she knew."

"How did you come to that conclusion?"

"I have ten grandchildren, Chief Leidecker. Like most children, they all know better than to talk to strangers." She leaned forward, her expression grave as she tried to get her point across. "Just before the car pulled away, I saw the driver reach over and wipe the little girl's tears and runny nose. She would not have let a stranger do that. Only someone she knew."

"How'd your meeting with the lawyer go?" Mike asked.

"I haven't even had a chance to tell Kate," Richard said. "My meeting ran late and I got home with just enough time to change before you two arrived with the pizza."

For Kate, the impromptu dinner was a blessing. She'd felt trapped in the house with too much time to think. However the sight of the food made her slightly queasy. She breathed slowly through her nose and reached out for a glass of water. She sensed Richard's scrutiny and took several tentative sips before glancing up to meet his eyes.

"You need to eat," he said.

She closed her eyes. Rebellion struggled against her natural acquiescence.

"Kate."

Richard's voice was close to her ear, the single syllable sharp and demanding. A spurt of anger flashed through her, but she fought it down. Her eyes opened and the sight of Richard's face, forehead creased in worry, banished her momentary revolt.

"Sorry," she said.

He smiled his relief and patted her arm as she took a forkful of salad. Placated, Richard launched into a summary of his visit with the lawyer.

"Thanks for putting me on to Stacie. Ms. Wolfram is pretty damned impressive."

"Agreed," Mike said. "She's a straight shooter and, despite the fact she looks about twenty, she's had plenty of experience."

"It really helped talking to her. I have to admit Leidecker had me panicked. Stacie told me to be totally cooperative. Not to take it personally. After all, whether or not I like the way the investigation's going, the most important thing is to find out who killed Jenny."

The bleakness in his voice touched Kate. She looked around the table and could sense a similar response in Mike and Chessy. When Richard picked up his wine glass, they raised their glasses too as if to seal a promise.

Richard continued. "After Stacie had calmed me down, she gave me a worst case scenario, walking me through it based on what she thought the police might do."

With dawning horror, Kate listened to Richard explain how much the police could invade their privacy and generally harass them. It mattered not at all that they were having enough trouble dealing with their own grief. Mike's face was grim, but he did not seem overly surprised.

Kate found her own state of shock echoed in Chessy's galvanized attention. It was the first time she had heard that Richard was under any suspicion, and the repugnance at such an accusation was evident in her expression. Blindly she groped for Kate's hand, communicating her sympathy through the steady pressure of her fingers.

Until Kate saw her own belief in Richard's innocence reflected in their eyes, she hadn't realized how hurt she had been that anyone could think him capable of such a crime. The remainder of the evening went well, and she managed to eat a slice of pizza and some more salad before they left.

It was nine o'clock when the phone rang. Kate winced at the shrill sound. She remained in the family room as Richard went out to the kitchen to answer it.

It was several minutes before she looked up to see Richard standing in the archway to the kitchen. His face was expressionless, his eyes unfocused.

"That was Carl Leidecker. He's on his way over to pick up the clothes I wore the day Jenny disappeared. He wants to have them tested."

# SEVEN

"WHAT DO YOU MEAN LEIDECKER wants to have your clothes tested?" Kate asked. "Tested for what?"

"He didn't say."

"This can't be happening, Richard. It's our daughter who's been killed, and they're treating us like it's our fault." Kate's voice shook in her agitation. "Besides, the slacks have been cleaned and the shirt's been washed. What if we can't find the right one? This is intolerable. Don't they need a search warrant or something?"

"Not unless I refuse to cooperate." Richard paced in front of the sofa. "The lawyer warned me that the police would probably ask for the clothes. Stacie said they would phrase it as a request. If I don't give them the clothes it looks like I have something to hide. That might give them grounds for getting a search warrant."

Kate tried to digest the nightmarish situation, but each new shock only added to her confusion. Richard turned away before she could comment. When the doorbell rang, she remained on the couch, letting Richard deal with Leidecker. She felt sick to her stomach.

When Richard returned, she noted the closed expression on his face and refrained from questioning him. Upstairs, she lay beside him. They were so close she could feel the heat from his body, but they might as well have been in separate beds. When Jenny died, they had drawn together in shared pain but as time passed they were becoming separated by their fears for each other.

\* \* \*

65

Monday morning brought no relief for Kate.

In only a week her body had established a rhythm of its own. In the instant before she opened her eyes, she didn't know that Jenny had been murdered. A moment of bliss, then it all crashed in on her. Pain tore at her. Raw physical pain, so all consuming that she had to grit her teeth together to keep from screaming. She fought her grief and when she was once more in control of her despair she got up and showered, forcing herself to begin another day.

Navy skirt, white blouse, white canvas shoes. Richard had laid out her clothes, as he did on most important occasions. For a moment, she hesitated, wanting to wear something less lifeless for their meeting with Leidecker. Knowing Richard would be annoyed if she changed, she shrugged and hurried into her clothes. Downstairs, Richard was just finishing his breakfast.

"Morning," she said. "Have I got time for some tea?"

He checked his watch. "Sure. I put the water on. Want me to scramble some eggs?"

"No." She shuddered at the thought, holding up her hand as he was about to speak. "I know. I have to eat something."

"Have I been lecturing? Come and sit down and I'll put in some toast." He stood up, holding her chair. When she sat down, he patted her shoulder as if she were a good child.

Kate pushed away the morning papers. Reading the newspaper used to be one of her favorite rituals after Jenny had gone to school and before she had to leave for her job at the library. Now she dreaded it. The *Pickard Weekly* was filled with stories about Jenny's murder, some factual and others pure conjecture. The Chicago papers were even worse.

Richard poured her a cup of tea. She sighed as the moist lemony aroma filled her nostrils and warmth began to seep into the chilled corners of her body.

"Jelly?" Richard said, setting the toast down in front of her.

"No. This is fine."

She forced herself to take small bites of the toast, content to watch Richard clean up the kitchen. By the time he had finished, she was amazed to see that she'd eaten both pieces of toast. Better than yesterday. She didn't even feel queasy.

"All set?"

"Yes. How is it out?"

"Pretty mild. All you need is a sweater or a light jacket."

He opened the door of the front hall closet, choosing her navy blazer. He helped her on with it, picking a piece of lint off the sleeve as he surveyed her. Her navy blue leather shoulder bag was on the hall table. She checked to make sure that she had keys to the front door since Richard was going to drop her back at the house and go in to work.

She was surprised at how formally he was dressed. Navy blue suit, white button-down shirt and a blue and yellow striped tie. He stood in front of the mirror to wrestle the knot into position, grimacing as if it were strangling him. He caught her eye and winked.

In silence they drove to the police station. A camera crew and several reporters accosted them when they arrived. Richard refused any comment, putting his arm around Kate, and shouldering his way into the building. Once inside, they were immediately ushered into Carl Leidecker's office.

Kate had never been to the police station before. She had little time to look around but got the fleeting impression of a modern facility with a subdued air that hinted at a well-run organization. The high-tech atmosphere was daunting. Pickard was such a small town that unconsciously she had been expecting something like the Mayberry police station.

One look at Chief Leidecker's face dispelled any ideas that they were dealing with Andy Griffith.

Carl stood up, shaking Richard's hand and nodding to Kate. "Thank you for coming. I know this can't be pleasant for either of you." He indicated the trim, gray-haired woman who had risen at their entrance. "This is Deputy Lieutenant Beatrice Johnson, the assistant chief of police."

"I prefer Bea."

The warmth that had been missing in Carl's expression was amply evident in the older woman's face. She held Kate's hand in a firm grasp as she expressed her sorrow at Jenny's death. And when she turned to Richard, Kate could see nothing in Bea's demeanor to indicate any antipathy. Perhaps she had imagined Carl's withdrawal. She stared at the closed expression on his face, dropping her eyes as he glanced in her direction.

"Why don't I explain what we hope to accomplish this morning?" Carl indicated chairs, but only Kate and Bea sat down. "In crimes of this nature, the murderer will frequently attend the wake or funeral of the victim. Sometimes he will return to the crime scene, especially if there is a crowd of people. He gets a kick from the risk of being there and from the opportunity to relive the experience."

Kate shuddered. Richard stood behind her chair, his hands on her shoulders. He squeezed firmly as if to remind her of his presence and to encourage her. Carl had stopped speaking. He too must have gauged her distress. For an instant, pity flashed in his eyes.

"Believe me, Kate. This will not be awful. It will only be pictures of faces. Just faces," he repeated.

"I'm sorry," she said. "I'm all right."

"We've gone through the film, both ours and the news media, and plan to show you each of the faces for identification. There will be friends, family, neighbors, and strangers. Your help in this will be invaluable."

He paused as if waiting for them to indicate their cooperation. Kate nodded. Behind her, she sensed Richard's agreement.

"It works best if we do one of you at a time and then run through one final time with both of you together in hopes that you can jog each other's memory. Kate, if you'll go with Bea she'll explain everything to you and stay with you in case you have any questions."

Kate could feel her stomach drop in a sickening free-fall sensation. What if she saw guilt on the face of someone she knew? She couldn't bear that.

"Come on, Kate." Richard took her hand, rubbing it between his own. "If you get moving, we'll be done in time for lunch. I'll buy you an avocado burger at Lynn and Diane's. We'll sit on the back deck and watch the birds."

"You know the right buttons to push," she said, forcing her mouth into a smile. Rising to her feet she followed Bea out of the room.

They went through the main room with its quiet bustle of activity to a hallway running toward the back of the building and a door marked FILM.

The room was spartan, painted a neutral cream color, no pictures on the walls to distract the eye from the viewing screen on the right hand wall. Rows of cushioned theater seats faced the screen. Close to the front, a young woman sat at a table that held a computer and a small lamp. The lamp with its mauve ceramic base and white pleated shade was incongruous in the otherwise colorless room.

She nodded to Bea, aware that the woman had been giving her time to look over the room. It was so nonthreatening in appearance that Kate could feel herself relaxing. Bea led her toward the uniformed policeman standing at the back of the room.

"Mrs. Warner, this is Lieutenant Walker, better known as Squint. He's in charge of all the photography and will explain how everything works."

Kate shook hands. Walker was in his early thirties, tall and angular, with intense dark eyes and blond hair pulled back into a ponytail. The crow's feet beside his eyes were evidence of the amount of time he spent behind a camera. With his long hair and a pomaded mustache with spike ends, a la Salvador Dali, he appeared more rebellious youth than policeman.

"He'll be controlling the computer images," Bea said, then escorted Kate to the front of the room.

"And this is Sue Byrne," she said, indicating the young woman at the keyboard of the computer. "When you identify a picture, she will enter the name. Sue's a student at Northwestern University, working here on an internship. We're hoping to spoil her enough so that after graduation she'll come back here to work."

The young woman grinned as Bea led Kate to one of the seats in the front row. As soon as they were seated, the lights faded except for the lamp on the computer table. Kate jumped as Walker's disembodied voice came from behind her.

"Mrs. Warner, I'm going to ask you a series of questions and then begin showing you pictures on the screen. Ready?"

Kate nodded then realized he could not see her in the dark and said "yes." Her voice sounded too whispery but apparently it was sufficient. He asked her several questions, then a series of faces flashed on the screen. Richard, Mike, Chessy, and several of her neighbors. After the first few identifications, she could feel her breathing slow to a more normal rhythm until suddenly she was looking at a man she could not identify.

Heartbeat pounding in her ears, she gripped the arms of the chair in rising agitation.

"Don't worry, Mrs. Warner," came Walker's voice. "This is Dr. Mitchell, my dentist in Seattle. I use his picture so you can get the idea that you're not going to recognize everyone. I had lousy teeth as a kid and I'm hoping someone will positively identify him as a car thief."

Even knowing it was a well-rehearsed quip, Kate could feel her body relax, settling against the back of the seat.

Face followed face in a mind-numbing array. Carl was right. There was nothing frightening about it. It was slow, tedious work. Once or twice Bea asked if she'd like to take a break, but Kate was anxious to get it over with.

"Thank you, Mrs. Warner."

Walker's voice and the lights filled the room at the same time. Blinking rapidly, Kate stared at her watch, amazed that an hour had passed.

Someone must have signaled to Leidecker because when Bea opened the door into the hall, Carl and Richard were just approaching.

"How'd it go?" Brow furrowed in concern, Richard stared down at her.

"Much to my surprise, it wasn't bad," she said.

She noted the strained expression on his face and wondered if Carl had been harassing him. She sensed a coolness between the two men. She was glad Richard would be with Bea for a while. The older woman's attitude was less threatening.

The door closed behind Richard, and Kate turned warily toward Carl.

"I don't know about you, but I could use some coffee," he said. He started down the hall, opening a door to a small lounge.

In contrast to the barren film room, the decor was positively homey. A small kitchen was on the left. Two easy chairs and two couches were upholstered in blue corduroy and looked comfortable.

"Coffee?" Carl opened a cupboard and took down two mugs.

"I'd prefer tea."

"Lemon, milk or sugar?"

"Just lemon."

Kate sat down on the sofa, watching Carl move around the kitchen. He poured himself black coffee, then brought Kate her tea, sitting down across from her.

"I'm not an ogre, you know."

His words startled her and she almost spilled her tea. She was embarrassed that her feelings were so transparent. She wanted to ignore his statement but decided that she might as well speak her mind.

"I thought you were our friend."

"Policemen do not have that luxury." He must have realized that his words were too sarcastic. "I have a job to do, Kate. I can't let friendship blind me to that."

"Richard could never have hurt Jenny."

Carl set his cup down and leaned toward her, his eyes intent on her face. His voice was harsh when he spoke.

"You believe your husband is innocent and that may well be true. It would be all too easy for me to see him only as a grieving father. However his actions have not been fully explained and until they are, I have to treat him as a possible suspect."

"You know Richard. You've talked to him. You've seen him in our home and around other people. Can you really believe he could do something so loathsome?"

"Christ, Kate," Carl said. "If you'd seen as much as I have, you'd realize that anyone is capable of evil. Mother, father, rich, poor. A momentary loss of control and even a saint can become a sinner."

"If Richard was in any way guilty, I would know it. Do you think I would be a party to such a crime?"

Kate held steady as Carl's eyes searched her face. It was a slow scrutiny as if he were weighing the possibility in his mind. When he spoke, he did not apologize for his hesitation.

"I am absolutely convinced that you had nothing to do with your daughter's death. You could not hide your surprise that Richard had not been at the office the day she died." With both hands he rubbed his eyes, sliding his fingers down his cheeks and tenting them at the base of his chin. He held her gaze. "There's one thing I don't know. If, and I am only saying if, Richard were guilty, would you protect him?"

Kate refused to comment. She simply could not deal with what she considered Carl's betrayal. She drank her tea in silence. He remained with her, prowling the edges of the room until the intercom announced that Richard had completed his session. He ushered her to the door of the film room, leaving her with only a polite goodbye.

"You've both done extremely well," Bea said as Kate sat down beside Richard. "Now you have a choice. We can either continue with the joint session or you can come back tomorrow."

"I'd rather get it over with," Richard said. He turned to Kate and she nodded her head.

When it was over, Kate asked Richard to take her home. Neither of them could face going out for lunch. The session at the police station had given her some awareness of the monumental task of finding Jenny's murderer. It was overwhelming.

"Don't get out," she said. "Just leave me and go in to work."

"Are you sure?"

"Positive. I'm exhausted. I'm going to grab a sandwich and lie down for a bit."

He leaned across and kissed her on the cheek. "I'll call you later."

Kate unlocked the front door but before she could go inside, she heard someone calling her name.

"Yoo-hoo, Kate. Up here, dear." Marian Granger's voice issued from a second-story window in the house next door. "Some flowers came for you while you were out. Is this a good time to bring them over?"

"Don't bother. I'll come and get them."

"It's no bother. I'm going out to the store as soon as I finish making the bed. I'm running late today. Are you going to be home for a while?"

"Yes. I'm here for the rest of the day. I'll leave the door open."

Inside, Kate dumped her purse on the hall table, hung up her blazer, and headed back to the kitchen. As she passed it, the wall phone rang and without thinking, she picked it up.

"Hello?"

"I saw him in the forest preserve."

The voice was a sibilant undertone.

"Who is this?" Kate's breath caught in her throat and she could barely get the words out. "What do you want?"

"He took her into the woods. I saw what he did. You knew, didn't you?"

Kate began to cry, sobbing with pain at the whispered words, but unable to hang up the phone.

The voice rose in anger. "You knew he did it."

"Who? Who did it?"

"Your husband. He bashed her head in with a rock."

# EIGHT

"I saw him in the woods. He killed her."

"No! No!" Kate shouted. "He didn't do it."

Kate shook her head with such violence that she lost her balance, falling against the countertop and sliding down the wooden surface of the kitchen cabinet until she sprawled in a heap on the floor, ear still pressed to the receiver.

"He killed her, and I saw it all. He'll pay for his crime."

"He didn't do it. He'd never hurt Jenny."

Her voice had fallen to a low moan, an echo of the evil whisper on the other end of the line. Words spewed from the caller. Vile words. Hurtful words. Sobbing now, Kate pushed the phone away, curling into a tight ball, rocking back and forth on the linoleum.

"Kate! Kate! What is it?"

She heard Marian's frightened voice, but she could not stop crying. Strong hands raised her to a sitting position and then Kate felt the older woman's arms around her. Marian held her, patting her back until her sobs became shuddering hiccups. Tremors shook her. Eventually they lessened and she was able to lift her head from her neighbor's well-padded shoulder.

Marian reached into a deep pocket of her skirt and came up with a square of neatly folded Kleenex. "Tissue?"

The use of such an old-fashioned word brought a sense of normality back to Kate. She shifted her position, leaning back against the cabinet, too exhausted to get to her feet. She blew her nose.

Marian stood up, brushing off her skirt as she leaned over to pick up the receiver. She listened to the dial tone then hung it up without comment. She opened drawers in the cabinets until she found some kitchen towels. Taking one out, she ran it under the faucet for a minute, wrung it out, and brought it over to Kate.

Kate sucked in her breath at the cool dampness of the terry cloth. Folding the cloth, she pressed it against her swollen eyelids.

"Just stay where you are, dear. I'll fix some tea." Cupboards opened and closed. Heavy sigh. "Ah, Lemon Lift. That's just the ticket." More cupboards opening. "And I suspect you've skipped lunch and it's well past noon. No wonder you're looking so white-faced. My mother always used to say, 'Marian, in a crisis, make sure you get plenty of protein.' It's strange because the articles you read nowadays stress carbohydrates."

The running monologue gave Kate a chance to recover. By the time the kettle whistled, she was ready to face her friend. Getting to her feet, she leaned against the countertop until her legs stopped trembling.

"Why don't we take this outside? The sun's shining and it looks to be a lovely day." Without giving Kate a chance to refuse, Marian picked up the wicker tray on the counter and started out to the family room. Kate unlocked the patio doors, holding the screen door open as Marian stepped out onto the deck.

In Marian, Kate had found the companionship she might have had with her own mother. It was easy to talk to her. She was well-educated, nonjudgmental, and had a wry sense of humor. She was very ladylike, almost prim. Her clothes had an understated elegance that minimized her plumpness. Her short hair was frosted, very striking with her pretty face and sparkling blue eyes.

They sat quietly drinking tea and Kate ate the sandwich Marian had made. When she was finished, Kate leaned back in her chair, raising her mug in a salute. "Thanks."

"Tea always helps." The twinkle in Marian's eyes faded as she stared across the table. "I assume that was an obscene call earlier."

Kate nodded.

"Right after Leah was born, I started getting calls late at night when George was out of town. The first time it happened, I was so stunned that I just let him keep talking. He said very nasty things. Eventually I learned to hang up. It went on for months. Then it stopped. I never did find out who was making the calls."

"It wasn't like an obscene call. This was different." Kate couldn't bring herself to tell Marian what the voice had said. "It was sort of threatening."

"You should tell the police."

"No!" Kate lurched, spilling tea on her skirt. She brushed impatiently at the wetness, shaking her head.

"Ah." Marian's mouth pursed in disgust. "I would guess whomever it was accused Richard or you or both of you of killing Jenny. Am I right?"

Kate's mouth trembled. She could only nod.

"There are such sickos in the world nowadays. People are frightened when crimes like this happen. They want someone to blame. You need to tell the police about the call." Kate raised her chin stubbornly, but Marian continued. "You don't have to describe what the man said."

Kate shook her head.

"Think about it, dear. It could have been the murderer."

At Marian's words, Kate caught her breath in sudden fear.

"The man who killed Jenny is crazy. He might get his kicks from making calls to frighten you. But no matter who it was, the police need to know."

Without pressing the point, Marian got to her feet and began to put the dishes back onto the tray. Kate sighed, rose to her feet and embraced the older woman.

"Although I hate to admit it, you're probably right."

"Of course, I am," Marian said. "And furthermore you really ought to have caller ID."

"That's what Richard said. We just haven't done it." Waving her friend toward the house, Kate picked up the tray.

Unnoticed until now, were the flowers, wrapped in florist's paper on the kitchen counter where Marian had left them. Kate ripped open the paper, sighing in pleasure at the basket of flowers. Yellow roses and daffodils. White daisies and babies' breath.

"It's from Chris Mayerling, Richard's boss. He's given Richard a great deal of support at work. He sent an arrangement to the funeral home and now this." Kate waved at the flowers. "I'm ashamed to admit I never thought he was particularly thoughtful. He's always so full of himself that I didn't think there was much beneath the blown-dry hair."

"People surprise you after a tragedy. You find new friends and old ones desert you. I remember how it was after George died. Sometimes life really stinks, so when you discover something good, don't knock it," Marian said, wiping her hands on a towel. "Well, my dear, I'm off. I'll check back with you later."

After Marian left, Kate stared at the telephone. Despite what she had told her friend, she couldn't call Leidecker. There was no way she could tell him about the phone call without revealing the contents. She wasn't a good liar, and he was intuitive enough to know she was holding something back.

She no longer trusted Leidecker.

More and more she got the feeling that he believed Richard had committed the murder. She didn't know who else the police suspected, but it was as if Carl was focused solely on Richard. Almost a personal vendetta. She wanted to scream at him to leave Richard alone.

*Richard didn't kill Jenny!*

She would have to hold to that belief if she had any hope of surviving.

Kate tried to remember the exact wording of the phone call.

*"I saw him."*

Now that she wasn't so stunned and frightened, she could think more rationally. She didn't know what information had been released to the media but other than the rock, the caller had mentioned no specific details. If the person had actually been in the forest preserve and seen the murder, he or she would have gone to the police.

It was hard to believe that anyone would be so cruel as to make such a call to her. However, a week ago she would not have believed that anyone could murder a child.

Kate pressed the palms of her hands against her eyes, sinking into the soothing darkness. If she called Leidecker and told him about the call she would only add to his belief that Richard was guilty. For now, she would let the answering machine pick up rather than risk hearing the obscenities spewed out by some twisted mind. Only if it continued would she consider talking to Leidecker.

*Finally she's asleep.*

He closed the bathroom door gently, wincing at the sound of the lock clicking into place. Heart sounds thudded in his ears. If she woke up, she would talk to him when he got back in bed. All he wanted was silence.

Opening the medicine cabinet he pushed the pill bottles aside so he could reach the bottle of castor oil in the back. The bottle had been in the cabinet for ages. She would never touch it. He unscrewed the cap, letting the contents spill out into his hand.

*My talisman.*

Index finger extended, he stroked the nest of delicate links, nudging the chain until it lay in a straight line across his palm. The wings of the angel charm appeared to move as the gold shimmered in the fluorescent lights.

*Arms spread wide, beckoning him.*

His breathing quickened and he touched the charm, increasing the pressure until the edges cut into his skin. The metal should have been cold but there was a warmth that seared him and he jerked back his finger, staring at the tip, amazed that it wasn't burned.

Once more he touched the charm.

A slight buzzing sound enveloped him and the room fell away. He was back in the forest preserve and he saw it all again, not in pictures, only in flashes of light that this time, instead of fear, brought heat and energy before disappearing into the secret recesses of his mind.

He had initiated many young girls. This time it was different and the difference frightened him.

In the beginning he had gone abroad for his pleasures. Other countries were not so restrictive, understanding that he had special requirements. The price was high but confidentiality was assured. He enjoyed the planning; the secrecy always heightened the experience. Then later, when it was difficult to get away, he knew people to call.

He had never taken a child off the street before. Was it the fear of discovery that made this time so special? Maybe. But there was something more.

*He had come at the moment of her death.*

Would he ever be able to duplicate the experience? Even though the incident had catapulted him to a higher plateau, it was far too dangerous to explore it. It must never happen again.

The intensity of sensations was a seductive lure but he would have to find a way to deal with the weakness of his spirit. He could not take another child. Far too risky. Repetition could lead to exposure. As if he could imprint the image of his decision on his skin, he tightened his fingers around the links of the gold bracelet. Holding the end of the chain, he lowered it into the mouth of the bottle, screwed on the cap and returned it to its position in the cabinet.

Closing the door of the medicine cabinet, he stared into the mirror, surprised to see that his face was unchanged. He had always believed in the mark of Cain, but realized now that it was just another myth left over from childhood. The bogeyman. No one would know to look at him; if there were marks, they were embedded deep within his soul.

His reflection mocked him. In the eyes there was knowledge of death and yet he was too cowardly to explore the subject. Had death triggered the rise in sensation and power? Would death alone give him the same pleasure? Coward! He glared back, wanting to refute the accusation.

*Sex or death?*

An intellectual challenge worthy of his talents. He ought to be able to find out which of them gave him the biggest thrill. He knew the risk he'd be taking. The investigation continued. The threat of discovery and arrest was constant. If he chose carefully enough, another death might be further protection against exposure. His mouth stretched in a grin. It was an obvious choice. Dangerous but it would be worth the risk.

His eyes glittered in anticipation.

# Nine

BEHIND THE CLOSED DOORS of the conference room, the bevy of activity in the center of the police station was muted. Even the ringing phones sounded less urgent, Carl thought as he reached for a cigarette. The compulsive action annoyed him and he snatched at the gum on the table and jammed a piece into his mouth. The vigorous chewing relaxed him and he leaned back in his chair.

Too bad Chief Corcoran hadn't lived long enough to see the new station. Patrick died two years after retirement. Everyone had known he had a bad heart, but it still had been a shock. Carl had consulted frequently with Patrick during the design phase of the new building. The old man had impressed on Carl the need for a conference room that could double as a war room in case of some major crime.

Carl yawned, staring down at his watch. Nine o'clock, Tuesday morning. A week since Jenny Warner was killed. The crisis team had been meeting for an hour.

"This coffee sucks," Diego Garcia said. Despite the comment, he stretched across the conference table for the thermos. His other hand reached for the tray of sweet rolls, taking two chocolate-covered donuts.

Carl noticed the slight tremor of his hands and debated whether he should talk to Garcia. The man had been divorced for a year. Perhaps his weekends really were the orgasmic marathons he bragged about, however the bags under his eyes and the pallor beneath the light tan told a different story.

Booze, at a guess, Carl thought. He ought to know. That's how well he'd handled his own divorce from Mary Clare. Drank himself into oblivion for several months. One night his partner, a big Irishman named Danny O'Sullivan, dropped by to tell him to get help. Danny wasn't long on finesse because when Carl told him to butt out, Danny punched him. By the time Carl agreed to go to an AA meeting, his eyes were swollen shut, two ribs were cracked, and every tooth in his head felt loose.

Carl went to the meetings. First, because Danny dragged him and waited outside in case he tried to skip out early. Finally, Carl stayed. He'd sworn to beat Danny to a pulp when he'd been sober six months. A month shy of the date, they'd been ambushed in an alley during a drug bust. Danny was gut shot. Died on the way to the hospital. Carl hadn't had a drink since.

"This is a summary of the interviews done at Mayerling's, the company where Richard Warner works," Bob Jackson said as he passed a stack of papers around the room. "The window of opportunity to snatch the kid is 3:10 P.M. to 4:00 P.M. Both Richard Warner and Christian Mayerling were unaccounted for at that time."

Bob had been a teacher for several years before joining the force and had never lost the habit of lecturing. He was the most conservative of the team, all too aware that as the highest ranking African American he had to be a role model. He had a tendency to frown on the raunchy humor of the other officers. Carl had rarely seen Bob in anything other than a suit. Even on summer days when the rest of the force was close to heat prostration, Bob never broke a sweat.

"Richard Warner's secretary said he'd been short-tempered in the morning. What she called post-presentation nerves. Said usually he's wonderful to work for. She was at lunch when he left. The reception-ist said it was about 12:45."

"Trains?" Bea asked.

"He could have caught the 1:26, which gets into Round Lake Beach at" — Bob flipped through his notes — "at 2:41. It would be tight to get to Pickard in time but Warner is definitely in the picture. Christian Mayerling's another possible. He's got little or no alibi. Had lunch at Debowski's in Chicago with his stockbroker. Verified. Then around two he says he went to the health club. Can't remember seeing anyone he knew. When I checked with the staff they said, he could've been there. He comes in a lot, but nobody could swear that he was there Tuesday. Could have been Monday or Wednesday. Mayerling says he was there until five."

"Background?"

"Inherited a bundle. Well connected in the city. Sexual preferences questionable."

"A fag?" asked Tony, speaking around the donut in his mouth.

Torrentino's homophobia annoyed Carl, but he put it down to the man's super-macho image. He was built square, very muscular, almost bullish. His dark skin was badly pockmarked and his mashed nose had little definition. Thick, black hair and heavily-lashed eyes were his only good features. He dressed the part of old time bootlegger. Powdered sugar dotted his black tie like snow.

Carl had grown up in the Hyde Park area where color and sexual preference weren't as important as education. Since becoming chief, he'd been at special pains to eradicate as much bigotry as possible in a police force made up primarily of whites. He'd hired blacks, Latinos, and more women. Pickard's police force was far more representative of the population than it had been.

Bob ignored Tony's comment. "Mayerling's fifty-five. Divorced. He was married in his late twenties. Lasted six years. No kids. According to the gossip at the office, he's got an ongoing relationship with a society matron. However, some thought it might just be window dressing."

"Opinion?" Carl asked.

"My guess is that he swings both ways. There's nothing overtly gay about him, but it's possible. His background is clean. He might just be one of those affected rich guys."

Tony grunted and shuffled through his papers. "I thought the witness said the guy had dark hair. Wouldn't she have seen the white hair if it was Mayerling?"

"Not necessarily," Carl said. "She only saw the back of his head and got the impression his hair was dark. Mayerling's hair is dark except for the white at his temples."

82

Bea spoke up. "Would Jennifer have gotten in the car with Mayerling?"

"I think so." Carl said. "Mayerling was at the Warner home frequently. Jennifer knew he was her father's boss, therefore a trustworthy authority figure. If his story was good enough, say an accident . . . let's say it's possible."

"What about the doc?" Diego checked his notes. "Kennedy? He's also at the house a lot, and he's her godfather."

"I interviewed him pretty extensively about Richard Warner," Bob said. "I figured he'd be able to give me a solid picture of the guy. Biased maybe, but I could adjust for that. He grew up an army brat. Couple postings abroad. Germany and France. At any rate he came back to the states for college. Cleveland, Ohio. He and Richard were roommates. Married a New Yorker after graduation. She worked to put him through med school, and then filed for divorce during his residency."

Bob checked his notes. "Since then he's had a series of live-in and live-out girlfriends. His current arrangement is with a Miss Chesapeake Chesney, one of the nutritionists at the hospital. He has a townhouse near the hospital, and stays at hers in Chicago a couple of times a week. According to the nurses at the hospital, he's — and I'm quoting here — a teddy bear."

"Guy that big looks more like a grizzly bear," Tony said.

Bob continued, "His specialty is geriatrics and, again according to the nurses, his patients adore him."

"Cut to the chase." Carl was getting impatient. "Does he have an alibi?"

"Looks like it. The shift change is three o'clock. Two of the nurses going off duty saw him at 2:45 on the second floor in" — Bob looked down at his notes — "a Mrs. Edith Olson's room. According to the night shift nurse, he was there at 3:19 when Mrs. Olson began having trouble breathing. He ordered an increase in her oxygen and stayed with her until she was stable. The routine is that when the new shift comes on the floor, they go around to each patient. Check vitals and see if there're any problems. On May sixteenth, there were only six patients. One of the nurses found Dr. Kennedy dozing in Mrs. Olson's room. She figures it was around 3:30 or 3:45. She didn't wake him. His beeper went off at 4:30. He left the floor after taking his messages at the nurses' station."

"The witness saw the kid get into the car at 3:10. Unless the good doctor can stop time, he's out of it." Carl flipped through his notes. "How are the school kids dealing with this, Ellen?"

"The younger kids don't understand, the older kids think they're invincible, and the rest are in between."

Despite her master's degree in social work, Carl had been reluctant to hire Fredricks. With her little mouse voice, long hair, and bangs, she looked about twelve. He hadn't thought she was tough enough for the job. Ellen had sensed his hesitancy and suggested he give her a month's probation.

She never spoke above a whisper yet somehow she established an immediate rapport with the kids brought into the station. Even the streetwise punks. They started out smart-mouthing her and ended up confiding their pissant life stories.

Carl hadn't waited until the end of the month; after two weeks he gave her the job.

"Have you got enough counselors?" Bea asked.

"Right after I was hired I set up a reciprocal deal with the Chicago Suburban Board of Education. Pickard sends three or four counselors when they're shorthanded. In return they supply us with a full-blown trauma team."

There were murmurs of approval around the table, and Ellen's cheeks pinked with pleasure.

"This is the first time we've needed help with a violent crime," she continued. "We're working with the parents as well as the children. And, I can tell you, anxiety is running pretty high. Everyone is afraid it'll happen again."

The sounds of assent were a low murmur around the table. Carl waited for the room to settle down. "Squint's in the lab, so he gave me his notes. The photo session with the Warners went well. They identified about fifty percent of the pictures. Another twenty were identified from various sources. That leaves thirty percent unknowns. Chicago is working on those. Bea has a list of those ID'd."

Bea picked up the narrative. "I've cross-referenced the names with the interviews we've done already. A team was set up to contact the rest. We did a brief background check, and if anything came up, it was added to the individual's file. Incidentally, two men with priors were here in Pickard the day of the funeral. Both repeat child offenders. Their pictures turned up in a crowd scene. I gave the names to Tony."

"The assholes were here all right. Said they happened to be in the neighborhood." Tony spoke out of one side of his mouth. His hamlike hands made chopping motions to punctuate his words. "Leaned on them but they had alibis for the day the victim disappeared. I don't think they'll be back."

"What about locals?" Bob asked.

Bea riffled through the papers in front of her until she found the one she wanted. "One convicted molester. Two more with complaints against them but never charged. A couple peepers. And one guy charged with stalking kids. You should all remember him. He's the one who said he was making a movie about the innocence of children at play."

"The guy was a faggot," Tony said.

"That don't mean he can't get it up." Diego made a hand gesture by way of illustration. "He told me he was going to be the next Walt Disney."

Carl rapped the table with the end of his pen. "You check 'em, Tony?"

"Better believe it. They were all pissed off, but in each case there was an alibi for some or all of the crucial time. Only one of the peepers I still got to talk to. According to his brother, he left town the moment he heard the news." Tony shook his head at the intent expressions. "Don't get your hopes up. The kid's nineteen and a computer nerd. The peeping was four years ago when he was fifteen. Raging hormones and no outlet. Roamed the neighborhood until he found someone stripping or screwing without pulling the blinds. Used to stand outside in the bushes and jerk off. He's got a girlfriend now."

"It'll save him from the dreaded rose rash. Talk about a sore prick."

85

"Really, Diego," Bob said. "Don't you ever quit?"

Diego's humorous contributions generally eased the tensions in a meeting, so Carl stayed out of it. Luckily the man was a first-rate cop. Great detail man. Intuitive during interrogation. He said it was his Latin side that gave him hunches and the ability to sniff out a lie. Carl didn't doubt it.

Pushing back his chair, Carl walked across to the windows. Hands behind his back, he stretched backward, rolling his shoulders to ease his stiffness. Outside the sun had broken through the clouds but the sunlight was anemic. He raised the window, letting in some of the fresh air.

A young mother pushed a stroller in the park across the street. Behind her, a girl of three or four hunkered down to investigate something on the ground. The mother's voice was sharp as she called the girl back to her side. Everyone in town was edgy.

Returning to his chair, Carl called the group back to order. "Diego, did anything come up on house to house?"

"*Nada*. Aside from Mrs. Doutt, no one looked out the front windows."

Carl cleared his throat. "The lab reports from the crime scene are in the packets I gave you. As you already know, the rape took place in the woods, probably just prior to the murder. Blood and hair samples were found on the surface of a rock at the scene. Positively identified as the victim's. It adds some credence to the theory that the murder was probably spur of the moment."

"Does that mean the chances for another kidnapping are minimal?" Bob asked.

"Maybe," Carl answered. "According to the profile we're working up, if this is a first-time offender he'll go one of two ways. He'll be so frightened by the enormity of his act that he'll never do it again. The worse case scenario is that, as we all know, the second time is always easier."

Gloom settled over the table.

"Yo, chief." Diego jabbed the point of his pencil on one of his notes. "I know we've been doing interviews over in the forest preserve with joggers and other people who use the trails. Have we put out the word to the gays who meet and greet by the south entrance shelter?"

Tony leaned across the table. "I thought you said the guy who killed the kid wasn't a queer?"

"He probably isn't," Diego shot back. "But the gay boys have eyes. And they mighta seen something. They're always looking around, afraid they'll get busted or bashed."

"Good point," Carl said. "We got anyone with connections to the alternate lifestyle group? Someone with a little discretion?"

"I know someone," Bea said, holding up her hand as Tony opened his mouth to comment. "No need to panic, Tony. He's no one you know, so we can count on the fact he's got some sensitivity."

"Was that a slam?" he said, cocking his head as he spotted the grins on several faces. "I can't help it if I got a thing about those guys. They give me the creeps. What I was going to say was that I couldn't find my summary of the crime scene." He continued to shuffle through a clutch of paperwork.

"I don't know how you find anything in that mess. I won't even mention your desk." Bob pointed to his own meticulous stack of folders. "You need to spend more time getting organized."

"Let's keep moving," Bea said. She leaned across the table and handed Tony her copy of the summary. "Was there anything in particular you wondered about?"

"Semen," was the blunt response.

"None." Bea's voice was brisk. "No stains on the clothing. Panties had been torn off and were lying separate from the body. No condom was found at the scene."

"By the way," Carl interjected, "I want all of you to take a good look at the photograph of Mrs. Warner's necklace. The charm is the same as the one on the bracelet that's still missing. Jenny's teacher confirms the girl had it on when she left the school. It could have come off on the way home from school, in the guy's car, or during the attack. The profile suggests the killer may have taken it as a trophy."

He pushed the pile of folders and loose sheets to the side and flipped open the cover of his notebook. "After a week, the only real suspect we have is Richard Warner. Do we have enough for a search warrant?"

"No." Bea's voice was sharp as she stared down the length of the table. The eyes of the others swiveled back and forth between the ends of the table. Carl raised his hands, palms toward the older woman.

"It's just a question," he said. Bea didn't comment; her stiff body language indicative of her thoughts. "Aside from the fact Warner lied about being at the office on the afternoon of his daughter's disappearance, does the rest of his statement check out?"

"With the exception of the period from 12:45 when he left work and 6:45 when he got home, everything he said is correct," Bob said.

"He could have picked his kid up at the bus stop, killed her, and had plenty of time to spare." Tony glared down at his tie, rubbing the spots of powdered sugar with his thumb. "He has the PF license plate. Did the background check turn up anything?"

"No. No arrests. No complaints. No speeding tickets." Bea kept her answers short.

"I'm inclined to think you might be off base on this one, Carl." Bob straightened his collar and smoothed his shirt. "I've gone over the interviews at Warner's office, the hospital, the neighborhood, and the church. I didn't pick up a thing."

"Then, God damn it, where was he Tuesday afternoon?" In his frustration Carl slapped the table with his open hand.

"My guess is that he's having an affair." Bob shrugged his shoulders at the skepticism on several faces. "I know it's hard to believe he'd lie, considering the gravity of the situation. In the beginning I think he lied to protect his lover. Now I think he's lying to protect his wife from further pain."

"Has the lab report on his clothes come in?"

"I'll check," Bea said, leaving the room. When she returned, she was holding a piece of yellow, lined paper. Her mouth was pursed as she reread her scribbled notes.

"I called the lab and they were just about finished with Warner's clothes. Some of the test results aren't in yet. As you already know, the slacks had been cleaned and the shirt washed. The preliminary findings on those two items show: no blood, no semen, no hair, no nothing. Prelims on the jacket show no blood and no semen. Five distinct hair samples were tested. Two are unknowns. In a preliminary test, the other three belonged to Richard Warner, his wife Kate, and the victim Jennifer. As you are all aware, the victim's hair could have come from direct contact or could have been picked up indirectly around the house."

Carl scribbled a note then asked, "Shoes?"

"They took minuscule scrapings from Richard Warner's shoes. The sample was tested against another sample from the parking lot of the forest preserve where the victim's body was found," Bea said.

"And?"

"It's a direct match."

# TEN

"THE DIRT SAMPLE FROM RICHARD'S SHOES matches the sample taken from the parking lot of the forest preserve," Bea repeated.

"Is that definite?"

"Yes." She sighed, obviously not pleased with the information. "I made a quick call to Seanne Buckwalter, the head of the forestry department. One week before the murder, the town sprayed a section of the forest preserve with an experimental weed killer. It's a special blend that Buckwalter mixes herself. The only way that Richard Warner could have gotten that particular chemical combination on his shoes was from the area where Jennifer's body was found."

Bea paused, staring around at the intent faces. She extended her arm, waving the pages in front of her.

"I have to stress again that this is a very preliminary report. We have nothing but circumstantial evidence against Richard Warner. No matter how it looks, we can't afford to get tunnel vision at this stage of the investigation. There's no evidence he was in the forest preserve on Tuesday. It could have been anytime during the week prior to his daughter's death. And even if he was there on Tuesday, it could be some bizarre coincidence that has nothing to do with the murder."

Carl knew Bea was right in saying that it was too early to make any judgments, but he would not make the mistake of accepting Richard's role of bereaved parent as proof of innocence.

The tension level in the room had risen with the results of the lab report. Carl changed the subject. "Ellen, what kind of psychological profiles are we working with?"

"If it's a pedophile who picked up a kid and then panicked and killed her," she said, "we're probably looking for someone either younger or older than Warner. Pedophilia's not generally a middle-aged crime. According to the experts, the peeping and flashing can be done to gather intelligence or it could be the foreplay to an event. The scenario: 'I see you but you don't see me' is very arousing to the serial rapist or pedophile."

"Bea, I want all recent reports of peepers or flashers flagged." Carl said, then moved to the next subject on his list. "What have we got on ButterSkots?"

Tony sifted through his paperwork until he came up with several pages clipped together. "The partially sucked piece of hard candy was found in the right-hand pocket of the victim's yellow jacket. It was wrapped in a clear cellophane sheet with the word ButterSkots in plaid letters on one side."

"Prints?"

"None. Only smudges." Tony looked up from his notes. "The candy is butterscotch flavored, made in Dundee, Scotland. It's a small company, family run. The individually wrapped candies, thirty of them to a metal tin, are sold locally. No mail order."

"I don't think she got it at school," Ellen said. "I checked with the teacher and the kids in Jenny's class. None of them recognized the name ButterSkots or the logo. I realize it's not conclusive but . . ." Her words trickled off into silence.

"Do you think the perp used the candy to lure her into the car?" Bob asked.

"Your guess is as good as mine." Tony shrugged his shoulders. "The prick could have offered it to her after she got into the car. To establish friendship or trust."

"If the killer gave her the candy it would argue against Richard Warner's involvement. According to Mrs. Warner, the girl hated butterscotch, and he would have known that." Bob was clearly in Bea's camp.

"He mighta forgot," Tony argued. "Someone ought to check if Warner's been to Scotland. I called the company direct, and they're going to send us a list of any American orders. At least I think they are. The babe I talked to had an accent, real thick. I could hardly believe she was talkin' English."

"She's probably saying the same thing about you," Diego said.

"I'd like to keep the info on the candy as tight as possible," Carl said. "The media would pick up on it and the next thing you know they'd be referring to the 'Butterscotch Killer'."

"What about the license plate info?" Tony asked.

Bea pulled out a thick sheaf of computer paper. "At this point we're not interviewing everyone with the plates, although it may come down to that. For the moment, it will be noted along with other information as we develop a prime suspect list. You'll be happy to know you made the list, Chief."

"You know my theory," Carl said. "Support local business. It pays your salary. And if you're wondering, I was home alone with my dog."

"You dating again?" Diego asked, earning a laugh from around the table. Carl grinned, saluting him with his coffee.

Tony leaned forward. "Does Richard Warner have the PF plates?"

"Yes." Bea's voice was neutral. "So does Mike Kennedy."

"How about Chris Mayerling?" Bob asked.

"No. He primarily drives a red Porsche convertible." Bea once more flipped through her notes. "However he does have a second car, a dark blue Seville. License number PE 4324."

"PF or PE. The old lady coulda mixed them up," Tony said.

The sound of a pencil scratching on paper filled the silence.

"Anything else?" Carl asked.

"Just one last item. I'd like you to take a look at this list." Bea dealt the papers out. "When we ran the printout of the people in town with the PF license plate, this group of names kicked out because they matched other criteria that's built into the system."

Carl read through the names quickly as he flipped the pages. "Are you saying we should consider this group as possible suspects?"

Bea shook her head. "No. Just be aware of them. They have PF plates, and for some reason they've come to the attention of the police department. It may be something as random as a burglary or jaywalking. Could be they called to report a lost dog."

"Did you run the names against the list of people the Warners know?" Bob asked.

"Yes, and four of them came up positive. They're underlined." Bea held the point of her pencil against the first name. "Edward Bushnell lives on the same block as the Warners."

Carl leaned forward. "Do you know who that is? Bushnell used to be the mayor of Pickard. Hell, it's got to be close to thirty years ago. Ed and his wife are very active in town. Lots of money and generous philanthropic tendencies. Before he retired, Chief Corcoran used to be pretty thick with Bushnell."

"I'll make a note of that but ex-mayor cuts no slack with me," Bea said. "He's seventy-three, retired, lives with his wife, and has no record. His name came up several years ago when we were running a sting on a mail-order house that was dealing in pornography."

"Old boy probably couldn't get it up and sent for some rubber goods."

Carl ignored Diego's aside. "Anything come of it?"

Bea shook her head. "No. The notes mentioned him in passing. Just said he was embarrassed and confused."

"I was at Warners' when Bushnell stopped by with a cake his wife had baked," Carl said. "He was at the wake. Came across as old and shaky. Upset but he seemed harmless enough."

"Pedophiles don't wear signs," Bob commented.

With a nod, Carl conceded the point, placing a double check mark beside Bushnell's name, and moved to the next one. "Buddy Fanning? The guy who owns the Jeep dealership?"

"That's the one. Mr. Sleaze himself." Bea grinned. "Two women customers accused him of fondling them while they were out for a test drive. Two separate incidents about a month apart. Neither pressed charges after Buddy Boy apologized, and offered a great deal on a new car."

"Just 'cause a guy tries to cop a feel doesn't mean he'd do a kid." Tony looked around the table for confirmation.

"I'm not making any accusations here. I'm just giving you the

93

facts," Bea said. "The next name is Nathaniel Nathanson. He's an insurance agent, and in his spare time volunteers for the park soccer league. He was Jenny's coach for two years. I don't know why his name came up. The reference name was Frank Mannino of the Rockford police."

"I know Frank," Tony said. "His wife, Marianne, is a cousin of mine. I'll give him a call and see what he can tell me."

"Good." Bea made a note and then moved on to the last name. "Wayne Zmudzki. He came up twice. Two teachers suggested he might be physically abusing his daughter. Beatings, not sexual. Nothing proved, and he denied everything. Wife backed him up, and the kid said he'd never hit her. He lives a block from the school, and his daughter was in the same class as Jenny."

"None of these sound particularly promising," Diego muttered.

"I know," Bea admitted.

"Okay then. Anything we've left out?" Carl asked. He looked around the table at the shaking heads. "The next meeting will be Friday at four, unless there's a break in the case."

Chairs were shoved back and they began to gather up their reports. Carl jotted a final reminder, closed his notebook, and rose to his feet.

"By the way," he said. "Make sure your teams stay visible. A strong police presence on the streets might discourage the killer from trying again."

There was little reaction to his words. Carl could see in the cynical expressions that the question was not *whether* it would happen again, but *when* it would happen.

"How's my girl?" Mike asked as he leaned over to kiss Kate on the cheek. He put his arm around her as they walked through the front hall to the kitchen.

She moved out of his embrace and pointed to the refrigerator. "Would you like something cold? Beer? Iced tea?"

"I'd love a beer, but I've got to go back to the hospital, so I'll go for the tea. My prize patient, Edith Olson, is well enough to be released. She's going to be eighty-five tomorrow, and wants to celebrate at home."

He pulled out one of the kitchen chairs and sat down at the table. He pushed the café curtains aside, unlocked the window, and raised the sash to let in some fresh air.

"It's stuffy in here. We ought to be sitting outside. It's a beautiful day." He nodded to the window. "Your daffodils look good."

"I hadn't noticed," Kate said. She placed a glass of tea in front of him, and stared out at the backyard, her face showing little interest.

"You know, Kate, it's natural to feel numb." He sipped the tea. "It's your mind's way of protecting itself against overload. In time it will pass."

Kate shrugged. Psychobabble, she thought. What did he know?

She moved away from the table and poured herself some iced tea. She leaned against the counter, too restless to sit down. Mike's unexpected visit made her nervous. Since Jenny's death, she'd been aware that he watched her, assessing her mental and physical condition. She didn't know if his concern was just normal for a doctor or if there was something more involved.

"What's up?"

"I was passing by and I thought I'd stop in." He raised his glass to take another drink.

"Give me a break."

Above the rim of the glass, Mike's face flushed, the freckles standing out starkly against his pink skin. It surprised Kate. She rarely saw him flustered.

"All right. All right. I wasn't passing by. I wanted to talk to you." He put the glass down on the table, moving it around, leaving a series of wet rings on the surface. "I tried to bring it up with Richard, but I thought it might be easier talking to you."

Whatever it was, the subject was obviously uncomfortable. "Could you give me a clue, Mike?"

"It's money."

He blurted out the words, looking relieved at the accomplishment, but leaving Kate still in the dark. "Do you need money?" she asked.

"No. No." He shook his head. "I'm doing this poorly, Kate. I'm sorry. I wondered if you needed help with legal expenses, that type of thing."

She was genuinely warmed by Mike's concern. Tears stung her eyes. She blinked rapidly, smiling at the look of panic on his face. He started to rise, but she waved him back.

"I'm not going to cry," she said. She brought her drink over to the table, sitting down across from him. She reached out, putting her hand into the large palm he extended. It was almost her undoing. His kindness broke through the defenses that she had erected in the past week and a half. Her voice was slightly shaky when she spoke. "I'm glad you were passing by."

Mike waited while she gathered her resources. She didn't feel rushed. Swallowing her tears, she smiled across the table. He released her hand.

"In answer to your question," she said, "we don't need any money at the moment. I don't feel I'm telling you anything Richard wouldn't, if you asked him. He gave Stacie $6,000. Her final bill will probably be pretty hefty, but we've got enough savings to cover that."

"Good."

Once more he appeared hesitant but this time Kate was more attuned to his thoughts. "You're wondering what will happen if Richard is arrested?"

"Yes. Richard appears to be the focus of their investigation. I'd hate to think they'd pin it on him for lack of any other suspect."

"It's happened before," Kate said.

"That's what concerns me. I know you're under a lot of tension and worrying about money will make things worse. I couldn't think of any way to bring it up with Richard. I don't want him to think that talking about arrest means I'm beginning to doubt him."

She pushed her iced tea away, wiping her wet hand on her jeans. "It's all part of the nightmare. You start weighing your words. You have to think about every action. How will it look? How will it sound? God, it's awful."

"It must be. I wish there was more that I could do. Chessy feels the same way. We've talked about it constantly trying to think how we could help. You know how practical Chessy is. She suggested I check on your finances."

"Chessy's a love. Both Richard and I are grateful for her support. Make sure you give her a hug from us."

"My pleasure." Wiggling his eyebrows, he twirled the ends of an imaginary mustache.

His antics made her smile. Talking to Mike was a welcome relief. She had been so mired in the effort to survive each day that she hadn't realized how many of her feelings were bottled up. She missed the give and take of discussions with Richard. Mike was only a substitute, but a blessed release for the moment.

"Look, Kate, I'm making more money than God these days. I spend a lot on golf and probably more on my clothes than Chessy does. I bought my townhouse when I moved out here and that's paid off. And I've got the cabin up at Beaverton Lake. As Chessy will be happy to attest to, I spend too much time at the hospital to run up any big bills."

He paused, then plunged ahead. "What I'm trying to say is that I've got plenty of funds that are yours if you need them. There's no need to mention it to Richard at this point, but at least it might relieve your mind to know it's available."

She had difficulty swallowing around the lump in her throat. "It helps immeasurably to know what good friends we have. It's strange. On one hand, the suspicions about Richard, getting a lawyer, and dealing with the police have been terrifying. On the other hand, they've given us a focus. A safe subject to discuss."

Mike nodded. "I suspect that for both of you, concentrating on Leidecker's investigation keeps you from having to deal with the pain of Jenny's death."

"But I feel so guilty," Kate said, crossing her arms over her chest as if she were cold. At the look of surprise on Mike's face, she tried to explain. "What I mean is that I feel guilty for not thinking about Jenny more. Everything I see and do is so wound up in thoughts of her, but I suppress the memories. The knowledge of her death is too much to handle, so I think about other things or just try to numb my mind. I'm such a coward."

"Good God, Kate! You ask too much of yourself. You're just being human. I suppose you could sink into a moaning pile of despair, but that won't be any help to anyone, let alone either you or Richard. It'll get better. After a while, it won't hurt so much."

"People say that, but I don't see how it can possibly be true. Just getting up in the morning is an effort. Nothing can bring Jenny back. And the simple truth is, Mike," she lowered her voice until her words were only a whisper, "I don't want to live in a world without Jenny."

Silence filled the kitchen. Mike cleared his throat as if to speak, but when she looked up his face was bleak. She remembered how good he had been with Jenny. And Jenny had adored him. Memories flooded Kate, and the sharp-edged pain of loss twisted in her chest.

"The average age of my patients, Kate, is seventy-eight, so I deal with death every day." Mike tipped his chair until all his weight was on the two back legs. He rocked slightly, staring at a spot above her head. "I can rattle off the stages of mourning, give you the pat sayings I learned in med school. As a doctor, I know all the answers except one. How to stop the pain."

"Enough, Mike." She couldn't muster the energy to be forceful. "Let's just leave it alone."

"Your reactions are normal. It takes time to move past the zombie stage. You need to fight the feelings of despair. No one, least of all me, expects you to deal with Jenny's death rationally. Anger comes before acceptance," he said. "Once you get angry, you'll begin to heal."

"I don't want to heal," she blurted out. "I want to die."

"And Richard?"

She felt a sense of abandonment that his first allegiance would always be to his friend. She squeezed her eyes shut, sagging in her chair. "What about Richard?"

"I think he's drinking too much."

She wasn't particularly surprised by Mike's comment. It explained some of Richard's behavior in the past few days.

"I wondered. He's been coming home later than usual. He says he's not hungry and either goes into his studio or dozes in front of the TV. I think he's just trying to blunt the pain of reality."

Mike leaned forward, bringing the front legs of his chair to the floor with a decided thump. "Blunting reality is considered one of the signs of a substance abuser."

"Will you stop lecturing me, damn it!" She glared across the table at him. With deliberation, he folded his arms across his chest. "What kind of doctor are you? You sit there so smugly, and you haven't the least idea of what I'm going through. I'm so tired of behaving correctly and doing what everyone wants me to do. I can't help Richard. I can't even help myself!" she shouted.

"Gosh you're beautiful when you're angry."

The old cliché was like a splash of cold water, bringing her back to her senses. She sucked in a gulp of air. She blinked several times, narrowing her eyes at the grin on Mike's face.

"You are an arrogant bastard, you know," she said conversationally.

"Thanks." His eyes sparkled above the wide grin. "Welcome back."

"If you're planning to follow up your performance with a reminder that this is the 'for better or worse' part of the marriage vows, I give you fair warning that I'll throw something at your head." Mike raised both hands in surrender. "All right, doctor, what do you suggest?"

His expression immediately sobered. "I'm not sure what to suggest. I think Richard's thinking and worrying too much. If you can't get him to talk, at least try to think of something to keep him busy." Mike waved toward the window. "The garden?"

She stood up, staring outside. Her neck was stiff and she massaged it with her hands. "I suppose that might work. The fresh air's bound to do us some good. It might even help us sleep through the night." She looked down at Mike. "How do you do it?"

"Do what?" He was immediately on the defensive.

"Deal with death. You know when you get a patient that you're probably going to watch them die. Doesn't that get to you?"

He shrugged. "I went into geriatrics originally because we're all going to get old, and I thought it might give me some pointers on how to get the most out of life."

"And has it worked?"

He chuckled. "Most of my healthy patients have low blood pressure and a cheerful outlook on life. That keeps me sane. Which reminds me I better get back to the hospital if I plan to get any cake from Mrs. Olson's going home party."

Getting up, he went around the table to hug Kate. She felt comforted, relaxing in his enveloping embrace. Before she could get too comfortable, she drew a deep breath and pushed him away. They walked to the front door in companionable silence.

"Chessy wants to get together again," Mike said, opening the door. "Are you going out at all?"

"Not much. Tell her to give me a call and we'll set up something. And thanks for stopping by."

She stood in the open doorway, breathing in the fresh air as he walked down the sidewalk. He pulled out his car keys just as Richard's car came down the street and turned into the driveway. Mike pointed to his watch and hurried to his car. With a toot of the horn, he drove away.

Richard unlocked the trunk and pulled out his leather portfolio. He smiled sheepishly at Kate as he came toward her.

"It occurred to me today that I've been neglecting you, so I decided to come home early."

"I'm glad," she said. "It's really beautiful out. We could have an early dinner. Maybe cook something on the grill?"

"Sounds good. What happened to the reporters?" Richard jerked his head at the empty street. There were no cars around, only two teenage boys on the sidewalk. "Don't tell me we've ceased to be newsworthy."

"Thank God for that."

A slight movement caught Kate's eye and she turned to look at the teenagers. One of the boys raised his hand.

"Look out!" Richard yelled.

An object smashed against the door panel beside her head. Richard dropped his portfolio and ran toward her but before he could reach her, something struck her in the center of her chest. She lost her balance, falling backward into the house.

"Oh, my God, Kate! You're bleeding!"

Kate looked down at the front of her white blouse, staring in horror at the splotches of red.

# ELEVEN

KATE CAUGHT HER BREATH at the red stains on her blouse. Her hip was bruised where she had fallen, but aside from that she wasn't in any pain. Beyond the partially opened front door she could see the teenagers shouting as they ran down the middle of the street.

"Don't move, honey." Richard knelt beside her, his face white with shock. "I'll call the paramedics."

He started to rise and she grabbed at his suit jacket to hold him in place.

"Don't try to talk," he said.

This is pure slapstick, she thought as she fought for breath to speak.

"I'm not hurt, Richard. It's a tomato."

"What?" He looked at her as if she were delirious.

"The boys were throwing tomatoes."

She pointed to the door. Lumps of tomato pulp were splattered on the panels, dribbling down in thick red streaks to puddle on the floor. At the sight, she began to giggle. It wasn't funny but she couldn't stop the waves of laughter that rose to her throat.

"Kate! Richard!" Marian Granger called from outside the door. "My stars, what a mess. I was just coming home when I saw those dreadful boys."

Richard rose to his feet, wavering between staying with Kate or going to the door. Even his indecision struck Kate as amusing. She covered her mouth to hold back the laughter and tears sprang to her eyes, rolling down her cheeks as she rocked back and forth.

Marian stood at the front door, staring in at Kate. "Good heavens, Richard, is she hurt?" she asked.

"No. I think she's hysterical."

Kate knew she was in trouble because she couldn't stop the laughter. She pressed her hands against her lips, but it only muffled the sounds bubbling up in an endless stream.

"Do something, Richard," Marian said.

Richard leaned over and pulled Kate to her feet. Her knees buckled and he supported her with one arm around her waist. With his other hand, he grabbed her shoulder and shook her.

"Stop it, Kate," he said. "Kate! Look at me."

It was the anger on his face that got through to her. Abruptly the laughter stopped and she began to cry, crumpling against his chest. He held her securely, his body absorbing each shudder of her body until the storm of emotion subsided. When she was quiet, he kissed the top of her head, leaning down until his mouth was next to her ear.

"This wasn't meant for you, Kate. They meant to frighten me. I should have told the truth. This is all my fault." Before she could even register his words, he turned her around to face Marian. "Can you take Kate upstairs? I'll clean up this mess."

"Of course. Come along, dear."

She didn't give Kate a chance to object. With an arm around her shoulders, the older woman led her upstairs to the bathroom and, as if Kate were a child, helped her remove the tomato-stained blouse.

"Kids can be very cruel," Marian said as she turned on the water in the sink and handed her a washcloth. "They're too young to understand how painful some pranks can be."

Kate grimaced into the mirror. Red dots covered her face and neck and her bra had soaked up some of the tomato juice. Even though she had not been hurt by the thrown tomato, she felt dirty. It was strange how things got turned around. It was the teenagers who were in the wrong and yet she felt ashamed, embarrassed to be the focus of the attack.

Unlike Marian, she did not think what the boys had done was a prank. The word itself indicated mischief not malice. This had been a deliberate attack. They had done it because they thought that she and Richard had somehow been responsible for Jenny's death.

She wondered how many other people thought the same thing. No matter what anyone thought, she was convinced that Richard had not killed Jenny.

Then why had Richard said it was all his fault?

"Don't think about it. It'll make you crazy," she muttered, shaking her head at the reflection in the mirror. She mustn't let words blurted out in shock affect her belief in him.

She dampened the washcloth and began to wipe away the physical evidence of the attack. The cool water revived her and she changed into clean clothes.

Downstairs, Richard and Marian had cleaned up the mess in the hall and were out in the kitchen. He smiled as she entered the room, wiped his hands on a towel, and crossed the room to Kate. He put his arm around her, leaning down to kiss her cheek and pull her close to his side.

"Are you all right, honey?" he asked. "You took quite a tumble."

"I'm fine. Just a sore hip."

Richard's mouth tightened and a flush of color rose to his cheeks. His eyes were overly bright as if he were running a fever. Without releasing Kate, he turned to Marian.

"It's five o'clock so the bar is officially open," he said. "What can I get you? I'm going to make a Manhattan."

"As long as you're making one, I'll have one too."

"Kate?"

"Just a Diet Coke," she said.

"Why don't you two go out on the deck? I'll bring the drinks."

With his arm still around Kate, he walked with them to the sliding glass doors. He kissed her once more before releasing her, then returned to the kitchen. Even though Marian's face was expressionless, one eyebrow was raised.

"His protective nature's been aroused," Kate said, in answer to the unspoken question. "In some respects it's good to see. Mike stopped by today to tell me he's worried about Richard. I suspect with good reason. Richard's been under so much pressure. You know how much he adored Jenny. Just the hint that he might be responsible for her death has hurt him beyond belief."

"Richard's a very private person. In my experience, men have a problem articulating their pain. It's impossible for them to express anger and pain in a therapeutic way." Marian's voice was thoughtful, her normally cheerful expression somber. "Are you going to report this to the police?"

Kate shook her head. "Neither the police nor the press need anything more to use against us. I suspect Richard feels the same way. Otherwise he wouldn't have cleaned it up. We'll just have to hope it won't happen again."

"This is such a stressful time. You should go back to the health club, dear. It's not just Richard I worry about, but you. You're used to swimming and especially now, you need the physical release."

"I'll admit I've missed it. I've been swimming most of my life. It was my father who got me into it. When I was fourteen, he found me crying about the fact I was never going to be pretty." Kate smiled in remembrance. "I had braces on my teeth and was covered with zits and a fair amount of baby fat."

"Ah, the wonderful teen years."

"Dad said being pretty wasn't important. Being healthy was. He marched me off to the local Y, and signed me up for the swim team."

Kate leaned back in her chair, staring up at the tops of the trees. It was soothing to watch the breeze swirl the leaves in ever-changing patterns. She sat quietly, just following the motion with her eyes. It was a few minutes before she spoke again.

"Over the years swimming has always been my solace, but this time I haven't tried it. I think it's somehow wound up with pleasure. How can I do something that's pleasurable when my whole life has fallen apart?"

"I felt the same way after George died. People told me time would make a difference. I hated them," Marian said. "Ah, here comes Richard."

Kate hurried across to open the screen door. Richard handed out the drinks then waited beside his chair until Marian had tasted hers.

She kissed the tips of her fingers. "You are a true master when it comes to Manhattans."

"I should be. Your husband taught me how to make them."

"George always said that the answer to every crisis was to make up a pitcher of Manhattans, then sit back and ride out the storm."

It was warm outside, even in the fading sunlight. Kate was thirsty. The cold effervescence bit into her throat as she gulped the Diet Coke.

Mike was right, Kate thought as she looked at the back of the yard. The daffodils were lovely. She had planted bulbs in the fall along the picket fence. The buttery yellow was perfect against the brown wood.

"I'd like to put in a rose garden," she said.

The abruptness of her words surprised Richard. "Roses? Well, I guess we could do that. Where would you put them?"

"In the vegetable garden. Then we can see them from the deck and the kitchen."

"Will there be room for vegetables?"

Kate shook her head. "This year I'd like flowers. Something beautiful."

"No cucumbers or beans? We always have those, don't we, Marian?" He turned to the older woman for help.

"I'll give you some of mine."

"It's not the same," he said, sounding like a sulky child. He eyed Kate and she kept her expression neutral. Finally, he tossed his head in defeat. "All right. You win."

"In this case we both win," Kate said. We'll have wonderful flowers and you won't have to spend endless hours in the garden. We could go to the nursery tomorrow."

"You seem in an awful hurry to get this project started. Do you think that's such a good idea?"

Marian jumped into the conversation. "I think it's a great idea. My mother had a rose garden. One Mother's Day, my dad bought her a rose bush. It became a tradition. Every year he gave her a new one until finally she told him she had enough."

"That's funny," Richard said as he took a slow sip of his drink. "My father grew roses when I was a kid. I'd forgotten all about them. I was never allowed to run around in the backyard with my friends for fear of trampling a bush. They were special roses. Maybe rare. I can't recall. All I can remember is my dad spent all his spare time with them."

"At your mom's house in Ohio?" she asked.

Richard nodded. "They were gone before we got married." He chuckled at some long ago memory. "You never met my mother, Marian. She was a very quiet, repressed woman. She taught Junior High math."

"She died the year after we were married. I was very fond of her," Kate said.

Richard reached over to take her hand. "You're going to love this story then. My father was a big man, overbearing. He was the office manager and head of accounting for an automotive company in Akron. It was summer and the roses had been particularly lush that year. Strange, but just telling this, I can smell them."

Richard paused to take a sip of his drink. Kate looked over at Marian who was leaning forward in her chair, waiting for him to continue.

"It was a weekday," Richard continued. "I'd been out playing with my friends. On the way home I cut through a neighbor's yard and jumped the fence. I was halfway to the back door when I came to a screeching halt, and looked back at the fence."

When he paused for effect, Kate groaned. "Come on, Richard. What happened?"

"The rose bushes were gone."

"Gone?"

"They'd been cut down to the ground. Stacked neatly in a pile beside the garage. I charged into the house to tell my mother. She was sitting in the living room, her face a picture of contentment. Her hands were folded in her lap on top of the garden shears."

"What did she say?" Marian asked.

"Nothing."

Like Marian, Kate was fascinated by the story. "Did you find out why she did it?"

106

"Not then. In fact one of the strangest parts of this story is that the roses were never mentioned in my presence. It was after my father died that I finally asked her." Richard laughed in genuine amusement. "She said she'd always hated the roses. She thought father spent too much time with them. He said a man needed a hobby. He worked so many long hours that he needed something to help him unwind."

"On that summer morning, mother was taking father's suit to the dry cleaners. She found a letter in his pocket. Apparently my father was involved in a long-standing affair. She put the letter on top of my father's dresser, put on a pair of leather gloves and cut down the rose bushes. She said a man didn't need two hobbies."

"Way to go, Mother Warner," Kate said.

Marian shook her head in awe. "Heavens to Betsy. Talk about a woman scorned. Your mother sounds like quite a gal."

"I suppose." Once more Richard looked thoughtful. "I never knew my parents very well. I was an only child, and they both worked. At the end of that summer I was sent to military school in Pennsylvania, and then I went off to college. I came home for the summers, but I didn't spend much time with them. I'd forgotten all about this until you mentioned the roses."

"We'll dedicate the garden to your mother." Kate held up her hands to make a square. "I can see the sign: The Blanche Warner Rose Garden."

"Her name was Blanche?" At Richard's nod, Marian smiled. "How delightful. There's a cabbage rose called Unique Blanche. We had one when we lived in England. It's white and has a million blossoms. It's an old rose, so I don't know if the local nurseries will stock it. I'll go online and see if I can't come up with a Unique Blanche. That'll be my contribution to the project."

Gratitude for Marian's thoughtfulness flooded Kate. She smiled at Richard when he leaned over and kissed Marian on the cheek.

"What a grand idea," he said.

Her cheeks pink with pleasure, she said, "If I can find one, you'll both love it. The flowers have a glorious fragrance. It'll remind you of your mother. As everyone knows, revenge is sweet."

\*　　\*　　\*

"I'm coming, damn it." Kate yelled as she fumbled to unlock the front door.

The key jammed and she gritted her teeth as the phone rang again. She was moving slowly, stiff from the weekend of gardening. Juggling three bags of groceries, her purse, and her keys, she shoved the door closed with her hip and hurried through the hall to the kitchen. The answering machine picked up the call.

She shoved two of the bags onto the counter, but the third caught on the edge and the plastic ripped. The contents spilled out, cans and boxes dropping and clattering across the floor.

It was the last straw. In a childish tantrum, she kicked as many of the soup cans as she could reach, watching in satisfaction as they slammed against the wall.

"Damn! Damn! Damn!"

Kate shouted the words at the silent walls of the kitchen. Her own voice brought her back to the present, and she looked in amazement at the dented cans scattered around the room. This was the first time she had reacted in anger instead of tears. She had been aware of the bottled up fury and had been afraid to let it loose for fear it would consume her. Yet, after her outburtst she felt only relief.

With a shuddering sigh, she stood up straight and opened the refrigerator. She grabbed a Diet Coke, popped the top, and gulped down half the contents. The caffeine gave her the lift she needed. She made a face as she surveyed the jumble of groceries on the floor.

"All told, it's been a shitty day," she said.

*Oh, Jenny where are you? Please don't be gone.*

She'd been in the middle of grocery shopping when she looked up and saw Jenny. Her response had been instantaneous. Her heart leaped with joy and her mouth stretched wide in a smile. She started to call out but when the child moved, Kate realized her mistake.

It wasn't Jenny.

Something about the pigtailed girl had reminded Kate of her daughter. It had happened before, and each time the letdown was excruciatingly painful. It brought home to her the fact that she would never see Jenny again.

"Damn! Damn! Damn!"

What a limited swearing vocabulary she had. She'd have to ask Richard for a new supply.

Reminded of Richard, she wondered if it had been his call that she'd missed. She pressed the message button on the answering machine. Hearing nothing, she turned up the volume and leaned closer, but there was no message. She was reaching for the delete button when she heard the soft disconnect sound and then the final beep. Puzzled, she pressed the message button and listened again. Long silence, then in quick succession, the disconnect and the beep.

The phone rang again.

She reached for the receiver, but then decided to let the machine pick it up again. Something about the call on the answering machine made her uneasy.

She fidgeted until the outgoing message finished, waiting for the caller to speak. Once again nothing. She strained to hear over the heavy beating of her heart. First the long waiting silence, then just before the final beep, the soft disconnect.

Glancing up at the clock, she noted the time. It was 2:15. She'd come in at 2:00. Would another call come at 2:30?

Fear crept through her body, chilling her. Trying to ignore it, she bent over to pick up the cans and boxes scattered across the floor. She put away the groceries, folded up the bags, and avoided staring at the clock.

The phone rang at 2:30 and again at 2:45.

Four calls fifteen minutes apart. Each call was the same. When the answering machine picked up, the caller listened to the message but didn't speak or hang up until just before the final beep.

The first time might have been an accident, but listening to the other calls Kate realized the disconnect was timed. The mental picture of someone watching the clock to gauge precisely the moment to hang up was disturbing.

Kate paced back and forth in front of the telephone, wondering what she should do. It was exactly a week ago that she had received the phone call from the person she thought of as the "Witness," who claimed to have seen the murder. It had been a frightening incident and she was relieved that it had not been repeated. Now these hang-up calls were as disturbing in their way as that first one had been.

The fifth call came at three o'clock.

Right or wrong, Kate picked up the receiver. "Hello?"

"I saw him," was the whispered reply.

Heart hammering in her ears, Kate tried to remember what she wanted to say. "You didn't see my husband. If you have any information please go to the police. It will help them find Jenny's murderer."

"I need to talk to him."

"He's not here. He's at work, but don't hang up. Please help us. Please go to the police."

She squeezed the receiver tightly against her ear. Her fingers ached from the pressure. Drawing air through her nose in a long, steadying breath, she waited for the voice to speak again.

Silence. And then the dial tone.

She began to shiver. Gritting her teeth, she replaced the receiver and backed away from the phone. She moved clear across the kitchen and out into the family room. Even that didn't seem far enough, so she opened the patio doors and stepped out on the deck. She needed to put distance between herself and the voice on the end of the phone line.

Was it the same person who had called before? The whispered voice could have been either male or female. There was nothing familiar about the voice. It sounded disembodied. No color or personality to give it substance.

What was the purpose?

The caller had wanted to talk to Richard specifically. The only question in Kate's mind was whether the person had any real information concerning Jenny's death.

No matter who the caller was or what the reason for the call, it was necessary to tell Richard about it.

Thunder rumbled in the distance. She shivered as she stared at the darkening sky, grateful that she'd made a decision. Back inside she dialed Richard's direct line. His secretary answered.

"Hi, Candy, it's Kate. Is Richard around?"

"You just missed him. He said he was going home early. If you want, I'll see if I can catch him at the elevator."

"I'd appreciate it."

Kate drummed her nails on the countertop as she waited. In no time, a breathless Candy was back on the line.

"Gosh, I'm sorry, Kate. He'd already gone down in the elevator. Was it urgent?"

"No. Thanks for trying." With a sinking feeling, Kate hung up.

Was it just a coincidence that Richard had decided to leave work early?

Of course it was. She either trusted Richard or she didn't. There couldn't be any halfway measures. She'd go right out of her mind if she began to second guess him. When Richard came home, she'd tell him about the phone calls. He'd be angry that she hadn't told him about the first call a week earlier. Well, that couldn't be helped. She tried to focus on the clock, wondering if the Witness would call again at 3:15.

It rang five minutes before she expected it.

"Hi, Kate, it's Chris Mayerling. Am I catching you at a bad time?"

"No, but Richard's not home yet."

"Actually I wanted to talk to you. I'm coming out your way, and I wondered if we could meet for a drink."

Kate frowned. Although Chris was always welcome at the house, it was as Richard's boss that they had any social contact with him.

"Would you like to come here?" she asked.

"No. I'd rather go someplace else." He chuckled. "I want to talk to you about Richard. I'm worried about him."

First Mike, now Chris. Bowing to the inevitable, Kate agreed. "Where would you suggest?"

"Do you know Dave's Place? It's on the north side of Pickard. The corner of Cumberland and Buckeye."

"One-story place with a deck and noisy beer parties in the summer?"

"That's it. Inside it's surprisingly respectable."

"Okay. What time will you be there?"

"I'm just finishing up some work now. The traffic won't be bad, but it looks like we're in for a storm. Is it raining in Pickard?"

Kate pulled the curtain back to peek outside. "Not yet. We've got thunder, but it's still dry."

"I'll try to get there by five. Is that okay?"

"That's fine. I'll see you at Dave's Place."

Kate hung up the phone. There was a cold feeling in the pit of her stomach. Despite Chris's light tone, an edginess to his voice warned her to prepare for some sort of bad news.

Dear God, how much worse could things get?

# TWELVE

HE STOOD SEVERAL FEET OFF THE MAIN PATH, motionless as the maple he leaned against. His face beneath the canopy of leaves was in shadow, and his dark clothing blended with the surrounding bushes. From where he stood, he had an excellent view of the circular path that ran along the edge of the open field.

He stared down at his watch.

Four-twenty. He made a mental note of the time, but knew it was futile. The moment he looked away, the numbers flickered like fading stars and disappeared without a trace in his memory until the next time he was forced to check again.

Tension had been building for the past two days; the anticipation was intoxicating. He could feel little bubbles of excitement rising in his chest, breaking and sending a tingle of energy along the paths of his nerves.

The feedback from his senses was heightened. The colors in the woods were sharp, tinged a yellowish green, throbbing with vitality in the late afternoon light. The sky was darkening and thunder growled in the distance. The loamy smell of decay rose to his nostrils and he breathed in the air, heavy with the imminence of rain. Sound was magnified. The first drops hit the leaves in a crisp staccato rhythm.

It had rained the last time his father had beaten him.

He was sixteen. Not a man yet, but taller than his father. It was summer, a weekend. He'd been out with his friends and he'd come home late, hoping the sound of the rain would cover his arrival.

No lights in the house. The old man would be passed out, his drunken snores a familiar rumble, muffled only slightly by the closed bedroom door.

The silence should have warned him.

His sneakers were wet and squeaked on the linoleum as he crossed the kitchen floor to the refrigerator. The old man always stocked it with beer on Friday. Swiping a few had gone unnoticed for several months. He knew stealing from the bastard was risky but despite the danger, or maybe because of it, each icy sip was ambrosia.

His heart pounded in his ears as he opened the door of the refrigerator. Careful not to hit the other bottles, he eased one out. With infinite care he closed the door. Plunged into darkness, he stood still, waiting for his eyes to become accustomed to the darkness. With one hand he twisted off the bottle cap and with the other he raised the bottle to his lips.

His father's cane crashed down on the bottle, shattering it. Pieces of glass cut into his skin and blood mingled with the beer as it rolled down his face.

Stunned by the attack, he shook his head to clear it. Another blow cracked him across the shoulders and despite the pain, he spun around to face the shadowy figure, cane raised to strike again.

Instinctively he lashed out. His fist struck bone. The physical sensation brought him to his senses and the chilling knowledge that for this latest sin the old man would beat him senseless. The thought was only a second in time, but in that instant he resigned himself to death. He cringed, bracing himself for the shattering blows of the cane.

In slow motion, his father doubled over, sprawling on the floor at his feet.

He held his breath waiting for the bastard to rise. When his vision blurred, he opened his mouth and the air burst out between his lips. In a daze, he reached for the light switch, squinting at the sudden glare flooding the room.

The old man lay in the puddle of beer and glass, his arm outstretched for the cane, which had fallen out of his hand. Curious to see if the man were dead, he prodded him with the toe of his shoe. A moan was the only response. He nudged him again. He kicked him but the softness of the sneaker deadened the sensation. Reaching down he picked up the cane.

He raised it over his head. His father's eyes were open, staring up at him.

Power surged through him at the terror on his father's face, and in the man's expression he read the lesson that would be his guiding principal through life. Domination was a matter of physical strength, nothing more.

He struck the crumpled figure with the cane. It wasn't a hard blow but the sound of wood against flesh was satisfying. He struck again. Straddling the drunken sot, he aimed carefully, hitting the old man so that every inch of his body would bear the mark of the beating. After this, his father would never dare to touch him again. When he finished, he broke the cane in half, throwing one piece down beside the sniveling figure. The other piece he placed on his bedside table, the last thing he saw at night and the first thing in the morning.

He had become a man, and the piece of wood was the outward sign of his rite of passage.

It was the first token he'd kept over the years to mark momentous events. It was only proper that he use the cane on this occasion. The short piece of wood was easy to carry and fit comfortably in his hand. He tightened his fingers. The wood was worn smooth from his handling it. He was not normally superstitious, but he believed that objects stored psychic energy that could be tapped when he needed a recharge. Standing in the misting rain beside the jogging path, he touched the pocket of his pants, drawing strength from the gold links of the bracelet.

The talisman.

From the first moment he had found it caught in the material of his jacket, he had sensed its power. Rubbing the bracelet brought instant arousal. Pressing the angel charm with his thumb caused an orgasm of cosmic proportion. Afraid of diminishing the potency, he'd rationed the number of times he'd tapped the source. Lately he had begun carrying it in his pocket, and wondered if the sense of danger would renew the power of the bracelet.

Danger. He would have to be careful. The COP was checking everything.

This time he wasn't acting on impulse. He'd planned it down to the smallest detail. The key was to think enough moves ahead so that he'd be safe. He was a better game player than the COP.

A shiver of pleasure slithered through his body.

The excitement was heightened because of the importance of this experiment. The subject had been chosen with particular care. No passion would be involved to cloud the issue. He would deal with nothing but the sensory input of the moment, and then he'd know the answer that had plagued him for almost two weeks.

Sex or death? Which would bring him most power?

Soon. He tightened his fingers on the piece of cane and looked at his watch.

Four-thirty. Would he come? The rain was still only a light mist. Not enough to be a deterrent; refreshing for a dedicated runner.

He caught his breath as a jogger appeared along the path on the far side of the field. Right on schedule. The air was heavy with moisture and the man seemed to appear out of a cloud, the noise of his approach muffled by the rain-dampened trail in the open area.

His secret knowledge added a certain piquancy to watching the jogger's movements.

He looked to see if there was anyone else around, then stepped out of the shadows, running in place for a moment before moving along the trail toward the jogger. He paced himself carefully so that he would intersect the man at the precise spot where the trail cut back into the woods.

His timing was perfect. The jogger moved from the open field into the darker woods, unaware of the approach of another runner until the two were only a foot apart. The first blow of the cane caught the jogger on the bridge of the nose, shattering his glasses. He staggered forward, stunned by the force of the attack. The second blow crashed against the back of his skull. The muscles in his legs gave out, and he collapsed.

Before his body hit the ground, the jogger was dead.

*   *   *

After a quick shower, Kate put on a green jersey sheath and green sling backs. Downstairs she grabbed her raincoat and scribbled a note for Richard. She didn't feel comfortable telling him that she was meeting Chris so she just said she was running errands. It was vague enough to salve her conscience.

Dave's Place was only ten minutes from the house. As she got out of the car, it started to rain. Although she hadn't been expecting much, the restaurant was surprisingly nice inside. The garden theme was pleasing with an abundance of plants and painted latticework on the walls. Cushioned booths circled the room and the lighting was discreet. The atmosphere amused her because it looked like a movie set for an illicit rendezvous.

It was just five and since Chris hadn't arrived, she chose a booth and ordered a white wine. There was little point in guessing why he wanted to talk to her. Leaning her head against the padded back of the booth, she sipped the wine and let her mind wander.

"Forgive me, my dear, for being so dreadfully late."

Kate had always loved the mellow tones of Chris' voice. His phrasing was old fashioned, almost formal, and his speech had the slightest suggestion of an English accent. She didn't know if he consciously cultivated such an affectation but to her mind the end product was very pleasing.

"You look lovely." He leaned over to kiss her cheek. "God! Traffic was truly nasty."

She smiled at the drama in his voice. He did look harried. His thick, black hair, usually styled to perfection, was matted down by the rain, the white at his temples muted. His cheeks were red as if he'd been outside in the wind and rain. When he shrugged out of his belted raincoat, even the shoulders of his jacket were wet.

"You're soaked, Chris. Is it raining that hard?"

"No, but it looks like we'll have quite a storm this evening." He hung his raincoat over the back of an empty chair and then sat down in the booth. "I got wet changing a flat."

"On the Porsche?" The red convertible was his prized possession.

"Heavens, no!" He looked shocked at the suggestion. The waitress came and he ordered more wine for Kate and a double martini. "I need a pick-me-up. If it had been my car I'd have called a tow truck. A young woman was pulled over on the side of the road, so naturally I stopped to be of service. It's been several years since I've changed a tire, but I eventually got the blasted thing done."

The drinks arrived. Chris saluted her with his glass before taking a sip.

"I won't waste your time building up to the subject," he said. "I have a great deal of respect for you, Kate, so I'll tell you straight out. I'm going to ask Richard to take a leave of absence."

His words shocked her, and the emotion must have shown clearly because he reached across the table and awkwardly patted her hand. His face was troubled, but there was an air of determination beneath the compassion. He waited until she had digested the news before he continued.

"You are probably damning me as a traitor, but hear me out." He pulled his hand back, running it over the side of his head. "Richard hasn't done much work since Jenny died. You must forgive me for being blunt. I don't mean to add to your pain, but you must understand what is happening."

"Don't keep apologizing, Chris. You have always been our friend. I've never doubted that. I was just stunned for a moment, and now I'm getting my second wind."

He nodded. "I am Richard's friend, and it is in his best interests to take some time off. He's always had a fine reputation in the advertising business. His judgment, his work ethic, his creativity are all impaired at this point. He's no good at his job right now. And worst of all, he knows it."

"But he loves the work. He needs it," Kate said. She winced at the pleading tone of her voice.

"If Richard only had to deal with a death in the family, I would expect a return to normality in a short time. But as you are well aware there is a cloud of suspicion hanging over his head. Richard knows people are talking about it and making guesses as to his guilt or innocence." He paused, tipped his head to the side as if taking her measure, then continued. "Two clients have asked to deal with someone else."

Kate closed her eyes to hold back the sudden rush of tears.

Poor Richard. It must be hell going in to work each day, when he knew people were talking about him. When she felt bad, she stayed in bed, pulling the covers over her head to block out the world.

"Don't cry, Kate," Chris said. "God, I'm a beast."

Kate took a deep breath and wiped her eyes with the tips of her fingers. "I'm all right. A momentary sinking spell. I can see why you think Richard should leave. Not just for his sake, but for yours." When he started to speak, she raised her hand to forestall him. "I hadn't really thought about the impact all of this would have on your business. Have you lost clients?"

"No. And I don't think it will come to that."

"I suspect more people are uncomfortable with the situation than you are aware of. I've noticed the same kind of polarization among our friends. Do you want me to talk to Richard?"

"No. I'll handle it. I didn't ask you here to turn over the problem to you. I needed you to understand and support my decision. Richard trusts your judgment. If he sees you are not troubled by this and don't see it as some sort of personal betrayal, neither will he."

"I understand." And she meant it. "You and Richard have been friends long enough that I don't think he'd ever question your loyalty. It was a lucky day when he met you."

He laughed, his face alight with mischief. "If you'd seen him then, Kate, you'd never have married him. He was in his college rebellious stage. Scruffy clothes, long hair, and a beard. Sort of the wild-man-of-Borneo look that was all the rage. You'd automatically judge him as a burnout. He was drawing when I first saw him. It was a very droll caricature. We got to talking and ended up at some god-awful workers' tavern drinking rotgut wine until dawn. Mostly we talked about art. With the difference in our ages, you can imagine our tastes were poles apart."

"And I know how Richard loves trying to make converts to the cause of modern art."

"He was eloquently profane in his arguments. I asked him if he was planning to be an artist. He said no, he was good, but didn't have the talent to be great. I was struck by his answer, surprised that at such a young age, he should be so self-aware and practical."

Kate found it difficult to swallow around the lump in her throat.

It pleased her that Chris would share his remembrances with her. She knew that Richard had that kind of effect on people. The first time he spoke to her, she had been under his spell. She smiled warmly at Chris who seemed slightly flustered that he'd been so forthcoming.

"Well, I certainly do run on," he said. "I guess it's an emotional time for everyone. I can't begin to imagine how you're surviving such an ordeal. Richard said over the weekend the police asked him to come into the station for another interrogation. Was it bad?"

Kate shrugged. "I assume so. He wouldn't let me go. He called the lawyer and she went with him. All he'd say was that it was more of the same. Nothing new."

"It must be infuriating that the police are handling the case like idiots. The thought that Richard could hurt anyone is positively ludicrous."

"You'll get no argument from me."

He cleared his throat. "Now, Kate my dear, is there anything *you* need?"

"I appreciate your asking, but there's nothing that I can think of."

"Promise you'll let me know if there is?"

Kate promised. They finished their drinks. Outside, the rain had gotten heavier. Despite the fact she had a raincoat, Chris insisted she wait until he got an umbrella out of his car. Sheltering her from the rain, he walked her to her car, waiting until she was inside with the motor running before he returned to his own. She honked as she passed the red convertible, wondering how he got his long legs into the little sports car.

All the way home Kate worried how Richard would take Chris's suggestion of a leave of absence. Even if Richard agreed with the reasoning, he'd be crushed.

It was almost seven o'clock. She hadn't realized how long she'd been gone. There weren't many lights on in the house, so she was surprised to see Richard's car in the garage. She hurried through the rain, fumbling with her key in the darkened doorway.

"Richard?"

No answer.

She looked in the living room and then Richard's studio, but he wasn't there. She checked the kitchen and the family room, but he wasn't there either. Back in the front hall she stopped long enough to hang up her wet raincoat, then started up the stairs.

"Richard?"

The stench of alcohol cut through the darkness, warning her of his presence before she made out the figure sprawled on the bed. Crossing the room, she turned on the bedside lamp.

Richard was fully dressed, lying on top of the comforter. His mouth was open and an occasional snore punctuated the heavy breathing. Kate leaned over him, reaching out her hand to shake him awake. When she touched his shoulder, she drew her hand back in dismay.

Besides being drunk, Richard was soaking wet.

She couldn't leave him in such a state. He'd catch pneumonia. It took awhile to undress him. His body was as limp as raw liver and, by the time she finished, she was sweating and feeling less than charitable toward him.

Returning downstairs, she put away the dinner she'd planned and fixed an omelet. She read for a while but had trouble concentrating. Finally at nine, she turned off the lights and locked up. She slipped under the covers, trying not to wake Richard. He rolled toward her, mumbling drunkenly.

"Never meant to hurt you, Kate."

"Hush, Richard," she said. "Go to sleep."

"Shouldn't have gone tonight. Shouldn't have gone."

In the darkness, she could feel him shake his head back and forth. She reached over to stroke his cheek. He nuzzled against her hand, still mumbling.

"Had to go. He was going to tell."

# THIRTEEN

The phone might have been ringing for a long time before the sound woke Carl. Blindly he reached for the receiver.

"There's been another murder in the forest preserve, Chief." The watch commander's voice came distinctly through the phone.

Carl rolled to the side of the bed and sat up, shaking the sleep from his brain. "A kid?" he asked.

"Thank the good Lord, no. An adult male, Caucasian, maybe forty-five."

Carl let out the breath he'd been holding. "Is that you, Jack?"

"Yes, sir. By the way, it's 6:12 and after I hang up I'll make some Chicago coffee, not that watery piss your suburban cops drink."

Carl snorted. Jack Witecki had worked the Chicago streets for fifteen years before following Carl out to Pickard. Nothing surprised the sergeant. He could be counted on to run things until the crisis team arrived.

"Call Bea and tell her I want her to cover the station. I want Squint at the scene and Bob Jackson. Tell Tony and Diego to work with Bea."

"Got it."

"Details?"

"Old fart walking his dog found the body and flagged down a squad car. Dennis Zack called it in. He says the skull's been bashed in. First stiff he's seen. Think he tossed his cookies. Had that thick voice sound." Jack chuckled. "Hope he didn't contaminate the crime scene."

Carl swore. "Ease up. This is Pickard, not Chicago. Most of my cops haven't seen shit, but that doesn't mean they can't handle it."

"Sorry, Chief. Just gallows humor."

"Where's the body?"

"Not far from where the Warner kid was found. Park on the north side of the Devon entrance to the forest preserve. You'll see the lights."

"Any hope the press hasn't got wind of this?"

"We're clear for the moment. The *Advocate* comes out today, so this is Blake's day to sleep in."

"Make the rest of your calls. I'm on the way."

Carl hung up the phone and headed for the bathroom. He turned on the shower and stepped under the spray, shuddering at the blast of cool water that hit him. It was a fast shower, just enough to wake him up. It was going to be a long day.

While he dressed, he considered the possibility that this was the second in a series of murders. His premise had been that the Warner murder was an isolated incident. On the surface, the finding of another body in the forest preserve might suggest the possibility of a series or spree killer. It was hard to believe there were two murderers running around the Pickard woods.

He'd been convinced that Jennifer Warner had been killed by her father. Bea had warned him about getting tunnel vision early in the game. He got into his car, wondering how much he'd screwed up the case by personally focusing on Richard Warner.

At the forest preserve a small crowd of people had already gathered. They huddled together in the damp morning chill, speculating and discussing each new arrival. They converged on Carl when he opened the car door.

A grandfatherly figure grabbed his sleeve. "We heard someone found a body. Is it another child, Chief Leidecker?"

Much as he was in a hurry, he stopped to speak to the bystanders. "Yes, a body has been found here. I can positively state that it is not the body of a child. I repeat, it is not a child. Beyond that I don't know a hellava lot more than you do. I urge you to go home because neither I nor any of my officers will make another statement here. And the sooner I get in there, the faster we'll have answers to all your questions."

With a wave of his hand, he tucked his leather notebook under his arm and closed the car door. The crowd parted before him. Carl lifted the luminous yellow tape that cut across the trail limiting admission to the crime area. He nodded to the officer who pointed along the trail.

The trees closed in behind Carl, muffling the sounds at his back, but as he moved down the muddy path, he could hear the activity ahead. It was 6:45. After the rain during the night, the air was heavy with an earthy perfumed scent.

A group of figures was gathered on the far side of the open field. With only nods of greeting, he took in the scene.

The body of the jogger was sprawled, face down, in the middle of the path, arms and legs at odd angles that only the dead could achieve. Carl leaned down, grimacing at the misshapen mound of bone and tissue that had once been a human head. As far as he could see there were no other injuries.

"Morning, Carl." Bob Jackson was beside him, impeccably dressed as always. "The M.E. thinks the man has been dead about twelve hours. Massive head injuries. Seems to be it. No weapon so far. Either the killer took it away or we haven't identified it yet."

"Clothes are intact," Carl said. "Was there any sexual interference?"

"Not as far as the M.E. could see."

"That's good. Maybe there's no connection between this and the Warner killing."

"Don't count on it," Bob said.

He led Carl out of earshot of the others.

"You probably noticed that all of the blows were to the upper part of the head. The jaw had dropped and the mouth was open. After the man was dead, the murderer put this inside the victim's mouth."

Reaching into his pocket, Bob brought out a plastic evidence bag, holding it between his thumb and first finger. Inside the bag, Carl could see a piece of candy wrapped in cellophane.

Clearly visible were the plaid letters: BUTTERSKOTS.

# Fourteen

The ringing of the phone woke Kate. For a moment she thought the sound was part of the series of nightmares that plagued her sleep.

It was morning. The bedroom was full of light and the phone continued to ring. She lay on her back, blinking up at the ceiling, letting the answering machine pick it up. A few minutes later it rang again. The third time it happened she realized the caller was hanging up and redialing. Someone was trying to get past the answering machine.

"Richard?" she called.

His side of the bed was empty and the house was silent. It was 8:15. He'd just be getting into Chicago. It had been close to three before she'd drifted off to sleep. She'd been so tired, she hadn't heard him get up. And besides he probably had been too embarrassed to wake her.

It had been years since she'd seen him so drunk. If the past were anything to go by, he'd have a vicious hangover.

What if Richard was trying to reach her? She sat up and swung her legs over the side of the bed. When the phone rang again, she grabbed the receiver.

"It's Marian, Kate. Is Richard with you?"

"No. He's gone to work. Is there a problem?"

"You obviously haven't looked outside. The reporters are massed on the curb again. Grace Peterman called to find out what was going on."

Kate hugged the portable against her shoulder, threw back the covers, and hurried across to the front windows. She cracked the blinds and gasped at the chaotic scene below.

It was just like the first days after Jenny died. Vans with antennae and dishes were parked all along the street.

"Oh my God, Marian!" Kate was so frightened her teeth began to chatter. "Do you know what it is? Has something happened to Richard?"

"Kate!"

Marian's sharp tone brought her back from the brink of panic.

"Stay calm. I don't know what's going on, but I'll call you as soon as I hear anything."

"No. Just come over. Please, Marian. I don't want to be alone."

"Ah, Kate dear. Of course I'll come. Give me ten minutes to do some checking, then I'll come around the back."

Kate hung up the phone. She washed, dressed, and straightened the room by rote. All she was aware of was the sounds of activity in front of the house. How could she have slept through such a hubbub?

She was coming down the stairs when the doorbell rang. From safety behind the living room windows, she could see the reporter smoothing his suit jacket, microphone in hand, cameraman and technicians at his back. She crossed the front hall, making sure the chain lock was firmly in place. She did not open the door.

Keeping well away from the other windows, she hurried through the dining room to the sliding glass doors. Even though she'd been expecting Marian, she jumped when she saw her. She opened the door and let her friend slip through.

Marian's face looked gray in the bright morning light. Without asking, Kate put on a kettle of water for tea. She was reminded of a similar scene a week earlier when she had gotten the call from the Witness. Then it was Marian who had taken care of her.

"What's going on?"

Marian nodded. "They found another body in the woods."

"Oh, God!"

For a moment Kate thought she might pass out. Marian must have thought so too because she jumped to her feet and hurried across to her.

"It's not another child," Marian said, reading her thoughts.

Hand at her throat, Kate shuddered in relief, then was appalled by her response. Marian squeezed her shoulder.

"That was exactly my reaction," she said. "I ducked over to Grace Peterman's house. I swear, Kate, I never see her talking to anyone and yet she always knows what's going on. She must use a ham radio to pick up the gossip."

"Richard says she gets alien messages."

"I wouldn't be surprised." Marian poured some tea. "According to her, a man walking his dog found a body in the forest preserve. It was an adult male who'd been hit on the head. It happened sometime yesterday."

"Was the man local?"

Marian shook her head. "No name's been released, but Grace thought he was from Pickard."

"But why are the reporters out front?"

Marian sighed. "They're convinced that it's somehow connected to Jenny's death. They're hoping to interview you or Richard."

"Richard. I better call him."

She caught him getting off the train in Union Station. She told him the little that she knew. There was silence on his end when she finished.

Finally he said, "I'm coming home. It'll be faster if I take a cab. I know this sounds heartless, Kate, but it just might take the heat off me. God, it would be great if it's long enough for the police to come up with a real suspect."

"I don't think it sounds heartless. I've been thinking along the same lines."

"I'll be there as soon as I can," he said. "Stay inside. I don't want you near those media vultures unless I'm beside you."

After Marian left, Kate was too restless to sit down. She puttered around the kitchen until she heard Richard's taxi. The reporters swarmed him as he got out of the cab, but he waved them away as he hurried up the front walk.

"How are you holding up?" Richard asked as he came into the kitchen.

One look at her face gave him his answer. He opened his arms and she stepped into the comforting circle. Arms around his waist, she rested her head on his chest. She didn't cry; she just held him while she drew strength from his presence.

"Could you make some coffee, honey? I didn't have much for breakfast."

It was strange how they were avoiding any discussion of the horrible event that had brought Richard home. Kate poured water into the coffee pot, listening as he talked about work. A new campaign for a breakfast cereal was just getting started.

He moved around the kitchen while he talked, straightening pictures on the wall, lining up the canisters on the counter, and moving the African violets on the windowsill. Although she was used to his rearranging her space to suit his own sense of order, it annoyed her. Every day she seemed to be filled with a greater need to control her own life. She tried to suppress it, but each time it was harder.

"I'm sorry I didn't wake you this morning." Richard massaged his forehead with one hand, looking sheepish. "I had an absolutely brutal hangover this morning. And yes, it serves me right. God, it's been ages since I've been stinking drunk."

"Where were you?"

"The bar at the train station. I stopped there after work. Then when I got home and you were out, I had a couple more drinks."

"I'm sorry I wasn't here. I left a little before five and when I got home at seven you were already in bed."

"What can I say? I was really tanked. Pressure's been building up, and I guess I just needed a release. Despite a massive case of the thumps, I felt less stressed when I woke up. Incidentally," he said, "I had a phone call from Chris on the train this morning. He wants me to consider taking a leave of absence."

"How do you feel about it?"

"I have to admit, Kate, that no matter how reasonably he made the suggestion, it came as a blow. He suggested finishing up this week and then taking a couple weeks off. He wouldn't let me argue my case or anything. He just said to think it over and we'd talk about it tomorrow."

"And did you think it over?"

"The shock was just wearing off when you called to tell me about this latest murder. I always thought some psycho killed Jenny. This just proves it."

"How?"

"It's pretty hard to believe that two killers are running around Pickard. Two deaths in the forest preserve, sure sounds like a psycho to me. I'm sure the police are rethinking the case now. Once the pressure is off me, I'll be able to work again, and there won't be any need for a leave of absence."

Kate understood Richard's euphoric mood even if she couldn't see any real justification for it. As far as she could see, nothing had changed except that someone else was dead.

The phone rang. Richard snatched up the receiver. The coffee was ready. She brought the pot to the table as Richard hung up the phone.

"That was Leidecker. He's coming over to talk to us."

Kate had the sensation of free falling in the pit of her stomach. She didn't know whether Leidecker's visit could be viewed as a good sign or a bad one. All she knew was that she was frightened.

"Did you call the lawyer?"

"Yes. On the way home," he said, taking a sip of coffee. "Stacie said Leidecker would likely call us. She said to be cooperative, but not talkative. If either of us feels uncomfortable, we're to call her. She gave me her pager number. I told her I'd call her as soon as we heard any details. Did you find out anything more since I talked to you?"

"Nothing. Marian even asked the the reporters. All I know is that a man's body was found in the forest preserve." She sat down next to Richard, noticing the dark circles beneath his eyes. Picking up his hand, she rubbed it between hers. "Are we going to need alibis?"

His body jerked at her question. He tried to pull his hand away but she held tight, staring back calmly as he glared at her.

"You mean, do I have an alibi?"

"Don't go defensive on me, Richard. Leidecker's going to ask."

The tension in his hand relaxed. "Sorry. You're right. The only trouble is we don't know when the man was killed. We'll have to wait and see." At the expression on her face, he tightened his hand on hers. "What is it, Kate?"

"We're sitting at the kitchen table calmly trying to figure out the time a man was killed. There's no reality to our lives anymore. The unthinkable has become commonplace." She pulled her hands away from Richard and pressed them against her cheeks, shaking her head in bewilderment. "It's like we're sliding down a hill on a toboggan. The speed is increasing and no matter what we do we can't affect the outcome."

"It's crazy, isn't it? Up until today I had the same feeling," Richard admitted. "Now I'm just praying this new murder will shed some light on Jenny's death."

Kate wished she could be as hopeful as Richard on that point. Currently she saw the world in shades of gray.

When Leidecker arrived, Richard let him in and brought him out to the kitchen. Kate offered a cup of coffee and he accepted, pulled out a chair, and sat down at the table. His uniformed figure looked out of place in the casually decorated room.

"I should have known the media would be here," he said. He pushed his notebook and hat to the far side of the table. "I promised them a statement when I leave, but I don't think even that will get them off your front lawn."

Kate sensed a difference in Leidecker, but at first she couldn't pinpoint the change. She was pouring his coffee when it struck her.

The police chief's air of hostility toward Richard was gone. He was not treating him like a suspect.

Blindly, she set the coffee pot down on the counter. Neither of the men noticed her agitation. When she returned to the table, Carl began to speak.

"Now before you hear all sorts of wild rumors," he said, "I'll tell you as much as I can without compromising the case. This morning a man walking his dog found the body of a jogger in the forest preserve not very far from the spot where Jenny was killed. The man died from injuries suffered through repeated blows to the head."

"Just like Jenny," Richard said

"Was it someone from Pickard?" Kate asked.

"We don't know yet," Leidecker said. "When I left the scene he had not been identified. For the moment we're assuming he's a local."

"Aside from the location of the body is there anything to tie his death to Jenny's?"

Kate could hear the strain in Richard's voice as he asked the question. For a moment Leidecker said nothing. His eyes stared across the table giving each of them a searching glance.

"Although I'm not at liberty to give you any details, evidence was found at the scene that definitely links this death with your daughter's."

Kate placed her hand on Richard's arm. He turned toward her, and she could see the glitter of excitement in his eyes. She supposed, after all the pressure he'd been under, it was reasonable to feel triumph at any sign of vindication. All too aware of Leidecker, Kate squeezed his arm in warning.

"Can you tell us when it happened?" she asked.

"Yesterday. In some places the ground underneath the body was almost dry. The medical examiner says he died no later than five o'clock because by then we had reports of rain in the area."

Kate nodded. It had started to rain when she got to the restaurant.

"The man was listening to an iPod while he ran. It was still hooked to his belt, but the earphones were missing. It's possible that the killer took them."

"Took them?" Kate asked.

"Sometimes a murderer takes something as a sort of souvenir. Kind of like the Indians taking scalps. The trophy is a symbol of the event. Focusing on the item can give him a high as powerful as any drug."

Kate was sorry she'd asked. "That's sick."

"Yes. The murderer is sick." Carl nodded in agreement. "And very dangerous."

Eventually Leidecker asked Richard how he'd spent the afternoon and early evening. It was not the antagonistic questioning that the police chief had subjected him to in the last week and a half. He wrote the responses down in his notebook, looking neither surprised nor critical that Richard had gotten drunk. He commented in an off-hand fashion that next time it would be better to take a cab from the train station rather than drive in such a condition.

Richard nodded. "At any rate, I got home around five. Kate was out, so I made a drink. Or maybe it was two." He rubbed his forehead as if to jog his memory. "I think I went upstairs to change clothes around five-thirty. The next thing I knew it was morning and I had a god-awful headache."

"And you, Kate?"

Kate was still listening to Richard's voice in her head so she didn't realize Leidecker was speaking to her until he repeated her name again. She was flustered by the shift of attention.

"What?" she asked.

Leidecker smiled indulgently. "I just wondered what you did yesterday afternoon. Just a formality," he added.

"Oh." She licked her lips and tried to organize her thoughts. "I went grocery shopping after lunch. I got home at two. Christian Mayerling called, and we arranged to meet for a drink at five."

"You were with Chris?" Richard asked.

Kate could feel the heat rising in her cheeks at his question and turned to speak directly to him. "He called because he was concerned about you. And he wanted to see how I was doing, and if there was any way he could help."

"You could have told me."

"When, Richard?" She could feel anger rising and fought to keep it out of her voice. "You were gone before I got up this morning, and then when you came home today, there wasn't a chance. Besides it was no big deal."

"Your note said you were running errands."

Disregarding Richard's aside, she turned back to Leidecker. His face was expressionless, but she knew he hadn't missed any of the by-play.

"I left the house at a little before five. We met at Dave's Place, that restaurant over on Buckeye. I had two glasses of wine and I came home. I got here about seven. Richard was upstairs, already in bed."

"Do you recall what time Mr. Mayerling called, Kate?"

"Yes. It was three-ten."

Leidecker looked up from his notes. "Exactly?"

His question flustered her. "Y-yes. I was watching the clock when the phone rang."

Leidecker didn't say anything, just stared at her. She noticed that when he was most observant, his face was expressionless. She held his gaze without blinking.

"Was Mr. Mayerling calling from Dave's Place?"

"No. From his car. He was on the expressway."

"And he arrived at five."

"No. He was a little late," she said. "I think it was about five-fifteen."

Once he had their statements, Leidecker finished his coffee and got up to leave. Richard went with him to talk to the reporters. Kate remained in the kitchen.

It seemed to her that all the sounds in the house were exaggerated. The footsteps were crisp and steady on the way to the front door. She heard the door open, the sounds of murmured voices outside, the sharp click of the latch. And then silence.

She remained standing, arms wrapped around her waist, thoughts inward. In her mind she played back Richard's answers to Leidecker's questions.

"When you left work a little after three, where did you go?"

"I stopped in the bar at the train station. I planned to just have one drink, but I got to talking and ended up having quite a few."

"What time did you leave the bar?"

"I don't know. All I can remember was having some drinks there, getting on the train, driving to the house, and then when I found Kate gone, having a few more drinks."

Kate closed her eyes, feeling cold and very frightened. She had been prepared to accept his story of getting drunk until she heard the lie in his voice. Now she didn't know what to believe. She remembered how she'd found him last night. Passed out on the bed, soaking wet.

The rain hadn't started until just before five. If Richard got home at five, how had he gotten so wet?

A voice in her head responded. He was standing in the rain waiting for the jogger?

# FIFTEEN

*Was it raining in the woods when the jogger was killed? Is that how Richard got wet?*

Hearing the questions inside her head, Kate panicked. She glanced at the door to the kitchen afraid that Richard would return at any minute. She knew she couldn't face him. Not yet. She went out on the deck, then wanting to get as far away from the house as possible, she went down the stairs into the backyard. She stood in the shade of the crabapple tree and stared up into the leafy branches.

I'm going crazy, she thought. I'm standing outside in the backyard, and going right out of my mind.

She felt as if her questioning of Richard was a betrayal. She knew he hadn't killed Jenny. That bit of soul searching had cost her dearly. Even though she had decided that he hadn't been involved in Jenny's murder, she had felt dirtied by the mental calculations.

And now she was faced with a similar situation.

She considered what she knew. Richard's suit jacket had been soaked. She remembered when she hung it up that the water had penetrated all the way through to the inner lining.

Richard had left the office after three. She had talked to Chris about the same time and he said it was not raining in Chicago. So if Richard went directly to the train station, he wouldn't have gotten wet. He said he drank at the bar and then caught a train to Pickard. So the only time he would have been outside was walking to his car on Main Street.

At a quarter to five there was only a light mist in the air. It didn't really start to rain until five.

The only way he could have gotten soaking wet was if he was outside for an extended period of time.

Where had Richard been?

Kate shook her head, biting her lip as she searched for answers. She thought back over the sequence of events. She'd forgotten all about the strange series of phone calls yesterday. She should have told Richard about them. Especially the last one when she spoke to the Witness. She'd tried. When she called to tell him, he'd just left the office.

What if the Witness had called Richard?

Even though the thought frightened her, it made sense. If the caller were out for blackmail, Richard would never want Leidecker to know about it.

It would also explain where he had been, and how he had gotten wet. They might have agreed to meet someplace outside. And then the storm caught them unawares.

Relief washed over Kate. The oppression that had weighted her down lifted as she realized what probably had happened. It didn't explain everything, but for the moment she'd just have to trust Richard. He was already upset with her over the meeting with Chris. This wasn't the time to ask him where he'd been. He was never very good at keeping a secret. Eventually he'd tell her.

Taking a deep breath of the summer air, she walked back to the house. Richard was just coming down the hall to the kitchen, wiping sweat from his face with a handkerchief.

"What an ordeal. You wouldn't believe the questions the reporters asked. Leidecker's really good with the press. Maybe it's because they're not hounding him personally." He blotted his upper lip. "God, I feel awful. I'm going upstairs to lie down."

As he started out of the room, Kate spoke. "Richard, you're not still upset about my meeting Chris, are you?"

He stopped in the doorway, but didn't turn around. "Perhaps a little. Maybe offended is a better word." He faced her then and she could see the hurt just beneath the surface.

"Chris was only trying to help," she said. "He's in an awkward position, and he wanted me to understand his motives."

"I hate it that everyone's talking about me. Even you and Chris."

He left the room, and Kate bit her lip to keep from crying.

*Why didn't Chris tell him about their meeting?*

She knew she was being unfair; it was her responsibility to communicate with Richard. She should have explained in her note that she was meeting Chris. The mere fact that she hadn't, added clandestine overtones to a simple situation.

Of course Richard had taken offense. Part of his anger stemmed from the surprise. The other part was too much pressure and a hangover. Eventually he'd see that their intentions were good, if misguided. The sad thing was that in their efforts to protect Richard, she and Chris had ended up hurting him.

And now Leidecker probably thought she was having an affair with Chris Mayerling.

"Get on the phone to Squint," Carl shouted over his shoulder to Bea as she left the conference room. "Tell him I want the pictures from the crime scene *now.*"

Carl directed his anger at Squint. He needed to give it a focus outside himself. He should have listened to Bea. She'd warned him not to settle on Richard Warner as the prime suspect. He had let his past experiences compromise his objectivity. It infuriated him that he might be responsible in some way for the second murder.

He had called a meeting of the crisis team when he got back from the Warners. When it concluded, everyone scattered to continue his or her assigned tasks. Thanks to the rain, they didn't have much to work with.

Pushing back his chair, he pulled out another package of gum and tore it open. He glared at the foil wrapped stick of gum as if it were to blame for all his problems.

He couldn't believe it was two in the afternoon and they still hadn't ID'd the jogger. The man wasn't carrying any identification. He wore a Velcro wallet around his wrist. Inside was a key. Nothing else. They'd run the jogger's prints but had come up empty. They'd given the media a description of the man and his jogging clothes. For the moment they were stymied.

Bob Jackson had been over the crime scene with his team. A spot had been located along the edge of the open field where the killer might have waited for the victim. From this vantage point, the jogging trail around the field was visible as well as the other trail that cut back into the woods. Broken branches and trampled grass suggested someone's presence, but the rain had erased footprints and other relevant clues.

Diego thrust his head inside the conference room door. "I think we may have an ID on the dead guy. Woman is on her way in. Pretty upset, but all I could get outa her is that she thinks it's her boyfriend. Sounds like the real thing."

"Great!" Carl started to rise when Squint appeared behind Diego's shoulder. He waved the man in. "Go ahead, Diego. Let me know as soon as you talk to her."

Squint hurried into the room. "Sorry, Chief. Trouble with the toner."

Without a word, Carl pointed to a cork panel on the wall, and went over to help the photographer attach the pictures. Once they were hung up, Carl moved closer to examine each one.

"Is the M.E.'s report in?" Squint asked.

"Preliminary only. You know Jack Mortimer. He won't submit a final report until every tissue sample's been tested for botulism and black plague."

Carl eyed the photographer, raising an eyebrow in question. His eyes thoughtful, Squint retied the blond ponytail behind his neck before he spoke.

"I need to see the report so I can check something." He shook his head at Carl. "Nothing to tell until after I've done some lab work. It's something I saw through the lens. Just a hunch."

Carl felt a jolt of excitement at Squint's words. The photographer saw more through a lens than most people saw with their eyes.

"Get the preliminary report from Bea."

Squint left.

After examining the pictures several times, Carl returned to the conference table. He swiveled his chair to face the windows, tilted back and put his feet on the end of the table. On the edge of his vision he could see the pictures of the body. He tried to imagine the series of events that led up to the man's death. In his mind he traced the jogger's path around the open field into the woods where the killer intercepted him.

According to the M.E., the jogger was moving when he encountered the killer. The attack was a surprise. There were no defensive bruises on the arms to indicate the victim had raised them to ward off the first blow.

If the murders were random killings, it would be hell to find some sort of link between the two before the murderer struck again. Dropping his feet to the floor, he picked up the folder marked "prime."

After Jennifer Warner was killed, a set of criteria was established. Make and color of car, PF license plates, acquaintance with child, time availability and other factors were considered in order to narrow down the possible suspects. The names fed into the computers were the people the Warners knew, and anyone who had been identified from the pictures taken at the funeral home and the cemetery.

Anyone who fit one or more of the criteria was placed on the "prime list" and ranked according to the number of categories they matched. With the discovery of the second body, the people would be contacted again and a new list compiled.

If the child and the jogger were randomly selected, the chances of finding the killer would be a matter of luck. In a community the size of Pickard, the prime list made a good starting point. If the crime was local, paths of even random victims would cross.

According to the original list, the three who ranked the highest were Richard Warner, Mike Kennedy, and Christian Mayerling. Warner and Mayerling had no alibi for the time when Jenny was killed.

Earlier in the day Carl had felt so guilty about his focus on Warner that he had practically absolved him from any involvement with his daughter's death. Aware of his own prejudice, Carl had turned Warner's file over to Bea who, throughout the investigation into Jenny's death, had argued for the father's innocence.

He turned to Christian Mayerling's file. According to Kate Warner, Richard's boss had called her on his car phone a little after three and had met her at Dave's Place around 5:15. Interviewed after the discovery of the jogger's body, Mayerling said he was delayed on the expressway when he stopped to change a young woman's flat tire. He hadn't taken down the woman's name or license number, so there was no way to verify his story. Dave's Place was about fifteen minutes from the forest preserve.

Even though Mike Kennedy appeared to have an alibi for the time of Jenny's death, he met enough of the criteria to remain on the prime list. Most abuse and abduction of children were committed by relatives and family friends. Since the doctor was a trusted figure, Jenny would have gone with him without question. For that reason alone, Kennedy was still on the list.

According to the doctor, he'd left the hospital at twelve-thirty for a two o'clock tee off at the Pickard Country Club. He'd had a drink and a sandwich in the bar with the rest of his foursome. With rain threatening, the game was canceled. He left the country club about 1:30 and went to the Sears store in the Pickard Mall to pick up some drill bits. He'd browsed through a bunch of the stores, bought a pair of shoes, then decided to catch the new Clint Eastwood movie. When the movie got out at five, he went home. No one had seen him, so for all practical purposes, Kennedy had no real alibi. The shopping mall was about a ten-minute drive from the forest preserve where the jogger had been killed.

Working down the list methodically, Carl went through each of the interviews to see if anything struck him as unusual. It was slow going. Too much information to absorb in one sitting. After an hour, his eyes burned and he squeezed them shut, rubbing his hands over his face. Shoving the papers back into the folder, he tossed them into the center of the table.

Squint entered without knocking. He brought in more pictures, and without a word began pinning them to the cork board. Carl pushed back his chair and crossed the room, standing silently until all the pictures were up.

"While I was taking pictures at the crime scene, I listened to the comments of the M.E. and the other cops," Squint said. "Conventional wisdom has it that we might be dealing with random killings. First the Warner kid and then the jogger. Some psycho who abducted the kid and then maybe returned to the scene and killed again. Right?"

"Maybe," Carl said. "Nothing's set in stone. We have to consider every possibility."

"The M.E.'s report said the man was struck once in the face and then several times across the back of the head. Any of the blows with enough power to be fatal. That's consistent with my photos. But there's something you need to see."

Squint pointed to the first picture that showed the jogger's entire body lying across the path. With his index finger, Squint tapped a spot beside the jogger's right foot.

"These are the man's glasses. They were broken by the initial blow. Shards of glass were embedded in his face. The glasses probably fell to the ground before he was hit on the back of the head. Otherwise they would have been under the body. Okay so far?"

"Yes."

Carl leaned closer, staring at the enlargement of the section showing the glasses. His scalp tingled as he began to get a glimmer of what Squint had seen. The photographer had been watching for his reaction.

"You see it too?"

"I think so," Carl said, studying the pictures.

The glasses were mangled pieces of glass and plastic. They were lying in an indentation on the path, pressed deeply into the mud.

"The killer struck the glasses twice while they were on the ground. In this picture you can see the two rounded depressions in the mud. The shape is consistent with the M.E.'s report that the weapon appears to have been the shape and size of a broom handle. My hunch is that the breaking of the glasses is significant."

After Squint left, Carl remained standing in front of the photographs. He was in no rush to leap to any conclusions. Even if Squint was right, it could be taken two ways. In the first case, the smashing of the glasses could have resulted from an excess of adrenaline in the killer.

The second possibility was more intriguing. The killer could have smashed the glasses out of spite because the jogger had seen something that he shouldn't have seen.

Carl turned at the sound of the opening door. Diego entered, his teeth flashing in a wolfish smile. He closed the door then strode across the floor, eying the wall of pictures.

"We've got our boy, Chief. His name is Walter Hepburn."

"Hepburn. Hepburn." Carl could feel the hair on the back of his neck bristle as he repeated the name. "Walter Hepburn was the name of the jogger who discovered Jennifer Warner's body. That's the dead guy?"

"You got it," Diego said, slapping a newspaper down on the end of the table. "This is a picture of Hepburn that appeared in the *Pickard Advocate* right after the kid's murder. Check the running suit. I think it's the same one he was wearing when he died."

Carl eyed the picture. It was difficult to tell if the man caught in the circle of reporters was the same person he'd stared down at in the woods. The sweatsuit looked to be identical.

"Who ID'd him?"

"A Carmen Hudson. Hepburn's girlfriend."

"This puts a different spin on things," Carl said. "Take a team to his place and see what you can find. Can we keep the lid on this for a while?"

"I think so. I've got Miss Hudson with Bea who's going to take a statement, and try to get as much background as she can on Hepburn."

"Okay, get over to Hepburn's before the media muddies the water."

After Diego left, Carl turned back to the pictures of the body. It was too much of a coincidence that the same man who discovered the first victim should become the second victim. Common sense told him it was impossible.

He stared at the blowup of the smashed glasses, considering various scenarios. If Walter Hepburn had seen Jennifer Warner's murderer, why hadn't he said anything? His statement had been that he'd lost his glasses and found the girl's body when he was searching. Perhaps he didn't realize until later that he'd seen the murderer or the murderer's car or something else that might identify the killer.

If that was the case, and Hepburn was killed because he posed a threat to the killer, how did the murderer know?

Carl hurried across the room to the telephone, punching the number for Bob Jackson. "Keep this under your hat, but we've ID'd the jogger. His name is Walter Hepburn, the guy who discovered Jennifer Warner's body."

There was a moment of silence and then Bob came back on the line. "What can I do for you?"

"I want you to pull the logs on Hepburn's phone. From the time of the Warner girl's death. Get the phone number from Bea. She's with Hepburn's girlfriend. You better check the girlfriend's phone, too. With this new wrinkle, I'm wondering if he might have tried a spot of blackmail."

"And ended up not rich but dead? Okay, Carl, I'll make it a priority."

"Call me if you turn up anything."

Carl remained in the conference room, making notes and working out ideas in his own mind. He tried not to look at his watch, but couldn't help be impatient. It was an hour before Diego returned.

"Lemme get a cup of coffee, Chief." Diego unbuttoned his shirt collar with one hand while he poured a cup with his other. He took a sip then grinned at Carl. "It was Hepburn all right. Fingerprints from the apartment match the body."

"What's his place like?"

"It's a two-flat over on Stonewood. He lived upstairs. We went through it and sealed it until we have more time. The gal who ID'd him lives a block away from his place. She's in her late thirties, very stylish. She was at work. Didn't hear the news right away. Tried to call him, and when she didn't get an answer decided to check with us. She's pretty broken up about it."

"How serious was the relationship?" Carl asked.

"According to her, they were planning on marriage." Diego looked skeptical. "The neighbors that I talked to said Hepburn had a long line of girls but never took the plunge. They thought Hudson could do better. Referred to him as the 'used car salesman type.' Definitely a negative response."

"What else did Miss Hudson have to say?"

"She said Hepburn jogged every day. Same time. Same route. When he found the Warner kid's body, it really spooked him. Didn't jog for a week. When he went back to it, he changed the time. Instead of leaving the house at six, he left at four. Joe Moore and I took turns running what we figured was his route to the murder scene. Took anywhere from twenty minutes to a half hour."

"If he left at four, it puts him at the scene four-twenty to four-thirty?"

"That's what we figure."

"It's consistent with the M.E.'s report as to time of death," Carl said. "Good job, Diego. Hold on to Miss Hudson long enough for me to get a statement ready."

Carl worked up a statement giving limited details of the identification. He was tempted to hold back the information on the role that Hepburn had played in the first murder, but suspected that Miss Hudson wouldn't be quite so reticent. Better if the information came from the police. He showed the statement to Bea, and suggested she handle it with Failing in publicity.

Back in the conference room, Carl reviewed the sketchy information on Hepburn. Much as he hated to make a snap judgment on the dead man, he had to admit it was definitely within the realm of possibility that Hepburn might have tried to blackmail the killer. And if he had, it was a fatal mistake.

After a cursory knock, the door to the conference room opened and Bob Jackson entered. Carl raised both eyebrows when he saw that Bob wasn't wearing his suit coat and his tie was undone, flapping against his white shirt like a banner.

"Was the blackmail angle a guess, Carl? If so, you must be psychic."

Bob pulled chairs away from the table so that he could lay out a series of computer printouts. Circled and highlighted entries were visible on the top page of each stack. When the papers were lined up to his satisfaction, he beckoned Carl to join him.

"These" — he tapped the first pile — "are the calls made from Walter Hepburn's phone since the Warner kid's death. We ran the numbers through the computer to see if there was a match to anyone involved in the case. No match. I even went through the calls made from his girlfriend's apartment." — he tapped the second pile — "Also nothing."

He pushed the first two piles into the center of the table. Picking up the next set of printouts, he set them down in front of Carl.

Bob was a puzzle freak, which was one of the reasons he was good on a case. He enjoyed explaining his thinking processes although Carl might have preferred a more succinct summary.

"I decided to attack it from the other direction." He tapped the pages in front of Carl. "These are the outgoing calls from the Mayerling offices for yesterday afternoon. Nothing significant. These are the incoming calls. Nothing particularly interesting except a call at five after three. It was from a pay phone in a strip mall at the corner of Stonewood and Saratoga. The mall is next to the two-flat where Walter Hepburn lived."

"Bingo," Carl said, his tone reverential.

Bob tossed the printouts into the center and pulled over the last set. "This is a log of the calls made from the pay phone yesterday afternoon. The circled one is a call to a direct line at the Mayerling offices at five after three."

"Whose line was it?"

"Richard Warner."

# Sixteen

"Damn it, Bob! It can't be Richard Warner." Carl felt as if he'd been personally betrayed.

"Why not?" Bob was clearly baffled by the about-face. "You were the one who was pushing to hang the guy."

"I changed my mind." Carl clamped his jaw shut.

"As Diego would say, 'Have you got some bug up your ass?'"

It was so rare for Bob to speak crudely that it jolted Carl, releasing his frustration. "This morning when it looked like we might have a random killer on our hands, I practically apologized to Warner for doing my job. I even went outside with him to talk to the press. We stood together, looking for all the world like the Corsican brothers, joined at the hip."

"That about it?" Bob had a smile on his lips but the sympathy in his eyes was evident.

"Okay. Let's get to it." Carl pushed his fingers through his hair and shook out the stiffness in his shoulders. "Are you absolutely certain that the call from the pay phone to Mayerling's was taken by Richard Warner?"

"Yes. It was his direct line. His assistant was in his office when the call came in and said he left immediately after that." By way of explanation, Bob added, "I gather since his daughter's death, the entire office is sensitive to Warner's every move. The assistant was worried that something else had happened because right after he left, Kate Warner called and was surprised not to find him at the office."

146

"Take a look at this," Carl said, as he pointed to a series of circled entries. "Five calls were made from the pay phone to the Warner house. The first call was at two o'clock and the rest were fifteen minutes apart. I thought it was strange that Mrs. Warner knew exactly the time that Mayerling called her. The fifth call to the Warner house from the pay phone was at three o'clock. If Kate knew the calls were coming every fifteen minutes, she would be waiting for another call to come in at three fifteen. She would be watching the clock, which would account for her accuracy on the time that Mayerling called."

"I wonder if she spoke to the caller and if she knows his identity."

"His or her identity," Carl said. "Other than the proximity to his residence, we have no proof that the calls were made by Walter Hepburn. At this point it's nothing but a guess."

"Agreed."

Eyes intent on the texture of the carpet, Carl paced across to the windows. "Let's assume for the moment that the caller is Walter Hepburn. He's trying to get in touch with Richard Warner. He calls the house but each time Mrs. Warner answers. Finally he calls the office. Warner answers and Hepburn identifies himself and makes arrangements to meet because he has information about the murder. Sound plausible so far?"

"Yes and no." Bob moved the phone printouts aside and leaned one hip on the end of the table. "This morning we pretty much agreed that the jogger was caught unawares. So it doesn't look like a meeting."

"OK, so what if Hepburn says he'll meet him in the woods after his jog? Warner goes early and kills him before the scheduled meeting."

"It still won't work," Bob said. "Unless Warner is acquainted with Hepburn, he wouldn't know that the jogger was the right guy."

"Hepburn's picture was in the paper."

Bob shrugged and nodded his head. "Not bad, Carl. Might have even happened that way. We got any proof for this 'Grimm fairy tale'?"

"Not yet. I've got Tony checking the bar in the train station to see if anyone remembered seeing Warner there." He looked down at his watch. "It's six o'clock now. Everyone's due back here to touch base at eight. Why don't we grab something to eat? Are you hungry?"

"Yes. As long as it's not Mexican." Bob rebuttoned his collar and tied his tie. "We going to work all night?"

"As long as we're making progress we'll stick with it." Carl could feel the tension in his neck muscles. "There can't be any mistakes on this one. I have no intention of railroading Richard Warner if he's innocent. But if he's guilty, by God, I'll nail that bastard to the wall."

He was restless. Unable to sleep. He opened the outside door and slipped into the darkness of the night. The heavy air surrounded him, clinging to his bare arms and legs. Sweat mingled with the humidity.

He'd always loved summer. A pear tree grew at the far end of the empty field behind the house. He'd burrow up inside the leafy heart of the tree. Once there, he could see to faraway places, could imagine exotic sights, and could relax in the safe shelter until he heard the voice.

If he heard the voice when he was in the tree, it was easy enough to slide down into the tall grass. He'd lay on his belly, soaking up the warmth of the earth. Smelling the moist, loamy smells and hearing his heart pound with fear.

In the grass, his father couldn't find him.

He could change position when the stumbling footsteps came too close. And if he got lost in his thoughts, as he had once, he could always outrun the old man.

Usually when his father called his name, he snarled it like a curse.

The angry voice meant only a beating. His mother said it would make him stronger. Easy to say when she wasn't the one getting beaten.

It was the soft, cajoling voice he feared.

When he was a child, he hated the night.

He never heard him enter the room. He would be deeply asleep, dozing off from sheer exhaustion while he listened to the infinite shifts and movements inside the house. He'd strain to hear and try to quiet the heavy pounding of his heart, and when nothing happened his terror would fade and he'd slide into sleep only to wake with an awareness of his father's presence.

In the morning his mother would turn her eyes away from his, ignoring the swollen eyelids and painful movements. She would move silently around the kitchen, flinching at every sound as if afraid it would draw attention to her existence. His father read the paper with total absorption.

It was difficult to know which one he hated more.

Now when the restlessness was on him, he tried to get outside, embracing the darkness, able to move in it with a fluidity that was lacking in the daylight. At the corner of the street, he stopped. The night air was warm. Not as fierce as the daytime. He opened his mouth, drawing in the heat, storing up the warmth for the cold times, the early morning hours when the memories of childhood returned in torturous dreams.

A trickle of sweat snaked down behind his ear, rolled to the back of his neck, and then slid down his spine to pool at the elastic waistband of his shorts. He shivered, reminded of how wet he'd been coming out of the woods.

The experiment had been a success. He had tried to be analytical and stay in the moment. He had been satisfied with the results even though he had not experienced the same sensory high that he had the first time.

He walked briskly through the night air, going over every detail, trying to discover the area of discontent. He heard again the rhythmic slap his footsteps had made as he ran along the trail. Smelled the wet decay rising from the muddy ground. Felt the muscle strain as his arm swung back. Saw the lips of the jogger open in a cry of agony as the bones of his face crumbled with the force of the blow. And then he knew what was missing.

He had not seen the jogger's eyes.

It was the visual record of pain that was missing. His own pain had always been muffled — he never heard it. In the morning the pain was only a buried memory, so he could not see it in the mirror. He needed to see the pain. It gave it reality, a personal verification.

Eyes. The mirrors of the soul.

He'd always been affected by what he saw in people's eyes. Even a quick glance could warn him of danger. He knew he had much to fear from the COP. His eyes were never still, always searching. The victim of the experiment had been chosen specifically with the COP in mind.

He'd worked so hard to make a good life. Protecting himself was his first priority. Mustn't get cocky. He had to take one more risk to ensure his safety from discovery.

The knowledge that the timing of the next event was so crucial added a layer of excitement. He'd gotten particular pleasure from the planning stage the last time.

He'd considered and discarded various objects for the new trophy. The jogger's earphones had been useless. He'd had high hopes when he took them. He thought that they would bring him the same pleasure as the charm bracelet, but they'd been useless as conduits of any source of power. They gave him nothing and he destroyed them. Perhaps the item had to be more intimately tied to the spirit of a person.

He stored the knowledge away. It was interesting how much he'd learned from each experience. Eventually he'd know all the elements required for maximum pleasure and minimal risk.

Kate looked out the bedroom window to see if a miracle had happened during the night and all the reporters had disappeared. The identification of the jogger had thrust the story back into the headlines. Now twice as many cars and vans were parked along the street.

*God, the neighbors must hate this circus environment.*

Angrily smoothing the comforter across the bed, she vented some of her frustration on the down pillows. If she went outside, she was accosted by the reporters; if she went anywhere in town, she was followed. She felt as if she were a prisoner.

Part of her frustration was that she hadn't had a chance to speak to Richard before he went to work. Late yesterday Mike called. He had heard on the radio about the identification of the jogger. Since Hepburn was tied in to Jenny's murder, Richard knew he would again become the prime suspect. Mike had suggested going to see the lawyer. He'd offered to make all the arrangements and pick Richard up around eight.

The rest of the day was agonizingly slow. Expecting a call from

Leidecker, Richard had jumped each time the phone rang. They ate dinner in virtual silence. Kate had watched Richard push the food around his plate, his thoughts far away. She'd wanted to say something reassuring, but her awareness that Richard had lied to her made her tongue-tied. When it was time to meet Mike, Richard had slipped out the side door, cutting through Marian's backyard to get to the street on the other side of the block.

Kate hadn't even offered to go with him. She was exhausted. By ten when they still hadn't returned, she'd taken a sleeping pill, and gone to bed. Even though she'd needed the rest she was annoyed that Richard hadn't wakened her when he got up. She wanted to know what the lawyer had suggested.

Downstairs she stopped in the doorway to the kitchen and frowned. Richard's cereal bowl was still on the table, the Raisin Bran a congealed mass of soggy flakes. His coffee mug lay on its side, a splash of brown staining the open newspaper.

The paper was open to the second page. On the right-hand side was a story detailing the murder of Walter Hepburn. Following that, was a recap of Jenny's murder and quotes from Mayor Etzel, Leidecker, and various other people in Pickard. Accompanying the article was a picture of Richard bending over to speak to Patrick Grange, the five-year-old who lived down the street.

Beneath the picture was the headline: No Arrest Yet in Child Murder.

Kate sat down and stared blindly out the window into the backyard. She let her mind float but eventually thoughts intruded.

In the first days after Jenny's death, neighbors and friends had rallied with food, flowers, and cards. Where words failed, these were the tangible evidence of friendship. Inevitably, life moved on and slowly people began drawing away.

Kate's eyes returned to the newspaper article. Now that she looked back she was aware that the calls and visits had slowed to a trickle and then stopped. Except for a small group of close friends, she and Richard were isolated. Kate suspected it would be like that until Richard was cleared of all suspicion.

She didn't know how long she sat at the kitchen table; her mind taken up with the bleakness of the situation. When the telephone rang, it startled her back to the present. It was Richard.

"I've got to go up to Milwaukee for a presentation," he said after only a cursory greeting.

"Today?"

"I'm leaving in about ten minutes." There was a pause. "We got a call from a guy who's thinking of changing agencies. Apparently, he was impressed with the ads we did for Yardmaster mowers. Wants to have a preliminary meeting. Just speculative. Chris and I are driving up together."

She was worried about Richard. He was speaking breathlessly, in bursts of energy, his sentences choppy, as if he had an adrenaline rush. "Do you have to go? I thought Chris wanted you to take some time off."

"That's on hold for the present. He thought it would be a break getting out of town."

"I saw the picture in the paper." Kate winced at the silence on the line. "Don't think about it. We'll talk about it when you get home. Will you be here for dinner?"

"No. If all goes well, we'll have a lot of details to work out. We'll continue right through dinner. And you know Chris. He prefers to stay over in Milwaukee rather than drive back late. I'll call you in the morning when I get into the office."

"I wish you were coming home, Richard, but the reporters are still gathered like vultures out front. It'll do you some good to be away from here for a bit. I hope your meeting goes well."

"Me too. Kate . . ." He started to speak then stopped.

"What?"

"Nothing. I love you, you know."

"I do know, Richard. Hurry home," she said.

Touched by his words, she caught her breath on a sob, holding the phone in her hand long after Richard had disconnected. It took her a few minutes before she realized she'd forgotten to ask what Stacie had advised. She debated calling him back, but decided he would have told her if the lawyer had anything of importance to recommend.

She was disappointed that he wouldn't be back until the next day. There were too many hours to fill. She spent the day cleaning. It wasn't as hot as the day before so she opened the windows and by late afternoon the house smelled of summer.

Periodically, she listened to the messages on the answering machine. It worried her that Leidecker hadn't called. His silence in the face of Hepburn's identification was ominous.

It was five o'clock when the phone rang. She was just rewinding the messages on the answering machine, so she answered.

"Hi, Kate. It's Chris. I just called to give Richard a message when he gets home."

"Isn't he in Milwaukee with you?"

"Milwaukee?"

"Didn't you go with Richard?" The silence on the line was palpable. Kate clenched her fingers on the receiver as she waited for Chris's response.

"No. I had to be in Springfield. Richard probably told me he was going up to Milwaukee, but it must have slipped my mind. It's been a really hectic week." His speech was slow as if he were weighing each syllable. "I tell you what, Kate. Don't worry about the message. I should have just put it on his voice mail. Sorry for bothering you."

Kate hung up the phone.

What was going on? Chris obviously knew nothing of a meeting in Milwaukee. He'd tried to hide the fact, but Kate knew he was covering for Richard.

She grabbed a bunch of bananas from the fruit basket and threw them at the refrigerator. They smashed against the door, falling in a messy heap on the tile floor. All the pent up anger came rolling out.

She was furious that Richard had lied to her again. The story of the Milwaukee presentation was reasonable and well thought out. Why had he thrown in the part about Chris going with him? Maybe so if she had a question, she wouldn't call the office? Now she wondered if Richard had actually gone to Milwaukee. But then, why did he need an excuse to be away?

*Maybe Richard is having an affair.*

Just the thought of it seared her soul. On top of everything else she didn't know if she could handle such a betrayal.

But it would explain where Richard had been the day Jenny disappeared.

Damn! In his own way, Richard was very old fashioned. If he had been with someone the day Jenny died, he wouldn't have mentioned it when he was first questioned.

The more Kate thought about it, the more sense it made. It hurt to think about it and she refrained from any conjecture as to who the woman might be. That kind of guessing would be truly destructive.

In fact there wasn't much point in dwelling on it. She'd only drive herself crazy if she did. She would have to wait until Richard got home.

Determined to stay busy, she mopped up the remains of the bananas. The cleaning was therapeutic. Finished with the kitchen, she got out her pruning shears and went out to the garden.

The new bed of roses lifted her spirits. She and Richard had bought six plants and spent the weekend getting them settled along the fence at the back of the yard. Marian's contribution was the Unique Blanche rose that she had found in a Wisconsin nursery.

She spent the remainder of the day working outside. For dinner she ate a small salad, and then with a fresh glass of iced tea went out on the deck. Legs propped up on the chaise longue, she lay back and watched as night closed in around her. To the southeast, the lights of Chicago illuminated the horizon, but in Pickard the stars were bright in a cloudless sky.

Physically tired, she dozed, but was startled awake by the sound of the doorbell.

In the uncertain light, she squinted at her watch. It was almost two in the morning. Her heart pounded in fear. Who could be at the door this late at night?

The doorbell rang again. She hurried into the house, turning on lights as she moved from room to room. She flipped on the outside lights and looked out the window. Carl Leidecker was at the door.

"I know it's late, Kate, but I need to talk to you."

She closed her eyes as fear closed in around her. With shaking hands, she unlocked the door and stepped back for Leidecker to enter.

"Is Richard here?" he asked.

She shook her head, unable to speak, as she saw the grim expression on Carl's face.

"Do you know where he is?"

"Milwaukee." She had to force the word out and her voice was too loud. "He's in Milwaukee."

"Have you talked to him today?"

"Yes. This morning. He called around nine to tell me he was going out of town."

"Did he pack any clothes?"

Kate shook her head. "I don't know. I wasn't awake when he left."

"Did he say where he'd be staying?"

"No. And I didn't think to ask." Her breathing was ragged with the rising tension in the hall. She couldn't stand it any longer. "What's going on, Carl? For God's sake, tell me."

"Richard's car was found in Chicago, parked in a lot at the Touhy Avenue beach. His clothes, the car keys, and his wallet were inside."

He reached into his back pocket and pulled out a brown leather wallet, which she recognized as Richard's.

"Police boats are patrolling the area along the beach . . ."

Kate cut him off. "Richard wouldn't go into the water. Even if it were a hot day, he knows it's much too early to go swimming. So maybe he drove back from Milwaukee along the lake and decided to stop and cool off."

"Then where is he?" Leidecker asked. "It's two in the morning."

"I don't know. Maybe he met someone he knew and is off having a drink."

"Without his clothes and wallet? Be reasonable, Kate."

"I am!" She spoke in anger. "Questions. Always questions. Badgering him. And Richard thought you were his friend."

"My job is to find the person who killed Jenny." Leidecker spoke without passion. "The Richard Warner you know is a good husband and loving father, an asset to church and community. To you, it is inconceivable that he would hurt his own child. But crimes are not always committed by drooling perverts and degenerate people. Nice people commit crimes. Good people can do bad things."

"Richard did not kill Jenny. He did not kill the jogger." She met

Leidecker's glance without flinching. "You've been against him from the very beginning, Carl. You and the media have hounded him. As I told you before, he called me this morning to tell me he was going to Milwaukee. He wasn't sure when he'd be back. I don't understand why he would leave his car and his clothes at the beach unless he was walking to clear his head. Did it ever occur to you that something might have happened to him? He might have been mugged."

"I don't think he was mugged."

She read compassion and sadness in Leidecker's expression. She shook her head violently, wanting to keep him from saying anything further "Let me tell you what I think could have happened, Kate," Leidecker said. "Sometime last evening Richard drove to the beach, parked, left his belongings in the car, and swam out into Lake Michigan."

"It's not true." Kate's voice held a pleading tone. "You know Richard. Why would he do anything so crazy?"

"He may have suspected that we were going to arrest him. He couldn't face that possibility." Leidecker's voice was steady, the words uncompromising. "The logical conclusion is suicide."

# Seventeen

"If Warner drowned, where's the body?" Tony Torrentino glared across the conference room table at Diego Garcia. "This is Monday. It's been five days already."

"What're ya yelling at me for?" Diego said. "I'm just telling you what the Coast Guard told me. You think you can do better? Why don't you offer to drag Lake Michigan?"

Carl had a headache and was in no mood for the usual squabbling. He slapped his hand on the table for silence.

"Don't get your balls in an uproar, Tony," he said. "We've been over this before. On Lake Michigan, anything's possible. If a body isn't found immediately, it could be days or weeks before it washes up either on the Illinois side or over on the Michigan side. And if it's caught on something underwater, it might never turn up."

"So I'm asking myself," Tony said, continuing as if Carl hadn't interrupted, "how do we know Warner's dead?"

"We don't." Bea's voice was matter-of-fact. "I realize that Warner's disappearance is a major setback, but we can't let it throw us off the track. We have a case to work on and one way or another we ought to be able to get closure. Now let's review what we have. Diego?"

"Like I already said, the Coast Guard found nada. They searched for forty-eight hours and then called it quits. No boats picked up anyone in the lake and no body washed ashore. The Chicago morgue had a couple floaters. All of them had been in the water for more than a week."

"Keep on it," Carl said. "Bring us up to speed on the evidence from Touhy Avenue beach."

"The watch commander called me at —" Diego ran a finger down his notes, "at 11:30. The Chicago police had Warner's car. The beach closes at 10:00, but it was a Wednesday night, and by 10:30 Warner's was the only car left. The cop on patrol flashed a light on the inside. When he saw the clothes on the front seat, he ran the license of the car. He recognized Warner's name from the news coverage. So Chicago called us. Me and the chief drove to Touhy Avenue beach where the cops were waiting."

Carl picked up the story. "Warner's suit coat was folded on top of the rest of his clothes. His watch, wallet, and the keys to the car were in the inside breast pocket. The beach lot has metered parking with a time limit of five hours. The car was ticketed at 9:00 for an expired meter. A patrol car goes through every hour."

"That doesn't tell us much," Bea said. "He could have been there as early as four."

"It doesn't matter what time he got to the beach. We have two witnesses who saw him at 6:00," Tony said. "So it's what happened after that that's important."

"How reliable are the witnesses?" Bob asked.

"Solid gold. I interviewed them myself," Diego said. "Peter and Julie Hills. Old couple, maybe seventy. They live in the building beside the parking lot. They saw the flashing lights, and the old guy came down to see what was up. When he heard someone mighta drowned, he came over to tell us about the man he'd seen going into the water."

"I was still in the parking lot and talked to him," Carl said. "Concise and positive. He picked Warner's picture out of a pack of six."

Diego was anxious to tell the story. "This Peter Hills and his wife had an early dinner and then took a walk along the beach. They saw a man in a bathing suit start into the water. It was cold and he sort of jumped backward onto the sand, bumping into Peter. The man apologized and, when the old lady said he'd freeze if he went in for a swim, the man said it was okay because he liked cold water. The old couple continued on their walk. They didn't see him when they returned about an hour later."

Bob raised his arms and scratched the back of his head. His expression was perplexed. "I have a problem here. Other than getting his feet wet, the witnesses never really saw him go into the water. In fact if it hadn't been for the man backing into the old guy, the Hills probably wouldn't have noticed him. But since they'd spoken to him, they were able to recognize his picture. See what I'm getting at?"

"No," Tony said.

Bob sighed. "If Warner was planning to fake his death, he'd need some evidence to indicate he went into the water. So he stands at the edge of the lake until he spots a likely couple. He stumbles into the guy and talks to them both for a minute or two. Perfect witnesses to his presence at the beach and his intention to go for a swim."

"How'd he know the witnesses would talk to the police?" Tony asked.

"It just seems a little too pat."

"Make a note of it and let's move on," Carl said. "Did the canvassing around the beach area turn up any more sightings?"

"Nada." Diego shook his head. "I've had someone, armed with pictures of Warner, in the parking lot and walking the beach every day since his disappearance. We'll keep at it through Wednesday, which will make a solid week. We got the usual people wanting to be helpful. Swore they seen him swimming, jogging, waterskiing, picnicking. My personal favorite was a guy who swore he spotted Warner in the front seat of a red sports car getting a blow job. He didn't get the license number."

"Charming," Carl said. Looking down at his notes, he asked, "Who had Warner's car?"

"Yo." Tony waved his pencil. "The car was dusted inside and out," Tony said. "Warner's prints are all over the driver's side. No clear prints of anyone else turned up in the car except for a partial palm print of Mrs. Warner on the passenger side armrest. A couple of Warner's prints on the leather wallet and the shoes."

"Exactly what clothes were left in the car?" Bob asked.

Tony read it off. "A suit coat and pants, a black leather belt, white button-down shirt, tie, black socks, and black leather tassel slip-ons."

"No underwear?"

"There wouldn't be if he was wearing his bathing suit under his clothes," Tony said. "And unless he had an extra set of shoes, he walked across the parking lot to the beach barefoot."

"I checked with Mrs. Warner," Bea said. "As far as she could tell, he hadn't taken any clothes with him. However she couldn't find his bathing suit."

"Way I see it," Diego said, "we got two possibilities. One, Warner committed suicide. Two, he faked his death in order to disappear."

"Or three, he was murdered." Carl's addition left silence in its wake.

"Murder?" Bob asked, jerking upright in his chair. "Has something turned up that might suggest Warner was murdered?"

"No," Carl said. "But it hasn't been ruled out."

He felt his own bias against Richard had influenced the conduct of the investigation. He had flip-flopped after the jogger was killed. Then, when it appeared that Richard was guilty, Carl was so infuriated that he had not issued an arrest warrant immediately, wanting to build an airtight case first. Warner's disappearance was a personal blow. His inaction enabled a murderer to escape.

Carl continued, "So far, all the physical evidence points to suicide. I should mention that Mrs. Warner says if Warner were planning to commit suicide, he'd never choose drowning. She's convinced that he either swam out too far and drowned by accident or he was murdered."

"Poor woman," Bea said. "I suppose if I were in her position, I'd say the same thing. It can't be easy. If she admits he committed suicide, she is almost labeling him a murderer."

"It's a tough call for everyone," Carl said. "What I'd like an opinion on is whether you think Warner is the type to commit suicide. The two consulting psychiatrists gave a split vote. Kristina Berg said no and Jen Puplava said yes. Even knowing Warner personally, I could make a case for either side. Give me some opinions. Why would Richard Warner commit suicide?"

Bob was the first to respond. "I always thought if he was responsible for the rape and murder of his daughter, it was a crime of impulse not premeditation. Pedophiles have an elaborate framework of excuses and dodges. If it was a spur-of-the-moment, one-time event, a guy like Warner wouldn't be able to live with the guilt."

"Or with the thought of going to jail," Tony added.

"So if he did commit suicide, we could close the case," Diego said. "Along with the evidence we got, it would prove he was guilty."

"Not necessarily," Bea said. Diego threw up his hands in frustration. "You've all met and talked with Richard Warner. He's self-absorbed, controlling, and appeared genuinely devastated by the death of his daughter. Both police and media consider him the prime suspect. Is it any wonder that he might have buckled under the pressure? He might have found the pain of Jenny's death too much to bear or decided death was preferable to arrest. Who knows?"

"Guilt or innocence aside, do you believe Warner committed suicide?" Carl asked. Bob and Tony nodded yes. "Diego?"

With an abrupt gesture, he thrust both thumbs downward. "No."

Carl turned to Bea. Her face was puckered in a grimace of indecision. After some thought, she heaved a sigh and shook her head.

"I don't think so," she said.

"Well we're just moving right along," Carl said. "So far, what have we got? Murder, unlikely. Suicide, maybe. Let's take a stab at a faked death and subsequent disappearance."

"At least if he went to the trouble to fake his death, it would prove he was guilty," Diego said, staring across the table at Bea. "If he was innocent, what would be the point of disappearing?"

"For just about the same reasons that I gave you for why he might have committed suicide," she said.

"You're really busting my balls!"

Bea wasn't offended. "That was part of my job description."

Carl smiled at the murmur of amused agreement around the table. He could sympathize with Diego. It was infuriating not to be able to come to any solid conclusions.

"I think it's entirely possible that Richard Warner couldn't handle the fact that people thought he'd killed his daughter," Bea continued. "Maybe disappearing seemed like the way out of an impossible situation."

Carl sighed. "I considered the same thing, but I decided against it.

He'd never desert Kate. Especially if he's innocent. I don't think he's the kind of bastard who'd deal her such a blow. My theory is that he's guilty and, if he didn't commit suicide, it's entirely believable that he'd fake his death."

"That brings up another point," Bea said. "Would Kate help him if he was guilty?"

"I asked her that once," Carl said. "She never gave me an answer. Kate Warner is the kind of woman you would describe with terms like: good, normal, responsible, moral. Until Jenny's death, I suspect she had no experience with evil. It would never occur to her that Richard might be guilty. When he became a suspect, she was forced to consider it. She obviously decided he was innocent. I know this is a long answer to your question, but if she thought he was guilty I don't think she would help him."

Bea pressed. "Assuming she thinks he's innocent, if he was going to be arrested, would she help him disappear?"

"Maybe," Carl shrugged. "If I'm reading their relationship right, Richard has controlled her throughout their marriage. I don't think she'd act on her own. I don't think she's a good enough liar to pull off this kind of a deception. In my opinion, she doesn't know any more about what happened to him than we do. His disappearance was a stunning blow. First her daughter is killed, then her husband is suspected of the crime, and now it looks like he's committed suicide. When I saw her yesterday, she was sedated and almost catatonic."

"I tend to agree with your assessment of Mrs. Warner," Bob said. "She believes in Warner, and the last thing she wants is his death. Dead, he would never be cleared of suspicion. Besides, she's too honest to continue to mourn for someone she knows is alive. It would be a betrayal of her own daughter's death."

"Agreed," Carl said. "So if he decided to fake his death, could he have done it on his own?"

Tony stabbed his finger on the top of his file folders. "No. He left behind his credit cards and his wallet with a hundred twenty-seven bucks. I checked his bank records and he hasn't taken out any chunks of dough. My read is that guys like Warner get used to the creature comforts. He isn't the kind of guy who'd walk away empty."

"Are we all agreed that if he disappeared he'd need help?" Carl asked.

Four heads nodded in unison.

"And a place to stay," Bob added.

"Okay," Diego said. "The way I see it, the two most likely candidates for Good Samaritan of the Month are Mike Kennedy and Christian Mayerling."

"Before you get into a discussion of opportunity," Bea said, "let me give you a sidebar. Warner is not staying in Mayerling's condo. We did a batch of interviews, and unless he's disguised as a fifty-year-old Hungarian maid, he's not there. I sent Jamison over to Kennedy's place. The complex has both townhouses and apartments. The manager is on the premises. According to him, nobody's been at the townhouse for at least a week, including Kennedy. He's been staying in Chicago at his girlfriend's along with Mrs. Warner."

"I can't believe Warner'd stay with either of those two guys," Tony said. "He'd have to know we'd check them out."

Bea shrugged. "We're not dealing with a streetwise criminal. I'm not sure that Warner would know how to disappear. I have the feeling if he went to a hotel, he'd register under his own name. One other possibility. Maybe two. Mayerling has a condo in Palm Springs, and Kennedy has a vacation place on Beaverton Lake up north of Madison."

"I'll put in a call to Palm Springs, even though it seems a bit of a stretch," Bob said. "My guess is if Warner disappeared he'd stay closer to home. Kennedy's place sounds more likely."

Carl leaned forward with interest. "I've fished Beaverton. It's a man-made lake. Real good fishing with lots of little inlets, bogs, and a hellish crop of killer mosquitoes. It's just three hours away."

"Might be longer," Bea said. "Kennedy's place is accessible only by boat."

"What's the doc own, an island?" Tony asked.

Bea laughed. "Not exactly. On the north end, the ground's low, intercut by springs and almost completely underwater. Apparently Kennedy bought a piece of this marsh. In the center is a high spot that has an old cabin on it. Pretty primitive. No electricity. No running water. And as the chief said, plenty of mosquitoes."

Diego cringed at her description. "Remember that scene in *The Deer Hunter* where the guys were kept in cages in the water. Kennedy's place sounds just like that. What the hell's he want with a place like that?"

"I guess he likes to fish and camp." Bea shrugged. "I called a friend of mine on the force in Madison, and had him check it out. Talk about a small world. His aunt owns a tavern and marina on the lake. When Kennedy comes up, he leaves his car at her place. He keeps a boat at the marina and uses it to get through the marsh to his place. She says he hasn't been up all summer and nobody else has either."

"Would she know?" Bob asked.

"Apparently she's a local character. In her seventies, and still goes out fishing every day. Knows everything that goes on."

"It doesn't sound much like the kind of place Warner'd go to hide out," Carl said. "He never struck me as the outdoorsy type. Motel with a pool would be more like it. Thanks, Bea. It's something to keep in mind at least. Now where were we?"

Diego was ready. "We were into who had the opportunity to help Warner. What was Kennedy up to last Wednesday? His friendship with Warner goes back a lot of years. If anyone helped Warner skip town, my money would be on Doctor Mike."

"I wouldn't bet big," Bob said.

He stood up and dealt several sheets of papers around the table. He remained standing in his lecturing pose, giving everyone time to look at the material.

Carl hid a smile behind his hand. One Christmas as a gag gift someone had given Bob a telescoping pointer. He'd been delighted and, to everyone's despair, had used it at every meeting until someone stole it. Broken into little pieces, it was left on Bob's desk. Wisely, he chose not to replace it.

"Since we haven't got an exact time of disappearance or death," Bob said, "I've made up a timetable for the whole of Wednesday, May 19."

Other than a groan from Diego, the room was silent. Carl reached for the thermos of water, poured a glass to wash down the aspirins in his hand, then waved for Bob to continue.

"Kennedy stayed in Chicago at the Conrad Hilton Tuesday night because Wednesday he was running an all-day symposium on osteoporosis. He was at the reception area at 8:45 for coffee and glad-handing. A series of panel discussions in the ballroom ran from 10:00 until 4:00. He had lunch in full view of the hundred or so people attending. Afterward he met with his committee until 5:30, and made it for cocktails in the ballroom at 6:00. The banquet started at 7:30, and Dr. Mike Kennedy was the keynote speaker."

"There goes that theory," Diego said.

Bob snorted in amusement. "Don't despair. Much as it looks impossible, I found a small window of opportunity. The banquet ended at 9:30. He had drinks in the bar with several people until 10:30, when he went up to his hotel room. It's a big hotel. He could have come and gone easily without anyone being the wiser."

"It's not a lot of time," Carl said.

"What about his car?" Bea asked. "If it was parked at the hotel, the garage would know if he used it."

"He left his car at his girlfriend's apartment," Bob said. "Miss Chesney was visiting her parents in Orlando."

"You're checking the taxis for a pick up at the Hilton anytime that evening?" Carl asked.

"If Kennedy was helping Warner get away, I don't think he'd be dumb enough to take a cab from the hotel." Bob shrugged. "I've got someone working on it anyway but it takes forever to check log books and interview cabbies and dispatchers."

"Keep at it, Bob," Carl said. "Now let's move on to Christian Mayerling."

Bob pointed down at the timetable, waiting until they'd had a chance to study it again before he continued. "Mayerling drove to Springfield on the day Warner disappeared. He left at 7:45 in the morning and got there around 11:30. He had lunch with Senator Crafa at a place called The Silver Stallion. Left there at 2:30 for a meeting with some of Crafa's constituents which lasted until 5:00. He says he wandered around until the rush hour traffic was over and then around six he headed back to Chicago. Said he loafed along and didn't remember what time he got back. The guy in the parking garage of his building logged him in at 10:45. He didn't use the car until morning, when he drove out to see Mrs. Warner."

"If he went out after 10:45, he coulda got a cab," Tony said.

"No go," Bob said. "The building's damn near impregnable. A security guard in front and back, surveillance cameras and two guys in the garage. If Mayerling was helping Warner, he had to do it prior to 10:45."

"He had lunch with the senator at 11:30," Bea said. "Didn't he stop to eat dinner somewhere on the way back to Chicago?"

"I asked him and he said he wasn't all that hungry. Just reheated some leftovers when he got home. On that basis he has no verification for anything past five and before 10:45. It's hard to believe it took him . . ."

"Wait a sec," Tony interrupted. "What about the guy getting the blow job?"

"Can't you stay with the program, Torrentino?" Bob said.

"I am! It was in Garcia's report."

"Don't blame me," Diego said, entering the fray. "What's that got to do with anything?"

"Not the blow job, you idiot!" Tony was shouting. "I'm talking about the red sports car!"

Carl felt a jolt of excitement. He sat up straight and narrowed his eyes in concentration. He rapped his knuckles on the table, speaking softly into the silence.

"Tony might be on to something. The red sports car. Could it have been Mayerling's red Porsche?"

# Eighteen

"The red sports car coulda been Mayerling's," Tony said. "Although it's a convertible, and if you'll excuse the pun, it doesn't have a lot of headroom."

"Good Lord, Tony!" Bea said.

Diego stood up. "The interview sheets are on the top of my desk." Without further comment, he left the room.

"Okay figure this," Tony said. "Say Mayerling left Springfield at five, directly after his meeting with Senator Crafa's constituents. Could he make it to Chicago in three and a half hours?" His words were more a statement than a question. "That's 8:30–8:45 at Touhy Avenue beach. He hooks up with Richard Warner at the beach parking lot and . . ."

"Remember," Carl interrupted, "Peter and Julie Hills saw Warner at the water's edge at 6:00. That's a long time for him to hang around the beach area in swim trunks."

"Nobody knows where he was from nine in the morning when he called the missus and 6:00 at night."

Diego returned, a clutch of papers in his hand. He leaned over the table thumbing through them until he found the one he wanted. Nudging his chair away from the table with his foot, he scanned the report before he sat down.

"This is the interview. Tyrone Rawlings. A dude to be sure. He was really strutting his stuff on the beach. Honest to God, women were practically wiping drool off their chins when they eyed him. We didn't exactly hit it off."

"Too much competition?" Tony asked with raised eyebrows.

"Before you boys start unzipping your pants to compare anatomical details," Bea said, "could we get back to the report?"

"Sorry," Diego said. "There's not much more in my notes than I already told you. Tyrone said on Wednesday, May 19, he saw Richard Warner in the front seat of a red sports car getting a blow job. At the time, I thought he was yankin' my chain so I didn't press him for a lotta details. He was vague about the time. I've got it written down as dark."

"It'd be dark at 8:30," Tony said, "which is the earliest Mayerling coulda got to the parking lot."

"No ID on the car?" Carl asked.

Diego shook his head. "I've got Tyrone's address and phone. I'll get to him today, and see if I can squeeze something more out of him."

"Take pictures with you," Carl said. "Include Christian Mayerling's, but don't force it on him."

"I got it. 'Cept I still don't think he saw nothing."

"Probably not." Carl tended to agree with Diego.

Tony waved his pencil for attention. "I know I brought this up, but I never got the idea that Warner swung both ways. The original reports said Mayerling might be a queen, but it never said there was anything between him and Warner. Am I wrong here?"

"No, you're not wrong," Carl said. "As far as I know, Richard Warner is straight. Mike Kennedy was his roommate in college, and said Warner put the sex in heterosexual. The thing is, Tony, this Tyrone may actually have seen a red sports car in the parking lot. And because he's an asshole, he might have thrown in the blow job for creativity points." He turned back to Diego. "I don't think I have to draw you a diagram. Play our friend Tyrone very carefully on the off chance he really did see Mayerling's car."

"Got ya, Chief."

"That covers everything I had on my list. Anyone have anything else?"

"One more thing," Bob said. "I was going through my paperwork, Bea, and came across that short list you gave us on May eleventh. Four names with PF license plates that had triggered an alert. Did anything come out of that list?"

Bea shook her head. "Sorry, guys. I must have dropped the ball. I don't have the foggiest idea what happened. Who was handling it?"

"Yo. I haven't got my notes typed up yet." Tony patted down his sport coat, reaching into the inside pocket and withdrawing a wad of crumpled papers. Unfolding them, he read down the list. "Four names. Bushnell, Danello, Nathanson, and Zmudzki. The last one you can count out entirely. He was the one accused of beating up on his kid. Got into a bar fight a week after the Warner kid was killed. He's been in a coma ever since."

"Sounds like a prince," Bea said.

"Real prick. Danello, the car dealer. He's also out of the picture. His wife caught him humpin' a customer in the back of a Jeep Grand Cherokee and she's suing him for divorce. The day of the murder he was in court the whole day. The little woman has a hotshot lawyer from the Chicago firm of Gill, McGuire and O'Keefe. By the time she finishes with Danello, he'll need a car jack to get it up. Nathanson and Bushnell are still on the active list."

"Part of this is my fault, Bea." Bob interrupted. He pulled a sheet of paper from the back of one of his files. "I told Tony I'd check into Bushnell. He's the old guy, neighbor of the Warners whose name came up in connection with a porno sting we were running. At any rate, he's never had any arrests but over the past couple years he's come under scrutiny. Always something on the sexual fringes."

"A latent molester?" Bea leaned forward, her curiosity piqued.

"Not sure." Bob shrugged. "I suppose an ex-mayor could be a deviant, but he seems more like an old dodderer who's interested in porn and ends up in the wrong place at the wrong time. Last week one of our guys was working an adult bookstore up near the Wisconsin border and happened to recognize Bushnell when he came in to buy a film. When he told me about it, I sent him over to Bushnell's for an interview."

"Did he have an alibi for the time of Jenny's death or the jogger?"

"Said he was at home. The wife was adamant that he had been in the house both times. The interview notes said he looked nervous and she was plenty ticked that he was being questioned. They've got big money and political connections. The wife kept threatening to call Mayor Etzel."

"As if Etzel wasn't already breathing down my neck," Carl groaned. "Anything else to link him to the murders?"

"No. Nothing except he's an odd duck and fits the profile for an old pedophile."

"Nice job, Bob. Ex-mayor or not, keep Bushnell on the active list. Who was the last one?"

"Nathaniel Nathanson, the soccer coach." Tony once more riffled through the crumbled papers. "I called my cousin's husband, Fred Weller, on the Rockford force. He's into computers in a big way. He says the Internet is one of the greatest opportunities for crime that's come along in years. Porn. Chat rooms. All without letting on your real identity."

"Does this have anything to do with Nathanson?" Carl was impatient for the meeting to be over.

"Yeah. Fred's set up some kind of Internet sting. He pretends he's a twelve-year-old boy. He's been keeping a list of people who've tried to contact him. Some are legitimate, but some sound questionable. Fred's got some source that can find out the real names and addresses. Nathanson's name came up."

"Did you check him out?"

"Briefly. He's twenty-eight. Single. Never been married. He coaches for the soccer league and is active with the kids' summer concerts. No alibi for the time of either murder. Has the PF plates. And last year he went on a vacation to England, Ireland, and Scotland, so he could have bought some of the ButterSkots candy."

"Anything to tie him directly to the murders?" Bea asked.

"*Niente*."

"Keep on this guy, Tony. Maybe he shouldn't be spending so much time around kids." Carl sighed. "Any other problems or comments?"

When no one spoke, Carl sat up straighter, leaning forward onto his elbows, his eyes registering the discontent on each face. "I realize that nobody wanted this sort of inconclusive solution to the two murders. In the long run, it doesn't matter whether Richard Warner is dead or alive. The main thrust of our investigation has to be to discover if he murdered Jennifer Warner and Walter Hepburn. Or if someone else did."

It was time to go home.

Kate heard Mike and Chessy fighting in the bedroom. Their voices were muted, but she could feel the tension in the clipped snatches of conversation. Since the night Mike and Leidecker had come to tell her about Richard's disappearance, she had been staying in Chessy's apartment on Lake Shore Drive. Knowing the amount of publicity Richard's disappearance would arouse, Mike had insisted that she couldn't remain in the house. Too stunned to fight, she had agreed.

It was just a week ago, and yet she could only remember bits and pieces of that awful night. Thinking about Richard's disappearance made Kate clench her teeth to hold back the pain.

Since arriving at the apartment, she had tried to block out all memories, existing in a cocoon of numbness. She had turned all the details of life over to Mike and Chessy. Except for visits from Leidecker and calls to Marian, she had isolated herself from everyone for the past week.

She slept. She ate a little. And she slept again.

Muffled voices behind the bedroom door reminded her that she had outstayed her welcome. Coming home from vacation to an uninvited guest, and one in an emotional crisis at that, had been hard on Chessy. She had been gracious, but the two-bedroom apartment was too small for Chessy, Kate, and a constantly hovering Mike. Kate's continued stay would push the boundaries of friendship.

Wearily she stood up, walking across the oak floor to stare out at Lake Michigan. She would miss the view. She had been comforted by her closeness to the water. Watching the boats moving on the surface, she convinced herself that the Coast Guard had not given up the search and eventually they would have news.

Six days, and still no word of Richard.

Had he committed suicide by swimming out into Lake Michigan?

Mike, Chessy, Chris, and Marian had all been too considerate to ask the question. Only Leidecker had asked. She'd hated him for asking. She didn't want to think about it. She accused him of hounding

Richard and blamed him for the depression that had settled over Richard.

Although she'd balked at saying the words out loud, in the darkness of the sleepless nights she acknowledged that Richard was dead. Since his disappearance, she had suppressed her emotions as she had in the days following Jenny's death. At least when Jenny died, Kate had a feeling of closure, if not acceptance. For a week she had been waiting for Richard's body to surface and when it didn't she was left in a state of limbo.

Even though she believed he was dead, the comforting ceremonies were absent. With no body, there could be no funeral. And worst of all, his guilt or innocence in his daughter's death would always be questioned.

She stared out the window, breathing deeply until she was calmer.

Even eleven floors above the city, she could feel the chill of the water. She turned away and went into her room. Keeping her mind purposefully blank, she stripped the bed linens, packed her clothes and checked the bathroom to be sure she hadn't forgotten anything. She called Marian to say she would be home later in the day.

"Good, dear. I'll turn on the air conditioner. It's really hot out today. I'm just on my way to the grocery store. I'll pick up some things for you, and then you won't have to go out for a few days."

"Thanks, Marian. I appreciate it. And thanks for everything the other night."

"Nonsense. What are friends for? The car doors woke me. I'm just glad I was there." The soft voice sharpened. "You come on home. I'll turn the lights on and get the place cooled off. Then I'll pop over tomorrow for a chat. You've been in my thoughts and prayers, dear."

Kate swallowed the lump in her throat. "Thank you, Marian. See you tomorrow."

After checking the room once more, she carried her suitcase out to the front hall. Mike and Chessy were in the kitchen, and Kate broke the news that she was going back to Pickard.

Mike met her announcement with anger. Chessy's reaction was a mixture of embarrassment and relief. She dutifully pressed Kate to stay longer, but they both knew it was time to leave. Mike was unconvinced. Right up to the moment he put her suitcase into the car, he continued to offer alternate plans. Once on the expressway, he drove in silence, his expression grim in the flicker of lights from passing cars.

How strange, Kate thought, as they drove down the streets of Pickard. So much had happened, yet nothing's changed. Somehow she expected the town to look different, perhaps reflect the despair and pain that she was feeling.

The car pulled into the driveway. In the glow from the front door light she could see new plants in the flower garden beside the steps and red-orange petunias spilling over the edges of the window boxes. Marian's way of welcoming her home.

Mike turned off the ignition. Kate reached over to touch his sleeve.

"After all you've done, I'm sorry I was so stubborn about leaving." She felt rather than saw the slight shrug of his shoulders. "Chessy was a lovely hostess, but it was time to go. I have to put my life back together."

"You don't have to rush into it."

"Let's not argue. Besides, you're bound to get mad all over again when I tell you I don't want you to come in."

"It would be easier if I did." Mike pushed a hand up through his hair.

"Perhaps. But I have to do this alone."

A tense silence filled the car. Kate knew how much Mike hated it when things didn't go the way he'd planned. She waited and was rewarded by a sigh.

"You win," he said. "Much as I want to, I can't protect you."

"No. Through everything, you've been an incredible support, but now I have to start functioning on my own. Decisions have to be made. If Richard is gone" — Kate's voice broke on the word — "I have to figure out what I'm going to do for the rest of my life."

Mike reached over and squeezed her hand. "I know you don't want to hear any of this now, but at some point I'd like to talk about your finances."

"You don't need to. Chris called me yesterday and talked about that too."

"Are you all right for immediate cash?"

"Yes. The money from my job at the library has always been in my name. Richard didn't approve of my working, and refused to let me use it for household expenses. There are legalities involved in Richard's disappearance, so for the time being I'll use that." A lone tear slid down her cheek and she brushed it away. "Sorry. Memories kind of sneak up on me. Time to get moving."

Before she could reconsider, she opened her car door. Mike carried her suitcase up the front steps. He had always had a key to the house but hesitated before he unlocked the door, staring down at Kate as if to ask permission. She nodded, a short jerk of the head. He unlocked the door, stepping away without opening it.

"When you get back to Chessy's, give her a big hug from me." Kate pulled on Mike's lapels until he bent his head and she could kiss his cheek. "I love you both, but I have to learn to get along on my own. I'll talk to you tomorrow."

Taking the suitcase from him, she slipped inside the house and closed the door, leaning against the wooden panels and listening as Mike started the car and drove away. The silence of the house closed around her.

With determination, she pushed away from the door and started toward the kitchen. She noted the yellow carnations on the coffee table in the living room and the white ones on the dining room table. In the kitchen was a vase of mixed flowers from Marian's garden. With each bouquet, Kate's spirits revived. By the time she reached the family room, she was able to smile at the showy blossoms of the Unique Blanche roses on the table beside the couch.

She stared at the flowers, remembering the day they had dug the rose beds. For a few hours, the shadowy suspicions had been held at bay. Richard had not been happy, but at least he had been less sad. Sinking down on the couch, she breathed in the scent of the flowers.

God, she was tired. Maybe tomorrow in the sunlight, life would not be so frightening.

Checking the lock on the sliding doors, she turned off the lights and the air conditioner, heading back into the front hall. Turning out the porch lights, she double locked the door, picked up her suitcase, and headed up the stairs.

She stopped at the door of the master bedroom, unable to cross the threshold. Her mind was flooded by thoughts of Richard. She was not strong enough to sleep alone in their room. Not tonight. Perhaps never.

Turning her back, she walked down the hall, past the closed door of Jenny's room and snapped on the overhead light in the guest room. The room had little personality and for that Kate was grateful.

The air was stale from disuse. She opened the window, letting in some fresh air. After the hermetically sealed atmosphere of Chessy's apartment, even the humidity smelled good.

A stranger in her own house, she placed her suitcase on the luggage rack and unpacked her nightgown and toiletries. She used the guest bath, the nightly rituals helping to restore her sense of security. At the last, she took a sleeping pill.

Once under the covers, she shifted around in the unfamiliar bed. She recited song lyrics to keep from thinking and waited for the muzzy feeling to steal over her as the pill took effect.

The shrill ringing woke her.

Kate struggled upright, clawing away the sheets as she tried to orient herself. In the humid night air, she was sticky with sweat. Bright moonlight streamed across the bed, falling on the bedside table.

The telephone rang again.

She didn't know what time it was, but she knew it was late. She was paralyzed by fear, and it took her a moment before she could reach out a hand. Finally, she grabbed the receiver and raised it to her ear.

"Hello?"

"Don't worry, Kate, I'm safe."

# Nineteen

Kate pressed the receiver to her ear. She squeezed her eyes shut, trying to bring the voice into sharper focus. "Who is this?"

Silence was the answer and she panicked. "Please don't hang up. Just tell me who this is?"

"I'm safe."

The words were whispered, and then she heard the click as the call was terminated.

"Don't do this to me. Damn you! Damn you! Damn you!"

In frustration she banged her fists on the bed, punching the soft surface over and over. The force of the blows exhausted her. She sat cross-legged in the center of the bed, bent forward so that her head touched the rumpled sheets.

She lay still, listening to the rhythms of her body. Her muscles were free of tension and her teeth weren't clenched. For the first time in three weeks, she felt relaxed. It was incredible. She had fought so hard to be strong, afraid she would fly apart if she let down her guard, yet instead of weakening her, the outburst had somehow made her stronger. It had broken through the paralysis that possessed her mind.

It appeared that she had two choices. She could sink back into the numbed state of mere existence until she withered away, or she could use her anger to motivate her survival.

"Damn! Damn!"

The bedclothes muffled the words, part sigh, part sob. She raised her head and straightened her back, each movement an effort. Sitting upright in the middle of the bed, she made her choice.

The killer was still free. She had to survive. She had to live long enough to witness his destruction.

Having made her decision, she considered the phone call.

The voice had been so low it was impossible to guess the identity of the caller. She had been so positive that Richard was dead. Could she be wrong? If he was alive, he had faked his death in order to put an end to the investigation.

"Richard did not kill Jenny. Richard did not kill Walter Hepburn. So Richard had no reason to run away. Therefore the call was not from Richard." She recited the words like a logic theorem. Perhaps she was blinded by loyalty, but if she conceded that Richard had faked his own death, she would have to reevaluate his role in Jenny's death. She couldn't do that. Richard's innocence was the one fact she had to believe in. Without it, she would not have the will to live.

Could the call have come from the person who'd made the calls after Jenny's death? The person she thought of as the Witness?

So few words had been spoken that she couldn't be sure, but she didn't think so. The other phone calls had terminated with the jogger's death, and she had always wondered if Walter Hepburn had been the caller. When she'd finally mentioned it to Leidecker, he confirmed the fact. According to Carl, Hepburn had been killed when he attempted to blackmail Jenny's killer. Naturally, his assumption was that the jogger had been trying to blackmail Richard.

This call wasn't like the Witness calls. This call had a specific purpose. It was meant to confuse her, torture her with the suggestion that Richard was alive.

Her heart gave a jolt as she wondered if it could be something else entirely. What if it was the murderer?

She felt very alone in the empty house. She swung her feet over the side of the bed. The moonlight was bright enough for her to navigate the stairs. She didn't want to turn on lights. She felt safer in the dark.

In the kitchen, she heated water in the microwave, then, still in the dark, she curled up on the couch in the family room with her mug of tea. She took several small sips, waiting as warmth flowed to the outer edges of her body. She began to feel less frightened.

Now that she was able to think more clearly, she realized there was absolutely no reason to believe Jenny's killer made the call. It was more likely to be a card-carrying member of the lunatic fringe.

*Oh, God, I can't stand this. Please help me. I've prayed and found no answers.*

What was she going to do? Where did she start in planning the future?

It had been comforting to be fussed over by Mike and Chessy, to hide away from friends and neighbors and to permit others to concern themselves with her finances and status, but now it was time to take control. As always, she wished she had family to rely on.

All her life she had been controlled by the men in her life. First her father and then Richard. And as much as she appreciated their support, if she permitted it, Mike and Chris would take over her life.

Even before Jenny's death, she had felt a sense of rebellion against Richard's control. When she was first married, it never occurred to her to question his authority. She felt loved and cared for. Once Jenny was born, she realized that she wanted her daughter to be in charge of her own destiny in a way that she had never been. Teaching Jenny to think for herself had created a restlessness in Kate, and an awakening awareness that her own life was not as rich as she had once believed.

Now circumstances had forced her to take charge of her own life. The anger she had felt earlier faded at the prospect that for the first time in her life she would not have someone to tell her what to do. Although the thought was intimidating, she felt ready for the change. She had lost everything that mattered, so now it was just a question of building a new life for herself.

First she would need a job.

She couldn't bear the thought of going back to the library. People would be unfailingly kind, anxious to help her work through the grieving process. And there would be speculative glances and interrupted conversations when she was around.

If she wanted anonymity, she could sign up with a secretarial agency. No one ever noticed temps. She had excellent office skills. And if she used her maiden name and kept to herself, people would see her only as a nameless, faceless worker.

Resolving to sign up in the morning, Kate felt as if she had crossed a major hurdle. It wouldn't be much of a life, but it would give her time to recover some of her strength. She would need to be strong to keep Leidecker from closing the case before the man responsible for Jenny's death was found.

Despite his antipathy toward Richard, Carl was essentially a fair man. Much as she hated his doggedness, it was this very quality that convinced her that he would search for the truth and find the murderer. Then Richard's name would be cleared, and he and Jenny could rest in peace. She wanted, if not revenge, at least justice.

He cupped the bracelet in his left hand, poking the golden links with the index finger of his right hand until he uncovered the charm. She lay in the valley of his hand, arms spread wide, her robe flared at the bottom as if she'd just twirled for his admiration. The wings caught the light, flickering in simulated motion.

He rubbed the angel.

The heat transferred to his finger and through his wrist, moving up his arm to the junction in his armpit. He pictured it there, building up energy before it radiated out through the rest of his body.

He only needed to touch himself with his finger to feel the power. The intensity of excitement was agony. He could feel himself expand and squeezed the bracelet to hold on to the pleasure. His skin stretched to the limit and when the pain became unbearable he climaxed. The release was so extreme it left him shaking.

That's how it should have been, he thought as he put away the bracelet.

He had tried the experiment again. It had not been a success. The subject had been chosen on the basis of expediency. He had not liked the choice, but felt if he was to ensure his safety it was necessary. Passion was not involved. If anything, sadness was the predominant emotion.

The COP had forced him to act. Always snooping. Always asking questions. Couldn't the bastard let it rest?

In some respect he enjoyed the challenge of the game. He had not expected the COP to move with such speed, but he could stay one step ahead of him. To do that it was paramount he remain in control.

It was the COP's fault the experiment had been such a failure.

The need to hurry was a contributing factor. He had planned with meticulous attention to detail, and the timing had been crucial. No chance to savor. No opportunity to let the knowledge of pain infiltrate the brain and shine with awareness in the eyes. Yes, he had seen the eyes but they never showed any emotion other than surprise. He felt no more than satisfaction for a job well done.

And the talisman he'd taken from the body had been useless.

He didn't know if the bracelet could withstand the constant drain and still maintain its power. Now that he was safe from discovery, he would have the time to analyze why the winged angel was so important. Each time he held it in his hand, he was afraid he would find the charm dark and lifeless.

If the talisman lost potency, he knew where he could find another one. Perhaps the second angel charm would be even more powerful than the bracelet.

Kate raised her face, closing her eyes tightly against the sharp sting of the shower spray. She turned to let the water strike her back, rolled her head on her neck, pulling her shoulders forward to ease her morning stiffness.

After she toweled herself, she used a corner of the thick terry cloth to wipe a circle on the fogged surface of the mirror. She stared at her unsmiling face. There were no tears, only a bone-weary sadness. She had not cried in the shower. For the third day in a row she had not cried.

Since Richard's disappearance she'd tried to bring order back to her life. She ate, slept, cleaned the house, and did the laundry according to a strict regimen. Her father, and then Richard, had always stressed discipline. Scheduling her activities kept her in balance. It enabled her to keep her emotions in check. Where there had once been sadness, now there was only anger.

Staring into the mirror, she remembered Mike's words after Jenny died. "Once you get angry, you'll begin to heal."

It was strange that she could think about Jenny's death but still referred only to Richard's disappearance. She knew he was dead, but the lack of physical evidence kept her from any real acceptance of the fact.

Richard had been missing for six weeks. In all that time, his body had not turned up. Leidecker told her that it was not uncommon. She tried never to think about Richard being trapped forever beneath the surface of the lake, although her dreams were peopled with horrific watery images.

Wrapping the towel around her body, she brushed her hair into a wet ponytail, returned to the bedroom, and dressed in a navy linen wrap skirt and a white blouse.

Downstairs the house showed the evidence of her disinterest. The rooms were neat but unlived in. She spent her time in the kitchen, family room, and the backyard. The rose garden had become a place of solace. She resented the rainy days when she couldn't sit outside after work, surrounded by the sights and smells of the flowers. She opened the doors to the deck for a quick check outside.

It was only eight o'clock and already it was hot. The weatherman had predicted possible nineties for the day, not untypical for the first week of July. She raised her face to the sun, feeling the heat penetrate her skin, spreading slowly through her body.

Signing up with the temporary agency had been the right course of action. The first two weeks she'd worked short assignments of one or two days duration. In her zombie state, it was exactly what she needed. All she had to do was show up, do her work, and go home. She was polite and cordial to the other workers, but kept herself detached from any more personal contact.

It encouraged her when she didn't see anyone she knew and no one appeared to connect her with the publicity surrounding Jenny's death or Richard's disappearance. Without makeup and with her hair pulled back behind her neck, she looked very different from the pictures in the paper.

With a quick glance at her watch, she cleaned up the kitchen, took her lunch and a can of soda from the refrigerator, and left. It was Wednesday and her assignment was for the full week with the added bonus that the office was just ten minutes from the house.

The offices of Garvey & Associates were in the center of Pickard, a one-story brick building across the park from city hall. Beyond the waiting room was an open area where the secretaries and assistants had work spaces opposite the offices of the three associates.

The final work space was outside Joseph Garvey's office. Unlike the others, it had windows with a view of the parking lot, unexciting but less claustrophobic. Opposite the door to Garvey's office was an arched doorway that led to the conference room and a small kitchen.

Paula Craig, the gray-haired office manager, was situated in an alcove that afforded some privacy from the rest of the room. Kate's desk was between Paula's and the two women who worked for Garvey. Loretta McCabe and Gail Richardson were both single and in their early twenties. They had been friendly, but they had little in common with Kate since they considered her ancient at thirty-one.

When Kate's service had given her the assignment, she had immediately recognized Joseph Garvey's name. He was a well-known corporate lawyer and one of Pickard's more celebrated citizens. His wife Lisa, a gracious sponsor of numerous charities, appeared frequently on the society page of the *Pickard Advocate* and the Chicago papers. Kate had met them only once, when they came to Jenny's funeral in Garvey's official capacity as assistant mayor.

She parked behind the building and once inside began work immediately. It was late morning before she paused for a break. She pressed against the back of the desk chair to ease the ache between her shoulder blades. Her fingers were clammy against the hard, plastic keys and she stopped typing to wipe them against her skirt.

Most of the work was correspondence. Nothing particularly interesting. One of the advantages of working as a temp was that she didn't have to stay long at an assignment. Thankfully, she would only be working for Joseph Garvey for a week. Paula had said he was a perfectionist. Petty tyrant, more likely.

Taking the letter out of the printer, she dropped it on the pile, pushed her chair away from the desk, and stretched her legs.

The door of the conference room opened, and Joseph Garvey bustled across the room to his office.

Garvey looked to be in his late forties or early fifties, stocky, bordering on the flabby. Understated suits with the fit of expensive tailoring gave him the slick look of *Gentleman's Quarterly*.

In contrast, his features had an earthy quality that was almost tangibly sensual. His lips were thick; his nose was finely cut, ending in plump nostrils. His nondescript hazel eyes were deep set, slumberous. He might have been handsome except for his acne-scarred complexion that was too white, as though he spent all his time in shadowed courtrooms.

Kate wondered if his air of importance was irritating to his fellow attorneys.

The only time Garvey had spoken to her was to criticize her work. It didn't bother her that he was particular about his letters. After all, the man was paying her salary. It was his manner that annoyed her. He never looked at her directly. He checked the letters, made additions or corrections, and then shoved the letters to be corrected across the desk without acknowledging her presence.

"Damn it, Loretta. I don't understand why this has happened again." Garvey's harsh voice broke into Kate's thoughts. The door of his office was open, so that his words could be heard distinctly in the outer room. "This is the second time in a month you've taken personal time during office hours."

Kate flinched at the sound of a hand slapping on a wood surface and pictured the lawyer glaring at his poor secretary. In the three days she had been at the office, she had been an unfortunate witness to several of Garvey's temper tantrums. She didn't know what else to call them. The man blew up at the most inconsequential things. She wondered why Loretta didn't quit.

"I'm really sorry, Mr. Garvey. I had a doctor's appointment."

"That's no excuse. If you wish to remain in my employ, you'll have to do better. You know the standards I require. I believe I explained it fully when I hired you. It's not like you're right out of sec-retarial school. You've been here almost a year."

A year working for that man! Either Loretta received an enor-mous salary or she needed a reference badly to put up with such verbal abuse. Kate stared at the computer screen and spotted a misspelling. She kept forgetting to use spell-check.

"Lunch time, Kate."

Paula's voice startled her, and she blinked several times to bring her thoughts back to the present.

"Lucky thing," Kate said. "My stomach's growling."

"I'm running down to the pancake house. It's beastly hot, but I like to get outside for a bit. You don't have to eat at your desk, you know. You're welcome to come along with me."

"Thanks for asking, but I think I'll stay in," Kate said, keeping her voice casual. "Go ahead. I didn't realize I was holding you up. I never even heard Gail and Loretta leave."

"Those two always keep one eye on the clock." Paula laughed, then wrinkled her forehead in uncertainty. "Are you positive you don't want to come?"

"I'm sure," Kate said. She opened the bottom desk drawer and held up a paperback in one hand and a brown bag in the other. "I promised myself I'd finish this book today. And I've a sandwich and a Diet Coke in here."

"Well, if you're sure you don't mind." The older woman stood un-certainly beside her desk, then nodded and left.

Kate sat perfectly still as the silence of the room closed in around her. In the outer offices there was some activity, so she didn't feel iso-lated, only blissfully alone.

She got up and walked through the archway to the kitchen. She took a plastic glass from the countertop and reached into the refriger-ator for some ice. Back at her desk, she poured the Diet Coke and opened the plastic bag, sniffing hungrily at the chicken sandwich. She stretched her legs out under the desk and began eating as she turned the pages of the historical saga she had been reading for the last week.

When she finished, she crumbled the plastic bag and the napkin, and reached for the brown paper bag. She hit the edge of her glass and for one heart-stopping moment thought it would topple over on the freshly printed letters. When the glass settled back into place, she pulled in a great gulp of air and blew it out slowly.

"Judas. That's all I'd need. Soda-stained letters."

She should have cleared off her desk before she started lunch. She got up, arranged the letters in a neat pile, and walked across the room to Garvey's office.

The office reflected the meticulous Garvey. The visitors' chairs were centered precisely in front of his desk. The wall on the right, facing the windows, was covered with diplomas and certificates, all framed identically, marching in two even lines above a credenza. Behind the desk were bookcases, filled with books, arranged apparently by size rather than content.

The desk was a contemporary rectangle of teak, the grain sharp contrasts of brown. There was a green blotter in the middle. Two pens in brass holders were set in a green malachite base, positioned on the edge of the blotter closest to the visitors' chairs.

Kate crossed the thick beige carpet, circled the desk, and leaned over, placing the letters directly in the center of the green blotter. As she leaned forward, she caught the cloyingly sweet smell of butterscotch.

The slightest whiff of the distinctive odor reminded Kate of the half-sucked piece of butterscotch found in the pocket of Jenny's windbreaker. Sinking down into Garvey's chair, she scrubbed her eyes as if to erase the memory.

Opening her eyes, she spotted a pile of candy wrappers in the ashtray. She reached across and picked up a handful. Her breath caught in her throat at the bright tartan logo. ButterSkots.

Closing her hand to hide the wrappers from sight, she pressed her fist against her bosom. Her whole body shook in reaction.

"What the hell are you doing in my office?"

# Twenty

"What the hell are you doing in here?"

Joseph Garvey's voice was so unexpected that a small shriek burst from Kate's lips. She shrank back in the chair.

"How dare you snoop around my office," he snapped.

Seeing the enraged man in the doorway, she was unable to speak. All she could do was stare. She stumbled to her feet, jamming the candy wrappers into the pocket of her skirt.

"I really am sorry for my intrusion, Mr. Garvey. I . . . I wasn't feeling well and I just sat down in your chair."

"Well, get out. You have no right to be in here."

It was the tone of his voice that brought Kate back to her senses. Anger boiled to the surface. "And you have no right to be so rude," Kate said.

"I pay your wages, miss."

"Not anymore."

Ignoring him completely, Kate brushed past him. She moved quickly across the room to her desk, picked up her book, opened the drawer and withdrew her purse. She did not look back as she left the office.

She drove home, still shaken by the ugly scene with Garvey. She unlocked the front door, dropped her keys on the hall table, and headed for the family room. Kicking off her sandals, she padded across to the couch and flopped onto the soft upholstery.

She couldn't believe how angry she was. Before she could change her mind, she called the temp agency and told them she wouldn't be going back to Garvey and Associates.

As she hung up, it started to rain. Fat drops of water splashed against the windows and she crossed to the patio doors to stare out at the backyard. The sky was dark. Thunder rumbled in the distance, and she could see the flicker of lightning against the black clouds.

Kate had always loved summer storms, and she had taught Jenny the joy of walking in the rain. As long as there was no lightning, they would pull on raincoats and boots and head outside.

She could still picture Jenny, face puckered as she turned it up to the leaden sky, her eyelashes trembling on her cheeks in spiky clumps and her tongue extended to catch the raindrops. Jenny would race along the sidewalk, jumping with both feet into any large puddle of water. Summer rain was a time of wild abandon for both of them. Now, a storm only roused a flood of sadness in Kate's heart.

With one finger, she followed a raindrop's zigzag path down the glass. God, she missed Jenny and Richard.

Silent tears rolled down her face, but she made no attempt to wipe them away. The pain was there as it always was when she thought of how much she had lost. She had to let it go. But God, it was so hard.

When the crying eased, she went out to the kitchen for a Kleenex. She wiped the tears from her face and blew her nose. Crumpling the tissue, she shoved it into the pocket of her skirt. She was surprised at the crinkle of cellophane and reached deeper to bring out the contents.

The ButterSkots wrappers.

She'd forgotten that she'd stuffed them into her pocket when Garvey appeared so suddenly in the doorway. She didn't want anything to remind her of the wretched man. Walking across the floor to the wastebasket, she opened her fingers and watched as the plaid ButterSkots wrappers fluttered down onto the trash.

Wanting to forget the whole incident, she decided to go to the health club. She'd gone back to swimming laps several weeks earlier, and she knew the exercise would be good for her.

It was seven o'clock when she returned to the house. Rain blew in giant sheets as the full brunt of the storm hit Pickard. Shaking out her umbrella, she propped it in the corner of the foyer. She was almost lightheaded from her workout. She'd run for an hour on the indoor track before she went down to the pool. It was satisfying to note that she hadn't even been breathless when she finished her laps.

The phone rang as she entered the kitchen. It was Leidecker.

"I hope I'm not getting you at a bad time," he said.

"No. This is fine," she said, her heart beating rapidly at the sound of his voice.

"Good. If you're going to be home for awhile, I'd like to drop by."

"It's raining." It was a stupid comment but she couldn't think of any polite way to put him off. She waited but when he didn't say anything, she grimaced. "I'm here now, but I may be going out later."

"Actually, I'm just leaving."

He had already hung up before she could respond. She had just flipped on the front door light when she heard the sound of a car. She unlocked the front door as footsteps hurried up the walk.

Leidecker stood in the rain. Kate clung to the edge of the door, blocking his entry.

She saw his eyes flicker past her shoulder to the dryness of the hall, but still she didn't move. She didn't want him inside the house. With Richard gone, admitting Leidecker seemed an act of disloyalty.

"May I come in?"

Leidecker's deep voice broke through Kate's paralysis. She stepped back and jerked the door open.

"I'm sorry," she said, glancing at the water streaming down his face. "I think the storm has me spooked. Come on back and you can dry off."

She hurried to the kitchen, got out several clean towels, and handed them to Leidecker.

He wiped his face, toweled his hair, and then combed it with his fingers. Wet, his hair was dark brown, the gray more prominent. In casual clothes he was far less threatening. He brushed the water off the shoulders of his shirt and then dried off his arms, blotting the watch on his wrist.

"Is it working?" she asked guiltily.

He looked across at her, raising an eyebrow as he caught her into-

nation. He didn't speak immediately but when he did, a hint of amusement was in his voice.

"It takes a licking but keeps on ticking," he said. "I never had
much use for expensive watches. All I want is one that tells me the
time. My wife wanted to buy me a Rolex once. I should have realized
then how incompatible we were. If I had, I wouldn't have been so surprised to end up divorced."

"I didn't know you were divorced," Kate said. "I'm sorry."

Her apology came from a sense of self-reproach because, even
though she had known Carl prior to Jenny's death, she had never
taken the time to learn anything about his personal life. In her defense,
he was a private man. His air of professional distance did not invite
questions.

"It was a long time ago," he said.

"Do you miss being married?" Her own loss made her ask the
question.

"Strangely enough, the thing I miss the most is going to movies."
His voice was reflective. "It's not the same watching videos."

It surprised Kate to discover a softer, more sensitive side to Carl.
He appeared almost approachable and she took advantage of it.

"Any kids?"

"No. It's my one regret. I wanted a batch of them, but after the divorce I discovered she'd been taking birth control pills the whole
time."

"Didn't she want children?"

"Yes. She just didn't want them to grow up fatherless." He smiled
in response to Kate's obvious bewilderment. "She never could get used
to my being a cop. She focused on the danger. Every time I went to
work, she was sure she'd never see me again. She wanted me to give it
up, but law enforcement suited me." He shrugged. "At any rate, she re-
married. Her husband works for a company that makes computer soft-
ware. Safe and financially rewarding. They live in Chicago and have
two kids. Boys."

Suddenly he stopped talking. He blinked his eyes, looking non-
plussed by his own candor. He turned away, dropping the towels on the
countertop.

"Can I get you anything?" Kate asked to bridge the awkward silence.

"No. I'm fine." He reached into his pocket and withdrew a small plastic bag. "I came over because I wanted to return this."

He held it out and Kate could see inside the gold necklace with the angel charm that she had given him after Jenny's death. She'd forgotten all about it; another event in her life she'd blocked out. She took the bag, closing her fingers over the necklace. It was several long seconds before she could speak.

"Thank you. I'm embarrassed to say, I forgot all about it. Eventually I would have missed it, but there's been so much . . ." She left the thought unfinished. Without opening the plastic bag, she put it in her pocket. "Did you ever find Jenny's bracelet?"

"Not yet. I'm convinced that if we find the murderer, we'll find the bracelet."

She nodded, at a loss for words. Sensing that he had more to say, she waited. He leaned against the counter, crossing his arms over his chest.

"I also wanted to stop by to talk to you. I'm going to release a statement to the press."

Kate tensed at the professional edge to his words. Leidecker was back in his role of police chief. "Has something happened?" she asked.

"No."

The expression on his face made her legs tremble. She read compassion and regret. Pulling out a chair, she sat down at the kitchen table. "What does the statement say?"

"That's why I came. To tell you." His voice was gentle. "The task force that was put together at the time of Jenny's death is being disbanded. Priorities are changing. There are very few new leads. It's a matter of sifting through the material we already have."

"You're closing the case?" She couldn't believe what she was hearing.

He shook his head. "No. We're not closing it. We'll still be following up on all the loose ends until we get some kind of a break. At this point we have no proof against any of the suspects."

Pausing, he waited to see if she had any other questions. When she remained silent, he continued. "Despite the fact there is no body, the official statement will say that Richard is missing, presumed dead. His death is being ruled a suicide."

She heard the words but at first the ramifications did not penetrate. When they did, she leaped to her feet, marching over to stand directly in front of him.

"You can't do that. Richard never would have committed suicide. I told you that before. Oh God, Carl, you can't do this."

"In this case, I can't do anything else. The coroner has made the ruling, based on the evidence we have."

"But don't you see that once you make suicide an official ruling, the consensus will be that Richard killed Jenny and the jogger, and then couldn't face the consequences of his actions." She gripped her fingers tightly together and pressed them against her chest. "You'll blacken his name forever. Damn it, Carl, you might as well close the case. The real killer will never be found. Everyone will be so convinced of Richard's guilt, they'll see every fact merely as confirmation of their prejudice."

"I realize you're disappointed."

"I'm not disappointed! I'm furious!"

Kate wanted to hit Leidecker. Instead she vented her frustration on the wet towels. She swept them off the countertop, and, with a slapping sound, they hit the wastebasket, tipping it against the wall.

Without comment, Carl walked over and straightened the wastebasket. He leaned over and picked up the towels, setting them back on the counter. His face was closed, eyes shadowed.

Furious, she snapped out the words, "You couldn't find anything to prove that Richard was involved in Jenny's murder, could you?"

"No. But we didn't find anything to prove he was innocent either."

"Go away. I have nothing more to say." She turned her back on him, trying to get her anger in check.

"Honest to God, Kate, the case is not closed," Leidecker said. "I swear to you I'll be working on it until we know exactly what happened to Jenny. I'm leaving my personal card on the counter. There's a number where you can reach me, night or day."

She didn't move when he left. She listened to his footsteps as he walked through the house. He closed the door quietly but her ears were straining so hard she recognized the sound of the latch clicking into place.

It was over.

Much as she had prayed since Richard's disappearance, God had turned a deaf ear to her. And no matter what Leidecker said, as far as she could see, there would never be an answer to the most important question.

Who killed Jenny?

A deep sadness overcame her anger. She knew from experience that the reporters would call to hear what she thought about Leidecker's statement. She pressed the button on the answering machine so that it would automatically pick up. A business card lay on the counter, blank except for Leidecker's name in large black letters and a phone number. She picked it up and crumpled it in her hand.

Upstairs in the guest room, she kicked off her sandals and crawled under the comforter. Her head touched the pillow and she closed her eyes. Sleep dulled the edges of her emotions, and she gratefully surrendered to the oblivion.

In her dream, Jenny was calling and waving her arms. The bracelet on her wrist glittered with the movement. The guardian angel was clearly visible. The charm grew larger, until it was life-size. She couldn't see Jenny anymore. Only the angel.

The angel's arms were spread apart. Reaching out to her. The wings fluttered then began to beat the air with frantic strokes. The face of the angel grew dark and menacing. Kate tried to run but her feet kept sliding on the surface of the ground. She looked back over her shoulder.

Huge wings blotted out the light from the sun. The angel's flowing draperies changed from light to dark. The black-robed figure was gaining on her. A wall rose up before her, blocking her way. She whirled to face her pursuer, seeing the skull-like face of death.

The death angel loomed over her and she woke.

She lay under the comforter, shivering in reaction to the dream. Then she remembered Leidecker's visit.

It wasn't as if she was surprised that the police had signed off on the case. She had been expecting it. The newspaper articles had indicated a lack of movement on the case. It was the announcement that Richard's death was being called a suicide that really hurt. It was tantamount to a judgment of guilt.

It was a convenient verdict to a case that had no conclusion.

She must have dozed because when she woke again the morning light was streaming in the window. She squinted to focus on the face of the clock on the dresser.

Eight o'clock! She bolted upright. Good Lord! Leidecker'd left about seven-thirty. She'd slept for close to thirteen hours.

She showered and made the bed, finding Leidecker's business card among the bedclothes. She propped it against the phone beside her bed. Maybe when she was less angry with him, she could call him for updates on the investigation. At least that way he wouldn't be able to forget it.

Downstairs, the light on the answering machine blinked insistently. She listened to the messages. Some were hang ups, but the others were from reporters wanting to know if she could be reached for comment on Chief Leidecker's statement.

She was just rewinding the tape when the phone rang and without thinking she raised it to her ear, relieved when she heard Mike's voice on the other end.

"I was just going to leave a message on the answering machine. How come you're home? I thought you were a working woman these days."

"I am. Or at least I was," she amended.

"Oh?"

"It's a long story that can wait for another time. How are you? How was the convention?"

"Good. I just got back yesterday. L.A. was cooler than this. It's stinking hot outside. The air's so heavy with humidity that it'll add at least five strokes to my golf game." Mike snorted in annoyance. "I called to see if you wanted to have dinner with me tonight."

She hesitated, wondering if he too wanted to discuss the police statement. "Not tonight. I'm afraid I wouldn't be good company."

"Studies have shown that people don't eat healthy meals alone. They eat junk food."

"I'll thaw some pork chops and fix a salad."

"Perfect. I love pork chops. I'll be there about seven."

Before Kate could respond, he had hung up the phone. "Presumptuous bastard!" she muttered.

She supposed she owed him a dinner. However, she was damned if she'd let him manipulate her. She opened the freezer and purposely pushed the pork chops to the back. Taking out a package of chicken breasts, she set them on the counter to thaw.

The storm had brought the humidity down, but it was still in the upper eighties when she got back from the grocery store. In the garden, she selected three yellow tea roses for the table. After setting them in a vase, she fixed herself a glass of iced tea, and returned to the deck.

A man was bending over the rose bushes. Kate caught back a cry of alarm when she recognized Ed Bushnell, one of the neighbors. She set her glass down on the glass-topped table. At the clink of glass against glass, Ed jerked upright and spun around.

"Oh, Kate. Y . . . you're home," he stammered. "My apologies for trespassing."

His face was red with embarrassment. He moved away from the rose bush as if he thought she might accuse him of trying to steal the blossoms.

"I'm glad you came over to look at my garden," she said. "I just poured some iced tea. Would you like a glass?"

Ed cast a guilty glance in the direction of his house and a flush pinked his cheeks. "Oh, please, don't go to any trouble."

"I'd enjoy the company," she called.

It was sad that people could live right down the street and yet be strangers, Kate thought as she got out another glass for tea. Marian had told her that Ed had once been the mayor of Pickard. It was hard to believe that such a mousy little man could have been a political force in the town. She doubted if she'd ever exchanged more than a word or two with him. As she carried the cold glass outside, she was surprised to see him still standing beside the roses. Picking up her own tea, she walked down the deck stairs and crossed to him.

Up close he appeared older and more frail than she remembered. He was stoop-shouldered with close-cropped white hair and Germanic features. Only when he smiled did she detect a slight twinkle in the quickly averted eyes. He reminded her of a henpecked Kris Kringle.

"Thank you," he said, as he accepted the glass. He took a slow sip and sighed. "It's very good."

"I made sun tea yesterday and added some mint from the garden."

"No wonder it tastes so refreshing." He took another drink then, without looking at her, turned his attention back to the flowers. "I've seen your garden when Mrs. Bushnell and I are out walking. I was curious about this white rose. I haven't seen one like it before."

"You know Marian Granger." Kate indicated the house next door and Ed nodded. "She gave it to us. It's a very old variety of cabbage rose. Would you like to take some home to Agnes?"

"No," he said shaking his head vigorously. If he had looked flustered earlier, he now appeared genuinely alarmed. "Mrs. Bushnell wouldn't approve."

Kate wondered if his wife didn't approve of roses or of Ed wandering around to other gardens. Agnes must keep him on a pretty short leash. Kate couldn't recall seeing Ed alone. He was always with Agnes. So much closeness must be claustrophobic. No wonder Ed had snuck off on his own.

"I don't know a lot about roses," Kate said, leaning over to smell one of the large blossoms. "I know this is the Unique Blanche because Marian told me, but the rest of the names I've forgotten. Do you have roses?"

"Only one or two. But mine don't bloom this early."

"I'm not a patient gardener. I chose these because I wanted flowers early in the spring and late into the fall."

"I have always loved beautiful things." Moving along the row, he stopped to admire each bush but seemed especially taken by the yellow roses. His hand tremors lessened as he cupped a dainty bud in his palm. "Like sunshine. So beautiful. But soon it will die."

His voice was pitched so low that Kate could barely make out the words. She was uncomfortable with the note of sadness in his voice and struggled to think of something to say.

"I'm glad you like them. You're welcome to stop by at any time to see the garden," she said.

"Thank you. I'd like to if it wouldn't be a bother."

"None at all." Kate smiled as he bobbed his head in response. "Would you like more tea?"

"No. No. I must be going. I shouldn't be here at all." Abruptly he thrust the glass at her and, without another word, hurried out of the garden.

What a strange man, she thought as she stared after the departing figure. She was ashamed to admit she was glad he was gone. His sudden appearance had thrown her off balance, and the longer she'd talked to him the more uneasy she had felt. Something about Ed Bushnell wasn't right.

Glancing down at her watch, she realized it was already five. The thought of a shower made her hurry into the house. Afterwards, she put on a white blouse with a blue chambray skirt and white sandals.

It had been a long time since she'd fixed a real dinner.

All too often she made a salad or heated soup, or skipped dinner entirely. The grief counselor had suggested having a small glass of wine to help her relax during the lonely evening hours. When one glass increased to two and then three, Kate decided it was time to go back to iced tea.

Knowing Mike's schedule, she had planned a simple dinner that didn't require split-second timing. He was almost always late. He usually stopped off at the hospital for a last minute check on his patients. It was this personalized care that made him such a good doctor. No wonder he'd never been able to sustain a long relationship, she thought. Any woman would resent coming second to his medical practice.

Kate suspected that Chessy was the latest casualty.

Mike hadn't mentioned her name at all for several weeks. Kate heard from Mike almost daily. He stopped by a couple times a week. When she commented that she was able to stand on her own two feet, he replied that Richard would want him to look after her. She hoped his preoccupation with her situation hadn't been responsible for the breakup.

Kate had to admit she'd missed Mike while he was in L.A. She hoped she wasn't getting too used to having him around. Since Richard's disappearance, she'd done her best to get on with her life. And Mike was just a temporary part of it.

Opening the package of rice, she checked the directions and set everything in readiness on the counter. She looked around the room, checking to see if there was anything else she could do before Mike arrived. She washed off the counter, picked up the empty rice box, and dropped it into the wastebasket.

ButterSkots. The plaid logo from the candy wrappers caught her eye.

What a bizarre coincidence that Joseph Garvey had the same candy that was found in Jenny's pocket after she died. Staring down at the wrappers, goose bumps broke out on her arms and she hugged herself as a chill rippled through her. She pictured Garvey as she had last seen him during the horrible confrontation at his office. The fury on his face was imprinted on her mind, and it frightened her. He had looked as if he wanted to kill her.

The idea was ludicrous. She might dislike Garvey on a personal level, but that hardly made him a killer. The man might be an overbearing control freak, but he was a respected lawyer, and an active member of the community. He was the assistant mayor of Pickard, a member of the school board, and a generous sponsor of several charity events.

Leidecker's words came back to her as if he were in the room. "Good people can do bad things."

What about the ButterSkots?

Could she possibly be thinking that Garvey was somehow involved in Jenny's murder on the basis of a handful of candy wrappers? She could imagine Leidecker's expression. He'd think she was crazy.

Maybe she was. She had to get a grip on herself.

Aside from the candy wrappers, was there a shred of evidence that tied Garvey to the crime?

It was inconceivable that Jenny would have gone anywhere with Garvey. She would have had absolutely no reason to trust him.

Kate rubbed her forehead trying to remember what else Carl had reported from the witness who had seen Jenny on the day she was killed. He'd given Richard a copy of the interview. She supposed it was still in the studio where Richard kept everything concerning Jenny's death.

Before she could reconsider, Kate left the kitchen, walking purposely through the living room to Richard's studio. The hinges of the door squeaked as she opened the door and stepped into the room. The draperies were drawn and in the early evening light the room was filled with shadows. And memories.

The easel still held the covered canvas that was going to be Kate's anniversary present. She wondered if Richard had finished the picture, and if she'd ever be brave enough to look beneath the shrouding cloth. She had seen the original sketches. It was a portrait of Kate sitting beneath the flowering crabapple in the backyard. Beside her, Jenny was sleeping, head resting against Kate's knee.

She turned away from the easel and looked around the room, searching for the box where Richard kept all the papers concerning the investigation. She spotted it beneath the drafting table. With only a momentary hesitation, she lifted it and carried it back to the family room.

Opening the top, she sat motionless on the couch, staring into the box. It was only half full of papers. How could such a small amount of paperwork represent the death of a child? It was such an enormous crime that it seemed to Kate there should be boxes that would reach to the ceiling.

Gritting her teeth, she picked up the first piece of paper.

It was the list she and Richard had drawn up, giving the names of friends, neighbors, business associates, and anyone else they came into contact with regularly. She started to look through the list, then realized she'd never get to the eyewitness report if she read everything. Taking out each packet of papers, she noted the contents and set it aside. About halfway down, she found the interview with Mrs. Doutt.

Now that she'd found what she was looking for, she felt foolish.

The whole idea seemed even more ridiculous than before. She reached down to replace everything then stopped. She might as well look at the interview with Mrs. Doutt. If she didn't, she'd always wonder about Garvey.

She scanned the information, but couldn't find anything that might point to Garvey specifically. Dark hair, suit or sport coat, dark two-door car. The description was so vague, it could fit anyone. Reading to the end, she was disappointed. There was nothing new, except she'd forgotten the car had Pickard Federal license plates.

The police had run a computer printout of every car in the state with PF on the license plate. She remembered Richard saying the list read like the Pickard phone book. He'd been angry because even with this list, the police had not come up with a likely suspect.

Looking down into the box she could see the long computer sheets. She reached in and pulled out the thick stack of papers. There were five columns on the top of each page: license number, make and color of car, owner's address, and owner's name.

Kate fanned the pages. It would have been a monumental task to check everyone on the list. She began to read the entries. Page after page of numbers and names.

In the middle of the fifth page, she stopped. Her finger traced the black letters on the white page: PF 7831. Lexus. Black. 419 Shell Lane, Pickard, Illinois. Joseph Edward Garvey.

# TWENTY-ONE

"PF 7831. JOSEPH EDWARD GARVEY." Kate read the words aloud, her voice just above a whisper.

She had been hoping to disprove her irrational fixation on Garvey. Instead, she'd found another piece of evidence that led to him. She ran the tips of her fingers along the computer entry, hoping her tactile sense would pick up some extrasensory vibrations.

The ring of the doorbell startled her back to the present. She didn't know how long she'd been sitting with the computer sheets spread across her knees. Quickly she folded the pages in half and dropped them into the open box. Her hands felt gritty, and she brushed them against her skirt as she hurried into the front hall just as the doorbell rang again.

She'd have to talk to Mike about using his key again. He'd always been free to come and go. Over the years, she'd gotten used to him wandering in whenever he was passing and saw the lights on. Since Richard's disappearance, he'd become more formal, ringing the doorbell and waiting for her to let him in. So much had changed, she thought, sighing as she opened the door.

"I know I'm late," Mike said, "but as a peace offering I brought wine. The guy in the liquor store said it would be perfect with pork."

He waved a bottle of white wine at her.

"We're not having pork," she said. As he backed away in mock horror, she grabbed the sleeve of his suit jacket. "Get in here before all the air-conditioning gets out."

He came in shedding his jacket and tossing it with unerring accuracy onto the newel post. His voice boomed, filling the empty spaces of the house, reminding her of how full of life he was. A wave of nostalgia hit her but she pushed it away, determined to enjoy the evening.

"What happened to all the reporters? I was sure I'd have to come through Marian's hedges again."

"I think the heat got to them. After several hours, even Leidecker's statement is old news."

"I told you Leidecker couldn't be trusted. He was so anxious to make the police department look good, he leaped at the chance to pin everything on Richard."

Kate held up her hand to stem further discussion. "How's a drink sound?"

"Like a call to paradise."

He followed her, pulling off his tie and tossing it on the back of a kitchen chair. He took over the bartending, muttering over the proportions of his martini and the inadequacies of the olives.

"Generic olives? Ye gods! Who'd have thought you'd have such little imagination? Next time I'll bring my own brand." He mixed a screwdriver for Kate and handed it to her before picking up his own glass. He took a tentative sip, eyes squinting as he evaluated the first taste. "Ah. The world is a better place since the invention of gin. Less sober, but definitely better."

"You told me you went out to L.A. for a conference. Must have been on the high seas. Your nose is peeling."

"I ducked out for a day of deep-sea fishing." Gingerly, he touched his nose. "I thought only lifeguards put that white gunk on their noses. Next time I'll be smarter."

"Aside from the burn, did you catch anything?"

"Nothing to write home about. I should have played golf."

Kate took a sip of her drink, then opened the oven door to check on the chicken. Mike peeked over her shoulder, sniffing appreciatively.

"Sit and relax while I get the rice started."

Kate picked up the recipe card as he left the room. After setting the casserole in the oven, she went out to the family room. Mike was standing beside the couch, staring down at the pile of papers on the floor.

"What's all this?"

"It's just some things I was looking through."

For some reason she felt as if she'd been caught doing something illegal. She hurried over, bending down to scoop up the loose papers and dump them into the box.

"I saw what it was, Kate. It's the box of reports from Richard's studio. He showed them to me after Jenny died."

"Oh."

"Oh, indeed." He took a sip of his martini, eyeing her over the rim of the glass. "What's up?"

"I was doing some cleaning."

"I think there's a little more to it than cleaning," he said. His voice was indulgent. "Why don't we sit down, and you can tell me why you've been going through all this?" He waved his hand in the direction of the box.

Without argument, Kate sat down on the edge of the couch, gripping her hands together in her lap. Her idea was so bizarre that she was embarrassed to even mention it. She suspected Mike would have the same reaction that Leidecker would. He'd think she'd lost her mind.

Mike sat down in the easy chair kitty-corner to her. "Well?"

She shook her head.

"Look, Kate, I'm only concerned for your welfare. Although you've been putting on a good front, I know inside you're still dealing with some pretty heavy issues. I wonder if it's a good idea to go through this stuff right now. Couldn't it wait for awhile?"

"No," she said, staring down at her lap. "I had to check something."

"I'm sure you have questions," he said. He set his drink down, and reached out to cover her hands with one of his. "It's a normal reaction after a death. Wait for a little longer when you've recovered more of your equilibrium. What could possibly be so important that you need to check on it today?"

"I thought I found a clue."

Her words startled her as much as they did Mike. His hand jerked away from her as if he'd been scalded.

"A clue? To what?"

"To Jenny's killer?"

Mike was staring at her as if she had taken leave of her senses. He reached for the glass that he'd set on the table and took a sizable swallow of the drink.

"You're kidding, right?"

His disbelief made her defensive. "I don't know for sure, but today I thought I might have come up with a possible suspect."

"A suspect. I see. Why don't you start from the beginning? Just tell me what happened to lead you to this —"

"Insanity?" she suggested.

"I'll be the judge of that." Mike leaned back, his face impassive. "Let's hear it."

Kate's mouth was dry and she licked her lips before she started to speak. At first she stumbled over the words, but each succeeding sentence came easier. She told him about the assignment at Garvey & Associates, and then spent some time trying to convey her impressions of Joseph Garvey.

She watched Mike as she told about finding the candy wrappers. He raised an eyebrow in surprise, but didn't interrupt. She tried to keep her voice matter-of-fact as she described Garvey's anger when he found her in his office. Finally she told him how she'd checked the computer printout and found Garvey's name. Even to her ears the whole story sounded idiotic.

Mike didn't speak immediately. He sat very still, staring down into his glass as if it held the answer to all the questions in the universe.

"It's not much," she said.

"No, it's not." He drained his glass, then set it on the table. He leaned forward and rested his elbows on his knees. He held a hand out, fingers splayed, but he did not touch her. "Two coincidences and a quantum leap."

"I know what you're thinking, and I'm not losing my mind."

He shook his head.

"I don't think you're crazy. I believe you found the wrappers and

Garvey's name on the computer list. I'll admit that his behavior makes him sound like a real asshole, but that's a far cry from being a murderer."

"I said, I thought he was capable of murder."

"Perhaps if I'd been there I'd think so too, but all I can deal with are the facts. I don't think even Leidecker would arrest Joseph Garvey for eating butterscotch and having a dark, two-door car with PF plates. Everyone we know has those plates. Richard had them. I've got them. I bet even that bastard Leidecker has them!"

Kate could feel hot color burning her cheeks.

"I know it sounds stupid, but I can't tell you how strong a feeling I have about the man." She grabbed her skirt in both hands, crushing the fabric in frustration.

"Do you really understand what you're saying, Kate? Listen to yourself. Are you saying that Garvey is some kind of psycho killer?" Mike's voice rose on the last word.

"Yes. I mean, no. Damn it, Mike, I don't know."

"Holy God, Kate! The whole thing's preposterous. Aside from the lack of any hard evidence, coincidences like this don't happen. It's a bit of a stretch to think you'd end up working for the man responsible for Jenny's murder. Can you imagine the odds of that happening?"

"I don't give a damn about the odds!" she cried. "All I care about is that my child is dead, and her murderer has not been brought to justice!"

Anger washed through her, and she jumped to her feet. She moved across the room to the patio doors and stared out at the back-yard bathed in the reddish-gold light that presaged the setting of the sun. Aware of Mike's silence, she could feel the muscles in her back tighten.

Mike shuffled his feet and she turned to face him, her back to the windows, chin raised in defiance. She was surprised that his expression was a mixture of confusion and apology.

"I'm sorry I barked at you." He rubbed his hands over his face then massaged the back of his neck. "We'll put my behavior down to sheer surprise and a real concern for you. If I try to make nice, will you come back and sit down?"

She did as he asked, sitting down on the edge of the couch.

"Don't be pissed at me. You've had all day to think about this, so don't expect me to leap right into the fray without showing the slightest bit of caution."

He waited while she considered his words. Hearing the sincerity in his voice, her muscles began to relax.

"I'm sorry too," she said. "My emotions still swing pretty dramatically."

Mike's mouth widened in a grin; part relief, part approval. "Let's call a truce. I definitely need another drink, some dinner, and a chance to digest some of what you've said. Okay?"

"Deal," she said.

He followed her into the kitchen, making another martini while she put the chicken and rice on the table and tossed the salad.

She waved him to a chair, then poured a glass of iced tea. She was reminded of all the other times Mike had eaten in the kitchen with her and Richard and Jenny. Pushing the memories away, she concentrated on her dinner.

He ate with great gusto. He'd told her once he'd never been able to get enough to eat when he was a kid. She could imagine him as a big awkward teenager with an endless capacity for food. It was a treat cooking for him because he ate everything with visible pleasure. Only when he was reaching for a second helping of chicken, did he look up and grin sheepishly.

"So I'm a boor." He shrugged. "What can I say? This is terrific and I was starving."

"I'm glad you're enjoying it."

The dinner continued in silence. Kate was relaxed, feeling no pressure to make conversation. She respected Mike's need to think over what she'd told him. However, by the time he pushed his plate away and folded his napkin, she had to admit she was getting anxious to hear his comments.

He stared across the table, eyebrows lowered in a frown. "Frankly, despite what you've told me, I'm having trouble accepting your theory." When she started to speak, he held up his hand. "Now don't get all defensive on me. I'm not saying you're wrong. All I'm saying is that

I can't accept the basic premise that Joseph Garvey murdered Jenny."

"I know that this whole thing sounds utterly impossible. But if you'd seen Garvey yesterday you'd have no doubt in your mind. There is something wrong with the man. I don't know how else to explain it, except to tell you that the man frightens me."

"That doesn't make him a killer."

She gritted her teeth at the reasonable words. She pushed her chair back and took a deep breath.

"I never asked you this, Mike, but now I have to." She swallowed convulsively. "Do you think Richard killed Jenny?"

He didn't speak immediately. He moved his chair away from the table, stretching out his long legs. With a sigh, he sat up straight, turning his body to face her.

"It's strange, but I've purposely not asked myself that question. I think there's a little part of me that's afraid to know the answer."

"I'm asking you, Mike. Just me."

He tilted his head on the side, his eyes searching hers. Finally he said, "I don't think Richard killed Jenny."

Just hearing him say the words lifted a weight from Kate's heart. Quick tears came to her eyes and she blinked rapidly to keep them from overflowing.

"I don't think so either," she said, voice a little shaky. "And if he didn't, someone else did. Which brings me back to my original premise. I realize it could be some total stranger but it could also be someone right here in Pickard. So why couldn't that person be Joseph Garvey?"

A pause. A grimace.

"God, Kate! You are one stubborn woman." He stared at her, shaking his head in annoyance. "All right. Just for argument's sake, assume I accept your wild theory. What do we do about it? Go to the police and tell them that Joseph Garvey's the murderer they're looking for?"

"No. They'd never believe me." Kate's answer was almost a moan.

"Aside from being abusive to his office staff, do you know anything about Garvey?"

"Not really," she admitted.

"Well, I do." At her look of surprise, he wiggled his eyebrows. "Honest to God, Kate, that's why I'm having so much trouble buying this. He may be an impressive lawyer, but the man's a cipher. His wife, Lisa, wears the pants in the family, which may explain why he's so nasty to his staff."

"Maybe. Maybe not. Murderers can be perfectly ordinary people. I remember when I went to look at the pictures at the police station, I was frightened that I'd see the face of the killer on the screen. Afterward it dawned on me that I'd been looking for some long-haired, unshaven, squinty-eyed monster. An easily spotted deviate."

She heard Mike let out his breath in a slow, steady stream.

"I could never understand why anyone would suspect Richard," she said. "I still don't. The thing is, if people could look at him and see a killer, then the normality of life is not a standard to gauge a person's potential for evil."

Mike sighed. "You're right. We all want the bad guy to look like a monster. If evil doesn't wear a strange face, then we might all have the potential for evil. I guess I can concede that point. But you still don't have any proof that Garvey's a killer."

"I know I don't have enough evidence to take to the police," Kate said, "but I was considering checking up on Garvey. It sounds stupid, but I might be able to find out something that could be helpful."

"This isn't like Colonel Garvey in the library with the hatchet. You're talking murder, and murder's definitely not a game." Mike's frustration was clear. "Sure you could go to the library and look up Garvey in the newspaper files. While you're at it, you could check into everyone in town with the PF plates?"

He stared at her for a long time before continuing. "Much as I hate to encourage your delusions, I can see you need to get this out of your system."

"I know you're just trying to humor me and I really appreciate it."

"Believe me, Kate, I'm not humoring you." His expression was serious, eyes flinty. "Jenny was my godchild. If there's the slightest possibility that Garvey was involved in her death, I'll kill the bastard myself."

Despite a jolt of fear at his words, she felt relieved that she'd finally be doing something active to find Jenny's murderer. She'd begin to check out not only Garvey but also everyone she knew on the license plate list. Maybe just asking questions would elicit new information that might help Leidecker in his investigation. What could it hurt?

Carl frowned at the clock on the squad room wall. It was ten after nine, and Tony still wasn't back. How the hell long did it take to measure skid marks at the scene of an accident?

He picked up the phone and punched Bea's extension. "Did Tony understand that I wanted to see him during this calendar year?" he asked.

"Yes, Carl. It's only been thirty minutes since I called him."

He hung up. He hated waiting. Picking up the mug on his desk, he took a swallow and grimaced at the mouthful of cold, bitter coffee. He pushed his chair back, pulled open his office door and, avoiding Bea's amused glance, stomped down the hall to the kitchen. The Pyrex container held a half cup of gritty coffee.

He snatched the Pyrex pot off the hot plate and rinsed it out in the sink. He filled it to the top with cold water. He flipped open the top of the coffee maker and pulled out the old filter. It caught on the edge, spilling coffee grounds onto the counter. Ignoring the mess, he dumped the rest of the grounds in the wastebasket. He started pouring in the water, but it ran right out the bottom, hissing and burping as it hit the hot plate.

"Dammit!" Still holding the half empty coffee pot, he pulled open the door and bellowed down the hall. "Bea! Get in here!"

Water sloshed on his shoes as he turned back to the coffee maker. A few more drops of water fell, bubbling and popping in the heat. Carl glared.

"What now?" Bea asked.

"That machine hates me."

Bea snorted. "Honestly, Carl, it's simple enough. Even Amy can make coffee, and she has to write out the alphabet in order to do the filing. You forgot to turn it off."

In no time at all she had a new pot of coffee brewing and she'd cleaned up the mess on the counter.

"Since you came in this morning, you've been a real prick." She stared at him and he shrugged. "If it's work related, maybe it's something I can help you with. If it's personal and you don't want to talk about it, I'll stay out of your face."

"It's the Warner case."

"I thought as much." She poured him a mug and handed it to him. "Try this."

Carl breathed in the coffee vapors. He took a tentative sip. It was hot. And it was good.

"That's terrific, Bea. I really appreciate it."

Back in his office, Carl waved Bea to a chair, but he was still too restless to sit down. He drank more of the coffee and with each sip felt less frazzled.

"I know you weren't thrilled about making the statement to the press about Richard Warner," she said. "I assume Mayor Etzel wanted it done."

"Actually he wanted me to say the case was closed. I wouldn't do that. So we compromised." He paced over to the windows and then back again. "I hate leaving a case dangling like this."

"I know you, Carl. You're holding something back. Does it have some bearing on the case?"

"I stopped over to talk to Kate Warner yesterday. I figured the statement would be another blow for her to handle, and I didn't want her to hear it on the news."

"She had to have been expecting it."

"It doesn't make it any easier."

"No. I don't suppose so." She waited but when he didn't continue, she prodded. "And?"

Carl glared at her over the rim of his mug. He came around the desk and sat on the corner. He took a last sip then set the mug down, and reached into his pocket.

"She took it pretty well. She was upset though and at one point threw a wet towel across the room. It hit the wastebasket that fell against the wall and some trash fell out. I went over to straighten things up. I found this."

Carl pulled his hand out of his pocket. He opened his fingers to show Bea the cellophane wrapper.

"Where do you suppose Kate got the ButterSkots?"

# Twenty-two

KATE SQUINTED AT THE SCREEN, eyebrows bunched as she turned the crank of the microfilm machine and searched for the correct entry. The filmed pages whizzed by in a blur of black and white. Occasionally she stopped to check the date.

She ran her finger down her notes. January 16, page 6. She found the correct page of the newspaper and adjusted the focus. It was an article on a fund-raiser for Pickard General two years earlier. The chair-couple was Lisa and Joseph Garvey. She scanned the article, but found nothing of particular interest.

She had decided to begin her background check of "suspects" at the library. Since Garvey was the prime target of her investigations, she had started with him. It was tedious work looking up each of the references to either Joseph or Lisa Garvey in the local media. Her eyes burned from reading text on the computer monitors and the microfilm screen.

Crossing out the last entry on the yellow, lined paper, she crumpled it up, and tossed it in the wastebasket.

It was surprising how much information she had been able to find. Unfortunately, her hard work had provided a skeletal picture of Garvey that meshed poorly with the suspicions she had.

According to everything she had found so far, Joseph Garvey was a respected lawyer, model citizen, faithful husband, and good father. A prince among men, Kate thought, as she flexed her knees and then her ankles.

Had she been wrong about Garvey?

She honestly didn't know. Starting at the front of the notebook, she leafed through the pages, reading the details of Garvey's life that she'd been able to locate.

He'd been born in Kenilworth, an ultra-wealthy suburb of Chicago. His father owned and operated a chemical company, which had profited handsomely during the Vietnam War and continued to prosper. His mother, an outspoken advocate of equal rights for women, was a judge. Garvey was the oldest of three children. His sister had married into an old-moneyed family from the North Shore. His brother worked in the family business.

Garvey had gone to all the right private schools. She'd found a reference to a party given for him on his graduation from Harvard Law School. After a stint in Atlanta with Farrington, Beard & Kruesi, he moved back to the Chicago area. He worked for eight years at Ginthner, Case, Seyer and Vlach, then went out on his own. Garvey & Associates had been in business for fourteen years.

Dry references that gave little insight into the man's character.

On the personal side, his life appeared equally blameless. During his last year in law school, he married Lisa Bowers. They'd been married for twenty-eight years. The Garveys had two sons. Mark was a lawyer, and Taylor, five years younger, was an artist slash actor.

Kate had looked at dozens of pictures from the *Pickard Advocate*. The Garveys appeared to be favorite subjects. Lisa was more heavily committed to the social scene. She was on several boards, not just a token, but also an active member. The Pickard Fine Arts Council and Pickard General Hospital were major recipients of contributions and volunteer help from Lisa. And to give Garvey credit, he was at her side in all the pictures, apparently proud of his wife's successes.

"Oh rats," Kate muttered, glaring at the picture of Garvey and Lisa at the benefit for the Youth Campus. "Mike'll never believe me now."

Everything she'd gathered showed Garvey in a positive light. The only information she had uncovered that might prove of interest was that two weeks prior to Jenny's death, Joseph Garvey had participated in a career day event at St. Madelaine's. Kate had always questioned whether Jenny would get in the car with a stranger. However, if

Garvey had been familiar from his visit to the school, Jenny might have seen him as someone in authority she could trust.

Aside from the school visit info, the sum total of two days work was exactly zero. All she had to show for her labors was some unexciting biographical data, and a handful of pictures of a smiling Lisa in various sequined gowns on the arm of a tuxedoed Garvey. And she'd only begun to look up some of the other people on the list.

"Damn it!" she said as she stood up and gathered her things.

"Is that meant for me?"

Carl Leidecker's sudden appearance in the study alcove startled Kate. She gave a small squeak of fright, which she quickly muffled with a hand over her mouth.

"I'm sorry," he apologized. "I thought you were talking to me, but I couldn't hear what you said."

"I was swearing."

Now it was Kate's turn to be embarrassed. She hadn't meant to be offensive. When she looked up at him however, it seemed that her blunt reply amused him.

"A lot of people swear when they see me," he said. He shifted the books under his arm. "But they're usually doing something they shouldn't be."

"How are you?" She was flustered, but she managed to get the words out without stumbling.

"Fine, thanks. And you?" Before she could respond he stepped closer, staring down at her. "I mean it. Is everything all right with you?"

"I'm okay. I'm sorry you were the target of my anger the other day. The frustration gets to me occasionally."

"I'm not sure you heard all that I said on Wednesday. The case isn't really closed. We won't have the same task force working on it as we had two months ago but it's still an active investigation."

"I appreciate that."

His eyes searched her face. She wanted to turn away, but refused to let him intimidate her. She held her ground.

"Everyone sees things through a cloud of their own prejudices and agendas," Carl said. "We make judgments based on our own viewpoint."

"That's human nature."

"But sometimes the viewpoint is wrong."

"In this case, you were wrong about Richard," she said.

"I dealt with the information I had."

He halted, as if waiting for some reaction. Suddenly the alcove seemed far removed from the rest of the library but before Kate could leave, Carl began speaking again.

"I will personally be in charge of the investigation. Sometimes one individual can get a better overall picture. If I had all the facts, I might be able to discover who killed your daughter." He reached toward her, but when she stiffened he withdrew his hand. "What I'm trying to say is that because of your loyalty, I think you've withheld information. You can't hurt either Richard or Jenny by telling me what you know."

"I don't know anything, Carl."

Afraid he would read too much in her eyes, Kate bent her head, hiding behind a veil of hair.

"Sometimes knowledge can be dangerous. And your input could be important."

"Please, Carl, I don't want to talk about it anymore," she said. Nodding her head in dismissal, she stepped around him.

"Just think about it, Kate."

His words followed her as she hurried away, but she did not respond. She was upset by her meeting with Leidecker. His attitude was different than it had been several days earlier. It wasn't the words so much as the expression on his face and the tone of his voice. He sounded as if he were warning her.

She wished she knew if Leidecker could be trusted. No matter what Mike and her own instincts told her, for a moment while she was talking to him in the alcove, she had almost told him her suspicions about Garvey.

On second thought, it was just as well that she hadn't. More and more she was beginning to wonder if she were losing her grip on reality. Mike could be right. Garvey might just be an ordinary asshole. Maybe tonight she'd get some answers.

She was a bit apprehensive about the evening ahead. Mike had called yesterday to invite her to an awards dinner at the Pickard Country Club to raise funds for the Fine Arts Council.

"It's a low-key event with some speeches and no entertainment."

"I don't know," Kate had resisted.

"You'll have to start going out." His voice was understanding. "This would be a good place to start. Besides I've got an additional incentive. Joseph Garvey and his wife are the chaircouple."

"Oh." Kate felt a flutter in the pit of her stomach.

"I thought that might pique your interest. You should see the man in some other context than the office situation. If nothing else, it'll give your opinion some balance."

"You could be right."

"I've been trying to get you for the last couple days. You're not avoiding me?"

"No. I've been spending a lot of time at the library."

There was an ominous silence on the line.

"The library?"

"I've been looking up things. You know. Checking on Garvey and the others."

"What others?"

Suddenly she felt defensive. "I just thought as long as I was spending time looking up Garvey, I might as well check on a few other people."

"Good Lord! Do you know how dangerous that could be?"

"I don't see that it's any more dangerous than looking up information on Joseph Garvey." Kate was annoyed. "I can't sit around doing nothing. For the first time since Jenny died, I feel like something I'm doing might be a help in finding her killer."

"I'm sorry, Kate," he said. "It's just that I'm worried about you."

"I'm sorry too," she conceded. "But I can't wait for Leidecker to come up with a solution. I have to actively do something or I'll go crazy."

"I understand that, but it's Leidecker's job to investigate. Not yours."

She pressed her lips together and made no comment.

"You're not going to give this up, are you?" he asked and she could hear the annoyance in his voice.

Mike had been a solid friend. For the support he'd given her, he deserved honesty.

"No. It's something I need to do. I'm sorry."

"You're a very stubborn woman, Kate." His words were not meant as a compliment. "I can't caution you enough to be careful. There are people out there who may be on the edge emotionally."

After a few less inflammatory comments, Mike had renewed his invitation to the Fine Arts dinner. She felt she had little choice except to agree. She hoped the concession would patch things up, and prove she wasn't always pigheaded.

Preparing for the evening, she wasn't sure it had been the right decision. She hadn't gone to a social event since Jenny's death. She felt very alone, and she missed Richard's companionship.

Aside from that, she was frightened about seeing Garvey again.

Eyeing her reflection, she wondered if there was any chance that he'd recognize her. She didn't think so. To all her temp assignments, she'd worn plain, matronly clothes to make her less noticeable. Tonight she'd chosen a sleeveless silk sheath with a sash belt. The light blue color accentuated her tan and the simple styling was youthful and very feminine.

She brushed her hair into soft curls and left it loose. She wore plain gold hoops and in the V-neck opening of her dress she wore the angel necklace. Staring into the mirror one last time, she touched the winged angel for luck.

*And don't break your neck*, she thought, as she navigated the stairs in her white sling backs. The doorbell rang and she glanced at her watch in surprise. Pulling the door open, she said, "Did the hospital burn down? I've never known you to be on time."

Mike stood in the doorway, his expression so unsettling that Kate glanced over her shoulder expecting to see something ominous behind her in the hall. Turning back to Mike, she was relieved to see a smile appearing on his face.

"For a moment, I thought I'd been transported back in time," he said, chuckling as he entered the house. "It's been a long time since I've seen you all dressed up."

Checking the patio doors and turning out some of the lights, she locked the front door and let Mike settle her in the front seat of his car.

He seemed to sense how nervous she was because he spent the drive telling her about the latest scandal at the hospital. The head of the anesthesiology department had been caught with one of the nurses in the X-ray processing room.

"He had to be pretty desperate to do it on top of a metal desk. For God's sake, it's a hospital! It was a slow week and there were at least eight rooms that were empty." Mike flashed her a grin. "Maybe I'm getting old. Comfort over passion any day."

Kate was still chuckling as they drew up at the front door of the Pickard Country Club. The dinner was being held in the dining room that ran across the back of the elegant old clubhouse. Beyond the wall of windows was the golf course, wide maple-lined fairways and manicured greens, a lush backdrop in the early evening light.

She nodded to people she knew as Mike steered her toward the bar. He took a sip of his martini as she raised a glass of wine to her lips. Mike touched her elbow and she followed him to a corner where they could survey the room. Because of his height, he was able to locate Garvey after one sweep of the crowd.

"I've got him." He leaned over, speaking quietly into Kate's ear. "Just to the right of the dais. See the hot redhead in the clingy black dress? Lordy. Lordy! Check that cleavage. Definitely implants. Looks like Wes Upton's work. A good boob man, but he tends to go for the bigger cup size. Find her, and then Garvey's in the group to her right."

Mike's humorous aside helped to ease Kate's tension. She found the redhead then the group on the right. She scanned the men's faces, jumping in reaction to her first look at Garvey. Mike squeezed her shoulder, leaving his hand there as if to reassure her of his presence.

Perhaps she had been expecting to see an ogre or monster because she had a sense of disappointment at the ordinariness of Joseph Garvey. She knew it was a cliché, but in his tuxedo with his stocky build he looked exactly like a penguin. Almost as if he'd read her thoughts, Mike patted her shoulder.

"He makes a lousy bogeyman," he said.

"Yes," she admitted.

Two people joined the group. She watched as Garvey was introduced. His mouth widened into a friendly smile.

"He certainly isn't very threatening. Tonight he just seems" — she shrugged. — "normal."

"Now you can understand why I've had so much trouble imagining him as some sort of homicidal maniac. I don't know him well, but he's always struck me as fairly harmless." He was silent for several minutes, then asked, "How'd you make out at the library?"

"I was doing fine until I ran into Leidecker," she said, earning a sharp glance.

"Leidecker? Was he looking for you?"

She shook her head. "Just bad luck."

"What did he have to say?"

"Not much." She stared down at her wine. "I'm not comfortable around Leidecker. Unconsciously, I blame him for what happened to Richard."

Harumphing, Mike said, "Don't feel bad. I have much the same reaction."

"He says the case isn't really closed."

Mike leaned toward her. "Be careful of that man, Kate. I've told you before I don't trust him. No matter what you think, he's not your friend."

Even though Kate herself had questioned Leidecker's motives, she felt the need to defend him. "I think you're being too hard on him. Carl's an honest man. Although I may have accused him of having a personal vendetta against Richard, I don't think he did."

"Maybe." His face was far from encouraging. "I'm just asking you to be careful around him."

"I will."

She was relieved when he dropped the subject, and led her over to their table and introduced the people they'd be sitting with. Members of the Fine Arts Council, she didn't know any of them. Mike talked easily to them, letting Kate fade into the background. She leaned back and sipped her wine, surveying the room.

She recognized Nate Nathanson cutting through the crowd. Mike had told her that he was one of the award recipients. She was pleased. She'd always been impressed with his enthusiastic coaching of Jenny's soccer team. The emphasis had been on fun rather than competition. She smiled at the look of surprise when he spotted her. He hurried around the table to greet her.

"How good to see you, Kate. How are you?" he asked, genuine concern in his voice.

"Fine. Every day a little better," she responded vaguely. "And you?"

"Good. Good. Very good."

He shook her hand in rhythm to his words, then stared at her as if unsure of what to say next. Since Jenny's death, Kate had encountered this reaction before and knew it would be up to her to take the initiative in the conversation. Gently she pulled her hand away, nervously fingering the angel charm on her necklace.

"Congratulations on your award, Nate. Mike told me about your work with the children's concert series. I'm ashamed to say I didn't realize that was your pet project."

"Yes." He beamed at her words. "I grew up in a small town and as a kid loved parades and band performances. Just a way of passing on my own fantasies."

"Well, it's a real plus for Pickard. The summer concerts in the park have been a big success. Must be a real labor of love."

He laughed self-consciously. "You've hit it on the head. And, of course, the kids are a great joy to work with."

"Congrats, Nate." Mike stood up and slapped him on the back. "You've done a fine job. Everyone on the council's really pleased with your award."

"I'm overwhelmed by all the praise." Nate inched away, putting some distance between himself and Mike's solid presence. "I enjoy everything I'm doing, so I feel sort of like a hypocrite."

The overhead chandeliers blinked.

"Thank God," Mike said. "I thought they'd never serve dinner. I don't know about you two, but I'm starving."

"You have more to fill up than we do," Nate said. With a wink, he headed for the dais.

"Should I be insulted?" Mike asked, glaring after the slender young man. "Scrawny guys like that are always making jokes. Little twerp."

Kate ate her dinner, surprised to discover that she actually was hungry. She let the conversation swirl around her, taking little part in it. By turning her head slightly, she was able to observe Garvey, seated on the dais beside his wife.

She'd never met Lisa Garvey. She looked older than her husband, but that might have been an unfortunate trick of the lighting. She wore a short emerald green sequined dress that did little to disguise the broad hips and thickened waistline. Outwardly the Garveys appeared to be a contented couple, although Kate noticed that they rarely spoke to each other.

When dinner was over, Lisa gave a brief welcoming speech and then led into the awards section of the evening. The awards were distributed and thanks given. At the end Garvey stood up and thanked everyone for coming and made a straightforward pitch for contributions to the Fine Arts Council.

After the applause, Kate remained seated, trying to sort out her thoughts about Garvey. She wondered if she had been completely mistaken about him. Surrounded by the elegance of the room and the beautifully dressed people, he appeared quite civilized. At this point she didn't know what to think. She was so engrossed in her thoughts that she jumped when someone placed a hand on her shoulder.

"So sorry, darling girl," Christian Mayerling said. "Didn't mean to startle you."

"Please don't apologize, Chris," she said, standing up to kiss his cheek. "I was daydreaming."

"Well, it's a definite bonus finding you here. You look quite lovely."

Uncomfortable with the compliment, she changed the subject. "I didn't know you were involved with the Fine Arts Council."

"I'm not. Although occasionally I've come out to one of their benefits." He nodded toward the dais. "Lisa Garvey and I are on the board of directors for the Kitchie Home for Boys. She convinced me I ought to come to this. Now that I've had a chance to see you, I'm delighted that I agreed."

After chatting with her for a few minutes, Chris gave her a final kiss, and wandered off. Kate took the opportunity to check on some of the other guests. The Pickard politicians were out in full force. Mayor Etzel and his wife were talking to Lisa Garvey. Joseph Garvey had his back to her, speaking to another group. Kate recognized several people as her eyes skimmed across the faces until suddenly she was staring at Carl Leidecker.

His presence in such close proximity to Garvey startled her. She didn't know why she was so surprised. As the assistant mayor, Garvey would obviously be acquainted with the chief of police.

Watching Carl, Kate doubted if she'd ever seen him so relaxed. He was laughing at something Garvey had said, his head thrown back and his eyes crinkled with amusement. He had a nice face when he wasn't frowning, she thought.

As if her gaze were some sort of magnet, Carl looked up and she found herself staring into his dark eyes.

He acknowledged her glance with a slight nod of the head but made no move toward her. His expression was unreadable. He neither smiled nor frowned. She forced herself to look away.

Mike was easy to spot in a crowd. He was leaning over the busty redhead in the black dress, his gestures expansive, and his face alive with warmth.

Kate decided to walk around until he was finished checking out all the available women. She eased her way through the tables and out into the hall.

The air was cooler after the overcrowded dining room. She headed for the water fountain against the wall. Leaning over, she took several sips then stepped away from the fountain and collided with a solid wall of flesh.

"I'm so sorry," she managed to gasp out.

"Are you hurt? I didn't mean to —"

"Why hello." Kate stared into the brick-red face of Ed Bushnell. "Sorry for plowing into you."

"It was my fault. I'm so . . . so clumsy," he stammered.

His face was a mixture of confusion and embarrassment. Kate was very conscious of his eyes fixed on her bosom. She could feel the angel necklace rising and falling with each breath. She took a step backward.

"In this case it was my fault, Ed. I wasn't looking where I was going."

"You're not hurt, are you?" he asked. His eyes were now raised to hers and he blinked owlishly at her.

"No. Please don't worry. It was a nice evening, wasn't it?" She glanced around. "Is Agnes here, too?"

"Yes. She sent me to get the car."

As if suddenly reminded of an urgent mission, he whirled around and, without another word, made a dash for the main entrance. Kate stared after him, wondering if she was the one who made him nervous or if he was just a very odd man.

"Kate? Over here, dear."

She turned at the sound of the voice and, as if she had conjured up the woman, saw Agnes coming out of the dining room beside Grace Peterman, Kate's neighbor from across the street.

"Agnes. Grace. It's nice to see you," she said, smiling at the two women.

"Glad to see you're getting out socially." Grace spoke in her usual staccato fashion.

"Actually this is the first time. I decided it was a good cause."

"Everything going all right with you, dear? Anything I can do?"

"No, Grace. I'm fine. Really I am," Kate said, unwilling to get into a discussion of her life. "I've been meaning to call you. I was wondering if you'd share the recipe for that rhubarb coffee cake you sent over."

"She brought one for me when I had my gallbladder out," Agnes said. "It really is wonderful."

"Pleased you liked it," Grace said. "I'd be delighted to give you the recipe."

"Great," Kate said, then turned to Agnes. "I saw Ed a minute ago. I nearly ran him down at the drinking fountain."

"Oh dear. I suggested he bring the car around to the door, and he just up and raced off. I suppose we better get outside or he'll start to fuss. He's such an impatient man." Agnes shook her head in exasperation.

Kate gave each of the women a hug and they bustled out the doors to the main entrance. Despite her words about Ed being impatient, Kate suspected it was Agnes who kept him in line. That might explain why Ed had been in such a hurry to get away.

Maybe she was becoming paranoid, seeing menace in everyone she met. All evening she'd had the sensation she was being watched.

Ever since Jenny's death, she had been under scrutiny by friends, the press, the police, and by strangers. She'd accepted that, even if she hadn't gotten used to it. Tonight it was different. It was as if the eyes watching her were unfriendly, even hostile. She shivered.

Returning to the dining room, she spotted Mike up at the dais. He motioned to let her know he was coming. The room was emptying out. She headed back to the table to pick up her purse.

A man stood beside her chair. He was half turned away, but she could see that he had one hand inside her white silk purse. She had just opened her mouth to speak when he raised his head and stared across the table at her.

It was Joseph Garvey.

"Is this yours?" He closed the purse with a sharp snap of the clasp. "I was just looking for some ID."

Despite his nonchalant words, it was obvious he was embarrassed to be caught rummaging inside her purse.

"I saw you earlier with Mike," Garvey said, his eyes narrowing as he stared across the table that separated them. "I feel as if I should know you, but I can't place the connection."

Kate turned her head, spotting Mike working his way across the room.

"Speaking of Mike, here he comes," she said, ignoring his comment.

When Garvey made no attempt to give her the purse, she moved around the table and extended her hand. He stepped close to her, his eyes holding hers as he placed the purse in the palm of her hand.

"I'm sorry you have to leave before I've had a chance to talk to you."

Kate shivered at the invitation in his words. She was short of breath and could feel perspiration beading her upper lip. Her suspicions returned in a flood and she shuddered, nearly dropping her purse in her agitation. She fumbled with it, and Garvey's hand shot out toward her. Not wanting him to touch her, she jerked away.

"Steady, Kate." Mike's voice penetrated her panic. "Sorry to tear this lovely lady away, Joseph, but I've got early rounds tomorrow."

Kate let Mike take charge, nodding as he steered her toward the door then led her outside, and seated her on the stone wall that edged the parking lot. She sucked in the warm evening air. The rapid beat of her heart faded.

"Are you all right?" he asked.

"I got a little lightheaded."

"Tension probably. After obsessing about Garvey, there you were talking to him." He shrugged. "No wonder you were hyperventilating."

"He frightens me, Mike."

"Don't dwell on it. It's been a long evening and you've got to be tired. How about I get you home?"

Driving home she felt unsettled. She didn't know if it was her running into Garvey or just the unfamiliarity of being out without Richard. She unclasped her purse, but Mike had his keys in his hand. He unlocked the door, and followed her out to the kitchen.

"Want a drink?" she asked.

"No thanks. I've got to be up early. I've got a golf game."

She rolled her eyes and he chuckled.

"Well, it was a nice evening," she said. "I hope my behavior didn't embarrass you. Honestly, Mike, I couldn't help myself. I had just decided that my suspicions of Garvey were groundless, when he got too close to me. Suddenly I got this creepy feeling, and it threw me into a tailspin."

Opening her purse, she reached inside to return the house key to the key rack. The small silk bag was full of odds and ends. She couldn't find the key. In exasperation she turned the bag over and poured everything out on the countertop.

Lying between the house key and her lipstick was a piece of candy. Printed on the distinctive plaid cellophane wrapper was a single word.

ButterSkots.

# Twenty-three

BUTTERSKOTS!

Kate reached for the brightly wrapped piece of candy. Even before she touched it, she could smell the overly sweet butterscotch aroma. She tightened her fingers and the hard round disk pressed against the palm of her hand. So much had happened that made her question her own sanity. She needed the tactile sense to be sure she wasn't imagining the whole thing.

"What is it, Kate?"

Sensing something wrong, Mike crossed to her side. Without a word, she held out her hand, opening her fingers so that he could see the tartan-plaid logo of the candy.

"Good God! Where did you get that?"

"It was in my purse. Someone put it there."

"Are you sure?"

"Yes, of course I'm sure."

Her lips were stiff, barely able to form the words. With a shudder of distaste, she dropped the candy back on the counter.

"When I was getting dressed tonight, I took the purse out of the closet. There was some loose change inside and I shook it out before I put anything inside."

"Can you remember what you did with it at the dinner?"

"Not really. I had it at the table. I didn't take it to the ladies room because I can remember muttering that I didn't have my lipstick."

"So anyone at the dinner could have put the candy inside," Mike said. "Only a moment's work. A simple clasp to open."

The word clasp triggered the picture in Kate's mind. She stopped her pacing and faced Mike.

"Joseph Garvey did it."

She could see by the wary expression on Mike's face he doubted her.

"It's not just my obsession with Garvey. I didn't realize it until now, but I actually saw him do it. When we were getting ready to leave, I went back to the table to get my purse. Garvey was holding it. His hand was inside. I literally caught him in the act. He said he was looking for ID."

"That doesn't mean he put it there."

"Who else," she snapped. "I'm not hallucinating, for God's sake. I talked to him for a minute or two. In fact, that was why I was upset. Both his conversation and his behavior were strange."

"How do you mean?"

She shrugged her shoulders. "It's hard to explain. It was just a feeling I got. All I know is that I was uncomfortable talking to him and had a panicky need to get away. Luckily you arrived and got me out of there."

"God, what a mess!" Mike smacked his hand on the top of the counter, making Kate jump. "I think I'll take that drink you offered earlier. Do you want one?"

At her nod, he moved to the liquor cabinet, and Kate got out ice and orange juice. In silence, Mike made her a screwdriver and then poured vodka into a glass and added ice. He took several healthy swallows before speaking.

"I know you've been saying all along that something was wrong with Garvey, and I didn't believe you. I've been going on the assumption that you were reaching for straws. The ButterSkots makes a difference. If Garvey put the candy in your purse, it looks like he might —"

Mike stopped, almost as if he couldn't bring himself to complete the sentence. The words hung in the air between them.

"Are you saying you believe me?"

"I said 'might.' Honest to God, Kate. I don't know what to think. I'm still sort of stunned. Do you think we should call Leidecker?"

Kate shook her head. "Leidecker believes I'd do anything to prove Richard's innocence. He'd suspect me of putting the candy there myself." She stared at Mike, her eyes steady. "I didn't put it there, you know."

"I believe that, Kate."

She was warmed by his words. Although it wasn't the total conversion she'd hoped for, at least it was a start. After several minutes of silence, she asked, "What do we do now?"

"Nothing."

The single word shocked her. "What do you mean?"

Mike took a long swallow of his drink, then reached for the bottle of vodka and added some more. He swirled the contents for several seconds. He took another long drink, then set it on the counter and folded his arms over his chest.

"I want you to give up the investigation."

"You can't be serious," she said, shaking her head in confusion. "After what we know? What about the candy in my purse."

When he spoke his tone was harsh.

"That's exactly why I want you to give this up. How many people do you think know the significance of ButterSkots?"

"Outside of the police, not too many," Kate said. "Leidecker said they were withholding that fact from the media. The only people who know about it are you, me, and Richard. I suppose he might have told Chris, but I can't think of anyone else who would have known."

"Except the killer."

Her shock must have been evident.

"Maybe now you can understand why I want you to give this up. Whether it's Garvey or someone else, the ButterSkots was meant as a warning."

"Why would he take the risk?"

"Maybe he gets off on the risks."

"I think he wants to frighten me."

"Well if it hasn't worked on you, it sure as hell has me scared."

228

Mike took a sip of his drink, and when he spoke he was under control but adamant. "Get it into your head that if the killer is Garvey, he's already killed twice and a third time wouldn't be any big deal."

His words penetrated Kate's sense of outraged justice. Thinking about it she knew he was right.

"I'll admit I'm scared," she said, "but I can't give this up."

"Do you know the danger you could be in?"

When she made no comment, he blew out his breath in a stream of frustration.

"Will you do me a favor? Just cool it for a few days? I know a couple people that I can question very discreetly. Let me do that. I should have some answers by Wednesday, and we'll talk then. Can you resist the urge to play detective until then?"

"Yes."

"In the meantime, you have to take this seriously. If you won't go to the police, you have to be extra careful. We can't ignore the fact there's a killer out there."

After Mike left, the house seemed too large and too empty. Her sense of security had been violated. Locking up downstairs, she took special care to check every window and door. If the purpose of the candy had been to frighten her, it had succeeded.

Upstairs in the guest room, she got ready for bed. She was grateful that the door had a lock and she felt a slight release of tension as she heard it click into place.

She climbed into bed and huddled under the covers. The more she thought about the purpose of the candy in her purse, the more she suspected it was not just a warning, but a message.

To Kate, the message was clear: I can get to you any time, any place.

He stood at the edge of the clearing, waiting for the moon to rise above the circle of trees. The silence of the forest surrounded him. He was wrapped in the security of night. He touched the outside of his pocket, tracing the outline of the bracelet. It had been his best talisman. A powerful token.

His first token had been a yellow ribbon. A bow from Adele's hair. Even after all these years he could close his eyes and feel the satiny fabric imprinted on the pads of his fingertips.

He had been ten the first time he saw Adele. Her parents were coming over to play poker, and when the sitter canceled, they brought her with them. His mother brought her to the basement and showed her where the toys were kept.

He was in his "cave" and watched her through a slit in the old woolen blanket that covered the card table. She was seven, her body soft with traces of baby fat. She had long, curly hair that bounced and shimmered in the overhead light. He wondered how it would feel to touch it. Holding her hair in place was a yellow satin ribbon, nestling among the curls like a golden rope. He was fascinated by her hair and the satin ribbon.

Even though he hadn't made a sound, she was aware of his presence under the covered table. She sat down facing him, spreading her legs in a wide V and setting the blocks on the floor in the space between. She built towers of blocks and when they toppled, she flapped her skirt with mock anger, exposing her underpants. Each time it happened she stared at the eyehole in the blanket, her eyes smoky with amusement.

She left when her mother called. She hadn't said a word to him, but when he crept out into the room the yellow ribbon lay on top of the pile of blocks.

At night, he kept the ribbon inside his pillowcase, rubbing it against his cheek to soothe away the pain from the night encounters. The next time she came, he was huddled in the cave recovering from a beating. She sat on the floor, holding the blanket apart with her two hands, and in the illumination from the basement lights, she saw the bruises and tears.

Without a word, she crawled under the table, dropping the blanket in place, enclosing them in darkness.

She cuddled up against him, plump hands brushing at his cheeks and touching his hair. She smelled of talcum powder and shampoo. The scent of cherries masked the musty woolen smell he was used to.

In the dark he stroked her hair, holding a handful up to his nose and inhaling the fruity aroma.

She ran her fingers over his body as if she were trying to learn how he was put together. He didn't like it when people touched him, but he would have let her do anything as long as she let him smell her hair. Strange sensations coursed through his body as her hands moved over him. When she tired of the game, he wanted to touch her in his turn.

One hand remained anchored in her hair and with his other he touched her face. His fingers skated across skin softer than anything he'd ever felt. He stroked her, and felt her stir beneath his hand. The movement excited him. He grew bolder. Sometimes she pushed him away but when he tightened his hand in her hair, she stopped struggling. He touched her everywhere. Places he had not known existed. Secret places.

After she left, he took out the ribbon. Holding it in his hand, he felt a jolt of energy fill his body as he remembered touching her. She had struggled but it was clear his show of strength had swayed her. He stared down at the ribbon, seeing and feeling each movement with renewed excitement. Power flowed into his body from the ribbon.

Adele didn't return to the basement. He used the ribbon until the memories began to fade. Over time the golden satin turned dark and limp and when he touched it he felt nothing.

His hand clenched around the bracelet in his pocket, bringing his mind back from the past. He held his watch up close to his face.

It was midnight. He'd chosen the time specifically even though he normally didn't believe in superstition. The clouds shifted and moonlight radiated down into the woods. Listening intently for any other movements, he walked to the very center of the clearing.

He reached into his pocket and withdrew the talisman. Even in the uncertain light, he could tell that the bracelet was not shimmering as brightly as it had been. He had noted it several days earlier, but dismissed it as imagination. Now he was certain.

The charm bracelet was losing its power.

Wings that used to flutter in the light remained stiff and unresponsive. The robed angel was dull, the golden face dark and forbidding.

He'd tried other tokens, but they didn't hold the power the way the bracelet did. Holding it by the broken clasp, he extended it toward the moon, as if the mere presence of the mystical crescent would rejuvenate the life force. He rubbed it against his body.

Before this, he could hold the talisman in his hand and, merely by recalling the events in the forest preserve, he was able to reach orgasm. The intensity of those memories was fading. Just like they had with the ribbon. Eventually the charm bracelet would lose all power.

He closed his eyes, picturing another angel. This one was larger than the one he held in his hand. He could see it clearly, nestled in the valley between her breasts. The angel necklace caught the light, shimmering as it rose and fell with each breath. When he needed a new talisman, he would take it.

Soon. It would be soon.

Kate parked as close as possible to the grass so that other cars could pass on the narrow roadway. Without looking out the windows, she turned off the engine, put the keys in her purse, and opened the car door. She stood on the tarmac, letting the silence of the cemetery seep into her body.

*I can't do it.*

Closing her eyes, she leaned weakly against the side of the car. She had not been to the cemetery since the day of Jenny's funeral. The memories of her daughter, alive and happy, had sustained her, and she knew the sight of the grave would bring her face to face with the long-term emptiness of a life without Jenny.

She'd found another message from All Saints Cemetery on the answering machine. It was the third request to inspect the engraving on the headstone to ensure that everything had been done correctly. This time she knew she had to go.

Standing beside the car, Kate stared blindly across the vast garden of granite stones, each as individual as the person they identified. How strange it was that the simple details surrounding death could be so incredibly painful. All she had to do was check two lines of writing on a gray-white rock. Why did it seem as if each cut of the engraving tool would open a gaping wound in her heart?

*You can make it, Katie. Kick harder.*

Her father's voice was clear, floating across the grass on a breeze. He always used to shout that at the swim meets. No matter how loud the crowd was, she always heard the words.

She squared her shoulders, and stepped onto the grass, weaving through the stones toward the top of the hill where Jenny was buried. They had chosen the spot because it was shaded by a flowering crab-apple tree and was the highest spot in the new section of the cemetery. Spring blossoms would flutter down around her and she'd catch the first drops of rain and feel the warmth of the sun for most of the day.

The first thing she saw was freshly planted daffodils just starting to open.

"Chris Mayerling," Kate said aloud. She remembered the basket of daffodils he'd sent to the house. How kind he was to take the time and trouble to plant the flowers.

And God knows where he found daffodils in July, she thought.

It had been good to see him at the Fine Arts dinner the other night. She felt guilty for not keeping in closer touch with him.

Knowing she couldn't put off the moment any longer, Kate raised her eyes to inspect the headstone. She reached for the trunk of the tree, afraid her legs would give out on her. Seeing the inscription, she had an overwhelming desire to close her eyes and never open them again. She tightened her grip on the tree, letting the roughness of the bark anchor her to reality.

JENNIFER LOUISE WARNER
SEPTEMBER 14, 1997 – MAY 16, 2006

She read the words, lovingly tracing the sharp-edged letters with her eyes. In the right-hand corner above the name was the fresh cut image of a winged angel. It had been Richard's idea; not hers. Jenny's guardian angel had not protected her in life, what good to guard a dead child? Kate glared at the crisp outline of the angelic face.

The Angel of Death.

Bitterness accompanied her down the hill to the car. She opened the door then turned for a last glimpse of the leafy guardian above Jenny's grave. She committed herself to continue her search for the truth. She'd return when justice was done.

Richard's name had to be cleared. The killer had to be identified.

Kate realized that those two goals were all that mattered to her now. For the moment, neither was likely to happen. The police hadn't been able to come up with the murderer. She was aware that Leidecker didn't have all the facts. His focus on Richard had frightened her so much that she purposely withheld things, afraid they would somehow make matters worse.

Was that what Leidecker was trying to tell her that day in the library?

She squinted up at the sky, trying to bring back his words. He had asked for her help. She remembered that much. And he'd said she couldn't hurt Jenny or Richard anymore. God what a quandary! What if she told Leidecker something that would prove conclusively that Richard was the murderer?

Could she take the risk? Slowly the answer came to her. In a sense, Richard had already been found guilty, so no matter what she told Leidecker it couldn't be any worse for him.

She got in the car and took out her cell phone. If Leidecker was at the station, she'd take it as a sign and agree to talk to him. She took a deep breath and dialed.

"Pickard police station. May I help you?"

"Is Captain Leidecker there? This is Mrs. Richard Warner calling."

The operator hesitated for a fraction of a second as she registered the name. "Just one moment. I'll check to see if he's in."

Kate could feel her heart hammering as she was put on hold.

"Kate?"

Leidecker's voice made her jump. She was breathing through her mouth, her lips too dry for speech.

"Kate," he repeated, "are you there?"

"Yes. I'm here." Once she got the words out, she didn't know what else to say.

"Are you all right? I can barely hear you."

"It's my cell phone. I've been doing some thinking." She stopped to organize her thoughts. "In the library the other day, you asked me to think about things and I did, and I thought maybe sometime when you were free I could talk to you."

"I'd really appreciate that, Kate." She sensed he was choosing his words, so he wouldn't sound too eager. "Would you like to talk now? I've been sitting here doing paperwork, and I have nothing scheduled for the rest of the day."

"I'm free for the day too. I'll come to the station." She swallowed her fear and checked her watch. "Is ten minutes all right?"

"Fine. I'll be here."

She didn't really know what she could tell him that would be helpful. And what about Garvey? Should she tell him about her suspicions? By the time she turned into the parking lot of the police station, she was no closer to a decision on Garvey. She'd just have to play it by ear.

She was nervous as she got out of the car and walked around to the entrance. Leidecker, dressed formally in his uniform, was sitting on a bench outside the front door. He got up at her approach, holding out a hand in greeting. Chatting casually, he led her into the station, whisked her through the main rooms and, once they were in his office, closed the door behind her.

She had only been in Carl's office once before and then she was too nervous to look around. The room was neat but not fanatically so. Diplomas, certificates, and commendations vied for wall space with pictures of fishing boats, fishing resorts, and endless strings of dead fish. On the opposite wall was a large bulletin board. Catalog cutouts of fishing rods and reels and notes of various sizes were pinned to the cork.

Leidecker stood behind the desk, one hand on the high back of the black leather swivel chair. It was obvious he had been watching her, but he made no comment. His eyes were direct, and he held himself straight as if for her inspection.

His walnut desk was big, old-fashioned, and battle scarred, looking incongruous in the otherwise modern office. A pile of papers and folders took up the left-hand corner. On the right there was a desk lamp, a daily agenda book, and the telephone. Telephone numbers and doodles were scribbled on the blotter. The only personal touch was a wood-framed picture of an older man and woman who were probably his parents.

She sat down on the chair in front of his desk.

"Do you want anything? Coffee? Tea? Water?"

"Water, please."

Picking up a tray from the computer table, he brought it over to the desk, pushing papers out of the way as he set it down. He unscrewed the top of the ceramic carafe and poured two glasses of ice water. He handed her one.

He sat down behind the desk. His posture was relaxed. As she looked at his face, she was reminded of the character, honesty, and sense of fair play she had noted in the early days of the investigation. She didn't know if she could tell him everything, but for the time being her level of trust was acceptable.

"I am afraid of you."

He blinked in surprise at her words. Slowly a thin smile softened his expression and lit up his eyes. "My sister's kids used to call me 'granite face.' After awhile they got used to me, and stopped fleeing the room when I came to visit."

She could feel her face flush with embarrassment. "I didn't mean to say that, but in part that's the reason I've come. You have a quiet tenacity that terrifies me. It's the kind of power, like water dripping on stone, that finally wears away the outer layers and reveals the truth. Only doggedness and determination will solve Jenny's murder. I thought about what you said the other day. I am willing to do what I can to help find the killer."

"No matter who it is?"

Although Leidecker's posture had not changed, Kate could feel the tension in his body. She sat very straight, staring directly into his eyes, knowing exactly what he was asking.

"No matter who it is," she said.

The ground rules were set.

Leidecker let the words hang in the air for several seconds while he examined Kate's face. Since Jenny's death, she had been less than forthcoming, caught between her loyalty to Richard and her desire to find Jenny's killer.

Something was different about her. He sensed a resolution, absent during the investigation. She appeared more alive than he'd ever seen her. Fear, excitement, and hesitancy all registered in his mind.

He had known all along that the best hope of solving the case was with Kate's help, but when Richard became a suspect that avenue was closed. Now that she'd had time to sort through her feelings, her loyalties shifted to finding Jenny's murderer.

"I'll be honest with you, Kate. I had a pretty good circumstantial case built up against Richard when he disappeared. I was planning to arrest him, and I think he knew it. But no matter how often I've gone over the evidence, I can't prove the case against him. I'm not as close minded as you think. Once I have all the pieces to the puzzle, I'm hoping to be able to fit them into one cohesive picture. I'm not absolutely sure I'll see Richard's face."

The glow in Kate's eyes was reward enough for Carl.

"I don't know how to begin."

"Can I make a suggestion?" She nodded. "I think you should start right at the beginning and tell me everything you can remember. It'll be easier and less painful than going back and forth. And you're less likely to forget something that might turn out to be important."

Kate nodded again. While she took a drink of her water, Carl reached for a pad of lined, yellow paper, setting it directly in front of him. He tried not to set his expectations too high. He didn't expect any revelations; the most he could hope for was an isolated piece of information that might give him new insights.

She began speaking, words halting as she talked about Jenny's disappearance and death. Once that hurdle was passed, the narrative went smoother. She faltered again describing Leidecker's interrogation after the funeral, and her realization that Richard was lying.

Carl leaned across the desk, trying to keep any judgmental tones from his voice. "Do you remember the exact wording of your question?"

"No. I think I asked him if he'd been in the forest preserve. He got

237

really annoyed at my questioning him. He said he'd driven around, but he hadn't gone near the forest preserve. I'm not sure I'm quoting him correctly. All I remember is that I was really frightened because I knew he was lying to me about something."

He could see that she was upset. Her hand shook as she took a sip of water. Guessing that she felt disloyal to Richard's memory, he let her catch her breath. After a moment she continued.

"When I'd had a chance to think it over, I realized that no matter what else Richard might have done, he would never kill Jenny."

"Do you still feel that way?" When Kate looked at him sharply, he said, "It's not a trick question. I need to know the answer."

"I am absolutely convinced that Richard did not kill Jenny."

Carl held her gaze for a moment. He heard the sincerity in her voice and accepted it. "All right, let's assume you're right. Can you think of any reason for him to lie about where he was the day Jenny disappeared?"

"I think he was having an affair. That would explain why he lied about where he was that day." She blurted the words out, then took a deep breath. "I know in this age of sexual freedom, that sounds stupid, but Richard was very old fashioned. He had seen the hurt his father's infidelity caused."

"Do you have any proof he was having an affair?"

"No. It's a guess. It was something that Chris Mayerling said. Or didn't say." She told him about the phone call from Chris the day Richard said he was going to Milwaukee. "I may be wrong, but I got the distinct impression that Chris tried to cover for him. Whether it was just because he didn't want to upset me or because he knew where Richard had probably gone, I don't know."

"Could it have been someone at the office?"

"Maybe. It's just like the joke about the wife being the last to know."

"Had he ever been unfaithful before?"

"I don't think so." Despite the tremor in her voice and her height-ened color, she didn't dodge his question. "Once Jenny was born, sex wasn't a priority for him. It was no longer a driving force."

Carl got the picture of an old-fashioned marriage, where Richard was in full control of all aspects of Kate's life. He began to see why she had never been assertive. The household revolved around Richard, and Kate had been content to follow his orders.

She presented a picture of vulnerability that appealed to a man's protective nature. A knee-jerk reaction he'd been guilty of himself. Listening to her quiet narrative of everything she'd been through, he could not believe how much strength of character it must have taken for her to survive.

Watching her now, it seemed to Carl that since Richard's disappearance she had begun to take the first steps to become an independent person. Where she had been ravaged by grief, she appeared to be energized by anger. He could hear flashes of it in her narrative.

She continued with her story, giving him some idea of how the pressure had built for her once Richard became a suspect. She held nothing back, describing how friends had abandoned them and others had rallied to their support. When she told him about the tomato throwing incident, he was appalled.

"Was it after the tomato thing that he said, 'I should have told the truth'?" Carl asked.

"Yes. He sounded forlorn, not guilty. It was as if he suddenly realized that if he'd told the truth in the first place, he never would have been a suspect. I felt he was apologizing to me for the ugliness of the boys' attack."

Kate looked at him, seeking confirmation for her theory. He could only shrug. He had no way of knowing what had been in Richard's head. When he made no comment, she continued.

"I'd like to tell you something that I couldn't tell you earlier. The night the jogger was killed, I had my meeting with Chris Mayerling. When I got home Richard was passed out on the bed. His clothes were wet. I might not have thought anything about it except I'd just left Chris who had also gotten wet changing a flat tire in the rain. Richard's jacket was soaking."

Carl sighed, and Kate glared at him accusingly.

"I know you see this as further evidence that he killed Walter

Hepburn, but I'm convinced he didn't. According to the accounts I read in the paper and what Richard and I guessed, someone who knew his identity killed the jogger. Right?"

He nodded.

"I saw Richard's face when he learned the jogger's name. It meant nothing to him. Nothing. He didn't have the slightest idea who Walter Hepburn was. Mike had to explain to Richard that it was the man who'd discovered Jenny's body."

"I'll reserve judgment on this point. Let's get back to his wet clothes. Did he give you any explanation?"

"No. When I got up the next morning he was already at work. When he came home, the reporters were out front and you were coming over. We only had a few minutes to talk before you arrived. To be perfectly honest, I didn't think about his wet clothes again until after Hepburn was identified. Even then, I didn't ask him."

"Why not?" Carl asked, studying her.

"You can't imagine what that day was like. For Richard, it was an emotional roller coaster. He was positive that the second death meant he wouldn't be a suspect anymore. Then with the discovery that the dead man was connected to Jenny's murder, he was convinced he was facing possible arrest. If I questioned him then, I knew he would think I doubted his innocence. I didn't know it would be the last time I'd see him."

She pressed the tips of her fingers against her trembling lips. He didn't rush her. Dark smudges ringed her eyes, giving her face a haunted quality. He knew nothing he could say would ease her pain. He was neither her friend nor confidante. He was her interrogator.

She blinked several times, and then continued speaking. "In Richard's statement to you, he said he had gotten home just after five. He knew that I left the house before five because I'd told him so before you arrived. But the rain hadn't started much before five. As wet as his clothes were, he didn't get home until at least six. Maybe even later."

For the first time since she'd made up her mind to talk to him, she was avoiding Carl's eyes. Her hands gripped the arms of the chair as if only the pressure kept her from bolting for the door. Much as he felt sorry for her, he knew he had to force her to tell him what she was holding back.

"If you keep it inside, Kate, it'll just be something else gnawing at your guts." He spoke from the heart and hoped she'd hear his sincerity. Her bottom lip trembled. When she raised her eyes, he could see how close she was to tears.

"He was very drunk. He was mumbling, talking to himself. I don't really know how aware he was of me. He said something about not wanting to hurt me. Said he shouldn't have gone and then he said —"

She swallowed hard but couldn't get the words out. Carl couldn't wait, afraid she'd lose courage.

"What did Richard say, Kate?" he asked, his voice a command.

"He said, 'I had to go. He was going to tell.' "

# TWENTY-FOUR

" 'HE WAS GOING TO TELL?' That's what Richard said?"

Carl kept his voice neutral, showing nothing but curiosity. He could understand why Kate had been reluctant to tell him this before. It was a damning statement.

"Yes. I don't know if they're the exact words but they're close enough."

"Did you draw any conclusions from what he said?"

"No."

He let it go. It didn't matter what she'd thought. Her situation had been a nightmare, and she'd coped the best she could. He gave her a chance to catch her breath while he looked back over his notes.

"As you think about the last couple months is there anything that strikes you as out of place. A little thing. Maybe a detail that nagged at you but didn't seem particularly important."

She thought for a moment, her gaze unfocused as she retraced the past. At one point her eyebrows jerked and then they both drew together. Carl tried not to get his hopes up. Finally she looked across the desk at him.

"Several things come to mind. One is a question. When I was going through Richard's office the other day, I came across the computer printout of the cars with PF license plates. Were all of those people checked out? Like for alibis?"

Without knowing what had prompted her question, Carl answered as fully as he could. "No. You've seen the list, so you know it wasn't feasible in the time frame that we had. Better than half the people in town have the plates."

He could see the disappointment on her face. "You must understand, Kate, that the possibility always existed that the car was stolen or borrowed. We used the printout as a cross reference for anyone who turned up on any other list. Is it important?"

"No. I was just curious."

Although he suspected she was holding something back, he didn't challenge her. "You said there were several things."

"Richard's knife is missing. It was a small Buck penknife. Black. I gave it to him one year for Christmas and he always carried it in his pocket. It should have been with the things that were found in the car the day he disappeared, but I couldn't find it."

Carl jotted the word "knife" on a Post-it and stuck it to the telephone to be dealt with later. "I'll check the list of things that were returned to you. If it's on the list then it may have just been misplaced. Either way, I'll get back to you."

"I'd appreciate it. The knife holds a lot of good memories." She reached for the carafe of water and filled her glass. She drank it slowly. "Ever since Jenny died, we've had crank calls but there were several that were different."

He listened as she described the first call from the person she called the Whisperer.

"I wish you'd told me."

"I couldn't. By then you already suspected Richard. If I said I'd received a call from someone saying he'd been in the forest preserve and seen Richard attack and kill Jenny, you'd have been convinced he was guilty. Admit it."

Carl pushed his chair back, too restless to remain seated. He walked to the window. Oblivious to the sunlit scene, he stared outside. She was right, and he knew it.

Turning, he faced Kate.

"You're right. If you had told me about that call, I would have taken it as further confirmation that Richard was guilty. I don't know if my opinion will change when I've sifted through everything we've talked about today, but I will promise to keep my mind open."

Her eyes were steady on his face, her expression closed. Whatever her assessment, she merely nodded her head and finished up the narrative by describing the series of phone calls on the day that Walter Hepburn was killed. He didn't tell her that he already knew about the calls to the house or the last one to Richard's office.

"Okay. For the moment, let's go back to that first phone call. You didn't recognize the voice?" he asked.

She shook her head. "It had no real substance. Just a whisper. Neither male nor female. It could have been anyone."

He pulled over the desk calendar. "It was a Monday when you got that first call, and the series of calls on the day Hepburn was killed was also a Monday. I don't know if it means anything, but it's curious. During the last call of that series when the person asked to talk to Richard, did you feel it was the same voice as the one you call the Whisperer?"

"Yes. I think so. But again I can't be positive."

"Did Richard ever mention any calls?"

"He never said anything, but when he was home he didn't like me answering the phone. And the ones later —"

It was the shock on Kate's face that tipped Carl off to the fact she had inadvertently let something slip. "Later than what?"

Kate's lips were pressed firmly together, spots of color dotting her cheeks. At first he thought she was embarrassed but when she looked at him, anger was clearly evident.

"Someone called a week after Richard disappeared. He wanted me to believe that Richard was still alive. His words were: 'I'm safe.' The second call came about a week later. Same words. Same whispered voice."

"Did you ever think the calls might actually have been from Richard?"

"Not for an instant. They infuriated me. It seemed like the purpose was to make me lose faith in Richard. I told you before that running away would not have been his style. So if he didn't run away, he had to be dead. Maybe Richard was so overwrought that he swam out too far and then between the cold and the distance couldn't get back to shore. Although it was an accidental drowning, I feel Jenny's murderer was just as responsible for his death as he would have been if he'd actually murdered Richard."

Carl had been staring down at his notes, and felt a spark of excitement at Kate's final words. Although at one time he'd given a cursory thought to the idea that Richard had been murdered, none of the evidence supported it. With some of the additional information that Kate had provided, it might be interesting to reconsider that possibility. He made a note, and looked across at Kate.

She sat perfectly still, a speculative expression on her face. He sensed that she was weighing whether or not to tell him something.

"You know, Kate, every piece of information helps in the investigation of a case. Small, random items can make all the difference when it comes to presenting a case to the jury. In a trial it's imperative to have a solid case in order to ensure a conviction. Have you any information you'd like to add?" he asked.

Her body language indicated her withdrawal. He knew the interview was over before she spoke.

"No. I can't think of anything else I need to tell you," she said.

Carl grimaced at her choice of words. He didn't know if it was something he'd said, but she'd decided against telling him anything more. Given time she might confide whatever she was holding back. He accepted the dismissal and came around the desk as she stood up and smoothed down her skirt.

"I appreciate your coming in, Kate. This has been incredibly difficult for you. You mustn't think of this as a betrayal of loyalty. What you've told me today may eventually lead to justice for Jenny."

He walked outside with her, chatting about the weather, letting the small talk ease her back into the real world. He waited until she had driven out of the parking lot before he returned to his office. He stared at the scribbled notes, circled several entries, and marked a star in front of the words: computer printout. Why had she asked about the printout?

Leaning back in his chair, he opened the top drawer of his desk.

He pulled out the crumpled piece of yellow, lined paper he'd found at the library the day he'd run into Kate. She'd looked so guilty when she first spotted him that he'd been curious about what she'd been doing. After she left, he'd looked in the wastebasket and found the piece of paper with the references to Joseph Garvey.

He placed the paper on his desk, smoothed it out, and reached back into the drawer. On top of the yellow paper, he set the cellophane ButterSkots wrapper he'd found in Kate's kitchen. She hadn't mentioned it.

Where did she find the candy wrapper, and why was she looking up information on Joseph Garvey? He glared at the starred item in his notes. What did Garvey, the candy wrapper, and the computer printout have in common? It wouldn't take long to check. He had a hunch about what he'd find.

He didn't know what to do about Kate, but to be on the safe side he'd better have a talk with Joseph Garvey.

Kate sat in the car outside the police station, wondering if she'd made a mistake. She'd sworn to tell Leidecker everything, but at the last minute she couldn't talk about Joseph Garvey. She'd been about to tell Carl her suspicions when he began talking about trials and convictions.

She remembered seeing Carl and Garvey talking together at the Fine Arts Dinner. Would Carl even take her accusations seriously? He said he wanted the truth, but what if it involved a well-connected member of the community?

Garvey was rich, and he had a ton of political contacts. He could afford an expert team of defense lawyers. Even if irrefutable evidence was discovered, she suspected he'd never see the inside of a prison cell. It had happened in too many high-profile cases. Even if a jury convicted him, he'd probably end up with a fine, two years probation, and fifty hours of community service.

What kind of justice was that for the life of a child?

God, how she hated the man who killed Jenny! It didn't matter if it was Garvey or someone else. Whoever it was, had to be stopped. If he wasn't caught soon, he might kill again.

Questions! Everywhere he turned there were questions. He should have known it would be like this. First it was the COP. He gave him the perfect solution to the deaths, but the man refused to close the case. The COP wanted every lead chased down, every detail nailed.

And now SHE was asking questions.

SHE was small and fragile looking. To look at HER, he'd never have guessed SHE had so much tenacity. SHE reminded him of the snapping turtle he'd gotten on his birthday when he was a kid.

Tortuga.

He'd seen it in the pet shop and the owner, Mr. Collins, let him play with it. The turtle wasn't big. Six inches across with a wrinkled neck and brownish green shell. He'd bite at anything. The best fun was to hold out a stalk of celery. The turtle would scuttle across the bottom of the box and snap at the celery. He'd cut it off clean. The crunch sound when the turtle first bit down made his heart jerk inside his chest.

His father had gotten drunk the morning of his twelfth birthday. Just before he passed out, the old man shoved a crumpled dollar bill into his hand and told him to get his own damn present. He bought the turtle and named it Tortuga.

Once he took Tortuga to school. The turtle was a big hit. He watched the girls squirm when he described how when the turtle bit down on something, it would never let go. It was a death grip. At recess he bet the other boys to see who could hold the shortest object within range of the turtle. They were all too afraid to get close to the turtle's beak. He'd practiced and he knew just the range that was safe. Easy money.

And then Bobbie came to visit.

He'd never liked his cousin. A first-class whiner. He never wanted to do anything but read or watch television. He stayed the weekend. During the day, Mother fawned over him.

During the night, Bobbie belonged to him.

Bobbie was terrified of the turtle. He begged him not to let the turtle loose in the night. In return he gave up all the spending money he'd brought with him. The second night Bobbie had nothing to barter.

Watching his cousin's growing fear gave him an erection. He

turned the lights out, and waited until Bobbie's sniveling eased into sleep, then put Tortuga under the edge of the covers on his cousin's bed.

Bobbie's first scream brought his parents running.

His father took one look at him and knew he'd set Tortuga on the bed deliberately. His father beat him until he bled, but he never uttered a cry. He ground his teeth together and pictured his father being attacked by snapping turtles. For years it was one of his favorite fantasies. His father, naked, writhing amid a swarm of turtles. Turtles hung from his lips, his nostrils, and his eyelids. Turtles clung to his nipples and his penis.

Tortuga died two weeks after Bobbie left. He'd reached in to feed it dinner and got too close to the snapping jaw. It caught the tip of his little finger, and when he couldn't shake it loose, he tore the turtle's head off.

He hadn't thought about the turtle in a long time. So many memories were coming back to him. Stirred up by the questions. He hated the memories.

If SHE kept asking questions, he'd have to stop her. SHE was afraid. He could always sense it, and the smell of it excited him. The power of the bracelet was fading. Each day the angel face grew darker; the wings had become limp and lifeless. Eventually the bracelet would be useless.

Then it would be time to collect the other angel.

Kate lay on the chaise longue too enervated to move. Since Saturday she had been sleeping fitfully, jumping at every creak and groan in the house. In the daytime she was able to put away her fears, but as darkness fell she was conscious of her own vulnerability. It didn't help that Mike called frequently to check on her. He tried to reassure her that she had nothing to worry about, however each call served to remind her of the possibility of danger.

"Yoo-hoo, Kate." Marian's voice floated over from next door. "Are you receiving visitors?"

"Sure. I'm on the deck."

The honeysuckle bushes parted, and Marian eased through the

narrow opening. As she walked across the grass, she brushed down her lime green linen dress, and picked a leaf out of her frosted hair.

"Those bushes are long overdue for a trim. A few more bridge luncheons, and I'll never get through that space." She kissed Kate's cheek and brushed off a wrought iron chair before she sat down. "How are you, my dear?"

"Hot like the rest of the world. I haven't seen you at the fitness center all week. Everything all right?"

"Yes. Delightfully so. Leah was in town for a couple days, and we spent most of our time in Chicago. Talking, eating, and shopping. My kind of mother-daughter bonding. I've spent an absolute fortune on clothes, and everything I've eaten was either bad for my weight, my digestion, or my heart. Now it's back to reality. I just took her to the airport."

"Oh, I wish I'd known she was coming. I'd love to have seen her."

"She was sorry to have missed you, too. It was a sudden business trip. We stopped by the last couple mornings, but you were already gone. I thought you were taking some time off from the temp agency."

"I was. I mean, I am." Kate was flustered. She hadn't told Marian anything about her investigations. She sensed that her friend would be convinced she'd lost her mind. "I had a lot of errands to run this week."

Marian looked over at her, her eyes searching. "Are you feeling well? You look flushed."

"I'm fine. I've been working in the garden, and now I'm waiting for enough energy to go in and take a shower. Mike's taking me to the Patio for ribs tonight. Would you like something to drink?"

"Nothing for me. I just dropped by to say hello. I'm glad to see you're getting out. Mike will keep you well entertained." The older woman chuckled. "I heard he took you to the Fine Arts dinner last Saturday as his date."

"His date! Good God, Marian! Wait a minute." Kate's eyes flickered over her friend's perfectly coiffed head. "Let me guess. You were at the beauty shop today."

"Stopped on the way back from the airport. You were the hot topic of the blue-haired set."

"That's sick. Do they really think that there's something going on with Mike?"

"Probably not. One of the downsides to living in a small town is that everyone knows everyone else's business." Marian's eyes were filled with compassion. "They don't mean to be cruel."

"Do you think I should cancel?"

"Uh-uh." Marian shook her head. "You can't live your life according to what the neighbors will think. I probably never told you, but right after George died your Richard was coming over to cut the lawn and do little things around the house. One of the women in my Tai Chi class wanted to know what it was like to be having an affair with a younger man."

"Dear God in Heaven," Kate gasped out.

"I told her that the Tai Chi kept me so limber that I was able to handle some of the more acrobatic lovemaking positions."

"You didn't!" One look at the raised eyebrow and smug expression on her friend's face and Kate burst into laughter. "You did. I just know you did."

"Well I couldn't let her get away with asking such a rude question."

"So that's why you hired that lawn service. Richard always thought it was because he refused to edge around the sidewalk." Kate grinned across at her friend. "That woman probably thought you wanted more variety."

Now it was Marian's turn to laugh. "So my point is, dear, don't pay any attention to the gossips. What time is he coming?"

"Around seven. You know Mike. He'll stop by the hospital to see one of his little old ladies and forget all about the time."

"Well, I won't keep you."

Marian got to her feet. Her forehead puckered as she stared down at Kate. "Are you sure you're feeling all right? You look edgy. I can't put my finger on it, but I have the feeling something's going on. You'd tell me if something was wrong wouldn't you?"

At Kate's quick nod, she tossed her head.

"I'll bet," she said.

Kate stared after her departing figure. She hated keeping secrets from her friend. It was obvious that Marian was picking up something of her emotional turmoil.

Marian's gossip about Mike unnerved her. How could they conceive of the fact that she was dating? Her daughter had been killed only two months ago and now her husband was gone.

Should she have a talk with Mike?

She'd never felt anything but friendship for him. He was probably feeling some responsibility for her now that Richard was gone. She didn't think he harbored any secret feelings for her. At least she hoped not. She'd have to stop leaning on him. Not easy, especially now that she had involved him with her investigations. Eventually she'd have to talk to him.

The Patio was a casual place she'd been to several times. The ribs were always good and the booths were cozy enough to encourage talking. Mike didn't appear to be in any hurry to bring up the discussion of Garvey and Kate was content to wait until the meal was over.

It was after the table had been cleared and Mike was wiping the last of the barbecue sauce off his fingers that his cell phone went off.

"Not to worry," he said, squinting at the number on his pager display. "It's the call I've been waiting for. Order me some coffee while I take this outside."

Kate had just taken her first sip of tea when Mike rejoined her.

"Everything okay?" she asked, noticing his distracted air.

"Yes. No."

He took a sip of coffee as if delaying until he could arrange his thoughts. Setting his cup down, he leaned forward and lowered his voice.

"It was a friend of mine on Hilton Head. Joanne Burgess. I've been trying to get hold of her for the last few days. She went to Harvard Law School the same time as Joseph Garvey."

"Was that her on the phone?"

"Yes. She was pretty tight with Garvey in the first year of school. They were in the same study group and hung with the same crowd. When she got engaged, they didn't see as much of each other, but she still was able to give a pretty thorough report on him."

Kate sighed. "I can practically hear the conversation. Joseph Garvey was an outstanding and dedicated student, a great drinking companion, and a law-abiding citizen. You're probably convinced now that he should be in line for sainthood."

"Don't be in too big a hurry to hand him a halo." His voice held a note of caution that piqued Kate's interest. "Some of that's true, but not quite as glowing. Garvey was only an average student, showed some potential as a litigator, and got along fine on the social scene. As far as Joanne knew he'd never been in any trouble. Except for one incident at the beginning of his last year."

"Incident?"

"That was the word she used."

"What happened?" Kate asked.

"According to Joanne, Garvey was accused of molesting a thirteen-year-old girl."

# Twenty-five

"GARVEY MOLESTED A THIRTEEN-YEAR-OLD?" Kate was so shocked she could barely get the words out.

"He was accused of it. Eventually the charges were dropped."

Mike looked around the restaurant. No one was sitting at the table across from them, and the high backs of the booth seats gave them a semblance of privacy. Despite that, when he continued, his voice was pitched just above a whisper.

"According to Joanne, the mother of this girl went to the police and told them that someone had attacked her daughter when she cut through the park on her way home from the movies. She had been molested and beaten. The attacker apparently warned the girl to keep her mouth shut because, as he put it, 'the police couldn't touch anyone at Harvard' and she'd only end up in worse trouble."

"Poor baby," Kate said, closing her eyes against the pain of her own memories.

Mike hurried on. "The mother wasn't about to let the guy get away unscathed. She took the girl to the police, and she told them she'd talked to the man several times in the park and knew his name. She identified Joseph Garvey as her attacker."

Kate leaned forward, her hands tightly clasped. "Why were the charges dropped?"

"He had an airtight alibi. A young lady came forward and swore he'd spent the entire day with her in a motel room in Boston."

"For a moment I thought we really had something."

"Just wait. I haven't gotten to the interesting part yet."

At Mike's words, Kate gave him a hard stare.

"The young lady who gave Garvey the alibi was a waitress he'd taken out a couple times. She was eight years older than Garvey and had to quit school when she was sixteen to go to work. By class, money, and education, she and Garvey were worlds apart. Her name was Elizabeth Bowers. Her friends called her Lisa."

"Lisa," Kate whispered. "Lisa Garvey?"

"Exactly." He waited while she digested this latest news. "He married her a month later, and she had a bouncing baby boy during spring break. In those days it was said to be premature. According to Joanne, gossip had it that the child might not have been his. At any rate once out of Harvard, Garvey moved to Atlanta with Lisa and the baby. Lisa must have been an ambitious little thing. In five short years she managed to get enough education and polish to appear as if she were born to the purple. With determination like that a gal might do anything to achieve her goal."

"Would he marry her just for an alibi?" Kate asked.

"If convicted he'd be bounced out of Harvard, do jail time, and bring disgrace to the family. Marriage would be cheap compared to that."

"I can't believe that Lisa would lie to protect a man who'd committed such a horrible crime."

"If she were pregnant and she wanted a better life badly enough, she might. On the other hand, maybe he convinced her of his innocence. Told her he was being railroaded. Who knows?"

"If this is true, do you see what it means?" When Mike shook his head, Kate reached across the table and grabbed his arm with both of her hands. "It would indicate some sort of pattern. If Garvey did molest that child, it would make it a lot easier to convince the police that he might have been involved in Jenny's death."

"Maybe."

"Do you think we could get any proof?"

"No."

The single syllable wasn't encouraging. She pulled her hands away.

"Why not?"

"According to Joanne, there were no police records."

"What about the girl?"

"She and the mother left town shortly after Garvey was cleared. Some thought there might have been a financial settlement to encourage her to leave. Even if we could find her, why would her story be any more believable now than it was then? Garvey had an alibi."

"Do you suppose we could appeal to Lisa?"

Mike snorted. "Not a chance. If little Lisa lied to advance herself when she had absolutely nothing, do you really think she'd tell the truth now? She has wealth, social position, and a reputation for good works. She could lose all of that, maybe even leave herself open to some kind of criminal charges."

"There must be something we can do." Kate tapped a spoon against the tabletop in frustration. "Do you think if we went to Leidecker he'd do anything?"

"I don't think he'd do a damn thing. It's our word against Garvey's that this ever happened. Face it, Kate, Joseph Garvey's an important man in this town. And Leidecker and Garvey are good friends."

"Then I'll just have to go back to my investigations."

When Mike made no comment, she looked up. She tried not to flinch beneath his searching gaze.

"You're never going to give this up, are you?" he said, a trace of sadness in his voice.

"I'm sorry, Mike. I can't."

"I don't want to frighten you anymore than I have to, but I'm worried that you're in danger. Someone put that candy in your purse on Saturday. It doesn't matter whether it's Garvey or not. Someone is interested in you, and I think we have to take some precautions."

"I'm being careful, Mike. What more can I do?"

"I think you should leave Pickard for a little while."

"You've got to be kidding."

One look at his face was sufficient to convince Kate he was serious. He must have sensed her shock because he reached across to take her hands, his grasp steadying not intimate. When she tried to pull away, he held her in place.

"Hear me out. I've been so worried about your safety that I can't think straight. Originally I thought the candy was just a warning to back off. But the more I think about it, the more I worry that you could become the focus of this man."

Kate shuddered.

"I think you should go away for a while. A week or two. Maybe more. Enough time to let any interest in you die down. It'll also serve a second purpose. Whoever it is must know you're asking questions, so just the fact that you'd go away might convince him that you're no threat to him."

"That's ridiculous, Mike. I can't leave town. Where would I go?"

"Chris has a place out in Palm Springs. I'm sure he'd let you use it. You could go out there for a vacation."

"And then what? I can't stay away forever."

"Damn it, Kate. It looks more and more possible that Garvey might be a suspect, but what if he isn't? It could be anyone. It's driving me crazy. I need to know you're safe. You and Richard and Jenny were my family. I couldn't bear it if I lost you too."

Kate caught the slight tremor in his voice and turned her hands so they were holding his in a reassuring grasp.

"You're not going to lose me, Mike," she said.

He cleared his throat, then smiled across the table. With a final squeeze he disengaged his hands, and drank the last of his coffee.

"With this Harvard story we know there's more to Garvey's life," Kate said. "What if we could find evidence of other incidents? If Garvey's guilty, he must have committed other assaults over the years. All we need to do is find one. Then we could go to Leidecker."

"I don't know where to look for information like that. Maybe a private detective would know. At least it's something to consider." He shrugged his shoulders. "Like you, I think we're close to getting at the truth. If we could sit down with no distractions, lay everything out, we might be able to see some way to proceed."

Mike fell silent. Suddenly he rapped his knuckle on the top of the table.

"That's it, Kate. That's exactly what we'll do. We'll both go away for a few days."

"Not that again." She threw up her hands in exasperation.

"This is different. We could go up to my place in Wisconsin. It's not very far and you'd be safe there. I'll admit it's nothing luxurious, but you'd be surrounded by water and trees and sky. What could be more healing?"

Seeing her hesitation, he continued.

"You look just as tired as I feel. With all that fresh air, you'd sleep and eat better. And knowing you're safe would make it easier for me to think clearly. Together we can work out a plan of action. No matter what we discover, you'll be stronger and better rested when you return. Today's Wednesday. We could leave Friday for a long weekend. Will you come with me?"

His excitement communicated to her and she could feel a lessening of the fear and confusion that had taken over her mind.

"I guess I could use a couple days away," she admitted.

Mike's relief was so apparent that it was evident how much he had been worrying about her. Conscious of her earlier thoughts about their relationship, she vowed to talk to him over the weekend.

His enthusiasm for the trip carried them through the drive back home. She agreed to a Friday departure and suggested he work out the details.

Getting ready for bed, Kate accepted the fact that she would have trouble sleeping. The fear that had jerked her awake at every sound in the night was replaced by anticipation for the trip to Wisconsin.

For the first time since Jenny's death, Kate felt in control of her life. She knew exactly what needed to be done. She thought about all that she had learned since she'd begun her investigations. The discovery that Garvey had molested a child many years ago was the piece of evidence she'd been searching for. She was convinced that he had murdered Jenny.

She suspected that Mike wanted her to get away so that he could convince her to give up her investigations. She had to admit that she was exhausted and needed to build up her strength. If she caught up on her sleep, she'd be able to think more clearly. Richard had always loved Mike's cabin. Surrounded by the peaceful beauty of the lake, her mind would be able to plan with precision, and her body would be prepared for action. Now that she was convinced of Garvey's guilt, there was only one thing to do.

When she returned to Pickard, she would kill Joseph Garvey.

Kate sat at the bottom of the steps, staring at the baggage stacked in the front hall. It was only nine-thirty. Mike wasn't due for an hour.

Although at first the idea of killing Garvey had appalled her, once she began to consider the options she could come to no other conclusion. In the last two days, she had come to believe that she had made the right decision. Not only did she want justice for Jenny but she needed to ensure that Garvey never hurt another child.

Making the decision was one thing. Executing it was another. She'd never realized how difficult it was to plan a murder.

She knew she'd only have one chance, so she'd have to find a method with the greatest degree of success. The plan would need to be simple and couldn't endanger anyone else. She had no illusions that she would be able to get away with it. It didn't matter. Garvey's death was the priority.

Since Wednesday, she'd considered and discarded a thousand schemes. She had no access to poison and had no idea how she could administer it. She didn't think she could stab him. She debated running him down with her car, but that wouldn't guarantee his death.

Aside from the fact that she didn't have the foggiest idea how to hire a hitman, she didn't think it was morally right to ask someone to kill for her. She saw nothing contradictory in her thinking. As Jenny's mother, she had the right to act as executioner. After much thought, she decided that shooting would be the easiest and most accurate method.

And she already had a gun.

The gun had belonged to Richard's father. In the early days of their marriage, Richard had taken great pains to show her how to assemble, clean, and use it. He'd been pleased by her accuracy, but Kate had been uncomfortable with the weapon. She'd worried about the safety of having a gun in the house after Jenny was born and insisted that he store it in the attic. When she went up to get her suitcase, she searched until she found the gun in an old trunk.

Kate's fingers stroked the soft tan leather gun case in her lap. She unzipped the case and took out the gun, grasping it firmly as Richard had taught her.

The Savage automatic was a thirty-two caliber with a high-luster, blue steel finish. The gun had hard, black rubber handgrips. Built to fit the hand, it was small; weighing a little over a pound.

Standing up, she carried the gun and the ammunition over to the hall table. Thanks to Richard's painstaking instructions, she had no trouble remembering how to load the pistol. She shoved the magazine into the butt. Pulling back on the cocking piece, she shot a cartridge into the firing chamber then set the gun on safety.

She was standing in the front hall with the gun in her hand when the doorbell rang.

Mike wasn't due for another fifteen minutes. Heart pounding, she shoved the gun into the leather case, fingers shaking as she zipped it up. She looked around for a place to hide it just as the doorbell rang again.

Her open duffle bag was at her feet, and she thrust the gun case between her raincoat and a sweatshirt and closed the top. Her hands were sweating and she wiped them against her shirt as she reached for the doorknob. Marian was just turning away from the door.

"Oh, you are home."

"I was upstairs." Kate sounded breathless to her own ears and she caught Marian's sharp glance. "I tried to call you yesterday, but I must have missed you."

When Kate didn't immediately invite her in, the older woman stood uncertainly in the doorway, "I haven't seen you for awhile. Have you been working?"

"No."

Marian raised an eyebrow at the brusque response. When she spotted the duffle beside the hall table, her expression changed to one of surprise. "You're going away?"

"Yes. I haven't had a chance to tell you. For a couple of days. A long weekend. With Mike. He thought a fishing trip would be good for me. Relaxing."

Kate knew she was making a muddle of everything, practically stumbling over her words.

"You're going fishing with Mike?"

"Yes. We're going up to his cabin in Wisconsin."

This time Marian's eyebrows rose almost to her hairline. "Have you ever been up there? I heard the place is a hellhole."

"Mike said it's pretty primitive. Sort of like camping." The comment made little sense, but Kate couldn't think of anything else to say. She pointed at her bedroll and the fishing rod leaning against the closet door.

"Camping at Mike's place. Sounds like nirvana."

The bite to Marian's words indicated she was aware that Kate was shutting her out.

"When I get back, we'll have dinner," Kate said.

"Of course, dear." Marian leaned over and gave her a quick hug. "In the meantime, have a good trip."

Without another word, she left. Kate stood in the doorway, staring after her, regretting the fact she'd hurt her friend. One part of her mind told her it was necessary to distance herself from Marian because, if she went through with her plans for Garvey, she didn't want anyone else involved in the consequences.

Before she could close the door, Mike pulled into the driveway. He was full of enthusiasm as he carried her things to the car, and they got underway. His running dialogue needed little response on Kate's part. She had slept only fitfully since the night she found the candy in her purse, and as exhaustion settled over her, she dozed during the drive to Beaverton Lake.

"About twenty minutes more and we'll be there," Mike said as she groggily stared out the window at the passing scenery. "I leave my car at the marina where I keep my boat."

Kate had been amazed to discover that Mike's place was located in the middle of a marsh. The only way to get to his cabin was by boat. For a man who treasured the amenities of life, she couldn't wait to see how he handled a more rudimentary existence.

"There's the lake," Mike said, pointing to a break in the trees.

Kate sighed with pleasure at the huge expanse of water. In the July sunshine the foliage on the shoreline picked up a golden tone, accented by the shimmering blue-green of the water.

She noticed that as they traveled farther north, the number of boats and water skiers lessened. Through the trees she could see houses along the shore, but these too thinned out as the ground got lower. The undergrowth thickened, cutting off her view of the lake. A few minutes later they turned into a road marked by a painted sign announcing Rice Resort and Marina.

A sprawling log building perched on the edge of a small bay with the lake beyond. A wooden deck, facing the water, ran the length of the building. Planked walkways led down to the marina. Mike pulled the car up beside a metal shed.

Kate got out, sniffing the lake air. After the air-conditioned drive, it was like stepping into a sauna. The weather bureau had predicted the mid-nineties and she thought it was close to that. Despite her white shorts and yellow cotton shirt, she was hot. She was grateful for the steady breeze off the lake.

The marina was a busy place. Boats were being gassed up at an ancient pump, while cars with trailers were lined up at the ramp ready to put in or haul out boats. At a touch on her arm, she turned and followed Mike into the tavern.

"Must be a hellava wind, Doctor Mike, to blow you all the way up here."

The words accompanied by a cackle of laughter boomed across the room. Coming in from the bright sunlight, Kate blinked several times before she was able to locate the speaker.

A tall, weather-beaten woman came around the end of the bar. She had a loose-jointed, shambling walk. Apparently years in the outdoors had taught her there was no need to hurry. Somewhere in her early seventies, her hair was white.

Kate hung back as the woman shook hands with Mike, pounding his shoulder in greeting. She was wearing a man's button-down oxford cloth shirt tucked into oversized jeans. Old white sneakers completed the picture.

When Mike drew Kate forward, she found herself staring into the steadiest, clearest blue eyes she'd ever seen. She held out her hand, unsurprised by the strong grip of the older woman. Kate guessed she'd probably never been beautiful but her face had character, the seamed and creased skin resembling tanned leather.

"I'm Daisy Rice. Just plain Daisy to most folks." She herded them toward the bar, setting out ice-cold bottles of beer. "About time you got here, Doc. Your boat's all gassed and ready to go. We'll fix you up with ice and some beer before you leave." She turned her attention to Kate. "Did he tell you how godforsaken his place is, honey?"

Kate laughed. "Mike says it's just like camping."

"Except there are more mosquitoes," Daisy added.

Since it was lunchtime, they ordered hamburgers and fries. Kate hadn't had much breakfast, so she was starving. She didn't say much during lunch, listening contentedly to the banter between Daisy and Mike. Lake conditions and a hot spot for bluegills were noted, but much of the discussion centered on the location of a new marina across the lake, and whether it would bring more people to the north end.

After lunch, Mike got the cooler to ice down the beer. Outside, a fourteen-foot aluminum boat was tied in the slip closest to the shore. Trying to stay out of the way while Mike loaded the boat, Kate walked to the end of the pier and looked out over the water.

"It's a beautiful sight," Daisy said at her elbow. "I never tire of looking at the water."

Kate hadn't heard the woman's approach, but nodded in agreement. "How long have you been here?" she asked, without taking her eyes off the water.

"Thirty-three years. This end of the lake hasn't changed that much since my husband and I bought the place. The south end's another matter all together. Regular honky-tonk. Water slides, sleazy bars, and noise."

"From the sound of it, I'll take this end. I like peace and quiet."

"Mike's place is closer to comatose. Who knows? If you can stand it, you'll get a good rest. It looks like the ends of the earth and it's a pain to get to but funnily enough it's not that far away. Couple years back 'round Fourth of July some kids found the place and decided to have a party. Got a little noisy, drinkin' and shootin' off firecrackers. Woke me up. My nephew's a cop, so I called him. About two in the morning, I led him and a batch of his buddies right to the door of the cabin."

"Must have been quite a surprise for the boys."

"Right you are, honey. They'd been skinny-dipping and were sound asleep. You shoulda seen them staggering around bare-ass naked, looking for their clothes. Haven't seen that many dimpled cheeks since."

Kate's chuckle echoed Daisy's amusement. "It was lucky for Mike you heard them."

"Believe me. Nothin' goes on around this lake I don't know about. Night or day." Her words sounded like a pledge. She paused, then continued in a softer tone. "I met your husband a couple times. Liked him. So did my husband, Ham."

"Thanks," Kate said, surprised that Daisy knew who she was. Mike must have filled her in.

"Death's never easy. Fast or slow, it don't seem to make much difference. My husband passed three years ago. Heart. Still miss the old bastard. Everyone around here knew Hamilton Rice. World was empty when he died. Seemed like nothing would ever fill the void."

Kate turned to face the older woman, grinning when she saw the red and black plaid wool hunting cap.

"It was Ham's," Daisy said, noticing the direction of Kate's glance. "I wear it winter or summer. Started wearing his clothes, too. Everything 'cept the shoes are his. The shirts fit okay but the pants and belts run big. Wearing his stuff makes me think he's somewhere close."

"Does it get better?"

Daisy tilted her head, staring at Kate beneath the peak of her cap. "Usually I say yes to that question, but I think you're smart enough to have figured out that it never does. A little more endurable, maybe. At my age, it's just a matter of killing time until I join him."

Instinctively Kate put her hand on the woman's arm. It was a gesture of understanding. Daisy smiled and pressed her fingers in acknowledgment.

"I know what it's like to grieve for a child. Buried two of my kids, so at times I get a bit impatient at how long I've been hanging around. A month ago I got word I've got cancer. Honest to God, Kate, all I could feel was relief."

Kate knew better than to offer sympathy. She stood beside her, mutely honoring Daisy's disclosure. Mike's call brought them back to

263

the present, and they walked back to the boat in companionable silence.

"The car's locked," Mike said, handing Daisy the keys. "We'll be back either Sunday or Monday."

"I'll be here," Daisy said. "And if the fishing's no good, come on back for dinner. Tonight's fish fry."

Mike snorted. "The local Icelandic cod?"

"You wish."

By the time Mike and Kate were seated and added the cooler full of beer and pop, the boat was riding perilously close to the waterline.

"You'd think a rich doctor could afford a bigger boat," Daisy commented, blue eyes alight with amusement. "Better keep that bailing can close to hand, Kate. One wrong move and you'll go down like a rock."

"We'll see you in a couple days," Mike shouted above the roar of the engine.

Daisy touched the peak of the plaid cap in a salute. Kate waved, her hair whipping wildly around her face. Mike eased the boat between the buoys marking the channel into the main part of the lake and then opened the throttle. Kate watched Daisy and the marina grow smaller then turned to face forward, squinting her eyes against the wind-tossed spray.

To Kate, the marshy area appeared to have few landmarks. Tree stumps, cattails, and marsh grass grew up through the water and in some places it was so shallow she could see the mud bottom. She turned to Mike in apprehension. In his shorts and open-neck shirt, he looked younger and more carefree than he had in a long time.

He seemed to know exactly where to go although she couldn't detect a channel. As they moved deeper into the marsh, she felt far removed from the resort atmosphere of the lake. The quiet was oppressive. Even the motor sound was muted.

"There it is," Mike said.

They had been traveling through an alley of tall grass when suddenly the channel opened up onto an enclosed lagoon dotted with weed beds. Off to the right, a muddy beach slipped backward in a gentle incline toward a flat, open portion of dry land. At the back, the undergrowth was thick, interspersed with tall jack pines and shorter, fuller evergreens. Tucked in under the trees, Kate could see a small log cabin. With its center door and a screened window on either side, it looked like a house drawn by a child.

Mike increased the speed, pointing the boat toward the bank. He cut the motor so that as the stern lifted, the momentum carried the boat to the shore, grounding it against the mud bank.

"It's not exactly the Ritz Carlton," he said, voice loud in the surrounding silence.

"I feel as if we're entirely cut off from civilization," Kate whispered, eyes darting around the area. "How on earth did you find this place?"

He leaned over to take off his sneakers. "My first year in Chicago, one of the other interns, Ben Kendall, invited me up for a weekend. I couldn't believe that anything this private could exist twenty minutes away from a busy resort area."

"I suppose it's good fishing back here," Kate ventured.

"Surprisingly not. Otherwise it would be crawling with fishermen. Ben told me something about a chemical leaking into the water in the area, but I don't know if that's true. All I know is fishing's lousy back here. When he moved out east, he sold me the place."

Barefoot, he stepped over the side of the boat. Although he sank into the mud, the water only came up to his knees. He walked to the bow, grabbed the metal frame and heaved the boat up onto the land until three quarters of it was out of the water. Without ceremony, he picked up Kate, deposited her on the shore, then headed for the cabin.

The ground was hard packed. She walked up the rise, following Mike to the front door. He unlocked the padlock, pulled the door open, and cautiously peeked inside.

"The first time I came up here, a family of raccoons had taken possession. The mother was plenty pissed at our intrusion. We had a hellava time getting her and the babies out."

Kate stood in the doorway while he did his inspection and opened the windows. The interior was roughly twelve by fifteen feet, divided into two rooms. The furniture in the main room consisted of a rectangular wooden table, four chairs, and a long wooden shelf along the wall. The back room was smaller. All she could see were two metal cots.

"I've tried to keep it simple. The only improvements I've made were the windows and screens. The mosquitoes around here are the size of tanks." He looked at her standing in the doorway and for the first time seemed to sense her uneasiness. His brow furrowed. "You look worried. I hope this isn't too rustic."

She shook her head. "No. I remember Richard telling me about the place, but I thought he was exaggerating. I didn't imagine it being so, uh secluded," she said, although she thought isolated was a better description.

"That's the beauty of it," he said. Then realizing that her comment might not be a compliment, he grinned. "It's deceptive. This marsh winds around behind Daisy's place. We're really not that far from civilization. Once you're used to the place, I think you'll like it."

"Don't count on it." She smiled to take the sting out of her words. She couldn't understand why he found the place appealing.

"Well, let's get unpacked," Mike said. "Then I'll take you for a tour of the lake before dinner."

In the back room Kate found a broom, and once she'd brushed away cobwebs and opened windows, the musty smell dissipated. She spread the bedrolls on the cots and the two duffle bags on the shelf along the wall.

"You'd better wear long pants tonight. The mosquitoes are vicious after dark," Mike shouted from the main room.

Reminded that she would be spending the night in a marsh, she changed into jeans and a long sleeved blouse. It was still hot, but the outfit would give her some protection against the bugs.

By the time she finished, she began to view the place in a more favorable light. She'd camped enough with Richard to feel undaunted by the lack of plumbing. Mike had set the cooler, a five-gallon water jug, and the rest of the equipment on the long shelf. The Coleman lantern was in the center of the table, warm light lending a bit of charm to the inside of the cabin.

"The place looks downright homey," she said as she turned over the bedroom to him.

"I hope you're hungry," he said. "The place we're going has the best walleye in the area."

She had just finished brushing her hair when she heard Mike swear. He came through the doorway from the bedroom, a puzzled expression on his face.

"I found this when I knocked your duffle off the shelf," he said, his eyes dropping to the unzipped leather gun case in his hands. "Where the hell did you get this?"

"From Richard. It was his dad's." Kate couldn't believe she'd forgotten to take out the gun before they left. She tried to appear nonchalant beneath Mike's searching gaze. "I thought it might be a good idea to do a little target shooting while I'm up here."

"What for?" he said as he set the case on the table.

"All right, I'll admit it. I've been scared ever since I found that candy in my purse. I thought I'd feel safer with the gun."

The cabin was silent as Mike digested her words.

"I've never even seen a gun up close and personal."

He reached out, but before he could touch it, Kate pulled the case across the table.

"Don't, Mike. It's loaded." She knew he was angry at her admonition, but she didn't waver. "It's not safe unless you know what you're doing. If you can find a place where we can shoot it, I'll show you how to use it. For now it's better left alone."

Folding over the leather flap, she zipped up the case, and then set it on the shelf behind the cooler.

"Will it be safe enough here?" she asked.

"Sure. We'll lock the place, when we go out."

"I'm done dressing if you want to change," she said.

Kate caught the speculative look on Mike's face, but he went into the bedroom without comment. She was left alone to contemplate her own stupidity. How could she have forgotten the gun? Although he hadn't challenged her, she knew the discussion of the gun was not over.

When he returned, he opened the front door for a quick check of the sky.

"It's starting to cloud over. We better close up the place before we leave. They're predicting a storm, but we should be back from dinner before it hits."

The answering machine clicked on and Carl swore, slamming the phone down. Judas H. Priest! Ten o'clock on a Friday night. Where the hell is Kate at this hour? Reaching for a stick of gum, he wadded up the foil and flicked it across his desk in the direction of the wastebasket. After a cursory knock on the door, Bea put her head inside.

"There's someone to see you," she said. "A Glen Sather."

"Sather? Can't place the name." Carl looked over her shoulder at the man standing in the waiting area. He shook his head. "Never saw him before. What's he want?"

"He wouldn't say. He asked for you by name. He said he had some information about the Warner case. When I suggested he tell me, he said he preferred talking to you."

"A kook?"

Bea chuckled. "It's always possible, but he didn't drool or foam at the mouth."

"Well, that's a definite plus." He gave a long suffering sigh. "Send him in."

Carl returned to his desk, opened his leather notebook, and set a freshly sharpened pencil on top of the yellow pad. He stood when the man entered.

Sather was in his late twenties, good looking although his features were so perfect that his face had an artificial look. He was dressed formally for this time of night, Carl thought. The rich tones of his flowered tie softened the severity of the starched white shirt, conservative navy suit, and the mirrored shine of his shoes. After a darting glance around the office, he crossed the floor and shook Carl's hand, his grip loose, a mere brushing of palms.

"Evening, Mr. Sather." Carl waved to a chair. "I understand you wanted to talk to me about the Warner case."

"Yes, I do." He sat down and crossed his legs, smoothing the material over his knee. "It's late, but when I discovered you were still here, I thought it best to see you. You're the chief of police so I wanted to speak directly to you."

Noting the nervous gestures, Carl nodded and leaned back, letting the man get comfortable with the surroundings.

"Now, Mr. Sather, was there something in particular you wanted to discuss?"

"Call me Glen. Then it won't seem so official," the man said. "I wanted to come in sooner, but Richard made me promise that I wouldn't. Since he's been declared dead, I don't feel bound anymore. I have evidence that will prove that Richard Warner did not kill his daughter."

Carl felt a tingling across his shoulders and up his neck. He'd felt all along that the only way Warner could be innocent was if a vital detail was yet to be discovered. He held perfectly still, convinced that the missing piece of the puzzle was about to drop into place.

"The day Jennifer Warner was killed, Richard was with me in Rockford," Sather said. "We spent the entire afternoon together at Napp's Motel."

# Twenty-six

THE LOW RUMBLE OF THUNDER growled closer. Outside the restaurant, the wind had picked up and a flash of lightning lit up the sky over the lake. The rain was falling in a light drizzle, but it was just a matter of time before the storm broke.

"I hate to rush you after such a good dinner, but I think we better get moving," Mike said.

Kate nodded, teeth chattering from the chill that invaded her body at the thought of the return trip to the cabin. She took Mike's hand and ran along the wooden planking to the boat.

He untied the boat, jumped aboard, and pushed away from the dock. Once the motor caught, he eased the throttle back and turned the boat into the wind.

"You may have to earn your keep." He spoke over his shoulder. "There's a bailing can up in the bow. You may need it if the storm hits."

"So this is how you entertain a girl. No wonder you're still single." She dug around under the anchor rope until she found the can.

"That's gratitude for you. You ate enough fish tonight to last you all week," he yelled above the sound of the motor. "I'll have to take on another patient just to cover the dinner bill."

Mike's humor lessened some of Kate's apprehension. The lake was choppy. The boat bucked up and down in the wind-driven waves. She clung to the sides of the boat, occasionally reaching up to wipe rainwater out of her eyes.

"It's not far now," Mike shouted as he pointed to the weed beds just visible on the far shore. "I think we can beat the storm."

As if on cue, the storm burst overhead. Huge raindrops pelted the boat, sounding like pebbles falling on a metal roof. Kate grabbed the bailing can, scooping the water over the side as it accumulated in the bottom of the boat.

She worked steadily, only vaguely aware of their progress along the shoreline. She stopped when she felt the boat turn and recognized the straggle of weeds at the entrance to the marsh. As if to reward them for finding their way back, the rain tapered off to a misting drizzle and then stopped.

Inside the channel, the night fog enclosed them in a gray-white world of blurred shapes. Kate had trouble breathing in the heavy air and sighed in relief when they broke through into the lagoon in front of the cabin.

The fog was less dense, dissipating slightly in the open space. Mike's expression, which had been tight with concentration, lightened as he steered toward shore. He gunned the motor then cut it off, running the boat up onto the mud beach.

The cabin, which had looked so forbidding the first time Kate saw it, had all the familiarity of home. While Mike pulled the motor out of the water, she stood up, wet clothes plastered to her body, and climbed over the side of the boat.

Her shoes slipped on the soft bank. Before she could grab hold of the side of the boat, her feet shot out from under her, and she landed on her stomach in the mud.

"Are you all right?" Mike yelled.

He scrambled over the side and the moment his feet touched the ground he too ended up in the mud.

"I'm fine," Kate said. "How about you?"

She was propped up on her elbows and grinned across at Mike. He tried to get to his feet but his shoes couldn't find a purchase and slid toward the edge of the lagoon. Laughing now, Kate reached up to brush the hair out of her eyes, leaving a smear of mud across her forehead.

Scooting backward, she slid down to the edge of the water. Struggling upright, she waded out into the lagoon, ignoring the sickening feeling as her feet sank into the mud.

When the water reached her waist, she dove head first, coming up several yards from the boat where the water was shoulder height. She stood on the bottom, rubbing her hands over her clothes to get rid of the mud.

"Great idea," Mike shouted. His voice was loud in the otherwise silent lagoon.

For an instant, Kate flashed back to a long ago summer when she and Richard had gone with Mike and his girlfriend of the moment to the Indiana Dunes. They'd camped in the park and gone to the beach for a picnic and a swim. When it got dark, they'd gone skinny-dipping, the four of them frolicking in the water like young otters.

With one final dip, she headed for shore, moving carefully so that the clinging mud didn't suck off her shoes. Mike splashed up behind her. He unlocked the door to the cabin, and she held a flashlight with shaking hands while he lit the lantern. The small flame expanded, spreading a warm glow of light around the room.

"Better get some dry things on," Mike said. "I'll heat some water."

Shoes squishing across the floor, she hurried into the bedroom. She pulled bath towels out of her duffle. Hurrying to the end of the bed, she peeled off her wet clothes, leaving them in a pile on the floor. She stood up, jumping when the cold angel charm slapped against her skin. Her fingers touched it for reassurance. She was lucky she hadn't lost it in the water.

She toweled her hair with shaking fingers then rubbed the terry cloth roughly over her body to increase her circulation. Once she'd wiped the mud from between her toes, she felt clean. Naked, she pulled on a fleece sweat suit, grateful for its comforting warmth.

"Water's ready," Mike called and she padded barefoot back to the main room.

He finished pouring hot water into two mugs on the table and flipped her a tea bag. She dunked it, warming her hands on the mug as she raised it. She took a sip, sighing as the warm liquid found its way to her stomach. Over the rim, she smiled her gratitude at Mike.

He added instant coffee to his mug, stirring it only minimally before he raised it to his lips. He took several quick sips. Setting it on the table, he pulled a bottle of brandy off the shelf and splashed some into his mug. He held it out to her, but she shook her head. The brandy must have cooled the coffee because he was able to finish it in several long swallows. He poured more water into the cup, adding the coffee and brandy together this time.

"You'd better change or you'll need a doctor," she said.

"I'm okay. The coffee's helping." He eyed her in the glow of the lantern. "You look bushed. Why don't you pile into bed? I'm going to sit up for a bit."

"Are you sure you don't mind? I really am tired."

"Go ahead. I'm too keyed up to go to bed. I'm going to have another coffee and read a medical journal. That'll put me to sleep for sure."

"It was a fun evening. Thanks for getting us back safe and sound."

With a final sip of her tea, she set the mug on the table and returned to the bedroom. She climbed into her sleeping bag, pulling the edges up around her neck. After being so hot during the day, she couldn't believe how cold she was. The hot tea was a center of warmth in her stomach, and she curled her body into a tight ball.

When Mike came into the bedroom, she was practically asleep. Nestled under the covers, she heard him change clothes and was surprised when he returned to the main room. The clink of glass against mug suggested he was having another brandy and coffee.

After all we drank at the restaurant, she thought, he's going to have a dreadful hangover in the morning. Her eyelids became heavier until finally her mind slipped away into sleep.

"Richard Warner was bisexual?" Bob Jackson slapped his forehead with the palm of his hand. "Is that why he was in the forest preserve the day Jenny was killed?"

"On the nose." Carl stared around the table. He could almost see them absorbing the ramifications of Richard's elimination as a suspect.

"Verified?" Diego Garcia asked.

"In part," Bea said. "Sather had receipts for motel bills and restaurant tabs. He also agreed to supply us with the names of two other men who'd had contact with Warner over the last two years. He's holding the names until we can give him assurance that the interviews will be strictly confidential."

"So Warner picks up this fag in the forest preserve." Tony was having trouble getting a handle on the story. His face indicated his repugnance for the alternate lifestyle. "They hotfoot it to a motel, do the bad-nasty then Warner runs home to the little woman, arriving at the time he normally comes in from work only to find the kid missing. The body's found in the very same forest preserve where he was knee deep, if you'll pardon the wording, knee deep in fruits. Sort of ironic, huh?"

"For once, Torrentino, think of the guy as an ordinary father." Bob glared across the table. "Give his pain some thought. You've got two kids. How would you have felt?"

Tony flushed and stared down at his notes. Carl spoke into the tense silence.

"According to Sather, over the years Richard had questioned his sexual orientation. He'd had several homosexual encounters in college, but it was only in the last two years that he'd begun to experiment in earnest. He'd never really come to terms with it and was terrified that someone would discover his secret. He loved his wife, was content with his marriage, and had a daughter he adored."

"It's easy to see why he lied about where he was on the day Jenny was killed." Bea, like Bob, was sympathetic to Richard's dilemma. "In the midst of such a tragedy, it was hardly the time to declare his sexual preferences. Besides, it probably never occurred to him that he'd become a suspect and need an alibi."

"Why didn't Sather come in sooner?"

"When Richard became a suspect, Sather called him to say he'd be willing to make a statement that they had been together, but Richard refused. He made Sather promise not to go to the police. Even when questions were asked of the gay crowd that hung out in the forest preserve, he held his tongue."

Privately Carl thought it was probably the fear of Sather going to the police that triggered Richard's drunken statement to Kate when he said "he wanted to tell."

"After the official statement declaring Richard's death a suicide," Carl continued, "and the general assumption that he'd killed himself out of guilt, Glen began to have second thoughts. He'd genuinely liked Richard and worried that his wife might think Richard had killed Jenny. In an agony of conscience, he came in to talk to me, albeit belatedly."

"If Richard is definitely innocent, why does so much of the evidence in the case point to him?"

"You think the murderer set us up?" Diego asked.

Carl nodded. "It looks like it. I've always been convinced that Jenny knew her killer, and both the person Mrs. Warner called the Whisperer and the killer knew a great deal about the Warners."

"The next two candidates on the prime list are Mike Kennedy and Christian Mayerling," Diego said.

"Consider this. As Warner's closest friends, wouldn't these two men have known about his sexual orientation? And if they did, why didn't they tell us in any of the interviews?"

"They might have been trying to protect his reputation."

"Maybe in the beginning, Bob, but once Warner became a suspect they had to know the fact that he had gay leanings would probably go a long way to clearing him."

"Why?" Tony was clearly puzzled. "He's married, so we know he likes women."

"Women, not little girls," Bea said. "A bisexual seeks relationships with mature adults of both sexes. For pedophiles, children are the preferred sexual objects."

"It's semantics," Tony muttered.

"No matter what it is, we need some answers," Carl said. "I want a microscope turned on both Kennedy and Mayerling. Go back to the interviews for the day of Jenny's death. Mayerling was at the health club and Kennedy was at the hospital. Regardless of an alibi, see if you can account for every second of their time."

"How much more of Sather's story needs to be verified?" Bob asked.

"Bea and I did a quick check," Carl said. "Bea's going to follow up on it. She'll let you know if anything important turns up, but for the moment consider it gospel. As for assignments, Bob, I want you and Tony to take Mayerling. Diego, you have Kennedy. Everything we've got on those two has to be reexamined in light of what we know now. Try and look at it a new way. Be creative."

"What about Nathanson, the soccer coach, and Bushnell, the neighbor?" Tony asked.

Carl shrugged. "Neither of them look very promising. However, I don't want to take a chance on missing anything. Who wants them?"

"I'll take them," Bea said.

After the meeting was over, Carl went back to his office. By one o'clock his desk was reasonably clean, and he called it quits. He decided to grab some lunch and then go over and talk to Kate. She'd be pleased when he told her that he would issue a statement exonerating Richard completely from any complicity in Jenny's death.

The nature of Richard's alibi was another matter.

Pulling his car into the driveway of the Warner house, Carl sat for a moment, thinking about Kate. He didn't know how she'd take hearing about Richard's relationship with Glen Sather. He was almost positive she didn't have a clue. He didn't relish being the one to tell her, but he didn't want her to see it on the news or read about it in the paper once the media got wind of it. Much as he'd like to, he couldn't prevent her being hurt by her husband's duplicity.

He got out, straightened his jacket and put on his hat, checking his reflection in the window of the car. He rang the front doorbell and waited. He wondered where she'd been all week. He'd tried calling last night until well after midnight. Maybe the reason she hadn't answered the phone this morning was that she'd gotten home so late and was sleeping in. He rang again.

When nothing happened, he opened the screen door and knocked. Still nothing. Walking back to the garage, he spotted flagstones going toward the back and followed the path to the backyard. On the deck, he knocked sharply on the patio doors.

"Chief Leidecker?" The voice came from the next yard, not the Warner house.

"Who's there?" he called. The bushes parted and Kate's neighbor appeared. "Mrs. Granger, isn't it?"

"How clever of you to remember. But call me Marian." She came through the bushes, her eyes darting up to the blank windows of the house. "Were you looking for Kate?"

"Yes. I gather she's not home."

"No." Her voice was hesitant. "Was there anything in particular you wanted?"

He knew from meeting her before, and from things Kate had said, that the woman was a good friend. At the moment she seemed ill at ease in his presence.

"Something's come up and I need to talk to her, Mrs. Granger, uh, Marian. It's rather important that I find Kate. Do you have any idea where I could reach her?"

"She's not in any trouble, is she?"

"Were you expecting her to be?"

"N . . . no." She shook her head. "I'm just concerned. I've been worrying about her."

Making a quick decision, Carl said, "To be perfectly candid, I have been too."

At the older woman's expression of dismay, he pulled out one of the chairs on the patio and offered it to her.

"Do you know where Kate is?" Her closed expression gave him little encouragement. "Look, Marian, no matter how you feel about my suspicions of Richard or my handling of the case, you must believe me when I say I have the highest regard for Kate."

Eyebrows furrowed in question, she searched his face then nodded her head as if she'd made the decision to trust him. "She's gone on vacation."

"Vacation?" He blinked in surprise.

"I dropped by yesterday because I hadn't seen her for quite awhile. She didn't invite me in." Her expression was bewildered. "We stood at the door talking. I didn't mean to pry, but when I saw her duffle bag I was so surprised that I asked where she was going. Truly, Captain Leidecker, I'm not usually so nosy."

"I know from what Kate's said you've been very supportive, Marian."

"My question flustered her. I suppose she felt guilty because she hadn't told me. Maybe thought I wouldn't approve, but really it's none of my business."

"And did she say where she was going?"

"Yes. She was going fishing with Mike Kennedy."

"Fishing? With Dr. Kennedy?" No matter what Carl had been expecting, that wasn't it.

"Yes. They were going up to Mike's place in Wisconsin. But really, Captain Leidecker, I can't imagine why she'd go there. It's very primitive, you know. If she wanted to get away, she could have gone to a thousand other places. Ones with air-conditioning and room service."

"I'm sure you're right," Carl said. "When did you say Kate left?"

"Yesterday. Mid-morning." She bit her lip. "I think she didn't tell me she was going away because of something I said the other day. I teased her about some gossip I'd heard about her and Mike."

"Did she say when she'd be back?"

"A couple of days. She didn't seem very sure. She's been edgy lately. I volunteer at the hospital and ran into Mike last week. When I mentioned it to him, he said he'd noticed it too and was worried about her."

"In what way?"

"He thought she was very depressed. She'd been overwrought since Richard's disappearance. He asked me to keep an eye on her."

Sensing that she had nothing more to offer, Carl stood up.

"Thanks so much for the info, Marian." He reached in his pocket and pulled out a card. "If you think of anything else, I'd appreciate it if you'd give me a call."

She tucked his card into the pocket of her skirt and walked with him down the steps into the yard.

"You know, Captain, I sense that you're fond of Kate. Mike's just an old friend, and she needs his support right now. Eventually she'll get through the raw emotions of mourning. If it's any consolation, I know she respects you, and she's not one to hold grudges."

Her words startled Carl, and he glanced over at her. Her blue eyes held a hint of amusement, but he chose to let it pass. "I'll keep that in mind," he said. "Thanks for the help."

"This is my day to answer questions about Kate," Marian said as they reached the front of the house.

"Someone else was asking about her?"

"Yes. He didn't introduce himself, but I recognized him anyway. I'm sure you know him. It was the assistant mayor, Joseph Garvey."

"Joseph Garvey was here?"

"Yes." Hand on her forehead to shield her eyes from the sun, Marian stared up at Carl.

"Did he say why he was looking for Kate?"

"No. Kate mentioned she'd worked in his office and, after a run-in with him, she quit. Maybe he wanted to straighten things out. I told him she was on vacation, and he said he'd get in touch with her at a later date."

"Doesn't sound as if it's anything important." He shrugged. "Well, I better get moving. Thanks again for your help."

Carl was anxious to get away, reaching for his cell phone as he hit the street. He punched the numbers to Bea's private line.

"I'm taking the rest of the day off," he said without preamble. "I'm at Kate Warner's house. Her neighbor says she's gone up to Wisconsin with Mike Kennedy. A sudden trip. It doesn't feel right. Besides now that Kennedy's back to being a suspect, I'm not too keen on her spending any time with him."

"Okay. If anything turns up, I'll call you."

"Do me a favor. Get hold of Joseph Garvey. If he's not at his office, try city hall. Tell him I want to know why he wanted to talk to Kate Warner this morning, then ask if he's ever heard of ButterSkots candy?"

"Garvey?" Bea's voice held surprise. "Is he a suspect?"

"No. Do you remember the wrapper I found? I think Kate might have gotten it from Garvey."

"From Garvey?"

"It was in her wastebasket the day she quit working for him. His name keeps coming up, and I need to rule him in or out."

"Okay. I'll check on it. Talk to you later."

Carl stopped at his house only long enough to change out of his uniform. Blue jeans, light blue knit shirt, and sneakers would look less out of place around Beaverton Lake. He slipped his gun into an ankle holster, pulling his pants leg down to cover it, and strapped his hunting knife to his belt. In twenty minutes he was back outside, heading northwest out of Pickard.

Perhaps it was stupid, but he was going to Beaverton Lake in order to bring Kate back to Pickard. He felt a sense of urgency to keep her in sight. He couldn't shake the conviction that Kate was in danger.

He tried not to analyze his motives. It was unlike him to become personally involved with anyone he came across in his job. From the beginning, he'd been drawn to Kate. First, out of sympathy for the tragedy of her daughter's death, then later by the woman herself. He didn't have a clue what form their future relationship would take. All he knew was that for now he wanted to protect her and eventually have some part in her life.

His cell phone rang.

"It's Bea, Chief."

"What have you got?"

"I talked to Joseph Garvey. He's in Chicago with his wife. He said to tell you he went to see Kate Warner because he thinks she's been following him. Does that make any sense to you?"

"Unfortunately, yes," Carl said, pressing the phone to his ear. "Remember I went to see him when I discovered Kate was doing research at the library about him. I asked if anything unusual was going on. He said he thought a woman had been observing him in court. He was nervous because he'd just fired a secretary for snooping in his office. I told him to change his schedule and see if she continued to follow him."

"You knew it was Kate Warner?" Bea asked.

"No. It was a hunch. I checked with Garvey's office manager. The woman he fired was Katherine Daniels. Daniels is Kate Warner's maiden name. I checked the temp agency and it was Kate. She'd been assigned for a week and quit halfway through. Some sort of disagreement with Garvey. I couldn't get any details. At any rate when Garvey didn't call me again, I assumed he'd been mistaken."

"Apparently he ran into her again at some dinner and decided either he was hallucinating or she was the woman he'd fired and the woman in court. He said he stopped by her house just to see if it was the same woman." Bea snorted. "Between you and me I think he was interested in her in a social sort of way."

"Makes you wonder, doesn't it?" Carl checked his watch. Another twenty minutes and he'd be at the lake.

"By the way. I asked Garvey if he'd ever heard of ButterSkots. Bingo. He said his wife gave him a tin of candy for his office. Neither of them have been to Scotland. He assumed she got it as a gift. Said he'd ask her about it."

"Good. Keep on everyone's tail until I get back."

After he rang off, he turned the various bits and pieces over in his mind. If Kate'd found the ButterSkots in Garvey's office, could she possibly have jumped to the conclusion that he was involved in Jenny's death? If so that would account for her library research, for watching him in court, and for her questions about the PF license plate printout.

With so little evidence, it would take a major leap of faith to believe Garvey was guilty of murder. Assuming she'd managed that, what next? And why did she suddenly go up to Wisconsin with Mike?

Where did Mike Kennedy fit in? Carl could understand that grief might have given Kate a warped sense of reality. But Mike?

Marian said that Mike was worried about Kate. Would she have confided her suspicions about Garvey to Mike? Mike knew Garvey and would see her theory as ludicrous. Is that why he had gotten her out of town? Hoping to talk some sense into her?

Questions, questions, and more questions. What bothered Carl most was, when she came to the police station, why hadn't she mentioned Garvey?

Kate opened her eyes, wincing at the bright light. She was feverish, her body hot and sweat-soaked. It was with relief that she realized she was bundled up in her sleeping bag in an airless room.

A loud snore jerked her upright. Mike was sound asleep, sprawled on his back on top of his sleeping bag. By the alcohol smell in the room, she guessed he'd been pretty drunk when he came to bed. She slipped out of her sleeping bag, tiptoed across the room, and opened the window.

Muddy clothes and towels were everywhere. Moving quietly she made a bundle of all the wet things. She gathered clean clothes and her toiletry bag then picked up the sodden mass, grabbed her shoes, and tiptoed out of the room. Reaching back, she closed the bedroom door.

Dumping the pile of wet clothes beside the front door, she lit the stove and set a pan of water for tea. Her watch was on the table. Ten. No wonder she felt so rested. She didn't know what time Mike had come to bed, but she'd gotten about ten hours of sleep.

Outside the sun was shining in a cloudless sky. The storm had passed through and, although it was hot, the humidity was lower than the day before. High eighties, she guessed. She washed up and changed into clean shorts and a cotton T-shirt. Her sneakers were streaked with mud, but dry.

Suddenly her stomach growled, an audible rumble in the silent cabin. After making tea, she dug out some cream cheese from the cooler and spread it on a bagel. Wanting to be outside, she took a chair and set it in the shade of the trees beside the cabin. She returned for her breakfast and the magazines she'd brought from home. It was well past noon when the heat of the day urged her to check on Mike.

When she didn't hear a hint of movement behind the closed bedroom door, she debated waking him but decided against it. For lack of anything better to do, she carried the pile of wet clothes outside. She located a rope in the cabin and after walking around the area, found two well spaced trees and strung a clothesline between them.

Mike's jeans were still muddy. She pulled out the leather belt and then turned to the pockets. Along with a handful of mud, she found a ring of keys, knife, pocket change, and his watch. She wrapped the grimy objects in a washcloth and set them aside.

She scrubbed everything in the lagoon, then hung it on the clothesline. The rope drooped with the weight of the wet things, but it held. By the time she finished, she was sweating in the heat of the afternoon sun. Back in the cabin there was still no sign of Mike.

How can he sleep this long? It was almost three.

She filled a plastic basin with water and set it on the table. Dunking Mike's belt buckle, she dried it off with a hand towel and put the belt on the seat of one of the chairs.

The watch was next. She rinsed off the expansion band and used a wet finger to clean off the face. The time was accurate, so maybe the watch was waterproof. She rinsed the coins and the ring of keys and set them in the center of the table.

The mud-caked knife was last. She dipped it in the water, just as she heard the first stirrings from the bedroom. Her fingers slid over the clean surfaces of the pocketknife. She pulled it out of the water and set it in the towel to wipe it off. Her eyes touched the sleek lines of the small Buck knife.

She recognized it immediately. It was Richard's knife.

# TWENTY-SEVEN

WHAT WAS MIKE DOING with Richard's knife?

The bedroom door opened. Mike stood in the doorway, mouth stretched in a yawn, shoulder propped against the frame. Kate could do nothing but stare at him. Her fingers closed convulsively around the knife and she dropped her arm to her side.

"God, do I feel awful," Mike said. When she didn't respond, he squinted to see her more clearly in the sunfilled room. "What's up?"

She couldn't speak. Her throat was frozen. All she could do was shake her head from side to side.

He raised his head as if he scented danger then pushed away from the door and walked purposefully toward her. His eyes darted around the room. He glanced at the things on the table, then the bowl of dirty water. She flinched away from him and he noticed her clenched fist. His hand shot out to grasp her wrist. He raised her arm, turning her hand over and squeezing her wrist until her fingers opened to reveal the knife.

"I should have thrown it away."

The tone of his voice was so conversational that at first the words didn't penetrate. When they did, the shock must have registered on her face. He thrust her arm away and the knife went sailing across the room to clatter against the far wall.

"Oh, God, no!" Kate shook her head from side to side. "Oh, God!"

Mike turned away from her, walked over to the stove and tested the water with a tip of his finger. Satisfied, he poured some in a mug and added coffee. He stirred it, his face expressionless.

"You couldn't leave it alone, could you, Kate? You had to dig and dig even after Leidecker was willing to close the case."

Her legs trembled and she clutched the back of one of the chairs to keep from passing out. It took every ounce of strength to keep from sinking into the darkness that swirled around her.

Silence filled the room except for the sound of Mike's spoon clinking against the side of the ceramic coffee mug. Kate pulled herself upright, her movements awkward as if she'd aged. Mike was staring at her, eyes sad in an otherwise expressionless face. She had to unlock her jaw before she could speak.

"Did you kill Richard, too?"

He didn't even blink at her question. "Yes."

"Why?"

A flicker of anger crossed his face. The muscles in his cheek popped with tension. "Damn it, Kate, I had to! Leidecker was relentless. He'd never leave it alone. Once he became suspicious of Richard, I knew it was the only way I'd be safe. It wasn't easy. Richard was my friend."

"You killed my daughter," she screamed.

Mike looked so offended that her fury increased and she picked up the flashlight on the table and threw it at him. Instinctively he raised his arms to cover his face. The flashlight hit his wrist and splashed hot coffee over his shirt. He threw the mug, smashing it against the wall and in three strides was across the room.

She curled her fingers to claw his face. She narrowly missed his eyes as he pulled his head back, snarling as he tried to capture her flailing arms. When he caught her wrists, she kicked his legs and pulled his hands toward her mouth so she could bite him. He released one of her arms and slapped her across the face.

It wasn't the pain of the slap that stopped her but the violence of the act. She had never been treated roughly before, and the trauma to her system was paralyzing. She flinched away from his upraised hand as he prepared to hit her again.

"That's better," he said. He dropped his arm, aware that all the fight had left her. "Sit down."

He jerked a chair out and shoved it toward her. She collapsed onto the seat, shaken by the realization that she was totally in his power. If she fought him, she suspected he would beat her to death. She shuddered, staring at the stranger who stood over her.

Victorious, he swaggered across the room, kicking the remains of the mug underneath the shelf along the wall. Seeing the leather gun case beside the cooler, he chuckled. He brought the case over to the table, opened it and stared in fascination at the gun. He picked it up, turning it from side to side as he hefted it, getting used to the weight.

Kate couldn't believe the change in Mike. His bloodshot eyes peered out of a pale, unshaven face. He was wearing bathing trunks and the shirt he'd slept in. His body smelled, a combination of sweat, alcohol, and dirt. College friend. Compassionate doctor. Friend of the family. Not a vestige of those remained. All gone, leaving behind a vicious killer.

"Don't look at me like that," he snapped. "It was all an accident. It never should have happened."

She covered her ears. "You monster."

Although she'd spoken under her breath, he heard her. Fury suffused his face. Gun still in his hand, he charged around the table. With his free hand, he grabbed the front of her shirt and dragged her out of the chair until only the toes of her shoes touched the floor. He laughed when she stiffened. He continued to speak, but now his voice was taunting.

"That's my girl. If you're good, I won't hurt you. But if you're a bad girl, I'll have to punish you."

His face was so close to hers that Kate saw the instant change of expression. One moment his eyes were wide with mockery and the next they'd narrowed in heightened perception. She couldn't hold back a groan at the flash of desire that crossed his face.

He set her down. Heart pounding in her ears, she kept her head bent, praying that he'd leave her alone, but his left hand circled around her neck, holding her in place. She felt the point of the gun scrape against her neck and looked down.

The chain of her necklace was looped over the barrel of the gun.

Mike raised the gun and the angel charm swung free. It twirled and twisted, the reflected sunlight sparkling on the gold surfaces.

Mike sighed, the sound a soft, drawn-out hiss. His grip on her neck shifted, thumb jammed beneath her chin. He forced her head up until he could see her face. His rasped breath touched her, and she closed her eyes.

"Open them."

He didn't shout at her, just squeezed her throat until she obeyed. Dropping the necklace, he raised the gun and touched the barrel to her temple. He grinned when she tried to pull away. He slid the gun to her ear then down her jawline to her chin. Retracing the path, he stroked down her neck to the shoulder then down her arm and across her waist. At her bellybutton, he paused.

His breathing was more ragged as he started upward, circling her breasts then teasing the nipples with the point of the gun. Kate whimpered and he cocked his head at the sound. He stared at her face, eyes focused on her trembling mouth. He raised the gun and pressed it against her lips.

"Open your mouth."

Despite the restraining hand at her throat, she managed to shake her head. His nostrils flared at her defiance. He tightened his fingers, cutting off her air until she started to lose consciousness. Her mouth opened as she fought for air.

He shoved the gun inside.

At the touch of the cold metal, she squeezed her eyes shut. Knowing she was going to die, she prayed silently.

"I'm not going to kill you, Kate." His whisper was close to her face, moist breath touching her skin. "Let me see your eyes. I need to see them."

She didn't respond immediately, and he tightened his grip on her throat. Afraid of losing consciousness, she gave in. Above her, Mike's face was covered with sweat and his eyes glistened with excitement.

His gaze intensified and he moved the gun.

He pulled it back until only the end of the barrel was between her lips then he slid it back inside. When the trigger guard bumped against her mouth, he began to pull it out again. He stroked the gun back and forth in her mouth. His breathing quickened. He moved faster, finally pulling the gun out and clutching her against his body as he bucked in orgasm.

When he released her, Kate slid to the floor. She breathed through her mouth to keep herself from throwing up. Her tongue was cut. The salty taste of her own blood made her gag and she spit the red-streaked saliva onto the floor.

"What am I going to do with you, Kate?"

It was a quietly spoken rhetorical question. Even if she'd wanted to respond, she couldn't. She curled herself into a ball and remained on the floor. He moved away, padding across the floor in his bare feet. When he returned, he nudged her with his foot.

"Get up."

Afraid his next kick would be more violent, Kate pushed herself into a sitting position. Mike stood over her, hands behind his back. He jerked his head toward the chair.

"Sit down."

Avoiding any contact with him, she inched onto the seat. He moved closer and she pressed against the back of the chair, relieved when he walked past her.

It was only when she spotted the gun on the table that she realized her mistake. It was too late. The rope dropped over her head and tightened around her neck. Her hands flew to her throat, clutching at the rope.

"Oh, God, don't tie me! Please don't tie me up!"

"Shut up."

He pulled the rope behind her head, tying it to the back of the chair. It was not tight enough to choke her, but it confined her movements. She couldn't bend over, stand, or move from side to side. She gasped for breath, her fingers tearing at the rope in a futile attempt to loosen it.

Coming around in front of her, Mike stood over her, watching her frantic movements with amusement. He didn't even notice when she raised her leg and lashed out, a direct hit to his knee. He staggered backward, falling heavily against the table.

She felt a momentary jolt of satisfaction, but when he roared to his feet, she knew it would cost her. He struck her across the face. Her head slammed against the back of the chair. First a flash of light and then darkness.

Kate woke up to pain. Her head pounded and one side of her face stung as if she'd been burned. It was an instant or two before awareness clicked in, and at the returning memory of where she was, she had to bite back a cry of despair.

She was no longer in the chair but lying on the floor, her back against the wall to the left of the door. Her hands were tied in front of her. Her feet were also tied and it didn't matter now that the rope was no longer around her neck. She lay on her side, knees pulled up to her chest. As far as she could tell, Mike hadn't hit her again, only tied her up.

Motionless, she assessed her injuries. Aside from a sore, swollen cheek, a bump on her head, a split lip, and various minor aches and pains, she was all right. At least for the moment. She had few illusions as to her fate.

Mike would kill her. But first, he'd rape her. Just like Jenny.

Keeping her breathing even, she opened her eyes a crack, shuddering at the sight of him seated at the table. While she was unconscious, he'd changed into a maroon short-sleeved shirt, navy Dockers, and boat shoes with no socks.

She was glad he hadn't shaved. The beard stubble made him look seedy and she could pretend he was a stranger. In truth, this was a man she'd never known. He was eating some bread and cheese, a can of beer close at hand. Two crushed cans littered the floor along with an empty bag of potato chips.

Staring at Mike, hatred formed in her heart. The paralyzing fear disappeared. Since failure meant death, she no longer had anything to fear. She'd have to watch for an opportunity because she'd only get one chance. In the meantime she'd have to find a weapon. Mike was physically stronger. She couldn't fight him. She'd have to kill him.

Keeping her actions slow, she tried to move her wrists. The rope wasn't cutting off her circulation, but it was tight enough so she couldn't get loose. She took a quick peek at the knot to see if she could use her teeth to untie it. A definite maybe. Next, she tried her ankles. She strained at the ropes and her shoe scrapped against the wall.

The sound was loud enough to alert Mike. He shoved his chair back and hurried over.

"Welcome back," he said. "You were out a long time."

She bit back a shriek when he reached for her. He picked her up as if she weighed nothing and set her on the chair beside the table. He handled her with a familiarity she found repugnant but she tried to hide her feelings, aware if she angered him, she would gain nothing and might precipitate more violence.

"I'm hungry and thirsty," she said. "Can I have something to eat?"

Her words surprised him. He narrowed his eyes as if expecting some kind of a trick. She hoped she hadn't overdone the whine in her voice. After a quick glance at the table, she hung her head and waited. The gun was nowhere in sight.

"Say please."

She cleared her throat to force back a flash of anger. "Please. Please, may I have something to eat?"

"That's better." He set the loaf of bread in front of her. The cheese was a block of cheddar, and she stared longingly at the small knife beside it. "And I suppose you want me to untie you."

"Please," she said without prompting.

She set her hands on the table, motionless as he untied the knot. She had an almost uncontrollable urge to snatch up the knife and stab him, but she knew he'd be expecting something like that. He must have read her thoughts because he grabbed her face and jerked her head backward until she was staring up at him. His fingers dug into her cheeks. She cried out at the pain.

"If you do one thing I don't like, you'll regret it. I won't just kill you, Kate, I'll hurt you in ways you can't even imagine."

Her body trembled in reaction to his words. He released her. Purposely turning his back on her, he went over to the cooler. With her ankles tied, she wasn't much of a threat. She focused on her breathing, and was calm by the time he returned with a can of Diet Coke. He sat down across from her, eyes intent on her every movement.

The thought of food made her nauseous. But she needed strength. She cut several slices of cheese for a sandwich. She took a bite, chewed it to a pulp and washed it down with a sip of the Diet Coke. She kept her voice neutral as she asked the question uppermost in her mind.

"How did you manage to kill Richard when you were at the Hilton all day?"

Mike grinned. "You've been watching too much television, Kate. It's the old let's-get-the-killer-talking ploy."

She shrugged her shoulder as if it were of little importance and went back to eating. It needed all her concentration to chew each bite and swallow without gagging. Mike fiddled with the beer can, sliding it around on the table top, then tipped his head back and finished it off. He crushed the can in one hand, tossed it on the floor, and crossed to the cooler to get another.

"Could I have another Diet Coke, too?" she asked, hastily adding, "Please?"

Kate gritted her teeth at Mike's chuckle. When he turned his back, her eyes darted around the room. Her heart skipped a beat when she spotted the gun, lying beside the Coleman stove. She kept her expression carefully bland when he returned to the table. He made no comment, but slid the can of pop across the table and opened the new can of beer.

"It was sheer luck that everything worked so well." Kate jumped as Mike's voice broke the silence. "I had a tight timetable. Actually Richard helped me figure out the timing of everything."

"That can't be true." She kept her voice calm, knowing any criticism would be met with anger.

"Do you remember the night before he disappeared, we went to see the lawyer?" She nodded and Mike continued. "That was just an excuse for Richard to get out of the house. He was positive that his arrest was imminent, so we went to a bar to consider his options. I convinced him that leaving town was the only way to stay out of jail."

"Richard would never have left without telling me."

"I told him if he told you ahead of time, you could be arrested for aiding and abetting. I said I'd tell you the moment he got away safely."

At the casual way Mike spoke, hatred rose like bile in her throat.

She twisted her feet to loosen the rope. It would be insanity to try anything with her ankles tied together. She took a sip of the Diet Coke, swallowing with difficulty. She had to keep him talking.

"H . . . how did you do it?" she asked.

As reluctant as she was to hear the details, she sensed that Mike was eager to tell her. He set his elbows on the table and leaned forward.

"The symposium was scheduled for all day Wednesday at the Conrad Hilton. Since I was a highly visible part of the event, I knew if I planned carefully, I would have an unbreakable alibi. The night before the conference, Richard and I drove up to the Touhy Avenue beach. I parked my car on the street about a block away. I gave Richard the keys to my car, and he drove me home."

Kate could barely stand to listen to Mike, let alone look at him. Watching the animation on his face, she couldn't believe that he was the same man she'd known for years. Did he always have a dark, bestial streak that none of them had seen? Could someone be a good, kind person one minute and a heartless killer the next without any noticeable transition? She understood the concept that good people could do bad things, but Mike's actions were far more complex.

"Pay attention!"

Kate jumped at Mike's shout. She hurried to appease the anger evident in the tightly clenched fists.

"I'm sorry," she said. "I was just thinking if I hadn't gone to bed early, I would have seen Richard when he came in. He might have told me what you were planning."

"I doubt it. I convinced him that he had to keep you out of it for your own safety. He came over to my place at the crack of dawn so we could finalize the plans. Everything was timed to the minute."

Pleased to have an audience, Mike was almost gloating. Yet he was full of nervous tension, fidgeting with the objects on the table. Too restless to sit, he began to pace, watching for her reactions as he continued.

"He drove me over to the Hilton to check in for the conference. I'm not sure what he did all day. He said he drove around for awhile after he called to tell you he was going to Milwaukee. I do know he went to the mall and bought new clothes. He was wearing his bathing suit under his clothes and he needed something different to wear from the beach to my car."

Kate pushed the bread and cheese away, leaving the cheese knife close to her hand. Mike was watching too intently. She'd have to wait for her chance.

"I never believed Richard would have chosen to commit suicide by drowning," she said.

"Too bad. If you'd left it alone, you wouldn't be in the predicament you're in now." He must have seen the agreement in her eyes because he chuckled. "Besides, Leidecker bought it."

He paced back to the table, picked up the bread and cheese, and put them back on the shelf. Returning, he stared at her for a long moment, then leaned over and, with deliberation, picked up the cheese knife and took it over to the shelf, well out of reach. She tried to keep the disappointment from showing in her body language, but he was far too interested in cataloging his clever machinations to notice.

"When Richard got to Lake Michigan, he parked, stripped down to his bathing suit, and then walked along the beach talking to people. We figured someone was bound to notice him and tell the police when they started searching the area. Once he felt he'd established his presence, he changed into the new clothes and walked down the block to my car. He was to meet me at Chessy's apartment at 6:30."

"At Chessy's?"

"Her apartment is only ten minutes from the Hilton." His tone was pragmatic. "I explained that she was away and he could stay in her apartment until I could get him out of town."

Kate was stunned. Mike had brought her to Chessy's apartment after Leidecker told her about Richard's apparent drowning. Had he still been alive, when she arrived?

"Now this is the beautiful part." Mike went back to pacing. "There was a cocktail party from six to seven-thirty for the banquet attendees. The moment I arrived, I began talking to people, mingling. Ten minutes later I left. Outside I found a cab and took it to Chessy's. Richard met me in the underground garage. No one was around. He parked my car in Chessy's space. I told him I had a suitcase in the storage area. I'd already unlocked the door to Chessy's locker so it was only a moment to get him inside. I knew I had to be quick so I hit him over the head with a hammer and covered him with a blanket."

"You beat him to death with a hammer?" She couldn't keep the horror out of her voice.

Mike's face reddened at her question. "Of course not. All it took was one tap. Once he was unconscious, I gave him an overdose of Versed. It's fast acting. Knocked him out immediately. He never felt a thing."

At least Kate had one thing to be grateful for. Richard hadn't suffered. It was painful but possible to picture the events surrounding his death. She couldn't even begin to consider Jenny's death. She didn't know how she'd ever be able to deal with it. Every time she looked at Mike, she was afraid she'd lose control.

"The timing was perfect. I was back at the Hilton before the cocktail party ended. I was the main speaker, and I was so pumped it went without a hitch."

"What did you do with Richard's body?"

"When I brought you to Chessy's I gave you a sleeping pill. While you were asleep, I put the body in the trunk of my car and buried it in that patch of woods behind my condo."

Poor Richard. At least she knew where he was. If she escaped, he'd get a proper burial. If not, it wouldn't matter. She felt a spurt of energy as the rope on her ankles slipped. She'd have to keep him talking until she could work her feet free. "What about Garvey?"

"You wouldn't give up on him." He shook his head, expression resigned. "I tried to get you to drop it, but you just wouldn't leave it alone. Finally I decided it would be safer to keep you focused on Garvey than have you wander off on some tack that might lead you to suspect me."

"But all those things I discovered about Garvey —" The words trailed away as she shook her head in bewilderment.

"You had a little help," he smirked.

"I don't believe it. I found the ButterSkots wrappers in his office before I ever mentioned Garvey to you. And I discovered his name on the PF printout."

He snorted. "I'll give you the license plate, but I take credit —

indirectly — for the wrappers. I gave Lisa Garvey a tin of ButterSkots for Christmas. Garvey must have taken them to the office. In any event it was interesting watching your growing suspicion of him. Luckily there wasn't enough so you could go trotting off to your pet cop Leidecker."

Kate was appalled by her own tunnel vision. She'd desperately wanted to discover Jenny's killer and once she found the wrappers, she couldn't see anyone but Garvey. Mike's opposition only served to stiffen her resolve. She clenched her fists at her own stupidity.

"Was the story about Garvey molesting the girl a lie?"

"Good, huh?" He took a gulp of his beer, his eyes smiling above the lip of the can.

"It wasn't Garvey. It was you?"

He nodded. "It was similar to something that happened when I was in school. But I didn't get caught."

Kate shuddered. Mike was silent. His eyes roamed over her and she tensed knowing he had more to say. Much as she wanted to shriek at him, she remained still, keeping the repugnance from showing in her eyes.

"I never meant for any of this to happen. One mistake. Then everything started to come apart. Leidecker kept asking questions. I only killed Richard to get him off my trail."

"God, you're sick!"

The words were out before Kate realized her mistake. Mike threw his beer can across the table. She ducked but it hit her on the side of the head and dropped to the floor as he lurched to his feet, face purple with rage.

With her ankles tied, she couldn't run. She doubled over, wrapping her arms around her shoulders to protect her body and pressing her face against her arms. Mike grabbed a handful of her hair and jerked her head back. Kate knew then she was about to die.

Rather than come through the lagoon, Carl had grounded his boat around the backside of Mike's property so he could cut through the woods and arrive at the rear of the cabin unannounced. He wanted to see exactly what Mike and Kate were doing before he made his presence known. For a moment, he frowned at the thought he might be interrupting some romantic getaway.

His shirt stuck to his sweaty back and his jeans were wet and streaked with mud from wading through the low spots. His gun was jammed into his waistband and he touched it to make sure it was still dry and secure. He was sorry now that he'd thrown away the ankle holster when it caught on a downed tree.

Clinging to the cover of the bushes, he made a quick survey of the area. Hearing voices inside the cabin, he crept over to the open window at the back. He raised his head slowly until he could see inside. The bedroom was empty. Looking through the open doorway, he spotted Kate. She was doubled over, arms wrapped around herself as if for protection.

He'd just glimpsed her when Mike roared into his line of vision and grabbed her by the hair. A chill of understanding ran through Carl as Mike swung his arm back and clenched his free hand into a fist.

Suddenly the sound of an outboard motor broke the silence, signaling the arrival of a boat.

"Yo, Doc," a voice called from the lagoon. "It's Daisy Rice. Are you decent?"

# Twenty-eight

"It's Daisy Rice, Doc. You guys ready for company?"

Kate opened her mouth to cry for help. Mike tightened his grip on her hair, leaning down to speak into her ear.

"If you scream, I'll kill her. Then I'll deal with you."

She slumped in defeat. It was one thing to risk her own life, but she couldn't let him hurt Daisy.

Mike tied her wrists again, scooped her up, and carried her into the bedroom. He dumped her onto the cot. She opened her mouth to gasp for breath and he shoved a handkerchief inside. Eyes narrowed, he glared down at her.

"One sound and you'll watch her die," he said as he left the room.

She heard him cross the floor and go out the front door. Then his shout of greeting.

"Howdy, Daisy. Did you get lonely for my company?" The rest of his words faded away as he walked down to the shore to meet the approaching boat.

Kate choked on the gag, afraid she was smothering and tried not to panic. This might be her only opportunity to get loose. She shoved the cotton handkerchief with her tongue, but it stuck to the inside of her mouth. She tried again. At first, nothing happened, then suddenly the handkerchief moved.

Something scraped at the window, and she rolled over to face the new danger. The gag muffled her scream. Carl Leidecker was outside, using a knife to cut the screen out of the frame.

Without much effort, he climbed in over the low windowsill. He tiptoed across to the bed. His eyes blazed with fury and his mouth was pursed tight. She held out her hands so he could free her.

He held a hunting knife with a carved ivory handle. The six-inch blade was sharp, cutting easily through the rope. He pulled the gag out of her mouth. Her jaw ached from being wedged open, and her throat was so dry she could hardly swallow. She used the wadded handkerchief to wipe away her tears.

Carl leaned over to cut the ropes on her legs. "Does Mike have a gun?" he whispered.

"Unless he took it outside, it's on the shelf beside the front door."

She took the knife from his hand and sawed at the ropes. He crossed the room, and peeked around the edge of the door.

"The gun's there."

"Don't let him see you through the windows."

He nodded, dropping to his hands and knees. The ropes fell away, and she swung her legs over the side of the cot. Gripping the knife, she turned toward the window, wanting to get as close as she could to her escape route. She raised her leg, shoving it out the window until she was straddling the sill. Holding onto the frame, she pulled her other leg up, ready to drop to the ground. Out front, the boat engine roared to life.

"Hurry, Carl!" she shouted knowing that Mike wouldn't hear her above the sound of the motor.

Suddenly her wrist was caught in an iron grip and the knife was ripped out of her hand. Mike dragged her out the window, whirled her around and, with one arm around her waist, lifted her clear of the ground and pressed her against his chest. He raised his free hand, the point of the knife at her throat.

Carl raced back into the bedroom. He knew Kate had been captured. He reached for the service revolver at his back. If everything went wrong, he didn't want Mike to have another weapon. He couldn't risk a search, so he shoved his own gun in a gap in the framework of the windowsill. He gripped the gun he'd found in the other room and stepped in front of the open window.

"Don't hurt her," he said. He held the gun steady in a two-handed grip, pointed directly at Mike's head. "Just set her down easy and I won't shoot you."

Mike's chuckle was almost lighthearted. "I'm a doctor, Leidecker. I know exactly where to cut her. She'll be dead before you finish pulling the trigger."

Carl was a good shot, but the risk was too high. The knife dimpled the skin beneath Kate's chin. As if to emphasize his point, Mike pressed harder and a drop of blood slid down the blade.

"Set the gun on the windowsill, and then climb outside."

Not wanting to give Mike any excuse for further violence, Carl followed the instructions. The fading sound of the boat engine emphasized the hopelessness of their situation.

"Put your hands in the air and step away from the window." Mike barked the words.

Carl took three steps, keeping his movements slow and non-threatening. Mike jerked his head and he moved back two more steps. From that distance he could still jump him if he got a chance.

Dragging Kate, Mike shuffled sideways over to the window. He lowered the knife and immediately threw Kate in Carl's direction, effectively blocking any counterattack as Carl tried to cushion her fall. Over her head, Carl watched Mike scoop up the gun, flick the safety lever up, and point it at them.

"All right, let's go around to the front door." Mike waved the gun to get them moving.

"Limp."

Carl said the word under his breath. Kate's expression didn't change, and he wondered if she'd even heard him.

"Start walking," Mike snapped.

Carl waved Kate ahead. She took several steps, then tripped, falling on one knee. Carl wasn't sure if it had been real, but he reached out to help her up.

"Don't touch her, Leidecker." Mike glared at Kate. "Get up and this time stay on your feet."

She struggled upright, crying out when she stepped on her right foot. Mike kept an eye on Carl, daring him to try anything. Kate limped around the side of the cabin. Carl came next, then Mike, knife in one hand and the gun in his other.

Inside, Kate hobbled over to a chair. She flopped down and leaned over, groaning as she massaged her ankle. Ignoring her, Mike kicked the door shut, and waved Carl over to the far side of the table.

"Well, Chief Leidecker, what brings you up to our neck of the woods?"

"A Glen Sather came by the station yesterday." The gun in Mike's hand jerked in recognition of the name. "The man had quite a bit to say. While my officers were looking into his story, I decided to have a talk with Kate. When I got to her house, I discovered you'd both come up here for a vacation. Thought I'd better drop in and say hello."

"How'd you find the cabin?"

"I fish Beaverton quite a bit. After Richard disappeared, I had the Wisconsin police check out the place to see if he was here. The next time I came up fishing, I tried to find the cabin. That marsh is a sonovabitch. I thought this time I'd come through the woods."

"Sorry you made the trip for nothing."

"Listen to me. Right now I've got an entire team focused on every facet of your life. By the end of the day there'll be enough evidence to take to the grand jury. When I called in to say I'd arrived at the lake, two of my men were on their way to the hospital to meet with both sets of nurses who were working the second floor the day Jenny died."

"What's that to me?"

"Trust me on this. If you thought we put a lot of pressure on Richard, imagine what it would be like if anything happened to either Kate or an officer of the law. You think I'm tenacious? My cops are as relentless as a pack of pit bulls."

Carl stared into Kennedy's eyes trying to read the man's reaction. He didn't want to panic him, only let him know that he was in real danger of being arrested. At the same time, he hoped to convince him not to hurt Kate.

He tried not to think about the blind fury that had made him careless when Mike attacked her.

"Can I get something for my foot?" Kate asked, breaking into the tense silence of the room. "My ankle really hurts."

"Stop your whining. It's just a sprain."

"Can I get some ice?"

"There's none left."

"I could use one of the cans in the cooler," she continued. "Please?"

"Oh, for God's sake! If that's what it takes to shut you up, go get one."

She staggered across to the cooler, wincing at every step. Lifting the top, she took out a can. Back in her chair, she propped up the sore foot and rubbed the can back and forth, sighing aloud. Mike stared at Kate, his glance speculative.

"Just out of curiosity, Doctor, how'd you figure out I was here?" Carl asked to draw his attention away from Kate.

"The old gal I was talking to out front owns a tavern down the shore. The bartender told her a guy came in while she was down at the marina. Said he was up fishing and was a friend of mine. Asked a load of questions about when I'd gotten up here, etc. The bartender told her the guy was a cop."

Mike pointed the gun at Carl and laughed. "After she left, I decided I'd better look around back. I was just in time to catch Kate making a break for it."

Mike set the gun down and picked up Carl's knife by the handle. Suddenly he glanced up.

"All right, Leidecker. Sit in that chair."

Carl moved the chair close to the wall so he'd have a clear path to Mike. He sat down and waited.

Putting the knife down, Mike reclaimed the gun. "All right, Kate. There's some rope on the floor under the shelf. Get it. And if you blink, Leidecker, I'll shoot her first."

Kate hobbled over and picked up the rope. He wagged the gun at her.

"Tie him up. And you better make it good, I'll be watching."

Carl sat forward the slightest bit so that when she looped the rope around his body, it looked tight but wasn't. She came around to tie his legs and as she leaned over she lost her balance, catching herself on his shoulder. Her head was beside his ear.

"The safety's on."

The words were only a breathy hiss, but he heard them.

Methodically he reviewed his actions. While Kate was climbing out the bedroom window, he'd crawled across the floor, and reached up for the gun on the shelf. He pulled it down and finding the safety lever, he pressed it down to take the safety off.

When Mike forced his hand, Carl had set the gun on the windowsill. He touched the safety lever but hadn't reset it. On the slim chance he could jump Mike, he wanted the gun ready to shoot. When Mike picked up the gun, he must have assumed that Carl had put the safety on, so he flicked up the lever. The significance hadn't registered. Carl snuck a quick peek at the gun. Kate was right.

The safety was on.

The trigger was locked in place. Mike wouldn't realize his error until he tried to fire the gun. When that moment came, Carl knew they would have their chance.

Kate finished tying him. She struggled to her feet and limped back to her chair.

"Can I get another soda?"

"Yes, and while you're there bring me a beer."

She gave him the cold can, and then sat back down to chill her sore ankle. Mike popped open the beer, tipping his head to drink.

"How did you manage an alibi for the time of Jenny's death?" Carl asked. "You were seen at the hospital at 2:45 and 3:19. Unless the nurses were covering for you, that's not enough time."

Mike's face lit up at Carl's obvious confusion. He took another gulp of beer then slapped the can down on the table. "It was the damnedest stroke of luck. I was in Mrs. Olson's room when two of the nurses going off shift came in. We chatted for a moment. They left. I noticed she was having trouble breathing. I stayed with her until she was more comfortable and told her I'd increase the oxygen. I made a note on her chart for the nurse coming on shift, and then I left."

Kate's hands were clenched on the seat of her chair. Her expression was a mixture of pain and fascination. Carl prayed Mike wouldn't get too graphic because he doubted if Kate could handle the details. He strained at the ropes, feeling them slip on the oily perspiration covering his skin. He was grateful for the heat in the room. If he sweated enough, he'd slide right out of the ropes.

Mike tipped his head back, staring into space. "I was driving down the street when I saw this little girl fall. At first I didn't even realize it was Jenny. When I did, I pulled over to the curb."

He scratched the beard stubble on his jaw, his expression pensive. His eyes were unfocused as if he were mentally watching the events unfold.

"Jenny had fallen and scraped her knee. She was crying. I rolled down the window and called to her. When she got in the car, she looked so sad I gave her one of the ButterSkots I had in my pocket."

He turned to Kate.

"I never meant to hurt her. I swear to you I had never touched her before. I was only going to bring her home. When I hugged her and she snuggled up to me, I just wanted to be with her for a little more time."

"She adored you, you bastard."

Carl held his breath. Mike blinked at the hostile tone and the moment of compassion was gone. He turned away from her and faced Carl.

"After it was over, I had to get away. And I knew I would need an alibi. I raced back to the hospital. I was just coming up the back stairs onto the second floor when I realized there was a code blue."

Mike's voice was devoid of emotion. Strictly conversational. Carl hoped it would stay that way.

"One of your patients?"

"No. A Joe Blalock. He was old Doc O'Brien's patient. Died." Mike shook his head. "At any rate, when I got on the floor, I ducked into Mrs. Olson's room. She was awake and wanted to know why nobody'd been in to see her since I left. I told her that because of the emergency down the hall, the new shift hadn't gotten to her yet. I was still pretty shaken up, so I picked up her chart to give myself a chance to calm down. I looked at my watch. It was 3:50. I had one chance to create an alibi. I changed the time I ordered the oxygen increase to 3:19, and told Mrs. Olson I'd sit with her for awhile."

"No wonder," Carl said, putting a touch of awe in his voice. "So when the nurse came in, she thought you'd been there all the time."

"Exactly." Mike smiled. "The moment I heard her footsteps, I pretended I was asleep in my chair. She tiptoed across to the chart, spoke to Mrs. Olson, and then left. When my beeper went off, I said good-bye to my patient and went out to talk to the nurses at the desk."

"Why did you bring me up here?"

Kate's question startled both men. She tried not to stare at the gun on the table. Mike was still too watchful. It wasn't the right time. She'd have to wait.

"The case was closed, but you wouldn't let it alone. Questions. Looking up things at the library. I knew I had to stop you."

"People knew I was coming up here with you. Marian knew. Were you planning to stage some kind of an accident?"

Mike laughed, but there was little humor in the sound. "Better than that. I wrote several prescriptions for you and talked to several people in the hospital about how worried I was about your depression. I even told Marian. You've been under a terrible strain, so I don't suppose it would surprise anyone if you took some sort of overdose. Of course, I'd have done everything to revive you but my efforts would naturally have been in vain."

Kate nodded. "That makes a certain amount of sense and might have worked. Now with Carl here you'll have to come up with another scenario."

"Yes, he's complicated things. I definitely need a new plan since it looks as if my time in Pickard is up. So we'll sit tight here until nightfall," Mike said. "Then I'll take the boat and make a run for it."

She didn't believe him. She glanced at Carl, and could see in his eyes the truth. Mike would leave, but he would kill them before he left. It was still daylight, but the sun would be going down soon. She guessed the time at six or six-thirty. A couple of hours before it was dark. That would be the time to make their move. Until then she needed to marshal her strength.

"If that's the case, I'd like to lie down. My ankle's still killing me, and I'm tired."

"You know, I'm getting pretty damn annoyed with your complaints."

His face reddened and his fingers twitched on the butt of the gun. Kate hurried to placate him.

"I'm sorry for all my moaning, but my ankle's throbbing."

Her apology seemed to appease him. "If you want to lie down, you can use the floor."

She lay down beside her chair, her back against the wall. Knees pulled up to her chest, she pillowed her head on her arm and closed her eyes. Richard's penknife was somewhere on the floor, but she hadn't been able to spot it. She wondered what Carl had done with his gun. Had he hidden it in the bedroom before Mike forced him outside?

She tried to think how they could get the gun or the knife away from Mike, but she really was exhausted. She tried to relax letting her body drift into a mindless trance.

"Get up, Kate."

The impatient call broke into Kate's semiconscious state. For a moment, she wondered why she was lying on the floor. With a jolt, she remembered where she was and raised her eyes to Mike sitting at the table, glowering down at her. She jerked her head. Carl was still tied to the chair, but she noticed he'd managed to work his feet free. His eyes were steady and encouraging as they met hers.

The cabin was filled with shadows. The edges of objects were beginning to blur, growing indistinct in the gathering dusk. The time was near when she and Carl would have to make a move.

"Light the lantern."

Kate jumped at the barked order. Tilting on the back legs of his chair, Mike waved the gun in the direction of the Coleman lantern. The stiffness of her body lent credibility to her awkward movements as she limped across the room. She picked up the lantern, set it on the corner of the shelf beside the stove, and lit a match.

Her fingers shook as the match touched the wick, the tiny flame a beacon of hope in the darkened cabin. She didn't need to see the message in Carl's eyes to know it was time for action. Turning, she faced Mike.

The gathering darkness had taken a toll on his nerves. His face was flushed and seemed bloated.

"Try anything, Kate, and I'll blow your head off." He pointed the gun at her face.

"I want to ask a question."

"What question? I don't have to tell you anything more."

"I know you don't, but it's something I still don't understand. Was Richard in the forest preserve the day Jenny died?"

He stared at her without speaking for a full minute. Kate remained motionless under his glance, afraid that her slightest quiver would put him off.

"Yes."

"Was he with you?"

His mouth slowly widened into a smile. "You don't know, do you?"

At his expression, Kate stepped back a pace, sorry now that she'd asked the question.

"Leave her alone," Carl said.

The interruption startled Mike who had been concentrating on Kate. He seemed to have forgotten they weren't alone. He whirled to face Carl, gun swinging back and forth between the two.

"Stay out of this, Leidecker!" he shouted. "If it hadn't been for her, the case would be closed. Her constant snooping has cost me everything. I had money, social contacts, and a position of respect." He swung back to Kate, his expression ugly. "If I'd known how much trouble you'd be, I'd have killed you a long time ago."

Kate held perfectly still. In Mike's present state, she suspected she was as good as dead if she so much as blinked. Carl must have sensed it too.

"Listen to me, Mike. Don't hurt her. If it hadn't been for Kate's absolute belief in you, we might have focused more carefully on you. Because of her, you still have a chance. Don't do anything in haste. If the police get here before you can get away, you can use us as hostages to negotiate for better terms. Hell, you can probably work out some kind of a movie deal."

The touch of humor got through to Mike. In relief, Kate watched the apoplectic color fade from his face.

"I'm sorry I made you angry," she said. "All I wanted to know was why Richard was in the forest preserve."

Mike turned to face her. His smile was nasty. "Richard was picking up someone."

"An affair?"

"More like a brief encounter. He wasn't interested in a relationship. He just wanted sex. And for that, any man would do."

For a moment she didn't understand. When it dawned on her what Mike meant, her face must have reflected her shock. Mike laughed.

"Shocked to discover your husband was a queen?"

"Chris knew, didn't he?"

"Knew that Richard swung both ways? Yes. I used to think that Chris was gay, but Richard said no. In my opinion, he is, but too afraid to act on it. Whether Chris knew it or not, he loved Richard and covered for him the last couple years while Richard was trying to decide if he preferred boys or girls."

"That Glen Sather Carl mentioned earlier. Was he Richard's —?"

"Lover?" Mike was enjoying her awkwardness. "Richard said Glen wanted to go to the police. I called Richard and used the whispery voice and told him if he didn't meet me, I'd go to the police, and tell them about Sather."

"That's why he was soaking wet. He wasn't waiting for Hepburn. He was waiting for a blackmailer."

So many things that had puzzled her were falling into place. No wonder Richard had lied. He couldn't face the consequences of exposure. And with the lie, he became a suspect in the rape and murder of his own daughter. A heinous crime committed by his best friend.

God, how she loathed Mike! She darted a quick glance at Carl. He blinked once. It was time.

An icy calm descended over Kate and her hands were steady as she picked up the lantern. She held it lightly, her fingertips caressing the smooth metal. With faltering steps, she limped across to the table.

She raised the lantern to set it down and with all her strength threw it directly at Mike.

The lantern struck him a glancing blow on the shoulder. The glass shattered, spewing kerosene and shards of glass across the floor. In a flash of light, the kerosene ignited.

Mike jumped up away from the flames. He leveled the gun at Kate's face and pulled the trigger. When nothing happened, he stared down at it. It took him several seconds to figure out why it hadn't fired. With a smile of pure malevolence, he pushed the safety lever down and raised the gun again.

With a flying leap, Carl slammed into Mike, knocking him to the floor.

As the men fought, flames raced along the floor and up the wall. Kate raced into the bedroom, grabbed her sleeping bag and used it to beat out the flames. She dropped the sleeping bag and raced back to the table. Her fingertips brushed the knife hilt just as the men careened into the table, overturning it. The hunting knife disappeared.

In the shadowed light inside the cabin, she couldn't even tell which man was on top of the grunting, heaving pile, fighting for possession of the gun.

A shot exploded, curiously muffled but still terrifying. Straining her eyes, Kate saw Carl's body jerk in a spasm of pain, but he still held Mike in a viselike grip.

"Get out, Kate," Carl shouted. "Run."

# TWENTY-NINE

"Run, Kate!"

With only a momentary hesitation, Kate whirled around, pulled the door open and raced outside. She ran down the bank and splashed into the water of the lagoon.

She didn't even consider taking the boat. The water was safer. The mud sucked at her feet and she hurled herself forward into a low dive. She dove again, heading for the weed beds. She gasped for breath but didn't stop until she'd wriggled into the concealing center of a clump of cattails. Knowing that her shirt would be easy to spot, she submerged her body up to her neck.

Another shot rang out, and she covered her mouth to muffle the sound of her sobs. Her breathing and the pounding of her heart were deafening. She began to shake and she put her arms around her waist, huddling down in the water.

Eyes at water level, she pulled the marsh grass apart until she could see the cabin across the lagoon. As if she were watching a play, the clouds parted and the stage was lit up with moonlight.

A figure stood in the doorway of the cabin, holding the sides of the frame. It was Carl.

He took a step forward, then another. Suddenly he dropped to his knees and in slow motion, crumpled sideways onto the ground. She waited but could see no movement. Hands over her mouth, Kate sobbed silently into the night.

Where was Mike? Was he dead too?

Frantic as she was to get away, she knew she had to wait until she knew what had happened to Mike. Suddenly she spotted the beam of a flashlight inside the cabin. Moments later there was movement at the door. Mike came out, carrying his duffel bag. His white face and bare arms stood out starkly in contrast to the maroon shirt and navy slacks that blended into the dark background. He stood motionless, staring out over the lagoon.

"Kate?"

Mike's voice was a breath on the wind and she recognized the sound of the Whisperer. She bent her head close to the water and closed her eyes so she wouldn't draw his gaze.

"Kate, I'm leaving. I'm sorry."

Head turned away, she remained where she was. She opened her eyes when she heard the motor drop into the water. The boat was in the lagoon and Mike stood in the stern, pulling the cord for the motor. It caught the first time. He feathered it lightly, then sat down, and steered the boat toward the wall of marsh grass that hid the channel. In an instant the boat was swallowed up, and all she could hear was the sound of the motor fading away.

When she could no longer hear anything, Kate swam out from behind the cattails. She treaded water while she stared at Carl, lying on the beach. He hadn't moved, but she needed to check if he was alive. She was reasonably certain that Mike was gone, escaping while he could, but she'd have to be careful. If he returned, she'd have enough warning to make a dash for the woods behind the cabin.

She swam to shore and after one more searching glance, she squished through the mud and up onto the bank. Running over to Carl, she dropped down beside him, rolled him over onto his back and felt for a pulse in his neck. Beneath her fingers, his heart beat slowly.

"Oh, thank you, God!" Taking only enough time to whisper another prayer of thanksgiving, Kate examined him.

His right side was soaked with blood. She pulled the knit shirt out of his pants, easing it up until she could see the wound. It wasn't as bad as she'd expected. The bullet had sliced across his ribcage, scoring a groove about four inches long. It wasn't deep, so unless a rib had been broken and there was internal bleeding, it wouldn't be fatal.

The other wound was worse. About four inches below his shoulder, a small hole penetrated the outside of his right arm. Turning the arm over, she gagged. The skin was shredded where the bullet had torn its way through. Ugly as the wound looked, at least it wasn't gushing blood. If she could bandage it up, he wouldn't bleed to death.

She was surprised that with all the pushing around Carl hadn't regained consciousness. His breathing was steady. She reached up to touch his forehead and her hand came away wet with blood.

Getting to her feet, she hurried up to the darkened cabin, searching the shelf beside the door until she found a pack of matches. Her hands were shaking so badly, it took her several tries before she could light one. Her eyes darted around the room. Everything was in a shambles from the fight.

Just before the flame went out, she spotted her little flashlight. She dropped to her hands and knees and crawled across the floor, wincing as the glass from the lantern cut her knees. She felt around until her fingers touched the plastic casing of the flashlight.

The beam came on and she flashed the light around the room. She spotted Richard's penknife on the floor. In the bedroom, she snatched several blouses out of her suitcase, and pulled Mike's sleeping bag off the cot.

She tossed the sleeping bag over her shoulder and hurried back into the main room. She picked up the water jug and started for the door.

In the beam of the flashlight she saw the first-aid kit on the shelf beside the cooler. She juggled the items in her hands and reached for it.

Back outside, she stood beside him, wondering whether she had time to bandage him before she went for help. If she didn't, he'd probably die of shock or loss of blood.

Using the penknife, she cut the back out of one of her blouses. She soaked it with water from the jug and washed off all the dirt she could see on the wounds. The right side of his face was swollen, but the cut on his head appeared to be only a shallow laceration. She opened the first-aid kit and found gauze dressings and adhesive tape. She dealt quickly with his head, then wiped away the blood on his ribcage and covered the groove with the dressings, taping them in place.

Carl's whole body was limp as she examined the bullet hole on his arm and taped dressings to the top. She used several for the ragged skin on the other side. With the last of her shirts, she tied the dressings securely.

Just as Kate finished, the moonlight disappeared behind a cloud. When her eyes adjusted to the change in light, she unzipped the sleeping bag and spread it out. Carefully she rolled him onto his side and slid the bag under him. Setting him back down, she folded the other half over him and zipped it up to his chest. With the last of the water, she wiped his face clean then let a few drops trickle across his partially open lips. She felt the muscles in his throat move as he swallowed.

Carl groaned and opened his eyes.

"Kate?" His voice was raspy, and she barely heard her name.

"I'm here. I'm going for help."

His throat worked. "Mike?"

"He's gone. Do you understand?"

His eyelids fluttered.

"Don't you dare die on me, Leidecker," she said. "I need you."

"I need you too."

Tears filled her eyes as she stared down at him. How had she gone from hating him to feeling that she would die if she lost him? She stroked the side of his face and he sighed.

"Careful."

He blinked several times, but then his eyes closed. His breathing was so soft she had to press her head to his chest to hear the sound of his heart.

Time to get help. For a moment she debated between the woods and the water. If she went into the woods she might lose her way entirely. In the water, she at least knew the direction to the main part of the lake. Leaving her shoes on, she stepped into the lagoon.

The moon came out from behind the clouds, shining magically across the water. She took it as an omen and smiled as she dove in, swimming toward the wall of grass where she hoped to find the channel. She had almost reached the entrance when the moon once more ducked behind a cloud. She felt disoriented. She stopped swimming, treading water until her eyes adjusted to the darkness.

In the silence, she heard the slap of water against the aluminum side of a boat.

Terrified that it was Mike returning to the cabin, she dove underwater, turning her body and kicking strongly toward the weed beds at the back of the lagoon. Once again she slithered into the concealing cover of the cattails. She was well hidden before the next patch of moonlight highlighted the area.

Chest heaving and breath whistling through her open mouth, she peeked through an opening in the grass, just as the boat slid from the channel into the lagoon. In the night silence, she recognized the hum of an electric motor and raised herself in the water to get a better look at the single occupant. Just before the moon disappeared again, she recognized Daisy wearing a green long-sleeved shirt and her trademark red and black plaid cap.

"Daisy?"

"Here."

She could barely hear the old woman's whisper over the pounding of her heart.

"I'm coming," she said.

She swam in the direction she'd last seen the boat. Without the moonlight, she overshot the mark. She spotted the outline to her left, silhouetted against the lighter background of the lagoon. She whistled as loud as she could. The boat turned toward her, and she waited until the bow loomed above her and then reached a hand up to grab the side.

Hands braced on the gunwale, she hoisted herself out of the water, and Daisy grabbed her by the seat of her pants. Her stomach cleared the side and she flopped over, landing in a heap at the bottom of the boat.

On her back she stared at the huge figure towering above her. Beneath the red and black plaid cap, Mike grinned down at her.

"Welcome aboard," he said.

He reached down to help her up but with a yelp of fear, she rolled away from him, coming face-to-face with Daisy Rice. Her mouth was open above the crescent of red. Her throat had been cut. Carl's hunting knife lay beside her head.

Kate was stunned by the senseless murder of the old woman. Daisy had been Mike's friend. Just like Richard and Jenny. Blinded by anger, Kate picked up the knife and lunged at Mike, slashing at his legs.

The move was so unexpected that he staggered backward. The tip of the knife brushed the leg of his pants. He fell against the side of the boat. The shift in weight tipped it over. Kate tried to dive clear but at the last second before they hit the water, Mike grabbed her. One arm was pressed across her nose and mouth. Frantically she twisted her body back and forth until his grip loosened slightly.

Opening her mouth, she bit him. With a bubbling cry, he released her. Bringing up her feet, she kicked him, swimming with all her might toward the protection of the weeds. She slithered in among the cattails then stopped, aware that Mike was somewhere in the water and any noise would give him a clue to her whereabouts.

She shook at the narrow escape. The hat and the change to a long-sleeved green shirt had given him the perfect disguise.

The overturned boat floated just a few yards away, its rounded back giving the impression of a whale at rest. She could see Carl lying on the shore, covered by the sleeping bag.

The moon ducked behind a cloud and darkness descended on the lagoon. She hadn't seen Mike. She strained, but she couldn't hear him either. He must be somewhere in the weed beds. Among the tall grass and cattails, it was so dark he could be only a foot away and she wouldn't be able to see him. For the moment, it was a stalemate.

She'd have to make the first move. The water and the darkness were to her advantage. Mike knew he had her trapped inside the lagoon. He could afford to wait until morning. Although she was the better swimmer, his strength would be more important than speed.

If Mike still had the gun, would it work now that it was wet? She had to assume it would. She stared at the hunting knife clenched in her hand. In the morning light, Mike would be able to shoot her without ever getting close enough for her to stab him.

She'd have to act soon.

It was too dangerous to go through the marsh. Even with a head start, Mike knew the way better than she did, and if she got out of the channel and into a patch of shallow water, he'd be able to close the gap and catch her.

Carl hadn't come through the marsh, he'd come through the woods behind the cabin. If she could find Carl's boat, she'd be able to get safely away. She'd have to go quickly. Carl needed help. Her energy wouldn't last too long either.

The peek-a-boo moon flooded the lagoon with pale light. The overturned aluminum hull of Daisy's boat shone like burnished silver. It had grounded on one of the shallow spots, rocking gently to the motion of the water.

Just beyond, Kate could see Daisy. Her body was floating toward shore.

Kate stared up at the sky. A cloud was heading for the moon, ready to swallow it up. If she timed it right, she could swim to the boat before the moonlight returned, then, when the next cloud blocked the light, she could reach Daisy and use the body to camouflage her approach to the shore. If everything went well, she'd reach land before Mike spotted her. Once out of the water, she'd make a run for the woods and try to find Carl's boat. Deciding it was her only hope, she got ready.

Trying to minimize her movements, she slithered through the marsh grass until she had a straight shot to the boat. She watched as the cloud reached the outer rim of the moon and inched across the surface. The light dimmed and was gone.

Kate was lying flat in the water and in the darkness ducked her head and swam underwater to the boat. She came up on the side closest to the cabin, keeping the boat between herself and the weed beds. The moon emerged. With only her head above water, she waited as another cloud approached. It was smaller than the first, but she didn't think she could wait for a larger one.

She watched Daisy's body. She knew she could reach it. Even if Mike saw her, she should be able to out swim him.

The breeze picked up, chill on her wet face. A quick glance at the sky told her it was time. The instant the moon was blocked, she took a deep breath and dove underwater, swimming toward Daisy. It was farther than she'd estimated. Her lungs were bursting and she came up for air.

She was two feet short.

The moon emerged, pinpointing her on the surface of the lagoon. From behind her, came Mike's triumphant cry. Now that silence was no longer necessary, Kate kicked her feet hard, diving beneath Daisy's body. She swam with all her strength toward shore. She knew she'd swim faster without the knife in her hand but she couldn't bear to let go of her only weapon.

She heard Mike thrashing his way through the water and risked a peek back over her shoulder. He must have been in the first row of weeds because he was only twenty feet away and gaining fast.

It was hopeless. She wasn't going to make it. For a second, she had a mad desire to give up, letting the water close over her head forever.

*Kick your feet, Kate. You can make it.*

Her father's voice shouted in her head. It was the spur she needed. She kicked hard, reaching ahead to pull herself through the water. She was almost there. Hurry!

"Give it up, Kate," Mike yelled.

Her downward stroke hit the mud bottom. She dropped her feet and tried to run. The mud sucked at her shoes and in panic she looked back. Just a yard away, Mike was getting to his feet.

"I've got you now!"

His voice boomed across the quiet lagoon. He lunged forward and grabbed her legs. Kate fell forward. She twisted her body and landed on her side, half of her body out of the water. Another foot or two and she'd have been safe.

Mike held onto her legs, crawling up her body until he was lying on top of her. His chest heaved with his exertion and his panted breath was against her face.

"You'll beg for death."

He straddled her. One hand circled her throat, pressing her against the mud bank. Arms out at her sides, Kate went limp, knowing if she fought him, he'd strangle her. Reaching underneath her shirt, he squeezed her breasts. She cried out at the bruising pressure of his fingers and saw the gleam of his teeth in the light of the moon.

He grabbed the waistband of her shorts.

It was the feel of his hand on her abdomen that brought her back to her senses. She reached her arms up to fight. Forgotten until now, the blade of the knife shimmered in the light. She raised it above his shoulders.

With a sweep of her arm, Kate brought the knife down. At the last second, Mike must have sensed danger. He ducked to the side until her body was free of his crushing weight, but his move came too late. She stabbed him in the back, feeling the blade scrape across his ribs then slide between two of them, sinking in up to the hilt.

Mike stiffened. Still on one knee and one hand, he hovered above her. She rolled out from under him as he brought his other hand down. Slowly he lowered his body to the mud bank.

"My God! You stabbed me!"

Kate scrabbled backward, breath rasping through her lips from exertion and the shock of her actions. She stared in fascination at the knife sticking out of Mike's back. The ivory handle gleamed above the green of the shirt.

She stared up at the sky. The clouds were gone. The moon lit up the lagoon and the entire area in front of the cabin.

"Kate, you have to get help." Mike's voice was a harsh whisper.

Gritting her teeth, Kate stared down at him. He was lying motionless, elbows at his sides, hands underneath his shoulders to raise his chest slightly above the ground. His head was turned toward her, his expression concentrated as he tried to assess his injuries.

"Kate?"

She moved into his line of vision.

"Kate, listen to me. Don't touch the knife. I think my lungs are filling up. If you take the knife out, I'll drown in my own blood. You have to go for help."

He stopped to catch his breath, then took several panting gasps. His pleading eyes held hers. Hearing a low moan, she cast a quick glance at Carl, lying so still just a short distance away.

"Take the boat. Go for help."

She struggled to her feet. His eyes followed her as she walked up the bank to where Carl lay. She knelt down and put her hand on his forehead.

His eyes opened and he stared up at her. The corner of his mouth turned up in a smile. Her chin trembled as she blinked away tears then watched as his eyes closed again.

She was no nurse, but she was confident that Carl was not in any immediate danger. She pulled the sleeping bag back over his chest, tucking it carefully in place. Taking a deep breath, she stood up.

Mike's eyes showed relief when she returned to his side. His breathing was a little more labored, but not critical.

"Hurry, Kate. I need help."

She stood above him, staring down at the man she had known for eleven years. The monster who had destroyed everything meaningful in her life.

"You need help? You killed Jenny. You killed Richard. You killed Daisy, and you even tried to kill Carl and me. God, how I despise you."

Raising her hand, Kate touched the angel charm, rubbing her fingers across the smooth gold figure.

"Where's Jenny's bracelet?"

Her question startled Mike. For one brief second, defiance flashed in his eyes, then disappeared at the realization that he was at her mercy.

"Inside pocket of duffel bag. Now will you go? Hurry, Kate."

"There's no need to hurry. We've got all night."

She knelt down facing him. Her fingers wrapped around the carved handle of the knife. With a quick jerk, she yanked it out of the wound.

"Oh, God! What have you done?" he cried.

She held the knife directly in front of his eyes. When she spoke, her words were formal.

"I sentence you to death, you bastard."

Kate raised the knife and brought it down, stabbing the blade into the mud directly in front of Mike's face.

He lifted his head. She could see the shock on his face. His mouth opened and he coughed. Foamy flecks of blood dotted his lips. She sat down across from him. She pulled her knees up and wrapped her arms around her legs. Her gaze never left his face.

Dry-eyed, she waited for him to die.